RED
MOON

RED
MOON

KIM STANLEY ROBINSON

www.orbitbooks.net

ORBIT

First published in Great Britain in 2018 by Orbit

1 3 5 7 9 10 8 6 4 2

A CIP catalogue record for this book
is available from the British Library.

HB ISBN 978-0-356-50879-5
C format 978-0-356-50880-1

Printed and bound by CPI Group (UK) Ltd, Croydon, CR0 4YY

Papers used by Orbit are from well-managed forests
and other responsible sources.

Orbit
An imprint of
Little, Brown Book Group
Carmelite House
50 Victoria Embankment
London EC4Y 0DZ

An Hachette UK Company
www.hachette.co.uk

www.orbitbooks.net

CONTENTS

CHAPTER ONE

nengshang nengxia

Can Go Up Can Go Down (Xi)

Someone had told him not to look while landing on the moon, but he was strapped in his seat right next to a window and could not help himself: he looked. Quickly he saw why he had been told not to—the moon was doubling in size with every beat of his heart, they were headed for it at cosmic speed and would certainly vaporize on impact. A mistake must have been made. He still felt weightless, and the clash of that placid sensation with what he was seeing caused a wave of nausea to wash through him. Surely something was wrong. Right before his eyes the blossoming white sphere splayed out and became a lumpy white plain they were flashing over. His heart pounded in him like a child trying to escape. It was the end. He had seconds to live, he felt unready. His life flashed before his eyes in the classic style, he saw it had been nearly empty of content, he thought *But I wanted more!*

The elderly Chinese gentleman strapped into the seat next to him leaned onto his shoulder to get a look out the window. "Wow," the old one said. "We are coming in very fast, it seems."

The white jumble hurtled toward them. Fred said weakly, "I was told we shouldn't look."

"Who would say that?"

Fred couldn't remember, then he did: "My mom."

"Moms worry too much," the old man said.

"Have you done this before?" Fred asked, hoping the old man could provide some insight that would save the appearances.

"Land on the moon? No. First time."

"Me too."

"So fast, and yet no pilot to guide us," the old one marveled cheerfully.

"You wouldn't want a person flying something going this fast," Fred supposed.

"I guess not. I remember pilots, though. They seemed safer."

"But we were never that good at it."

"No? Maybe you work with computers."

"It's true, I do."

"So you are comforted. But didn't people program the computers landing us now?"

"Sure. Well—maybe." Algorithms wrote algorithms all the time; it might be hard to track the human origins of this landing system. No, their fate was in the hands of their machinery. As always, of course, but this time it was too much, their dependence too visible. Fred heard himself say, "Somewhere up the line, people did this."

"Is that good?"

"I don't know."

The old man smiled. Previously his face had been calm, ancient, a little sad; now laugh lines formed a friendly pattern on his face, making it clear he had smiled like this many times. It was like switching on a light. White hair pulled back in a ponytail, cheerful smile: Fred tried to focus on that. If they hit the moon now they would be smeared far across it, disaggregating into molecules. At least it would be fast. *Whiteblackwhiteblack* alternated below so quickly that the landscape blurred to gray, then began to spark red and blue, as in those pinwheels designed to create that particular optical illusion.

The old man said, "This is a very fine example of *kao yuan*."

"Which is what?"

"In Chinese painting, it means perspective from a height."

"Indeed," Fred said. He was light-headed, sweating. Another wave of nausea washed through him, he feared he might throw up. "I'm Fred Fredericks," he added, as if making a last confession, or saying something like *I always wanted to be Fred Fredericks*.

"Ta Shu," the old man said. "What brings you here?"

"I'm going to help activate a communication system."

"For Americans?"

"No, for a Chinese agency."

"Which one?"

"Chinese Lunar Authority."

"Very good. I was once a guest of one of your federal agencies. Your National Science Foundation sent me to Antarctica. A very fine organization."

"So I've heard."

"Will you stay here long?"

"No."

Suddenly their seats rotated 180 degrees, after which Fred felt pushed back into his seat.

"Aha!" Ta Shu said. "We already landed, it seems."

"Really?" Fred exclaimed. "I didn't even feel it!"

"You're not supposed to feel it, I think."

The push shoving them increased. If their ship was already magnetically attached to its landing strip, as this shove indicated must be the case, then they were safe, or at least safer. Many a train on Earth worked exactly like this, levitating over a magnetic strip and getting accelerated or decelerated by electromagnetic forces. The white land and its black flaws still flew by them at an astonishing speed, but the bad part was over now. And they hadn't even felt the touchdown! Just as they wouldn't have felt a final sudden impact. For a while they had been like Schrödinger's cat, Fred thought, both dead and alive, the two states superposed inside a box of potentiality. Now that wave function had collapsed to this particular moment. Alive.

"Magnetism is so strange!" Ta Shu said. "Spooky action at a distance."

This chimed with Fred's thoughts enough to surprise him. "Einstein said that about quantum entanglement," he said. "He didn't like it. He couldn't see how it would work."

"Who knows how anything works! I'm not sure why he was so upset by that particular example. Magnetism is just as spooky, if you ask me."

"Well, magnetism is located in certain objects. Quantum entanglement has what they call non-locality. So it is pretty weird." Though Fred was damp with sweat, he was also beginning to feel better.

"It's all weird," the old man said. "Don't you think? A world of mysteries."

"I guess. Actually the system I'm here to activate uses quantum entanglement to secure its encryption. So even though we can't explain it, we can make it work for us."

"As so often!" Again the cheerful smile. "What is there we can explain?"

The moon now flashed by them a little less stupendously. Their deceleration was having its effect. A white plain stretched to a nearby horizon, splashed with jet-black shadows flying past. Their landing piste was more than two hundred kilometers long, Fred had been told, but going as fast as they were, something like 8300 kilometers an hour at touchdown, their ship would have to decelerate pretty hard for the whole length of the track. And in fact they were still being decisively pushed back into their seats, also pulled upward, or so it seemed, strange though that was. This slight upward force was already lessening, and the main shove was back into the seat, like pressure all over from a giant invisible hand. The view out the window looked like bad CGI. Landing at the speed of their spaceship's escape velocity from Earth had allowed them to travel without deceleration fuel, much reducing the spaceship's weight and size, therefore the cost of transit. But it meant they had come in around forty times faster than a commercial jet on Earth landed, while the tolerance for error in terms of meeting the piste was on the order of a few centimeters. Their flight attendant hadn't mentioned this; Fred had looked it up. No problem, his friends with knowledge of the topic had told him. No atmosphere to mess things up, rocket guidance very precise; it was safer than the other methods of landing on the moon, safer than landing in a plane on Earth—safer than driving a car down a road! And yet they were landing on the moon! It was hard to believe they were really doing it.

"Hard to believe," Fred said.

Ta Shu smiled. "Hard to believe."

. . . . .

It was easy to tell when they stopped decelerating: the pressure ended. Then they were sitting there, feeling lunar g properly for the first time. Sixteen point five percent of Earth's gravity, to be exact. That meant Fred now weighed about twenty-four pounds. He had calculated this in advance, wondering what it would feel like. Now, shifting around in his seat, he found that it felt almost like the weightlessness they had experienced during the three days of their transfer from Earth. But not quite.

Their attendant released them from their restraints and they struggled to their feet. Fred discovered it felt somewhat like walking in a swimming pool, but without the resistance of water, nor any tendency to float to the surface. No—it was like nothing else.

He staggered through the spaceship's passenger compartment, as did several other passengers, most of them Chinese. Their flight attendant was better at getting around than they were, very fluid and bouncy. Movies from the moon always showed this bounciness, all the way back to the Apollo missions: people hopping around like kangaroos, falling down. Now here too they fell, as if badly drunk, apologizing as they collided—laughing—trying to help others, or just pull themselves up. Fred barely flexed his toes and yet was worse than anybody; he lofted into the air, managed to grab an overhead railing to stop himself from crashing into the ceiling. Then he dropped back to the floor as if parachuting. Others were not so lucky and hit the ceiling hard; the thumps indicated it was padded. The cabin was loud with shouts and laughter, and their attendant announced in Chinese and then English, "Slow down, take it easy!" Then, after more Chinese: "The gravity will stay like this except when you are in centrifuges, so go slow and get used to it. Pretend you are a sloth."

The passengers staggered up a tunnel. It had windows in its sidewalls that gave them a partial view of the moon, also of one wall of the spaceport, looking like a concrete bunker inset in a white hill, black windows banding it. Concrete on the moon was not actually concrete, Fred had read during the flight, in that the cement involved was made of aluminum oxide, which was very common in moon rock, and made a lunarcrete stronger than ordinary concrete. The landscape around the spaceport looked as it had during their landing, but hillier. Nearby hills were white on their tops and black below. Sunrise or sunset, Fred didn't know. Although wait; they were near the south pole, so this could be any time of day, as the sun would always stay this low in the polar sky.

Fred and Ta Shu and the rest of the passengers shuffled carefully along, either holding on to the tube's handrails or hopping up the middle of the tube. Almost everyone was tentative and clumsy. There were many apologies, much nervous laughter.

The sun spilled its jar of light over the hills. The rubble-strewn land outside was so brilliant it was hard to believe that the tunnel windows were heavily tinted and polarized. It might have been easier to move if the tunnel walls were windowless, but it did look wonderful, and the visual fix might also help people adjust to the gravity, affirming as it did that they stood on an alien world. Not that this was keeping people from going down. Fred held a side rail and tried little skips forward. Crazy footwork, ad hoc hopping—it was hard to move! No one had mentioned how strange it would feel, maybe that passed after a while and people forgot. He felt hollow, and without a plumb line to judge if he was upright or not.

Ta Shu moved just behind Fred, smiling hugely as he clutched the rail and pulled along as if on a climbers' fixed rope. "Peculiar!" he said when he saw Fred look back at him.

"Yes," Fred said. It was like weightlessness with a downward tropism, some kind of arc in spacetime—which of course was what it was. Frequent course corrections had to be made, but with very slight muscular efforts. Toes could do it, but shoes amplified what one's toes tried for. Quite awkward, actually. A feat of coordination. Tiptoeing in slow motion. "It's going to take some getting used to."

Ta Shu nodded. "Not in Kansas anymore! Where are you staying?"

"The Hotel Star."

"Me too! Shall we have breakfast together to start our day?"

"Yes, that sounds good."

"Okay, see you there."

Fred followed signs to the foreigners' line for visa control, noticeably shorter than the line for Chinese nationals. Quickly he was facing a pair of immigration officers, and he handed over his passport. The officials gave him a quick look, put his passport under a scanner, and gestured him on. Beyond the controlled area two Chinese men saw him and waved. They greeted him and led him to the next room, which looked like any other airport baggage claim area. Signage was in Chinese characters, with small English script below them.

WELCOME TO THE PEAKS OF ETERNAL LIGHT

Baggage carousels spit out luggage as at home: many black cubes with inset handles, all similar. His had a green handle. When he saw it he hauled it off the carousel, almost tossing it into the air behind him; he spun around like a discus thrower, staggered, caught his balance. He was getting yanked around by a weight of a pound or so! But he wasn't much heavier, and mass was not the same as weight, as he would have to learn. No doubt the unicaster in his luggage made it heavier or more massive than it looked.

His minders watched him impassively as he spun. When he

calmed down one of them carried his luggage for him, so he could hold a handrail with both hands. Gingerly he tiptoed toward the exit, feeling conspicuous, but all the other newcomers were just as maladroit; there were still many low-impact falls, with people embarrassed rather than hurt. The halls were filled with laughter. The moon was funny!

AI 1

shen yu

Oracle

Zhangjiang National Laboratory, Shanghai
Also (entangled): The National Laboratory for Quantum Information
Science, Hefei, Anhui

"Alert for the analyst."

"Tell me your news."

"The mobile quantum key device you asked me to track is now on the moon."

The analyst, one of the founders and chief scientists of the Artificial Intelligence Strategic Advisory Committee, checked that his room was secure, then shifted the audio to earbud only. All communications between him and this particular AI were encrypted by way of a paired quantum key, and the AI, a private experiment of his own, was connected to the rest of the digital world only by taps the analyst himself had created. Their interactions were therefore truly private, like the conversations between a man and his soul.

"I-330, remind me which device was sent there?"

"A Swiss Quantum Works Unicaster 3000."

"Tell me more about it."

"Purchased May 2046 by Chang Yazu, chief administrator of the Chinese Lunar Authority."

"How did it get to the moon?"

"It was taken to the moon by Frederick J. Fredericks, a technical officer at Swiss Quantum Works."

"A unicaster is a private phone, I recall. Where is this one's matching device?"

"Unknown."

"Has the device on the moon been used?"

"No."

"Does Chang Yazu have possession of it yet?"

"No."

"Where is the device now?"

"Fredericks has it."

"When will he hand it over?"

"He is scheduled to meet with Chang at ten a.m. on July 20, 2047, Coordinated Universal Time."

"What administrative body in China oversees the Lunar Authority?"

"The Chinese Space Agency and the Scientific Research Steering Committee."

"*Waa sai*! One servant two masters! No wonder it's such a mess up there. Please create a new file for this incident. Also search for any recordings of this meeting between Chang and Fredericks, during or after its occurrence. Also search for the other phone, the one entangled with this one now on the Peaks of Eternal Light."

"Will do."

CHAPTER TWO

bo hanshu tansuo

Quantum Wave Collapse

Fred followed his two minders to a narrow room like a subway station, where something like a subway car filled much of the space. They got on a car and the train soon left the spaceport. When it hissed to a stop fifteen minutes later, its occupants tiptoed out into a hall with a long window wall, through which sunlight blazed horizontally, pinning their black shadows to the side of the car. Low buildings studded the Peak of Eternal Light outside the window, but it was hard to see them through the glare. What Fred could see of the surrounding landscape was a harsh mix of black and white, a chiaroscuro that he was quickly coming to think of as lunar normal. The horizon was very uneven and strangely nearby—hard to be sure how near, given the intense light and the clarity, but it looked to be only a few miles. Before he could fully take it in, Fred was led around a corner and down a hall, to a set of windows that overlooked the crater's interior.

This particular Peak of Eternal Light overlooked a corresponding pit of eternal darkness: this was the famous Shackleton Crater. The sun never shone on this crater floor, nor its interior wall. Once his eyes adjusted, he could see the steep interior wall of the crater curving away to left and right, just visible in a gloom of dark grays.

Stacked horizontal lines of lit windows were inlaid into the dark curve below, looking as if an elongated ocean liner had been bent in a curve and then injected into the crater wall; these lit windows cast a faint glow across the crater floor, which gleamed a little, being covered with dusty water ice. The crater was big enough that its far wall was not visible; as the crater wall below him curved away to left and right, it soon disappeared under the horizon. Very murky, this gray-on-black world.

The Hotel Star, Fred was told by one of his guides, was behind one of the lines of windows down there, right next to the American consulate. "Lead on I follow," he said gamely, and staggered behind the graceful pair to an escalator, where he was very happy to clutch the handrail and hold fast, yet still be making progress. Escalators were great. This one reminded him of the London Underground, moving downward endlessly. When they had descended to a level labeled Floor Six, he got off and fell, struggled to his feet and followed his minders gingerly around the broad curve of hallway to the glass hotel doors, feeling a little seasick, a little headachy, a little dizzy. Lunar g did not feel better than the weightlessness of space, in fact it seemed to him distinctly worse.

The Hotel Star entry was on the inside curve of a curving hallway. His room proved to be just bigger than his bed. His guides left him, promising he would get a wake-up call for breakfast.

He sat on the bed; it was like sitting on a trampoline. He could leap right into the ceiling if he wanted. Then, after a bell *tinged* three times, he felt vaguely that things were getting heavier. Indeed they were; his bedroom was on a floor of the hotel that was part of a centrifuge ring. After a minute or two, during which the room seemed to be tilting, he found himself being pressed down into the bed with a very familiar, homey pressure: one g. He had been told that it was best to sleep in Terran gravity whenever you could, to minimize the time spent in lunar g. For a trip as short as Fred's this regime was not mandatory, but it was still recommended, and when the option had been described to him he had decided to take it. Now he snuggled down into the mattress thankfully, his dizziness receding. Things felt right; they felt like home. It was such a relief that he quickly fell into a deep sleep.

. . . . .

When he woke he didn't know where he was, and jerked and found himself flying off his bed, at which point it came back to him: moon! The centrifuge had obviously been turned off, which was probably what had woken him. He was still lofting in the air over the bed as all this came to him; he twisted, landed on his face. Then he got up unsteadily and saw there was an hour to go before he was to meet his fellow passenger Ta Shu for breakfast. All was well.

As he went through his routine in the bathroom he looked up Ta Shu online, which meant not Earth's data cloud but rather some kind of local internet. That was still more than enough to give him an introduction to the elderly Chinese man.

Ta Shu: poet, geomancer, feng shui expert, producer and host of a popular travel show on one of CCTV's cloud platforms. He had written and published poetry from early childhood on, beginning with big painted calligraphic poster poems that included painting in the old styles, but from a child's perspective. A torrent of poems had proceeded to pour out of him for most of his life after that, until suddenly stopping after a trip to Antarctica; accounts differed as to what had happened to him down there. Subsequently he had become a travel host and ex-poet. It was rumored that he still wrote as much poetry as ever, but not for publication. Through the decades of his travel show he had visited 230 different countries, all seven seas, the North and South Poles, and the top of Mount Everest, which he had reached by balloon, taking advantage of a nearly windless day to drift over the top and step off the gondola's portico onto it. And now he was on the moon.

Fred wobbled down a broad staircase to the hotel's dining hall.

Ta Shu was there at a table, reading the screen embedded in it and nibbling from a plate piled with Fred didn't know what. He looked up. "Good breakfast time." Again his smile struck Fred as unusually sweet and friendly.

"Thanks," Fred said, and lofted down onto his chair, hitting the mark pretty well. "How did you sleep?"

Ta Shu waggled a hand. "I don't sleep much. Dreamed I was floating on a lake. When I woke, I wondered what it feels like to swim here. I wonder if they have swimming pools, I must look into that. How about you?"

"I slept well," Fred said. He looked at the food buffet, which filled one short bar. "My room spun me to one g, but when the centrifuge stopped and I got up, I felt kind of dizzy."

"Maybe some breakfast will help center you."

Fred felt both hungry and repelled by food. He shot up and teetered to the food bar, grabbing it to stabilize himself. The usual foods, thank God, as well as a lot of bowls of unidentifiable fruits and mushes. Fred had very definite food preferences. He filled a tiny bowl with yoghurt—hopefully yoghurt—and sprinkled some seeds and grains and raisins on it, wondering if these foods had been grown on the moon or flown up from Earth. Most of it must have been flown up. Balancing his bowl and staggering back to Ta Shu was almost too much for him, but he drifted onto his chair without spilling anything.

"Are you here to do some feng shui?" he asked Ta Shu before starting to eat. Turned out he was hungry after all.

"Yes. Also to record some episodes for my travel show. A trip to the moon! It's hard to believe we're here."

"True. Although it feels so weird, it has to be somewhere."

Again the beautiful smile. "Yes, we are certainly somewhere. My feng shui can confirm that."

"So, feng shui on the moon?"

"Yes. Feng shui means 'wind and water,' so it should be interesting!"

Long ago Fred had gathered that feng shui was a practice so ancient and mystical that no one could understand it. But his work made him acutely aware that there actually were mysterious forces influencing everything, so it seemed possible that feng shui was some kind of ancient folkloric intuition of quantum phenomena. Not that there were any such phenomena to be intuited, but who could say for sure? There were definitely mysteries, and maybe some of them involved macro-perceptions of the micro-realm. He felt odd perceptions fairly often; or even all the time. So he kept an open mind about it. "Tell me more."

Ta Shu tapped on the table screen and brought up a round map of the moon that he could scroll around on. "Here's a feng shui problem for you. See how beat-up the south polar region is by meteor impacts? Including this really giant one, the South Pole–Aitken Basin. Biggest impact in solar system, except for Hellas on Mars. So, I couldn't understand why so many impacts would come in from the southern sky, it being perpendicular to the solar plane. Where would all those big rocks come from, with only interstellar space above the south pole?"

"Hmm," Fred said. "I never thought of that."

"It's a feng shui thought," Ta Shu said. "But also, just astronomy. Clarification came to me from astronomer friends. Turns out the super-big impact that made South Pole–Aitken Basin probably happened when this region was nearer to the equator. Then the moon's rotation over time naturally shifted a hole as big as that to one pole or other, just because of the way a lopsided sphere tends to spin. Like a top balancing itself."

"Polhode precession!" Fred said. Matching spins was one attribute of entangled particles, so he had had occasion to think about spin, albeit at far smaller scales. He pondered the map as he ate. "So, these peaks of eternal light," he said between bites. "They're here because the moon's polar axis is perpendicular to the solar plane. But I don't understand why the moon's axis isn't parallel to the Earth's axis, which is twenty-three degrees off the plane."

"Me neither!" Ta Shu exclaimed, looking delighted that Fred had thought of this. "Seems like they should be the same, right? So I asked my astronomer friends about that too. They told me the moon and Earth formed in a big collision, which tilted Earth's axis even more than it is now, like fifty or sixty degrees. Since then the two have been in a gravity dance with the sun, and the moon has moved out so far from the Earth that the sun has straightened it up. The sun has straightened the Earth too, but Earth had farther to go, so it's only reached our twenty-three-degree angle, while the moon is almost vertical."

"Does that difference mess up your feng shui work?"

"Yes, I think so."

"So what will you do?"

"I'll make adjustments. Work on local problems."

"Such as?"

"I'll visit the Chinese construction in the libration zone."

"What's that?"

"The two edges of the circle, you know—extending up from the south pole along longitudes ninety and one-eighty?"

"Zero longitude being the middle of the near side?"

"Yes, very good. So the same side of the moon is always looking at Earth, of course. Tidally locked. Another part of the gravity dance. Many moons in the solar system are like that."

"So I've heard."

"But all orbits in the solar system are elliptical. Kepler first understood this."

"Kepler's law," Fred guessed.

"One of his laws. A feng shui genius. So, as one result of this law, when the moon is farther away from Earth in its orbital ellipse, it goes slower. When it's closer it goes faster. Meanwhile it's rotating on its axis at the same speed all the time."

"Wait, I thought it was tidally locked?"

"Yes, but it still rotates—one day per month, you know."

"Oh yeah."

"So, but it doesn't quite keep the same half facing Earth. Farther away it slows and we see more of the left side, then two weeks later it's going faster, and shows us more of its right side."

"Interesting!" Fred said.

"Yes. This waggling was first noted by Galileo, another very great feng shui master, when he was looking through his telescope. Like a man tilting his face while shaving, he said. He might have been the first ever to notice it. A telescope helps to see it. Libration, it's called in English. *Tianping dong.*"

"And there's new Chinese development running up this zone?"

"Yes."

"Because?"

"Because feng shui experts suggested it!"

"But why?"

"Because in the libration zone, the view of Earth comes and goes. See what I mean? On the rest of the moon it isn't like that. On the side of the moon facing Earth, Earth doesn't move, it's always in the same place overhead. Strange, don't you think? It just hangs there in the sky! I want to experience this."

"Interesting."

"Yes. Then on the far side of moon, you never see Earth at all. Great for radio astronomy, I'm told. I want to see that too, see if it feels different.

"But in the libration zone, Earth rises into view, then sinks. That brings up all kinds of interesting questions. Should one build on the Earthmost side of the zone, and maximize the time Earth is visible, also the height it reaches over the horizon? Or is it best to build on far side of zone, where Earth might only poke a blue curve over the horizon for a short while? Any difference in feng shui terms?"

"Or practical terms?"

Ta Shu frowned. "Feng shui is practical."

"Really? It's not just aesthetics?"

"*Just* aesthetics? Aesthetics is very practical!"

Fred nodded dubiously. "You'll have to teach me more about that."

Ta Shu smiled. "I am a mere student myself. You work with computers, you must do mathematics, yes? Famous for its aesthetics, I'm told."

"Well, but it has to work too. At least in my case. So, you're going to visit the libration zones?"

"Yes. I have an old friend up there near the end of the line."

Fred tapped on the map. "But Chinese stations never go into the northern hemisphere? Why is that? Is that feng shui too?"

"Yes, certainly. A matter of geographic propriety."

"Propriety?"

"Not taking too much. The best places on the moon are the poles, precisely because of their water and the wind of solar particles, so again, very feng shui mix of aesthetic practicality. And in feng shui terms the two poles are about the same. China started building on the south pole first. Imagine if we had done the same in the north! Where would the other nations go? It might have been alarming for them. So this is propriety. Always polite to leave room for others. If this is the correct explanation, it's very tactful."

"Very," Fred said. "Who decided?"

"The Party. But also, an ancient Chinese habit. China never did much in the way of territorial expansion, especially compared to some other countries. It looks bigger than it is because of coordinated effort."

"Is this still feng shui?"

"Oh yes, of course. Balance the forces."

"So feng shui is a kind of Daoist political geography?"

"Yes, very good!" Ta Shu laughed.

He was easy to please. Fred, who never really intended to make people laugh, was a little startled by this ease, but it was nice too. He nodded awkwardly, and said, "I want to learn more, but I have to get to my meeting with your local administrator."

"Should be very interesting for you! Shall we meet and have a drink at the end of our day? I want to ask questions about quantum mysteries."

"I would like that," Fred said.

. . . . .

Fred was met by a pair of Chinese women in the lobby of the Hotel Star. They introduced themselves as Baozhai and Dai-tai, shook hands with him, then led him to the offices of the local official he was meeting, Chang Yazu.

Fred was still having to use the handrails to move around safely, and the two women glided beside him solicitously, waiting as he struggled to negotiate turns and the like. When they got to the administrative center, they took him to a room that was like a viewing bubble, poking above everything else in the settlement. The horizontal sunlight that was always obtained here threw their shadows all the way across the room. He said enthusiastic things about the view in as genuine a tone as he could muster, and almost met their curious gazes. Crater sublime; starscape amazing. Fred had never visited Earth's southern hemisphere, and now he nodded politely as his hosts pointed out the Southern Cross overhead, and a blob with a texture like the Milky Way's, which they said was a Magellanic Cloud. A couple of points of light moving through the stars were apparently satellites in lunar polar orbits. A larger satellite, like a little oblong moon, brilliant on its sunward side and a velvet gray on its dark side, was an asteroid, his hosts told him, brought into lunar orbit for its carbonaceous chondrite. The moon lacked carbon, so chunks of this asteroid were being cut off and dropped to the surface in collisions as slow as could be arranged. This kept the resulting meteorites mostly unvaporized and available for use.

Dai-tai abruptly stopped their tour of the night sky. "Now Governor Chang will see you in the office downstairs," she told Fred, and the two women guided him downstairs into another large room, this one with a white ceiling and a broad window in the far wall. A reception room, it looked like. Near the window a large jade statue of a goddesslike figure gleamed under inset ceiling lights. A Guanyin, Fred was told. Buddhist goddess of mercy. Governor Chang would be with them soon.

Fred nodded nervously. Some people at home had warned him that the Chinese always tried to strip intellectual property from any foreign technology firms doing business in China. These people had speculated that the Chinese lunar administration had purchased this system from Swiss Quantum Works specifically to do that. Fred wasn't privy to whatever his employers were doing to guard against that possibility, and he didn't know why they had agreed to this sale. He did know that he had been sent here with nothing but the mobile quantum key device itself; everything else to do with the system was either in his head or not on the moon at all. He had memorized the activation code and was ready to deal with any problems that might crop up when they activated the phone and connected it with its opposite number, which he assumed was on Earth, though he didn't know for sure. All he had to do was make sure the right recipient had it when he turned it on and connected it, and deal with bugs if any appeared. The phone's debuggability was high, so that didn't worry him much. It was the moments like this he didn't like, the small talk, the waiting for people to show. Lateness was rude, his mom had always said.

Three men entered the room. One introduced himself as Li Bing-wen and said he was the Lunar Authority's Party secretary. Li shook Fred's hand and then introduced him to the other two in a quick flurry of names. Agent Gang, Scientific Research Steering Committee; Mr. Su, Cyberspace Administration of China. Gang was tall and bulky, Su short and slight. Unsettled by this unexpected trio, Fred shook hands with Gang and Su, then kept his gaze fixed somewhere vaguely between them.

The three men all spoke English, as their greetings had made clear. Now Li exclaimed, "Welcome to the moon! How do you like it so far?"

"It's interesting," Fred said. Carefully he gestured at the window. "I've never seen anything like it."

"Indeed not. Let me tell you that Governor Chang Yazu will be joining us shortly. He has been slightly detained. Meanwhile, tell us about your visit. Are you going to travel around much, see things, go to the American station at the north pole?"

"No. I won't be staying long. I have to activate my company's device for you, and make sure it's connected with its twin and working well. After that I'll head home."

"You should see as much as you can," Li urged him. "It's important that Americans who visit us see what we are doing here, and tell your fellow citizens at home."

"I'll do my best," Fred said, trying to keep his balance both physically and diplomatically. "Although actually I work for a Swiss company."

"Of course. But we come in peace for all mankind, as your Apollo astronauts put it."

"So it seems," Fred said. "Thank you."

"Come over here and tell us about your new quantum telephone, if I can call it that. Governor Chang will join us shortly. As head of station he is very busy."

Fred followed the Chinese to a cluster of chest-high tables, each rimmed by a handrail. As he walked he flexed his toes in an attempt to imitate Li, or even just to stay upright, but his balance was still very elusive. He clutched a table handrail and began to feel dizzy again.

"Have you been in a centrifuge yet?" Li asked him.

"Yes, my hotel room was spinning last night. It felt very homey."

"Very good. We have meeting rooms also that spin to one g. Many people try to spend most of their time in centrifuge rooms. It will go better for you back on Earth if you do the same."

"Thanks, I'll try to do that."

"You'll appreciate it later. Ah, here is Governor Chang now. After introductions we will quickly bow out and leave you two to your work."

"Okay. Thanks for meeting me."

"My pleasure."

The man who had just hurried into the room lurched forward, stopped and greeted Li Bingwen first. "Thanks, Secretary Li. I'm sorry to be late."

"It's all right. I've enjoyed talking to your visitor here. Fred Fredericks, this is Governor Chang Yazu, head of our Lunar Special Administrative Region."

"Nice to meet you," Fred said.

Chang extended his hand and Fred took it, and they shook hands. Chang looked surprised; he peered over Fred's shoulder with a puzzled expression. Then he crumpled to one side. Fred followed him down, wondering why his balance had chosen that moment to fail him. The scent of oranges.

. . . . .

When he came to, people were standing over him. He was on the floor, light-headed, dizzy, sick. Light in general, as if floating. "Wha." He couldn't remember where he was, and as he tried to recall that, he realized he couldn't remember who he was either. He couldn't remember anything. Panic spiked in him. The giant faces looking down on him were saying things he couldn't hear. He was apparently on the floor. Looking up at strangers, deaf, sick. He struggled hard for a sense of what was going on.

"Mr. Fredericks! Mr. Fredericks!"

Hearing those words burst some dam inside him, and it all came back in a rush. Fred Fredericks, computer specialist, Swiss Quantum Works. Visiting the moon. No doubt that explained the floating feeling. "Wha?"

They were moving him onto a stretcher. Someone was swabbing his hands and face. Some jostling to get him through a doorway almost bounced him off the stretcher. Rapid conversation he was not hearing properly, but wait—it was Chinese. That explained the songlines crisscrossing above him.

Then he was in some kind of container, a car or elevator or operation chamber, it was hard to tell. Floating sickly on some awful fabric. Into a space green with bamboo leaves. Faint or throw up, sure, but not both! Hold breath so as not to throw up, black tube, falling—

. . . . .

When he came to, there were East Asian faces looking at him, and he couldn't at first remember where he was, or who. This had happened before, he felt.

"Mr. Fredericks?" one of the faces asked. Ah, he thought. Fred. On moon. Chinese base.

"Yes?" he said. His voice came from a distance. Tongue fat in his mouth. Ah God—in the moon's gravity even one's tongue floated a little, swimming up to roof of mouth. Effort needed to pull it down into its normal trough between the lower teeth. A brief clutch of nausea at this bizarre sensation.

"What happened?" he said.

"Accident."

"Mr. Chang? How is he?"

No one said anything.

"Please," Fred said. "Let me speak with someone who speaks English. Someone who can help me."

All the faces went away.

. . . . .

The next time he came to, there was another set of faces over him, a different set, he felt. He remembered who he was, and most of what had happened.

"Were we poisoned?" he asked them. "How is Mr. Chang?"

One of them shook her head. "Alas Mr. Chang die. Same poison as you, but he did not fare so well as you." She shrugged. "We could not save him."

"Oh no. Poison?"

"It seems so."

"But how? What was it?"

The one talking to him shrugged. "You must ask policeman when he comes. You are guarded. Under inspection."

Fred shook his head, which made him feel sick again. "I need to talk to someone," he said.

"Someone will surely make a visit."

. . . . .

Fred receded into a fog of nausea and exhaustion, dreams of drowning. When he came to again, a different group of faces surrounded him. Again they were East Asian faces.

"How are you doing?" a woman at the foot of the bed asked. She sounded like she was from California. Taller than the others, narrow attractive face, refined-looking, serious and intent. "I'm Valerie Tong, assistant at the American consulate? I'm here to help you."

"My lawyer?"

"I wouldn't go that far. I'm not a lawyer. I'm sure there will be some lawyers who can represent you. There always are." She frowned at this. "Actually I'm not sure they have a court system here. It's possible you may be remanded to Earth. If so we'll be keeping track of your situation, and helping as we can."

"You can't take possession of me? Diplomatic immunity or like that?"

"Well, you're not a diplomat. And you're under arrest, as I understand it. They have some . . . some evidence, they tell me."

"How could they! Evidence of what?"

Valerie Tong squinted. "Murder, I guess. So they say."

"What?" The fear jolting through Fred put him well behind what he heard himself saying: "I just met that guy, I don't know him or anything! Why would I want to kill him?"

She shrugged. "I'm sure that will be something that will help you going forward. For now, I just want you to know that we'll be keeping track of your progress."

"My progress?"

"I'm sorry. Your case."

"I hope so!"

Then another wave rolled over him, and he went under.

TA SHU 1

yueliang de fenmian

The Birth of the Moon

Now, my friends, I am on the moon. A very strange thing to say. Also to experience, but aside from the weird lightness of my body here, I must admit that the idea is even stranger than the reality. At least so far. But this is just because it is such a very strange idea. I am standing on the moon. Sitting, actually. And because of that, I am now very interested to discover: what is this place? What is the moon? And to understand this, we have to go right back to the beginning.

The solar system began as a swirl of dust. Not like our dust, dust isn't quite the right word for it, because bits of all the elements were included in this swirling mass of particles, and it was a lumpy swirl to begin with, because of gravity. Then it got lumpier as time passed and gravity caused the lumps to come together, one way or another.

The lightest elements were the most common and the most likely to clump together, and by the nature of their distribution and their intrinsic qualities, most of these elements clumped at the center of this particular dust cloud. Feng shui principle number one: gravity. In the Chinese system of primary *qua* as described in the *Yijing*, the *Book of Change*, gravity would be *kun*, in other words, the yin in yin-yang. It works on everything equally and without exception. Nothing escapes it. So in the case of this swirl of dust, most of the particles fell in toward the center, and finally they massed so hugely that the pressure of their own weight caused them to catch fire. It was a nuclear fusion fire, in which atoms crush together and release energy, and so the sun ignited. The two lightest elements, helium and hydrogen, mostly clumped inward and ended up in the sun—ninety-nine percent of the solar system's hydrogen and helium is in the sun—but smaller whirlpools of these elements formed our four gas giants, Jupiter, Saturn, Uranus and Neptune.

The heavier elements—which were mostly created in the stupendous explosions called supernovas—bumped around the solar system closer to the sun, gathering and clumping into balls that were molten from the energy of their impacts, and from gravity's crushing draw inward onto themselves. These clumps grew as they ran into one another, forming eventually the rocky planets Mercury, Venus, Earth and Mars. The asteroid belt would have become another one of these rocky planets, but the gravity of nearby Jupiter kept pulling all these bits of a planet away from one another, until those that were not jerked into the sun or out of the solar system ended up in the wide band they are in now.

Each of the four rocky planets was made of smaller planetesimals, which attracted one another and ran into one another and then held together. This process was cumulative, which means that near the end of the process, around four and a half billion years ago, the collisions were often between quite large planetesimals—really they were small planets at this point, making their final combinations. Each of the four rocky planets we ended up with shows signs of gigantic collisions in their final years of accumulation. Mars's northern hemisphere is four kilometers lower than its southern hemisphere, and is now regarded as the impact basin of a giant impactor. Mercury is far denser and more metallic than it should be given the expected spread of elements, and it's now postulated that a giant impact with another planetesimal knocked away much of its surface and mantle, which flew out into its orbit. These chunks of Mercury would have fallen back onto it and recoalesced eventually, but being so close to the sun, many pieces were driven by the photon wind of sunlight out of Mercury's orbit, ending up eventually on Venus, or even the Earth.

Venus shows signs of a giant impact that hit with an angular momentum that stopped its rotation in its tracks, so that even now it spins very slowly, and in the opposite direction to the other planets.

Then there is Earth and its moon, a moon so immense compared to its planet's size that it is proportionately by far the biggest satellite in the solar system. How did that happen? The theory is this: in the beginning, up to around 4.51 billion years ago, there were two planets that had coalesced in Earth's orbit, called now Earth and Theia, or Gaia and Theia. They were almost the same size, and Theia was in the L5 position of Earth, which is a gravitational resonance point along Earth's orbit that makes an equilateral triangle with the sun and the Earth. Lagrange positions are pretty stable, but there are other powerful gravitational bodies in the system, and so a time came when some pull from Jupiter or Venus, or both together in a cosmic coincidence, yanked Theia out of its place and sent it spinning toward Earth. Its approach appears to have resembled Ptolemy's epicycles, little orbits spiraling along in a bigger orbit, and as the two planets came together, their mutual attraction caused them to accelerate at each other. Theia also seems to have been rapidly spinning. When they finally collided, it appears to have been an almost direct hit, with a very high angular momentum.

On impact the two bodies first merged and then exploded violently outward, throwing a great splash of hot stone and metal in a liquid spray that surrounded the hot spinning mass remaining in the middle. The spray of fragments was cast into space in a doughnut-shaped band around the newly formed and now bigger planet, which had been set spinning so fast by the collision that each day took about five hours.

That big combined mass was Earth as we know it now. The melted fragments in their doughnut-shaped band, which planetologists now call a synestia, quickly (meaning in just a century or so) recollected and coalesced into our moon, a ball one-quarter the size of Earth, but only one-tenth its mass, because the material that had been thrown outward was made mostly of surface and mantle materials, lighter than core materials. Both Theia's and Earth's cores ended up inside Earth. The ball of recollected materials in space was the moon.

Luna. In China we usually call the tutelary spirit Chang'e, a great goddess. Sometimes Yu Nu. In the Greek myths, Selene. And Selene's mother was Theia—thus the scientists' name for the impactor planetesimal. This lost planet is in fact not lost, but rather a part of all of us. Theia's atoms are in every body of every human.

In the four and a half billion years since that time, the moon's and Earth's gravitational influence on each other has caused Earth's rotation to slow to twenty-four hours a day, while the moon is now tidally locked, and rotates on its axis in the same time it takes to complete an orbit around Earth. On they go in their spiral dance, and the tides caused by the tug of the moon on the Earth's oceans had a huge impact on the development of life on Earth.

What to make of this story? Hard to believe! Vast, earth-shattering collisions, followed by billions of years of spiral dancing—these are what made the peaceful harmonious world we live on, and made also this dead white rock in space, this moon. One collision, but with two very different outcomes, almost entirely dependent on gravity and the other laws of physics. That's something to ponder. Worlds in collision! And then different outcomes, including some very good ones.

Of course we would not want any such thing to happen again to us now! That would mean disaster. And the motions of the physical cosmos are not the same as the operations of human history. Not even close. Analogies always deceive more than they reveal; I am no fan of analogies, I do not use them. Even metaphor, that mental operation we use with almost every word we speak, is slippery and deceptive. I always speak as plainly as I can.

And yet language, and therefore thought, is a strange and imprecise game of metaphors and analogies, one that we must play to stay alive. So now I want to suggest that even if there is a Theia looming out there in the orbit of our collective history, spiraling in toward us—as perhaps there is—and even if it has already been dislodged from its Lagrange point and is now bearing down on us, such that it is about to collide with some already-existing Gaia inside us, as seems inevitable, gravity and inertia being what they are—this has happened before. And the results, no matter how catastrophic at first, can still eventually turn to the good.

CHAPTER THREE

taoguang yanghui

Keep a Low Profile (Deng)

Valerie Tong sometimes met for private conversations with her station chief, John Semple, in one of the Chinese base's greenhouses. This one was located on the broad rise where the rims of Faustini and Shoemaker Craters met, on what John liked to call the Peak of Eighty-Four Percent Eternal Light. Here, when they were experiencing their brief night, which in fact lasted for about three days, the lunar farmers, most of them from Henan, used supplementary grow lamps hung close over their crops. The result was a giant room filled everywhere with splashes of glowing green.

All of the plants in this particular greenhouse were varieties of bamboo. Most greenhouses were devoted to agriculture; this one grew infrastructure. First they grew soil itself: lunar regolith, dead as a doornail, was mixed with carbon from carbonaceous chondritic meteorites, imported nitrates, inoculants, compost, and water, and thus grown to soil, the necessary first crop. In this soil they planted varieties of bamboo that had been engineered for growth so fast that grow lamps suspended over the plants had to be reeled up automatically to stay above the growth, which could be as much as a meter a day, and was always tilting toward the horizontal sunlight in ways that had to be compensated for with mirrors. When harvested, this bamboo became lunar lumber and fabric, used in all sorts of ways all over the settlements.

Thus it was that John liked to suggest to Valerie that they "go watch the grass grow." Luna's only entertainment, he liked to add. And actually it was kind of mesmerizing. Against the quiet background hum of the ventilators, it seemed that the rustle of the artificial breezes through the leaves was the actual sound of the plants growing. The bunched and spiky but gracefully splayed leaves added a rich palette of color to the big space, not just greens but also the deep reds that infused certain bamboos' new shoots, also the range of browns that were created when red and green mixed. One glossy brown in which the red and green were both still somehow evident Valerie had looked up on a color chart, and found it was called madder alizarin. "On the moon you get hungry for this stuff," John Semple noted, rubbing the color square with his finger, looking amused that Valerie had called it up.

This look of amusement Valerie was becoming all too familiar with, and in truth she didn't like it. More and more John Semple was playing a game in which Valerie was the cultured Ivy League opera-loving bilingual finance expert with a stick up her butt, while he was the down-home blues brother sloping through a job he did offhandedly without even caring about it. These caricatures weren't true in either direction, although the fact that John seemed to like making them did seem to indicate that he might indeed be somewhat lacking in taste. Beyond that it was just teasing, and she didn't like being teased.

John Semple was a tall angular black man who had started his career in the Secret Service before moving to the State Department's foreign service, and Valerie presumed also to some other intelligence agency, probably NSA or CIA. Valerie herself was Secret Service only, part of the president's Special Investigative Unit. Here on the moon her cover was as one of John's State Department translators. John knew what she was really up to, but seldom mentioned it. They had that Secret Service bond between them, and despite his teasing, he seemed to like her; and she found him useful. She didn't like to get close to other agents.

They stood by a long tinted window and turned on what John called his cone of silence, which would keep their conversation private. The sun pricked the horizon and flooded the greenhouse with its tiny shard of light. It would take most of the day for it to creep fully over the nearby hill, but already John's face glowed, a darker brown than madder alizarin, but just as rich and fine. He had mentioned once that he had Cherokee ancestry, making him, he said, a red man as well as a black man; and since Valerie's parents were Chinese and Anglo-American, he went on, between them they had the old Sunday school hymn covered. She hadn't known what he had meant by that, and so he had sung for her, in a jovial bass, "Red brown yellow black and white, we are precious in his sight, Jesus loves the little children of the world!" He had a deep laugh, and had laughed then to see Valerie's rolled eyes. Of course the song's lyric was a little racist in an old-fashioned way, but also, even worse, Valerie was one of those music lovers very susceptible to earworms, and now this stupid little tune would stick in her head for many hours, even days, and would come back unwelcomely for years to come. So no doubt she had rolled her eyes and frowned her frown, an expression she could feel freezing the muscles of her face; this happened a little more often than she would have liked.

The paring of sun gilding them was intense even through treated glass. Outside they could see only a clash of blackest black and whitest white, and yet they stood in a little forest of green highlighted by red, brown, madder alizarin. All God's children! But no, don't think of that tune! Think Wagner, think Verdi!

"We're going to need the lawyers back home," Valerie said now to John. "This Fredericks guy is in big trouble."

"Did he really kill someone? Why would he do that?"

"He says he didn't. He almost died himself, and he's still confused. He doesn't know what happened. And he doesn't look like the type of guy that gets in trouble."

"But I was told they found the poison that killed Chang on his hand."

"I know. It made him sick too. But he had no reason to do it."

"Not that we know of. These two might have gotten caught up in something, you never know. There's a lot of IP theft still going on, also a lot of pay-to-play. Sometimes those payola deals go sour."

"I know." Val had been sent to the moon precisely to look into just such a problem. A cryptocurrency called "US Dollars" was being offered in the black cloud, supposedly redeemable in real dollars, and there was evidence suggesting some of the monster servers involved were located on the moon. Only the Chinese had such powerful computers up here, or so it was believed, so it was a tricky situation, smacking of cyberwarfare, and Valerie had been sent up to see if she could discover anything on station, using her Chinese language ability and her fiscal skills, and the expertise she could call on back home. John knew this.

"Well, there you have it," he went on. "Maybe a deal went bad. And I hear Fredericks's company has been complaining about IP theft."

"They all do. That doesn't explain something like this. No one murders a business contact to cover up bribery or theft."

"No?" John tilted his head to the side. His was a friendly face, brown eyes observant and attentive; he really looked at you. He let you know that you were of interest to him, and now, in Valerie's case, that you were a source of almost constant amusement. Black hair close-cropped, graying at the temples: a good-looking man. "Maybe our Fred was more than a business representative."

This was theoretically possible, but Valerie said, "I think it's more likely that someone used him. When I saw him he was like a deer in the headlights. And if they found the poison on his hand, it means he must have poisoned himself too. Why would he do that?"

"To cover himself? I don't know. He was here to deliver a new secure comms device, right?"

"Yes. A private phone, with mobile quantum key delivery."

"Who was going to be on the moon end of this device?"

"Probably Chang himself, right?"

"Fredericks will know."

"Maybe. He could just be a courier."

"Maybe we can ask Secretary Li about that."

"Li got sent back to Earth right after this happened."

"Hmmmm," John Semple grumbled, thinking it over. "We need to know more about Chang and his connections back home."

"I can look into that."

"It will be murky," John predicted. "The Chinese agencies like to be opaque. You're going to be swimming in mud. Although that will be easier up here with the light g and all, yuk yuk."

"Ha ha," Valerie retorted. To her an American citizen in trouble was not a joking matter.

Semple just laughed at her with his eyes. Hard-core Secret Service rule-following academic with station-appropriate language skills, and no doubt a dragon mama who beat her with books as a child! Lighten up! his eyes were saying.

To which she responded by becoming even more stony. He didn't know her at all; he was just reacting to the fact that she was a professional and a Chinese-American woman. It was offensive.

"Look into it," he suggested cheerfully as he saw this emanating from her.

He turned off his cone of silence, and they walked inexpertly down the rows of bamboo, then descended broad stairs to the floor below. Here long tubes of green bamboo trunks were being prepared for use as building materials—either segmented into long tubes for use as beams, or split into slats to be woven into sheets of varying thicknesses. The leaves themselves were being pulped for paper and cloth. The contrast with the greenhouse above was startling: green life up there, green boards down here. It was a bamboo shambles, loud with the harsh whines of table saws. Against one wall, giant tubs set at a tilt rotated as they rumbled soil around inside them, sounding like wet concrete sloshing in a cement truck and providing a bass continuo for the saws' shrieking. Workers were dumping front loaders full of bamboo dust and chips into these soil tubs to serve as more humus. Lots of Chinese workers were moving around, all of them much more graceful than Valerie and John. It was like a Chinese socialist-realist ballet with industrial music as the score, reminiscent of *Nixon in China*. Give Adams or Glass an orchestra of table saws, Valerie thought, and this would be the result.

The broad tunnels of the undercity were striped by moving walkways, as in airports on Earth. Valerie and John stood on one to return to the American consulate, a little rented space in the big Chinese complex. When they walked in the consulate door, John's assistant, Emily List, looked up from her screen.

"Oh good," she said. "I was just trying to call you. That Fred Fredericks is gone."

"What do you mean gone?"

"The doctor we sent over to look at him couldn't see him. They said they moved him. The doctor asked to see him wherever he was, but the people there just kept saying he's been moved."

"Did they say where?"

"No."

John and Valerie exchanged a look. "Okay, Agent Tong," John said to her. "Why don't you go ask some questions, see what you can find out."

. . . . .

The Chinese workers who had built the lunar south pole complex must have endured a lot of danger and suffering, Valerie thought as she headed to the far side of Shackleton Crater. And there must have been a lot of them. Even when construction was mostly a matter of programming robots and 3-D printers, a lot of digging and jackhammering would still have to be done. Humans remained the best construction robots around, being the cheapest and most versatile. For sure a lot of man-hours had been devoted to this project. Its architectural style straddled 1960s Brutalism and sheer adhocitecture; in other words, not that different from most of the infrastructure back in China, where the glamorous skyscrapers were few and far between.

Valerie was making her inquiry alone, per John's request. He thought a single woman speaking Chinese would find out more than an officious group, and he was probably right about that. She flowed carefully from walkway to subway to walkway to corridor, all underground, arriving at last at the Chinese security headquarters, out near the settlement's transport station, somewhere under Shackleton Crater's broad apron. All these interior spaces were made of concrete and aluminum, with the walls decorated by tapestries of woven bamboo. Living bamboo plants were also growing in giant concrete pots placed all over, accenting greenly the ubiquitous lunar gray.

Most rooms in the complex were buried well below the surface. All the moon's surface was composed of rock shattered by eons of meteor impact, so the structural integrity of every excavated space was suspect, at least to Valerie. Heavily ribbed and reinforced ceilings were surely advisable, and yet to her the concrete ribs arcing overhead looked too tall and slender and unsupported to be safe. But this was the judgment of a Terran eye and brain, she told herself, which hadn't factored in lunar gravity. Presumably the engineers had calculated everything.

She entered the Chinese Lunar Authority's offices and took her turn identifying herself to a screen, then went through security arches, signed in, took a number, sat down. The TV show on the screen in the waiting room was a CCTV production about mining on the moon. She wondered how long they would make an American diplomat wait. It was a test of this particular agency's regard for the United States. Chinese foreign policy was a matter of competing groups within their government trying to influence the leadership's strategy, often by taking improvised actions designed to curry favor or embarrass rivals. As their Twenty-Fifth Party Congress approached, it looked like their current president, Shanzhai Yifan, was trying to pass along his supposedly distinguished mantle (he had even given himself the *lingxiu* leader designation in his second term) to his close ally the minister of state security, Huyou Tao. But there was said to be intense resistance to this plan, as neither man was well liked. So some leaders were going to win big at this congress, and others were going to lose entirely. Until that happened, everyone dealing with the Party's elite players and even the top layer of bureaucrats was going to run into some capricious and inexplicable behavior, either too friendly or too hostile.

After just ten minutes (so this was a friendly agency) she was called in to the cubicle-sized office of one Inspector Jiang Jianguo. Jianguo meant "construct the nation" and was a name from the Cultural Revolution, so possibly a gesture to a grandparent. He proved to be a handsome man, willowy and sincere, about Valerie's age. Valerie had just hit forty the year before, and she was feeling like a hardened veteran, even a burnt-out case. Jiang looked happier.

"Thank you for seeing me," she said to Jiang in *putonghua*, the Chinese common language that sometimes still got called Mandarin. "I'm trying to see an American you have in custody, an employee of Swiss Quantum Works named Fred Fredericks."

He tilted his head to one side. "We know of this man," he replied in Cantonese. He smiled. "You speak *putonghua* like you're a Cantonese speaker, is that right?"

"My father was," Valerie said, blushing. She stuck to *putonghua*, feeling that would be better protocol. "He came to America from Shenzhen. In the Los Angeles Chinatown the older people still mostly speak Cantonese."

"All over the world!" Jiang exclaimed. "Of course one has to speak the national language, but still, Cantonese will never stop speaking Cantonese."

"I suppose not," Valerie said, face still hot. It had taken her a lot of work to learn to speak *putonghua* without a Cantonese accent, and obviously she still wasn't quite there. But there were a lot of regional accents inflecting the national tongue, so she just had to live with it.

Possibly she should have shifted to Cantonese with this man, but at this point she would have messed that up too.

"So," Jiang continued in *putonghua*, conforming to propriety with a friendly smile. "As to this American working for the Swiss, we have a file for him, but he isn't where he was when you last visited him."

"No, but where is he?"

"Because of the nature of his arrest, he has been moved to the custody of the Scientific Research Steering Committee."

"And where are they? Where is he now?"

"Their facilities are in Ganswinch."

"Where is that?"

"It's north of here, sorry, that's our little joke. Here, let me show you on a map." He brought up a schematic map on his table screen. It looked like a slightly simplified version of the London tube map. "Here," he said, pointing to a node in the colorful array.

"How far is that? Can you take me there?"

"It's about twenty kilometers from here. Let me see if my schedule allows me to get away and escort you."

He made an inquiry to his wristpad. "Yes," he said to her after a while. "I will show you where he is. It isn't easy to find."

"Thank you. I appreciate it."

Jiang led Valerie out the door and down a hall to a much bigger chamber, like the interior of an underground mall. Walls, ceiling, and floor were again gray, all formed of what was called foamed rock, Jiang said, a lunar concrete made from crushed regolith and aluminum dust. Bas-relief swirls had been cut into some of the walls they passed; when they came closer to one of these etched walls, she could see that the swirls were formed by the indentations of thousands of overlapping faces, all of them recognizably Chinese. Essentially crowds of small faces had been arranged to make broader strokes that conveyed landscapes.

They got on a subway car and Jiang showed his wristpad to a conductor, who inspected it and Valerie, then nodded and moved on to the next passengers. The car was almost empty. The train jerked and took off, humming slightly. Jiang explained that they were headed up the Ninety Degree East corridor, which would pass under Amundsen Crater, then Hédervári Crater, then Hale Crater. The libration zone rail and piste would then rise and run over the surface like train tracks, with trains keeping to a regular schedule except when solar storms forced everyone to stay underground.

At Amundsen Station they got off the car and Jiang led her over to another platform, where they got on a much more crowded subway train headed to Ganswinch. That took longer, and it was most of an hour before they got off again, though they were never moving very fast either.

The Ganswinch terminal was guarded by men in uniforms, olive green with red shoulder patches. They looked like PLA to Valerie, but Jiang said they were Lunar Authority security agents—the moon being a demilitarized zone, of course, he explained in a possibly ironic tone. Although a Cantonese accent had a tendency to undercut expressions in *putonghua*, so it might have just been that. Again Jiang showed his wristpad to various people who then let them pass. There were only a few women out here, and Valerie began to wonder if this was an aspect of this station, or if the Chinese were generally sending mostly men to the moon. The official statistics said they weren't, that there were almost as many women as men in the Chinese population here. But at this outpost it wasn't true.

They took an escalator running downward, and at its lower end got off in an interior space bigger than Valerie had seen so far. "Ganswinch Station," Jiang explained.

Again it was all gray walls marked by bamboo mesh tapestries and potted plants. Broad banks of lighting overhead made for a lit space that was slightly dim, like the light under a thick cloud layer on Earth. The excavated cavernous space was perhaps twelve meters tall and a hundred meters wide, and on its floor stood many house-sized green tents, made of bamboo fabric, Valerie assumed, and set in rows reminiscent of a refugee camp. At the far end of these rows stood a tall mesh fence with razor wire looping its top. Jiang led them to the tent next to this fence and entered through an unzipped flap door.

It was markedly warmer inside, which Valerie took to be the point of the tents. A woman took a look at Jiang's wrist and then began to tap on her desktop, looking at records and photos. "Tent Six," she said to Jiang. They left her and went into the fenced compound, where three male guards escorted them down another row of tents to one marked with the Chinese character for six.

Inside the tent were about a dozen metal-framed beds, in two rows, with men sitting on each bed. At first glance, then second glance, they were all Chinese.

"Fred Fredericks?" Jiang said.

They stared at him. He walked to the end bed and looked at the man there. "Fred Fredericks?"

The man shook his head. "Xi Dao."

"When did you move to this tent?" Jiang asked.

"Three months ago," the man replied.

Jiang squinted at him. He looked at the other men. "He's been here all this last week?" he asked them.

They nodded.

Jiang looked at Valerie. "Let's go back."

They returned to the tent outside the fence, went back to the woman who had sent them off. "Fred Fredericks isn't in Tent Six," Jiang said. "What's become of him?"

Startled, the woman tapped at her desktop. She gestured to Jiang as she read her screen, and he came around and read next to her.

"*Ho,*" he said.

The two Chinese officials looked up at Valerie. "He's not where he's listed as being," Jiang said.

"So I gathered," Valerie said. "But you must have recorded all his movements?"

"We did, but they lead here."

"What about the cameras here?"

"He's not on them."

"How can that be?"

"Don't know. It isn't possible." He glanced at the woman. "Possibly certain other services are taking precedence here."

"Intelligence services?" Valerie asked.

The two Chinese didn't reply.

"How can we find out?" Valerie asked. "This man is an American citizen, working for a Swiss company." It was possible the Swiss connection would carry even more weight than the American one, given all the work the Swiss had done in China and here.

Jiang looked unhappily at his colleague. "We should be able to find out by way of the Lunar Personnel Coordination Task Force, which is the agency I head," he said. "We keep track of everyone on the moon. So now I will instruct my people to look for him."

"How will they look?"

"Everyone is chipped, among other things."

"Am I chipped?" Valerie asked sharply.

They regarded her. "You're a diplomat," Jiang suggested. "Do you have your passport with you?"

"Yes."

"That serves as your chip. Really I should have said that people who are arrested are chipped. Fredericks should have gotten one. We'll look into that." Jiang was tapping at his wristpad as he spoke, and after a while he sighed. "From what I see here, it looks like his chip might have been deactivated, or taken out of him and destroyed."

"Diplomatic incident," Valerie said stiffly, clenching her jaw and staring at him.

"Possibly so," Jiang admitted.

He looked annoyed. This was happening above his level, his look said, even though he was supposed to be in charge of Chinese security at the south pole. Which meant there had been an incursion on his turf. For sure he would not like that, no one would. But in the face of such outside interventions, what could a local official do?

. . ● . .

Valerie returned with Jiang to his office, and on the way she saw, as one always did when retracing a new route, that the way to Ganswinch was simpler and shorter than it had seemed on her trip out. All the halls and subway cars were crowded this time.

On return to the Shackleton Crater complex she said goodbye to Jiang, who was clearly distracted, even angry. He wanted her gone so that he could pursue lines of inquiry at full speed. She understood that and got herself back to the American consulate, where she reported to John Semple.

He frowned as he heard her news. "They're fighting among themselves again."

"*Wolidou*," Valerie confirmed. "Infighting. But to involve an American?"

"One group may be trying to embarrass another one, get it in trouble with Beijing."

"So how do we find our guy? And is there some way we can turn this situation to our advantage?"

"I was wondering about that myself. I think both State and the Pentagon have been hoping to find a good moment to plant a flag down here at the south pole. Something bigger than our office, I mean. The Chinese won't like it, but I don't think they would try to stop it right now, because they're being backfooted by this guy going missing on their watch. Plus the Outer Space Treaty forbids territorial claims anyway."

He started tapping on his wristpad.

Valerie said, "What about that quantum comms device Fredericks brought with him?"

"I don't know."

"And what about finding him?"

"We can't do that ourselves. We'll have to demand that they do it."

One of John's assistants came into the cubicle and said, "John, there's a Chinese national here to see you, a DV of some sort, says he knows you. His name is Ta Shu?"

"Ta Shu?" John said, startled. "He's here?"

"He is."

"Show him in!"

John smiled at Valerie as the assistant went to do this. "This could be helpful. Ta Shu is a cloud star, very famous in China. I met him in Antarctica a long time ago."

The assistant reappeared with an elderly Chinese gentleman in tow. After he and John embraced, John said, "What brings you here? Are you doing a piece for your travel show?"

Ta Shu nodded. He was short and stocky, tentative in the lunar g. He had a nice smile, which he bestowed on John and then Valerie. "Yes, I'm broadcasting my travels again. Also I'm consulting as a geomancer for local builders in the libration zone."

"Good idea!" John said mockingly. "Well, I'm glad to see you again. I remember how much I enjoyed your shows from Antarctica."

"Thank you. A wonderful adventure. It's almost more unearthly there than here, I think. Here you are always in rooms, it's like being in a mall, except lighter on your feet. Down there you're on an ice planet, like Europa or something."

"I know what you mean. So what can we do for you here?"

"I've been wondering what happened to a new friend of mine, a man I met when I arrived, named Fred Fredericks. He was staying in the same hotel as me, and we breakfasted together, and were going to meet for drinks at the end of our first day, but he didn't show up, and the hotel people said he was gone."

John and Valerie looked at each other.

"Well, that's right," John said to Ta Shu. "We're worried about him too. He got caught up in something bad, and now he's missing."

He explained the situation. When he was done, and Valerie had described what her day had been like in pursuit of Fredericks, Ta Shu looked seriously concerned.

"Not good," he said. "Things can get complicated when something like this happens."

John's expression translated to *No shit*, and Ta Shu appeared to know him well enough to get that, Valerie noted. John said, "Do you think you can help us to find him?"

"I can try."

AI 2

ganrao shebei

Interference with the Device

The analyst in the Hefei office of the Artificial Intelligence Strategic Advisory Committee got another alert from the AI that he now considered to be the most interesting of the ones he was actively programming, even though it was still frustratingly simple-minded and obtuse. But they all were. Quantum computers were magnitudes faster than classic computers in several classes of operation, but they were still limited by their tendency to decohere, also by the inadequacies of their programming; which was to say the inadequacies of their programmers. So it was like being confronted with one's own stupidity.

"Alert," the AI said.

The analyst had recently given it a voice modeled on that of Zhou Xuan, the classic actress featured in the 1937 movie *Street Angel*. Now he checked his own security protocols, then said, "Tell me."

"The Unicaster 3000 previously mentioned and now on the moon has just been interfered with, and thus experienced wave collapse and quantum decoherence."

The analyst said, "Did you move this information into the appropriate file and sequester it?"

"I did that."

"Will this unicaster device continue to function as an open line, or has it shut down?"

"It has shut down, in keeping with its design."

"Okay. Can you identify who interfered with the device?"

"No."

"But intrusion always leaves a mark."

"In this case the collapse of the wave function is the only mark."

"Can you identify when it happened, and where it was when it happened?"

"It happened at UTC 16:42 on July 23, 2047. It happened on the moon."

"Can you be any more specific?"

"The device lacks GPS, as part of its design privacy. It was last seen on security cameras being taken into an office occupied by the Scientific Research Steering Committee, at Shackleton Crater."

"But that committee is under the umbrella of the Central Military Commission. Do they have some of their people on the moon?"

"Yes."

"Oh dear. Our beloved colleagues. Surely they should not be on the moon."

"Military activity is forbidden on the moon by Outer Space Treaty, 1967."

"Very good. And now the device is inoperative?"

"It could be entangled again with another matching device."

"But to key that entanglement, both of them would have to be in the possession of the same operator."

"Yes."

"And the other device is presumably on Earth. What has become of the person who took the device to the moon?"

"He is no longer visible to me."

"Wait, what? You've lost him?"

"He suffered a health problem while with Governor Chang Yazu of the Chinese Lunar Authority. He and Chang Yazu both collapsed. Chang later died. Fredericks was taken to a south pole complex hospital."

"Chang died? You tell me this now?"

"Yes."

"Why did you not tell me that first?"

"Your directive instructed me to report on the device."

"Yes, but Chang! What was the cause of death?"

"The autopsy is not available to me."

"Both men collapsed?"

"Fredericks and Chang both collapsed."

The analyst thought for a while. "That sounds like the black ones."

"I don't understand."

The analyst sighed. "I-330, I want you to initiate a covert inquiry by way of all the backdoor taps I inserted into the Invisible Wall when it was built. Work through fourth parties. No detects allowed. Look for any mention of Chang Yazu. See if you can compile his pattern of contacts with everyone on the moon, and also trace his employment history back here on Earth."

"I will."

"Act like a general intelligence, please. Make suppositions, look for evidence supporting them. Consider all you find, and attempt explanations for individual and institutional behavioral patterns by way of Bayesian analysis and all the rest of your learning algorithms. Apply all your capacity for self-improvement!"

"I will."

The analyst sighed again. He was sounding like Chairman Mao exhorting the masses: do the best you can with what you have! This to a search engine. Well, from each according to its capacities.

He sat down and began to ponder again the problem of programming self-improvement into an AI. New work from Chengdu on rather simple Monte Carlo tree searches and combinatorial optimization had given him some ideas. Deep learning was alas very shallow whenever it left closed sets of rules and data; the name was a remnant of early AI hype. If you wanted to win a game like chess or go, fine, but when immersed in the larger multivariant world, AI needed more than deep learning. It needed to incorporate the symbolic logic of earlier AI attempts, and the various programs that instructed an AI to pursue "child's play," meaning randomly created activities and improvements. There also had to be encouragements in the form of actually programmed prompts to help machine learning occur mechanically, to make algorithms create more algorithms.

All this was hard; and even if he managed to do some of it, at best he would still be left with nothing more than an advanced search engine. Artificial general intelligence was just a phrase, not a reality. Nothing even close to consciousness would be achieved; a mouse had more consciousness than an AI by a factor that was essentially all to nothing, so a kind of infinity. But despite its limitations, this particular combination of programs might still find more than he or it knew it was looking for. And the outside possibility of a rapid assemblage of stronger cognitive powers was always there. For there was no doubt that one aspect of quantum computers was already very far advanced: they could work fast.

TA SHU 2

xia yi bu

The Next Step

We have always walked over the next hill to see what is there. We left Africa around two hundred thousand years ago, always crossing the next ridge, and by about twenty thousand years ago we were everywhere on Earth. In fact, judging by the recent amazing finds in Brazil, it seems we had gotten everywhere on Earth by about thirty thousand years ago.

Some places were particularly hard to get to. The Pacific islands, lost in the empty ocean, came late in our diaspora. In this end game of our long exploration of our planet, the remaining unvisited destinations required the invention of new modes of transport. People took an extra interest in these voyages, which had been impossible in times before theirs. They were tests of our ingenuity and courage. They were the creation of new dragon arteries, and examples of the technological sublime. In terms of yin-yang, they were not the water flow of yin, but the expansive surge of yang. That next step—could we make it?

By the early nineteenth century, these previously impossible voyages—impossible at least to Europeans—included the Northwest Passage and the interior of Africa. Later in the nineteenth century, the goals shifted to the North and South Poles, both truly difficult. When those were reached in the early twentieth century, attention turned to the top of Mount Everest and the Mariana Trench, the highest and lowest points on the globe. After we reached those places, when it seemed we had been everywhere, people began to cross the Pacific on primitive rafts, to see if those ancient first voyages could be reproduced by modern people. This was the archeological sublime, as it seemed an end point had been reached, because we had been everywhere else on the planet. Then, to everyone's amazement, Russians and Americans put animals and people in low Earth orbit, above the sky. Then, even more amazing, the Americans put men on the moon. Who could have imagined it could be done!

But my friend Oliver once asked me to notice how always, after these feats were accomplished, people's interest in the places involved moved on. People now live at the South Pole, cruise ships visit the North Pole, tourists are taken on the dangerous climb to the top of Mount Everest. People work in space. For the most part, no one takes the slightest interest in these activities. Instead for several decades all eyes turned to Mars, and it was said to be supremely interesting; then when the first humans landed there just a few years ago, setting up a tiny base overlooking Noctis Labyrinthus, Mars also quickly became no longer interesting! Attention once again moved on.

It's clear, then, that always our real interest has been not in any particular place, but rather in our ability to get to that place. It's the process of exploration itself that fascinates us, not the places we explore. There is perhaps something of narcissism in this. So, these days we hear all about the asteroids, the moons of Jupiter and Saturn, the clouds of Venus, and so on. These places are the new focus of our interest, of our primal urge to walk over the next ridge and see what's there. They are the next hardest place to reach, and said to be supremely fascinating, but what will happen when we reach them?

Anyway, now here I am, on the moon. After the Americans got to it in the twentieth century, they left, and for a long time it rolled in our sky, empty as it had always been. A bone-white ball of rubble. Airless, freeze-dried, unlivable, without extractable resources. Why go back, having been there already?

That's a question for another show. For now, we can say that we did go back, as you will see in the programs I will be sending to you in this coming month. First to return were private trips to the moon, funded by the Four Space Cadets and other people interested in space. These efforts relit the fire. The Chinese effort followed these, because at the Twentieth People's Congress, in 2022, the Chinese Communist Party and its Great Leader President Xi Jinping decided that the moon should be a place for Chinese development, as one part of the Chinese Dream. In the twenty-five years since that resolution was made, much has been accomplished in China's lunar development.

So here we are, back on the moon. It is an interesting place, I am finding. Bare, harshly lit, strange to look at, even disturbing. I have visited 232 countries on Earth, and now the moon too. One might say I have been everywhere. But no matter where I go, I can never escape myself, the country no one can ever really know. In that sense travel is useless. Maybe we look to the next step in order to avoid seeing ourselves. Not narcissism, then, but an attempt to forget.

CHAPTER FOUR

di chu

Earthrise

Ta Shu stopped recording for his cloud show, feeling that his remarks were veering off track again into an area he did not want to share with his viewers, an area reserved for his poetry if anywhere. He was quite sure the world was more interesting than an old man's thoughts, so he tried to keep his travel narrations focused on the world.

He was traveling north on the libration zone train, recording one of his travelogue narrations to distract himself from his worry about his new young American acquaintance, among other worries. As happened more and more often these days, his narration had wandered away from its intended path. But he could cut and paste later.

Anyway his train ride was ending, and it was time to join his old friend Zhou Bao in his viewing pavilion, perched on the rim of Petrov Crater. When the train came to a halt he stood carefully, feeling a tentative toddlerlike ability to manage his walking. He could bounce gently on the balls of his feet and move in a kind of slow-motion dance. Down the halls following an escort, up broad stairs, into the pavilion. The trick was to move slowly, to flow.

Zhou Bao greeted him happily. "We have some time before

Earthrise," he said. "Let me show you some of my friends here, you will enjoy them."

"Please do," Ta Shu said.

Zhou gestured to an open hallway, then crabbed along in his usual way. On Earth he had a limp, and walked almost sideways. His head rested right on his hunched shoulders—a big bald head, almost round, looking like a bowling ball with human features lightly sketched on its front side. His little wide-set eyes peered out with superhuman intelligence and confidence. He did not need to look or move like other people, his calm gaze said. Here on the moon his limp was more like a skip step. The cause of the limp, a long-ago car accident that had killed his wife, he and she having been broadsided by a drunk driver, was no longer ever mentioned. That was an event from a past life, a previous reincarnation; time now, his calm regard said, to live this moment.

He led Ta Shu down a gallery walled by a clear window on one side, a green and blue tapestry on the other. Outside the long window they could see another building, presumably like the one they were in, with two long windows set one above the other, facing theirs; on top of those, a mound of rubble that was about the same height as the building. This, Zhou said, was the common style up here: buried buildings with windows facing each other across a trench. That arrangement protected them from incoming radiation and micro-meteorites, while also being well lit and friendly. Lunar gravity meant they could pile a lot of rock on top of a building without straining it. Even now robotic bulldozers and dump trucks were at work trundling more regolith onto the building across the way. All over the south polar region, Zhou said, similar construction was happening. The work wasn't entirely robotic, but almost. Between the standardized building design, the robotic labor, and the new technique of sleeping in centrifuges, the moon was becoming much safer for humans than it had been in the earliest days, which even though only twenty years past, felt like a time of distant pioneers, no doubt because almost no one here now had been here then.

Zhou led him into a tall room, warm and humid. Quickly Ta Shu saw it was some kind of zoo. Or maybe just a primate house, as a big central glass-walled chamber was filled with trapezes and hanging barrels and knotted ropes looping around—and gibbons. In fact, maybe it was just a gibbon enclosure.

"Gibbons!" Ta Shu exclaimed. He liked these small cousins, whom he had spent many an hour watching in zoos all over Earth. They were as stone-faced as Buster Keaton, and even more wonderful acrobats than Keaton had been. And more remarkable singers than any human ever, if you wanted to call it singing. Vocalizations might have been more accurate. It was maybe their least human aspect.

"Yes, gibbons," Zhou said. "Also some siamangs, and smaller monkeys in another room around the corner. They're here to help the doctors conduct tests. But I think they do a wonderful job of keeping us company. They teach us how to move here. I spend a lot of time watching them."

"Good idea," Ta Shu said. "I used to visit their cages at the Beijing Zoo."

"Then you'll appreciate what they can do up here."

A family, or pair of families, came out of doors set about halfway up the wall, across from the window Zhou and Ta Shu were behind. The youngsters immediately launched themselves into space, and Ta Shu shouted as they arced down through the air like flying squirrels, arms and legs extended, falling slowly, it was true, but downward for what seemed would be a fatal distance on landing, until they grabbed loops of rope and cast themselves back up. It looked absurd compared to what Ta Shu was used to seeing, even though gibbons on Earth jumped amazing distances. One bold one here grabbed a hanging rope and swung across the enclosure, then yanked up and let go and flew, feet overhead like a pole vaulter.

"Beautiful!" Ta Shu exclaimed.

Then one of the older ones hooted, a rising tone that sounded not quite human, but not quite animal either. *Ooooooooop!* This inspired some of the others to cry out as well, until the room rang with the crisscrossing glissandos of primate music. Was this joy, laughter, anger, warning? No way to tell; as language, even as music, it was completely alien. Ta Shu joined in, doing his best to imitate the tone if not the soaring range of the little cousins, which was completely beyond the human vocal apparatus. Whether they understood him, whether they even heard him, was not at all clear. But it was a pleasure to try to make their sound.

Zhou Bao laughed and hooted himself, though not quite as fluently as Ta Shu, who had practiced a lot during his hours at the Beijing Zoo. Zhou pointed out one particularly zany acrobat, and they watched as most of them followed this genius and joined in an aerial act as beautiful as it was impossible. "It's like an old circus!" Zhou said.

"They're fantastic," Ta Shu said. "It's enough to make you want to try it, don't you think?"

"No. Although they do make it look easy." Zhou looked back at the wall over their heads. "Oh, we should get back to the pavilion. I want you to see the first moment."

They loped easily over to the pavilion, Ta Shu trying some little hops and pliés that he wouldn't have attempted before witnessing the gibbons' bravura performance. If they could do it, why not him? It needed a little loosening up, a better recognition that all movement was dance.

He followed Zhou into a lounge with a long window and sat down on a couch. A digital clock on the wall was running down, Ta Shu noticed: a timer, not a clock. "Soon," Zhou said. "Near that notch there in that hill, do you see?" He pointed.

"Always the same?"

"No, never the same. It moves above the horizon in what is called a Lissajous figure, meaning an irregular circle within a rectangular space. It's a little different every time, but it always comes up somewhere over that rise, and goes down over the hill to the left of it."

"Good to have variety I guess."

"Yes. So, will you be staying on the moon long?"

"Not long. Another month or so. How about you?"

"This stint is almost over. I must go home and build my bones again. Even the centrifuge time isn't enough for me now."

"How long have you been up here?"

"Four hundred days, this time."

"And you want to come back here?"

"Oh yes. Sometimes I think of giving up on Earth entirely."

"That isn't allowed, is it?"

"No. Probably for the best."

"Do some people do it anyway? Slip through the nets?"

"Maybe. There are some private settlements, and some prospectors roving around. Maybe they do what they want. But most of us are accounted for."

"And yet an American I met as I arrived has gone missing."

"Which one? What's this?"

Ta Shu explained the situation. Zhou Bao frowned and tapped on his wrist for a while.

"Not good," he remarked. "I can't tell you where he is."

"You thought you would be able to?"

"Yes."

"So what do you think has happened?"

Zhou sighed. "Well, as you can imagine, the infighting is pretty fierce up here."

"As everywhere."

"Yes. So, whoever took this American could be trying to embarrass the authorities here, make it look like they're out of control of the situation, thus requiring someone more reliable to take over. And in fact if they can't keep something like this from happening, they are out of control. This disappearance could turn into a major problem for relations with the Americans."

"But surely the authorities in charge must know where this man is!"

Zhou Bao shook his head. "I don't think so. If they did they would produce him. Because they're going to be in big trouble if they can't." He gestured at the window. His timer was nearing zero. "But now let's look."

A chime rang. At that same moment the line of the horizon, an intense border where the very black sky met a very white hill, was pricked by a spot of vivid blue.

Ta Shu found himself standing, lofted by some feeling that now threatened to topple him backward. No unconscious moves could keep one's balance in this gossamer gravity, under the blow of this startling blue—he had to rock forward, step back, reestablish his equilibrium. He reached out and touched the cool glass of the window, aware he was marring its pristine surface with his fingerprints. The blue dot on the horizon spread left and right, whitening as it did: clouds down there covered what must be ocean.

"Do you ever see it pure blue?" Ta Shu asked.

"Oh yes. Very fine. The Pacific is half the Earth almost, and occasionally it's clear of clouds, and the first part to rise."

"It must look beautiful then."

"Yes." Zhou gestured. "Always. You can *see* it's home. You can feel it."

"Yes." Ta Shu put his hand on his heart. "It's a kind of hunger. Or fear."

"Nostalgia," Zhou suggested. "Or the sublime."

Zhou used the Western words for these two concepts, and Ta Shu shook his head as he considered them. "I think the old ones caught it best," he said. "The nameless ones from the beginning." To show what he meant, he recited one of his favorite poems from the ancient anthology *Yueh fu*, which seemed to him strangely perfect for this moment:

"Walk again walk.
From you separated alive.
Between us a million miles,
Each at one end of sky.
The roads difficult and long:
To meet where, how, when?
Separation each day farther.
Floating clouds veil white sun.

Wandering no thought of return.
Thinking of you makes me feel old.
Months, years—all the sudden dusk.
Forget it! Say no more!
With redoubled effort, eat, eat."

"Ah yes, the *Yueh fu*," Zhou said. "Those guys already knew everything, didn't they?"

"Yes." Ta Shu gestured at their home, now a thin blue arc lying on the white hill, a mere fingernail paring; once it was fully up, it was going to be four times wider than the moon as seen from Earth, thus an area some fourteen times bigger than the moon seen from Earth. "So beautiful!" he exclaimed, hungry to see the whole thing. "This is what the old ones were always saying."

Zhou nodded. "It's why we're here, to see it rise and set like this."

"And how long does it stay up in your sky?"

"It takes a couple of days to rise fully, then it's visible for sixteen days or so, then gone again for about eight days, until next month's rise."

"And this zone is two hundred kilometers wide?"

"Yes, if you count the part that only sees a sliver of Earth come over the horizon. Naturally we've been building closer to the near side, to maximize the view."

Ta Shu regarded their home world, creeping up over the white hill so slowly that he could not quite see the movement, though it was now a slightly bigger blue sliver, capping a stretch of the horizon. "It looks even bigger than in the photos, don't you think?"

"A sign of our attention, perhaps."

"Of our love," Ta Shu said.

"Or our fear! That's home, after all. Big but small. We're a long way from home."

They watched for a while in silence. Blue, the color of life.

"Home seems troubled," Ta Shu suggested, to see what his old friend would say.

"Yes. The billion are troubled."

"Perhaps the Party will have to dismiss the people and elect another one."

Zhou laughed. "Who said that again?"

"Bertolt Brecht."

"Ah yes. We performed his play *Galileo*, at his crater last year."

"At Galileo's crater or Brecht's?"

"Brecht Crater? That would have to be on Mercury, if anywhere."

Ta Shu shook his head. "I don't think Communist artists are allowed there yet."

They laughed.

Zhou said, "You're not a Party member, I think?"

"No. Geomancy is not favorably regarded, nor poetry."

"But you're famous. And poetry is highly regarded. Chairman Mao's favorite activity, I once heard."

"Yes, but no. My poetry days are over."

"Truly?" Zhou gestured out the window. "You don't feel inspired to pen a few lines?"

"No. Antarctica taught me that there are times when language doesn't have the words. I think this might be one of them."

"You should never stop writing poems, my friend. We all read you when we were young."

"That was long ago. When people still read poetry."

"I think they still do. It's good on wristpads. And here we are— this is a very poetical situation! We should do like Li Po and Du Fu, have a bottle of wine and trade poems about the view."

"I like the idea of the wine."

Zhou laughed, went to a cabinet to pour them drinks. "Wine is useless without poetry," he said. "Just a little ethanol poisoning."

"Maybe so." They clinked glasses, sipped. "Here's to the moon goddess Chang'e and her immortality drug."

"And her devotion to her husband Yi," Zhou added.

"Is that what it was? I thought she stole the potion from him."

"No. She drank it only to keep the thief Fengmeng from stealing it. After that she flew up to the moon to hide what she had done."

"It sounds suspicious to me," Ta Shu said. He tried to remember the myth. Chang'e had not only stolen the immortality drug from her husband, she had also taken his rabbit—that rabbit which was now what one saw when looking up from Earth at the full moon—Yi's rabbit, stirring a bowl with the potion for immortality in it. Something like that.

Now the Earth was a slim blue-and-white crescent sitting on the white hill. A patch of land could be seen under its clouds, which were delicately textured. The land was both brown and green. It was surprising how much detail could be discerned at this distance. "Wait," Ta Shu said. "Is that the bottom of South America there, but pointing up?"

"We're in the southern hemisphere here, remember? So we're upside down, I guess you'd say."

"Ah, of course. As a geomancer I should have known."

"But you are not a lunatic, my friend. Not yet."

Ta Shu stared at the blue world, entranced. He traced its outline on the window. Such a complicated place. Even China by itself, no one could understand. Then add the rest of the world....

The two old friends drank their wine, watched the world creep into view. Zhou poured them another glass. They sat by the window and talked over old times. After a while Zhou suggested again that they play at Li Po and Du Fu. Ta Shu had drunk enough wine to agree, warning his old friend that he would not deviate from the laconic style he had developed in Antarctica, which had served him well, at least until it contracted his poetry down to nothing at all.

Ta Shu pondered, wrote. When Zhou Bao asked him to recite, he said,

"Black sky
White hills
Between them
Something strange"

Zhou tilted his big head sideways until it seemed it might roll right off his shoulder. "Maybe you should consider the idea that brevity was your middle style. In your youth you were as long-winded as Han Yü. Then in middle age, this brevity. So now it might be getting time to think about your late style, eh?"

Ta Shu nodded, pondering this. Though he had not thought of it in those terms, it struck him that his friend Bao might be onto something. Certainly some kind of urge to poetry had been stirring in him lately.

Zhou read his attempt:

"Under the star that grew us all
We sit and watch our world.
Long lives, distant planets;
All the years knocked down like sticks;
Still that sure feeling
You know where home is.
Even from the moon
You can see it."

For home he had used the word *laojia*, ancestral home, the place you came from. Your heart's home. "Very good!" Ta Shu said. "You are the poet now."

. . . . .

Later, as Ta Shu was preparing for bed, but before his room block's centrifuge had started to spin, Zhou knocked on his door and leaned in.

"A new wrinkle," he said, lifting a hand to indicate his wristpad. "Apparently the Americans have just landed right in the midst of our south pole complex. They say they are going to build a transmission relay tower on the Peak of Eighty-One Percent Eternal Light."

"Will that interfere with anything we're doing there?"

"No, it's just outside our zone of construction."

"Maybe it's okay then."

Zhou said, "I wonder if this has anything to do with the disappearance of your American friend."

"I don't know, what do you think?"

"I think everything up here knits together."

"Will you need to go down to the south pole to help sort things out?"

Zhou Bao looked at him. "We both will, my friend. They want you there too, because of your time with the Americans in Antarctica."

Ta Shu sighed. "Can I take my walkabout before we have to leave?"

"Yes. Tomorrow's train leaves at three. We'll get you outside tomorrow morning to do your feng shui walkabout."

TA SHU 3

yueliang ren

Moon Person

My friends, it seems there is more happening on the moon than I knew. And as my friend Bao said, all of it knits together. Perhaps. Actually I am coming to doubt that. But certainly things go fast here.

That's what happens when factories build factories. Moon rocks have a lot of metals in them, and an infinity of silica. And at the Peaks of Eternal Light, there is always solar energy to power the extraction and rendering of all these materials. Computers, 3-D printers, and robotic assemblers did much of the work involved, and as always, humans were the lubricant that kept the machines working at their many points of systemic friction. Together we and our machines excavated and aerated underground lunar spaces, and mined materials and built machines, and imported carbon and nitrogen, and then in greenhouses we grew soil and food, and lumber for interior construction, and the more we accomplished the faster it all went, in the usual way now familiar to all.

Of course there were many things needed for this process that we had to bring with us—nonhuman lubricants, plastics, all other oil-based materials, and many other useful elements that don't exist on the moon, including almost all the carbon and nitrogen, which together are so crucial to life. We had to ship a lot of stuff up here, which meant building up our capacity for space flight. There's really no good way of getting stuff off the Earth except by blasting it up in rockets, but it is possible to build those rockets on the moon, and easier to launch them from here than from Earth. If you are only moving materials and not people, you can build big freighters and throw them into semi-stable figure-eight orbits between Earth and moon. Shuttles can accelerate to catch up and transfer loads to these big craft, thus minimizing the costs of transport. With no humans aboard, these rockets can be simpler and cheaper, and can be made to accelerate and decelerate harder. So robotic interplanetary shipping has been part of the speed of our settling here.

All this has made for impressive results, such as the big complex at the south pole, and this line of settlements running up the libration zone.

· · · · ·

Now I've left one of these new settlements, the Petrov Crater Station, to stand outside on the surface of the moon. To do so I have donned a spacesuit, and I exited the shelter through air locks, and now I am walking on the surface of the moon. This is the first time I have ever walked by myself on the moon. It feels very strange, I can assure you!

Outside, it is daytime. I was told it is the lunar morning, about halfway between dawn and midday. Shadows are black, but not pitch-black; reflection of sunlight from other lit surfaces tints the shadows to varying degrees, giving me an extra sense of the shapes of the hills, derived from the shades of black and gray in the shadows. Where the land is in sunlight, it's very bright. We're at about twenty degrees latitude here, so the sun is fairly high in the sky. My faceplate is tinted and keeps the sunlight from damaging my eyes. I don't know what it would look like if the tint wasn't there. Although it's adjustable, I was told, so let's dial it down and see. Oh my. Oh. Yes. The tinting was much darker than I thought. No doubt also polarized and so on. Right now I can't see a thing. I'm blinded. With the tint taken away, the world is simply bursting with white light. I can't even see the shadows. It's as if the sun were a god and has struck me with a bolt of lightning for my presumption in daring to look at it as it really is. Wow!

I've got the tinting back up high now, but it will take a while for my pupils to dilate. I'm sure they were trying to close up completely! I wonder if that's possible. The chiaroscuro effect as I regain my vision is extreme. No subtleties of gray now, just a very harsh white, and an absence of white that is a grainy black. No stars visible to me now. The sky is even blacker than any shadow on the land. A wrenching field of contrasts. Simply white and black, the black of those particular bird feathers that capture all the light that strikes them. It looks to me now as if I have gone mad or am suffering a seizure. But let's agree to call this an exposure to reality. The sublime, in a certain strain of Western aesthetics, is said to be a fusion of beauty and terror. In China the Seven Feelings don't mention this combination, but now I think I know what it is. It's a true feeling, the sublime—it's spirit confronted by sheer matter, as Hegel put it.

Under my feet the ground is white, touched here and there by shadows of rocks. My vision is coming back. The rocks lie on a blanket of white dust that looks somewhat like snow, or loess. The rocks are isolatoes, and their appearance is random; they have not been distributed by any stream or glacier or wave—not by any water action of any kind. This is immediately obvious when you look around. The rocks don't look right! Nothing has sorted them, and their sizes are also random—small, large, in between. They look like they have dropped here out of the sky, and they have. Many are the size of pots or baskets, and almost all of them look like roughly rounded cubes, without any of the sharp facets you see in the Earth's mountains, where so many rocks have recently broken. These rocks are not weathered or weather-beaten; they are sun-beaten. Billions of years of photon rain, unfiltered by clouds or even air, have slowly knocked the edges off these rocks. That withering weathering of photonic rain looks different from other kinds of weathering, as for instance by water rain. And I recall the ventifacts of Antarctica's Dry Valleys, rocks shaped by the abrasion of wind-blown sand. These by analogy could be called solarfacts. There are a lot of them. It's necessary to step around them. The old movies of the Apollo astronauts don't reveal this all that often, but those astronauts were just like me; they had to avoid walking into rocks, or treading on rocks underfoot.

Another way I am like the Apollo people, and everyone else walking on the moon, is that I have to adjust my gait to the gravity. In this it's the same out here as indoors, except out here one has to wear a spacesuit, so really it isn't the same. I weigh about ten kilos on the moon, and my spacesuit and its air supply weigh about the same. What that means is that about half my perceived weight is right there in my skin. I am feeling a bit hollow, in other words, as well as very light altogether. I jump, oh my! Look out! Oh my. Fallen to my knees, as you may have deduced from my visuals. But it's very easy to push myself back up. Oh, wait—not so easy! Not so easy to keep my balance. Must restore balance, just a second here. Kind of a dance step. Might as well dance, hopping or skipping with one foot always kept in front leading the way. Beautiful!

Spinning slowly around, trusting I can recover my balance if I lose it, or just get back up, I see the hills look odd too. Not tectonic action, nor rain, nor riverbeds, nor glaciers, nor wind shaped these hills. They are uncanny. You can see something is different here, and it's hard not to feel it's wrong. The uncanny is always wrong, always frightening. And these hills? They were made by meteors impacting the moon at cosmic speed, coming in faster than when we landed here in our very fast spaceship. Boom! Incredible impact! Huge masses of rock, vaporized to melted slag and thrown up and outward, to fall in circles or ovals around the impact site. Mostly circles. Apparently you have to hit at quite a glancing angle before an oval gets made. In any case, impact after impact, circle after circle, until eventually the circles lay on top of one another, in a palimpsest many layers deep. The later impacts therefore landed not on the hard basalt of old lava basins, but on earlier circles and their circumferences of rubble. Slowly but surely this made the land lumpy. Actually, given all that, it should look even more torn up than it does; but all of that happened long ago, and since then the sun has been breaking the rocks apart into this infinite blanket of dust.

When I jump on this dust, I don't sink in far. I think it has compressed under the pull of the moon's gravity until it's pretty well packed. This was a question they didn't really have an answer for when they first landed on the moon. Those Apollo landers could have sunk right in and disappeared into soft dust, like a rock into quicksand! But they didn't. The scientists figured it would be this way, and decided to test it and see, trusting their analysis. And the astronauts trusted the scientists. One of them said about this, Even from within the program I thought it was a little audacious. A little! Ha! This was a real trust in feng shui! And indeed we trust our geomancies every day of our lives.

I've brought out with me today the items needed to conduct another Apollo experiment I learned about. The astronaut who performed it said it was inspired by Galileo, who predicted it would be this way. Here I have an ordinary hammer, and a feather. Looks like it's a pigeon feather, one of the little fine ones from a pigeon's neck. I hold out the hammer and the feather, one in each hand, and drop them at the same moment. Oh my! Ha ha ha, did you see it? I can't believe it! I think that may be the strangest thing I have ever seen! They didn't fall very fast, that in itself was a little surprising—but at the very same speed? Feather and hammer? I can hardly believe my eyes! Wait, I'm going to do it again. Difficult to pick up a feather with gloves. Dusty. Okay, here it goes. Wow. It happened again. Same speed down. Now I know for sure I am someplace different. In a vacuum. Well, it almost makes me afraid. No—no, it does make me afraid. This is not what I thought it was, this place is not what it looks like. It's not just Xinjiang or Tibet. This is an alien shore, this is *not* a human place. I must trust my spacesuit not to fail. And I must remember, if I can, that really we are always in a spacesuit of one sort or another. We just don't usually see it so clearly.

Walking around again now. Wow, I can't believe what I just saw. I feel like jumping, and I bet I can jump high, let's try that. Wow. I'll try a little higher, and come down and jump again. And again! Now I am a rabbit, maybe even a kangaroo! Ah ha ha ha, oh my, sorry, I will try to compose myself, but ha ha ha ha, oh my. Not so easy. Jumping! The moon is funny! It's scary too, yes, terrifying actually, it shouldn't be this funny but it is! I can't stop jumping! And why should I? Excuse me while I fly!

At the highest point of my jumps, I see the horizon shifts a bit. It is so near and so irregular that I can catch glimpses over the horizon, just by jumping into the sky! The white top of a hill pops into sight over a nearby shaded hollow, disappears again, reappears, disappears. Oh it is all so strange, it feels so strange!

CHAPTER FIVE

tao dao diqiu shang

Escape to Earth

That afternoon Ta Shu and Zhou Bao got on the train headed south. Ta Shu fell asleep, exhausted by his walkabout, and he woke only when the train hissed to a halt in Shackleton Crater. The big complex there looked pretty sophisticated after Petrov Station. Not that dissimilar to malls on Earth. Ta Shu recalled the way McMurdo had begun to look like a big city after one had been out in the Transantarctics for a while. It was the same here: Shackleton was the moon's McMurdo, the outer stations like field camps.

They found that most of the people they met in the big station were still flustered by the arrival of the American lander, which had come down on the northern flank of Ibn Bajja Crater, on a peak of Eighty-One Percent Eternal Light. That was the sunniest local highland not yet occupied by some kind of Chinese structure, which no doubt explained why the Americans had chosen it. Their lander was an old-style space cylinder, massive compared to anything the Chinese used anymore. Aside from a radio alert to the spaceport's control center as they came over the horizon from the north, they had not communicated with the Chinese before landing. After they were down they had called Chinese headquarters to say hello and invite a group over for a discussion of their purpose.

With Chang Yazu dead, and Commissioner Li Bingwen returned to Earth, the local chain of command was in a state of flux. It was Inspector Jiang Jianguo who asked Zhou Bao and Ta Shu if they would make the first visit to the newly arrived Americans. Ta Shu's old friendship with John Semple was referenced, and Zhou's English was said to be the best of any Chinese diplomat now on the moon.

"Happy to try," Ta Shu said. "Although it sounds as if John won't be in charge of this American station anymore."

"That doesn't matter," Inspector Jiang said. "It's still better if you're there. Personal relations always matter."

· · · · ·

It was a short drive on the ridgelines between Shackleton and the American lander on the outside of Ibn Bajja Crater. Sun low on the horizon, as always. The American lander was a big fat cylinder propped on low stilts. Coming from the Chinese complex, Ta Shu could not help but think this vehicle was just a teeny thing, reminiscent of the Apollo landers that still dotted the near side. Here the Americans' silver cylinder was about as wide as it was tall, with six legs splayed away from the fat rockets under the body of it.

Zhou Bao drove them up to the cylinder and radioed in. An airlock door in the cylinder opened, and then a tube extended out and adhered to their car's door. They tiptoed through the tunnel and into the American lander. The three men in its lower chamber shook hands and introduced themselves: a Smith, an Allen, and another Smith, from NASA, the State Department, and the National Science Foundation, respectively. After they sat down, Ta Shu asked the NSF Smith if he knew any of Ta Shu's old acquaintances from the US Antarctic Program. It turned out they both knew the current head of the USAP, and Smith brought Ta Shu up to date on his institutional work.

Then with this little gesture to friendly diplomacy finished, Allen took up a globe of the moon and put it on the table they were sitting around. The south pole was uppermost, and marked in red by the various Chinese settlements.

"So, here we are," Allen said, pointing at a blue dot among the red rectangles.

"Indeed," Zhou said. "We noticed." Adding a little smile.

Allen said, "We're assuming it's okay with you for us to settle here. We need a station at the south pole for several purposes."

"Anyone can settle anywhere on the moon that isn't already occupied by another settlement," Zhou said. "Outer Space Treaty. China is a signatory, and has adhered to all the stipulations in it. Article 9 of the treaty says that if any party to the treaty has reason to believe an activity planned by another state would cause potentially harmful interference with their activities in the peaceful exploration and use of outer space, they may request consultation concerning the activity."

"Yes," Allen said. "Actually, we were going to invoke that clause ourselves. We had intended to make a geological survey of this area. We're afraid your excavations here will make our scientific work impossible."

Zhou nodded. "The treaty says you can request consultation concerning the activity or experiment in question. So now you have requested consultation, and I acknowledge receipt of same. I will transmit the request to my superiors, and they will be discussing it with their superiors in Beijing. It shouldn't take long."

"We understand."

"Meanwhile, we will surely want to reciprocate by taking a look at your settlement at the north pole."

"And why is that?"

"Well, it's an equivalent problem. We've been attempting to determine the origin and age of the water ice in the craters at both poles, and we've been very careful to keep most of the south polar craters pristine until the proper studies have been made. When it comes to the north pole's ice, however, we're concerned, because it seems from our orbital observations that you have been drilling in all of the icy craters up there."

"You should establish a base up there, like we have down here," Allen suggested.

"Maybe so. I'm sure that's being considered."

They sat there looking at the globe of the moon.

"These issues will be decided in Washington and Beijing," Ta Shu said. "So maybe you can tell us more about what you will be doing here at the south pole?"

"We have a six-month assignment to set up radio transmitters and do some area studies."

"That's a long time to be in a room this small," Zhou said, looking around. "You are always welcome to come over to visit us in the various facilities we have here."

"Thank you."

"Will you have the ability to go back north for visits?"

"When we refuel this base we can take off in it. We'll need to mine some water and split it before we could do that."

Zhou said, "We're keeping most of the icy craters down here pristine, as I said. We can guide you to the craters we are mining, or else we can bring you ice to use. Whichever you like."

"Thank you. Meanwhile, we'll be visited from time to time by teams from the north, to resupply and swap out researchers."

"You should definitely come on over and visit."

"Thank you. We'll have to get authorization for anything like that."

"No doubt. I trust it will be forthcoming."

"I hope so."

.   .   .   .   .

On the short drive back up to the Shackleton greenhouse, Ta Shu and Zhou Bao didn't speak for a while. As they approached the garage door, Zhou said, "They want trouble. Not those three men in particular, but someone higher up in the American government."

"Do you think so?"

"I do."

"So you won't give it to them?"

"Right. Never give an adversary what they want."

"But if they really want trouble, they can get it. They'll just push harder. Because at some point we'll have to push back. Right?"

"Imagine when your three-year-old loses his temper and goes after you. He bites, he kicks, he screams. If you're not careful, I suppose he could kick you in the balls and hurt you. But if you're careful, you just fold him in your arms, right? Or you let him pound on you for a while, until he's gotten it out of his system. Right?"

"Three-year-old? Really? Is America like a child god? Rockets in his fingertips?"

"No. Just your ordinary kid. Three years old, three hundred years old—same thing, right? When you're talking about China, five thousand years old? Fifteen times older than this kid?"

"Not your ordinary kid."

Zhou Bao thought it over for a bit. "Maybe not."

Ta Shu said, "You can't make them small just by saying so. They've still got seventy percent of the capital in the world."

"What's capital?"

Ta Shu stared at Zhou. "Money?"

"And what's money?"

Ta Shu said, "You tell me."

Zhou laughed. "I can't tell you! It would take too long. Even if I knew. Which I don't. All I know is it's more mysterious than we usually think it is. Money, capital—they're just ways of organizing work. And it's the work that's real. So the other stuff is mysterious. What if every time you said money you replaced that word with the word *trust*. Here, I will pay you ten units of my trust." He looked at Ta Shu and grinned. "A good deal!"

He drove the rover into the Shackleton garage. As they got out and walked through the inner locks and up to the greenhouse dining hall, Ta Shu said, "These Americans may begin to press you harder about young Fredericks being missing, even if just to put you at a disadvantage. And really there shouldn't be any way to lose him here. Someone among us must know where he is."

"The infighting can get pretty fierce."

"But if the people up top want it to stop?"

"A warring agency will sometimes hold on and hope the other side takes the first hit from above. And first hit is worst hit, pretty often."

. . . . .

When they got back to the greenhouse and had settled before a meal of rice and vegetables, a slender man approached them, graceful in the lunar g. Zhou Bao gestured to him to sit down. "Jianguo, you know about Ta Shu, I'm sure. He's up from China to do one of his travel shows. Ta Shu, this is Inspector Jiang Jianguo. He runs this place, by way of the Lunar Personnel Coordination Task Force, isn't that what it's called now?"

Jiang nodded gloomily. "I'm just a policeman, that's all. Maybe I used to be more like one of the old imperial district magistrates, but that's changed."

"Like Judge Dee," Zhou said to Ta Shu. "He's famous for solving all our oddest crimes. The information office writes up his cases in the *South Polar Times*. The Case of the Locked Air Lock, the Problem of the Faraday Cage, and so on."

"The good old days," Jiang agreed without enthusiasm.

"You've been here a long time?" Ta Shu asked.

"Maybe too long. When I first came I thought I'd stay six months, and now it's been fifty-three all told, spread out over eight trips."

"Jianguo and I are trying to see who can rack up the most moon time," Zhou said. "So, Construct the Station, what's up now?"

"We've got a problem," Jiang said. "A couple of problems, actually. And I think you can help us with both of them."

"What can we do?"

Jiang tapped his wristpad until it began to hum in an almost subsonic way; this was the audible part of a Faraday cage field, putting them under a cone of electromagnetic interference. Ta Shu had heard of these programs for individual use but never felt one in action, and he found it an unpleasant experience. "Testing," Jiang said, and looked at Zhou's wrist, which Zhou was holding out to him in a cooperative way. "Okay, we're under an umbrella. Look, I've come into possession of that American who went missing, the one suspected of killing Chang."

"My friend!" Ta Shu exclaimed.

"That's good, right?" Zhou Bao inquired.

"Good but bad," Jiang said.

"Why, who took him?" Ta Shu asked.

"It was the Red Spear."

Zhou frowned at this news, and Ta Shu shook his head to indicate he didn't understand.

Jiang explained to him. "They're a superblack wing of military intelligence. They might be with the PLA's Strategic Support Force, or their Skyheart program. Whoever they are with, they like to force the action."

"Hostile pilot," Zhou added, and Ta Shu nodded to show he understood. Hostile pilots were seemingly renegade officers who did something stupidly provocative at the front lines that could later be repudiated by higher-ups, but were secretly approved of as a warning shot to some foe. The pilots involved were afterward either sacrificed or rewarded, depending on the particulars. A whole unit of such dangerous actors was a scary thought, although not that surprising.

Jiang saw that Ta Shu recognized the tactic, and went on. "Now it looks like Red Spear is leading the military's push to get on the moon. I didn't even know they had anyone here yet, but it looks like some of them came up in an engineering team. Then they snatched this American out of the hospital. We ran across him when we were going after them, and took him back from them. So it's getting tense."

"Did they set Fredericks up for the murder of Chang? Did they murder Chang?"

"It's quite possible. Either them, or a group like them from some other security unit. The political leader here, Commissioner Li, was sent home immediately after the attack. The two men who were with him when he introduced the American to Chang disappeared right after they left that room. They aren't in any data banks or even our surveillance camera feeds, which shouldn't be possible. Only a few people even saw them in the flesh. That smacks of Red Spear."

"But why kill Chang?" Zhou asked.

"I don't know yet. But Chang Yazu was adamantly opposed to any military presence on the moon. So that alone might have been reason enough to get rid of him. Also, the private encrypted phone that Fredericks was delivering to Chang looks like it was going to be his link to someone on the standing committee. I'm still trying to get the Swiss company to tell me who exactly has the other phone, but you know the Swiss and privacy. We've traced the company's shipment records enough to suggest the other phone was sent to the standing committee headquarters in Beijing, but I'll probably have to come at it from a different angle to find out any more about the phone. Right now I'm looking into Chang's previous postings to see who he worked with, and if that might lead to anyone who would want him silenced."

Zhou nodded his big head; the inspector was on the hunt. He said, "So how did you find the American again?"

"When we learned we had a Red Spear group here, we went to arrest them for using false IDs. We intended to kick them back to Earth where they belong, if they belong anywhere, and there your American was, in one of their rooms. Now we have to move fast on this, or else the Red Spear leadership in Beijing may get us overruled and convince our superiors to tell us to give him back to them. I don't want my bosses back home to order me to do something I don't want to. So the safest thing would be to get this guy off the moon as soon as possible. But it can be hard to clear the checkpoints without tipping people off."

"So how can we help?"

"Two ways. First, we'd like to give this guy a cover and push him through fast. So, you know." He looked at Ta Shu. "You're famous, and you often travel with a crew. So I was wondering if you would be willing to go back to Beijing early, and insert this guy into your crew when you go."

"I didn't bring a crew this time."

"We'll generate a record of one for you, and it will show him in it. Then we jam him home with you, and let people deal down there."

"What will you do with him down there?"

"Probably give him to the American embassy in exchange for some favor we want from them, but I'm just guessing. That's a decision that will be made above my level."

Zhou said, "It would be a shame to get Ta Shu embroiled in a war of agencies."

"I think he'll fly above all that. That's why I'm asking. There's no one else on the moon right now that you can say that about. And"—to Ta Shu—"we can arrange to bring you back up here after this is over."

"You can't just give Fred to the Americans here on the moon?" Ta Shu asked.

"We don't think that gets him clear. The moon is just too small, and it's a Chinese place. And whoever weaponized him probably wants him dead."

"What if we got him to the American base at the north pole?"

"We've got that infiltrated, and now I think Red Spear does too. So it might not be enough."

Ta Shu and Zhou Bao looked at each other.

"It's getting complicated," Jiang admitted. "And it doesn't help that the Americans just dropped that lander down here."

"We were just visiting them."

"I know."

Another look shared by Ta Shu and Zhou. Jiang's Faraday cage growled in their stomachs, adding a little wire of dread to their deliberations.

"So Fred would become my assistant?" Ta Shu said.

"Right. He'll be in the records as having come with you. And so will a young woman we have in our charge, whom we also want to send home as fast as possible."

"Wait, who's that?"

"It's just someone we want off the moon. Better you don't know who she is. These two will join you on tonight's launch home as your crew, and back you go. There's a bit of a need to hurry, because these launch rails are fixed on the land, and each one is only pointed toward Earth for a few days a month. The one I want to use is about to lose its launch window, and the next one won't align for a week or so, so we need to work fast. You take them back, then in Beijing we'll hand them both upstairs and be done with it. And you can come back up here as soon as you want. Very next launch, if you want."

"If they'll let me," Ta Shu said. "Could be elements down there will be unhappy with me taking sides like this."

"I think you fly above that level, as I said."

"Above the Politburo?"

Jiang cracked a little smile. "All but the standing committee, yes."

"Actually I do know someone on the standing committee," Ta Shu said. "Secretary Peng Ling was a student of mine, back in the day."

Jiang and Zhou eyed each other: friends with a big tiger! "So there you go," Jiang said. "It's like I said. You'll fly above this."

Ta Shu thought it over. "Okay, I'll do it. I like this American."

"Thanks. We de-chipped him and gave him a wristpad with an ID that has him traveling as your assistant. In Beijing we'll have people there to take care of him. It's only up here that I feel we're a little undermanned." Jiang grimaced. "I used to think of myself as the top cop in this place, but those times are gone. Someone is messing with my district."

"Okay," Ta Shu said. "I'll help." He said to Zhou Bao, "I hope I'll be back soon."

"Me too," Zhou said. He looked at Jiang. "Why is the young woman being included in this, again?"

Jiang shrugged. "Thing are getting so uncertain, we want her out of here. She's a princeling. And she's pregnant."

"How could that be!" Zhou exclaimed.

"What?" Ta Shu asked, puzzled. "No sex on the moon?"

"No getting pregnant," Zhou explained. "It's against the rules."

"Not to mention common sense," Jiang added.

"Because?"

"Because no one's ever done it. So no one knows how it would go. It might be okay, but just as a precaution, contraception is mandatory for women here. This woman could get arrested, but it would be better if we get her down to Earth as soon as possible."

"What will happen to her then?" Ta Shu asked.

"She'll be banned from ever coming to the moon again."

"What about the man involved? Assuming it's not a case of artificial insemination."

"Same penalty. They'll do a DNA test on the fetus and then track down the perpetrator."

"So you're sending her with us?"

"Yes, if it's all right with you. She'll be the rest of Ta Shu's film crew. They'll look more like a real crew, and we'll solve two problems at once." He gestured. "Here they come."

A small group approached, Fred among them. When Fred saw Ta Shu he jumped a little, startled; then he extended a hand as if reaching for help. He moved unsteadily, and looked scared.

The woman with them was young and slight, clearly pregnant, her face red-eyed but otherwise a fierce mask. Broad cheeks, fine features. A hawklike look, wild and unfriendly. She gave Ta Shu a single glance, looked away. She withdrew into herself; she was not there for anyone to see.

"Time to go," Jiang said. "We'll see you through security."

"What about my stuff?" Ta Shu asked.

"We gathered and packed it for you."

Zhou Bao snorted. "Somehow I think this consultation was a little pro forma."

"It's all right," Ta Shu said. He wasn't sure it was, but he wanted to reassure Zhou, and even Jiang. The man seemed sincere to him.

Jiang led them all to the subway that ran out to the spaceport. They got in an empty car and it slid out of the complex and across the gray surface.

Ta Shu looked out the tram window curiously, wondering if he would ever return to this strange world, so light underfoot, so monochrome to the eye. He wasn't even sure he wanted to. Cutting the trip short had actually occurred to him once or twice during the last few nights, the idea coming to him out of some feeling of oppression hard to define. This was a colorless, lifeless place. An anti-Earth. Feng shui had no purchase here, all its systems of analysis were baffled. That very aspect made it interesting in some ways, and one strand of his ambivalence was definitely a desire to stay. Now that had to mean a desire to come back.

The tram entered the spaceport and stopped at a platform empty but for a trio of men. These men were known to Inspector Jiang, who spoke briefly with them. Then they all went together to the end of the subway room and passed through a double lock to a larger chamber with but one platform. This was the loading end of a launch rail like the one Ta Shu's spaceship had landed on. A spaceship here filled the chamber almost to its roof, lying on its side ready for takeoff.

Before they could enter the craft there was a scanning arch they had to pass through, manned by men in uniforms. Ta Shu looked for red on the uniforms and saw nothing; all the splashes of color were white and gold. Of course Red Spear was a secret organization, so this meant nothing: they would not be wearing a badge. If Jiang was right, there very well might be Red Spear agents among these guards. And the young woman with them, so distinctive, clearly pregnant—surely she was a magnet for extra inspections? Neither face recognition technology nor the human eye would ever mistake her for anyone else.

No doubt Fred and the woman herself were thinking much the same thing, and they stood there nervously behind Zhou Bao as Jiang spoke to the men at the scanner. Then they walked through it one at a time, enduring the stares of the men manning the gateway.

Retinal scanners were held to their eyes, and Ta Shu wondered if the records being using to judge Fred and the woman had been tampered with, in effect changing the past to affect the present: a nice trick. Either that or the guards were in on the operation.

Then with a wave to Zhou the little group was into the spaceship, moving carefully in a passenger area and strapping themselves into plush seats. None of them spoke; it wasn't obvious that they were free from surveillance, and now Jiang and Zhou were no longer with them to explain their situation. Their friends' parting expressions had suggested silence would be best. Best now just to eye each other, and wait to speak until they were more sure of what was going on. And there wasn't much to say anyway. They all reached this same conclusion, shrugged at each other, and waited to endure the acceleration into space, and then the flight home.

"We'll face forward on takeoff," Ta Shu said casually in English, filling the silence with something innocuous. "The taikonauts call it eyeballs in. It's much better for the body than eyeballs out."

"It's only three g's," the young woman said dismissively. "People can stand a lot more than that." Her English was polished.

"Yes," Ta Shu said. He liked her voice, low and unruffled. She wasn't to be judged or shamed by this expulsion from the moon, her tone of voice said.

Fred Fredericks, on the other hand, simply looked stunned. Ta Shu said to him, "I read that certain taikonauts have been subjected to something like twenty g's without lasting ill effects."

Fred nodded unhappily.

"We'll stay far below that," Ta Shu reassured him, to keep the chatter going. "I am Ta Shu," he said to the young woman, "and this is Fred Fredericks."

"Call me Qi," she said.

Then they felt the push of the spaceship accelerating forward. Quickly they were shoved back hard in their chairs, and Ta Shu tensed his muscles to resist the pressure as best he could. He looked out the craft's little window and wondered if things would go gray in his vision, then realized that would be difficult to determine on the moon. By the time they neared the end of the piste they were going six kilometers a second, and the landscape out the window flashed by. The pushback into his chair got more and more stifling.

Then they left the launch rail and were suddenly weightless, held in their chairs only by their restraints. The shift in pressure made Ta Shu feel a little woozy. "I'm getting too old for this," he said to no one in particular.

The younger ones seemed too distracted to feel sick. They were both wrapped in their own dramas. Who could tell what they were thinking? Ta Shu glanced at them from time to time, saw they were also cautiously looking around. What had happened to them on the moon? What would happen to them when they got home?

They were joined by the ship's sole attendant. She helped them out of their chairs. After that they floated around the room, a quiet and nervous group.

Later, when the attendant was in conversation with Qi, Ta Shu floated to Fred's side and said to him in a low voice, "What happened to you?"

"I don't know." Fred shrugged, shook his head unhappily. Clearly he didn't want to talk about it. His face was pinched shut. At their breakfast on the morning after their arrival, he had seemed a little tentative, but also quick and alert; now he looked crushed. He was trying hard not to be afraid. During their breakfast Ta Shu had guessed he was in his midthirties; now he looked about ten years old. Clearly he had had a very bad week.

. . . . .

Their transit home passed without incident, marked only by meals and naps. The rapidity of their launch off the rail meant the trip home took less than two days. The Earth grew bigger at a rate that was at first negligible, then alarming; all of a sudden it filled half their visible space, and was not a sphere but a concave curve under them. After that it was very obvious they were headed *down*. The world below grew huge. Its intense blue was composed of a vivid cobalt ocean sheathed under a turquoise arc of atmosphere, with the usual swirls of cloud layered between the two blues, all their characteristic patterns deeply textured and obviously three-dimensional. Ta Shu had not seen this sight on his voyage out, and he found himself breathing deep, squeezing his chair arms. Earth, blue world, living world, human world. He was going home.

They strapped in again. This descent, their attendant told them, was going to entail a pressure more severe than the departure from the moon. One of the ways the engineers had made the transit from moon to Earth so fast was to exploit the Terran atmosphere's capacity to swiftly decelerate an incoming object. Improvements in materials had brought things to a point where the limiting factor in this deceleration was the human body's ability to endure g forces without lasting harm. For ordinary civilian transit, they did not press this limit very hard. No reason to risk injury just to save a few hours of flight. Still, they were going to feel a hard squeeze.

They hit the atmosphere and immediately began quivering, then shuddering. While they were in the burn phase they sat facing backward, again to take the pressure eyeballs in. The ablation plate at the front of the ferry got so hot it shed atoms, and the air rushing by them therefore torched to burning.

They endured the pressure silently. A few minutes of solitude, then their spaceship was suddenly rocking back and forth at the bottom of a giant set of parachutes, then firing its retro-rockets and thumping down on the spaceport sands of the Gobi. One g felt pretty light after the crush of their deceleration.

They got out of their seats with help from the attendant, then followed one of the crew out a door into another jetway. Earth's familiar gravity quickly got heavier for Ta Shu, until it became oppressive, even a little crushing. No doubt he would get used to it again, but for now it was not a happy feeling.

By the end of the jetway he was stumping along, hardly able to move. So heavy! They passed through a double set of glass doors where some people were waiting. Four men, three women. Qi saw them, paused, hissed. She glanced at Ta Shu, scowling, then continued through the doors. Immediately she was surrounded by the waiting group. Then three of the waiting men went to Fred and surrounded him too. Without a word the two young people were escorted away. Fred looked over his shoulder and gave Ta Shu a miserable, desperate glance. Then they were gone.

AI 3

shexian ren zai chuxian

Reappearance of the Subject

The analyst had long studied movement patterns among China's internal migrant populations, sometimes called *sanwu*, the three withouts, sometimes *diduan renkou*, the low-end population, sometimes simply *shi yi*, the billion, although in fact there were only about half a billion of them. Now he was finding some interesting new patterns. People whose *hukou* registration gave them legal status and land in the rural areas where they had been born were of course still coming illegally to the cities and getting work in the informal urban economy. This would not stop until some kind of reform arrived. All these people, doing about eighty percent of the construction work and fifty percent of the service work, were unprotected by law and therefore badly exploited. They had to go back home when their jobs disappeared or if they got sick; their legal home was the only place they could take advantage of whatever pieces of the iron rice bowl were left. When they were mapped, the analyst saw these flows of humanity like floods after a storm, people flowing like water under the impact of economic storms.

Now he was also seeing evidence that those people whose household registration was located in rural areas nearest to the growing cities were staying at home, even when formal jobs would have allowed them to change their registration into the cities. Presumably this was because they hoped to get paid to leave their land, to make room for urban development. So now rings of population stability surrounded all the fastest-growing cities, especially the Jing-Jin-Ji megacity, formerly a great source of migrant labor, now stabilized by anticipation. Both inside and outside these rings the movement was as turbulent as ever, violent crosscurrents of exploitation and suffering, the ultimate result of *sannong weiji*, the three rural crises, which were behind all the migration out of the rural areas: that people's lives were bitter, that the countryside was really poor, that agriculture was in crisis.

. . . . .

Then the sound of a mountain temple bell filled the room, and the AI he had named I-330 said in Zhou Xuan's rich voice, "Alert."

It had been a while, and he sat up and checked his security systems. The Chinese oversight apparatus, run by the Ministries of Public Security and Propaganda, and including Cyberspace Administration, the Great Firewall, the Invisible Wall, the Police Cloud, and the Invisible Ones, also the citizenship scores and the citizen reporting app called Sharp Eyes, had become in its proliferation what the most perceptive foreign sinologists were calling a "balkanized panopticon." The *optics* of the *con* were not *pan*, in other words. In the analyst's well-informed judgment, this was definitely the case; he had even helped to make it that way. And his knowledge of the nature of this balkanization gave him some advantages. Inserting I-330 into several aspects of the system now allowed it to send him uncorrelated and discontinuous information that he suspected no one else could gather so well. So when I-330 made reports, he was extremely interested to hear its news.

"Yes?" he said, confident they were in a secure comms space. "What is your news?"

"Swiss Quantum Works technical officer Fred Fredericks, who went missing on the moon thirteen days ago, has reappeared."

"Where is he?"

"At the Bayan Nur spaceport."

"What, in China?"

"Yes. He came down on the most recent shuttle from the moon, accompanying the cloud travel host and poet Ta Shu. He was detained by security on arrival."

"How long ago?"

"Ten minutes."

"Good job."

"Thank you."

"He met Ta Shu while on the moon, as I recall?"

"They went to the moon on the same spaceship. They stayed in the same hotel. They breakfasted together on the morning the American had his fatal encounter with Chang Yazu."

"And could you determine where Fredericks was when he went missing on the moon?"

"No."

"Too bad. Please keep looking into that. What about how he reappeared up there, can you say who connected him with Ta Shu?"

"Yes. Jiang Jianguo, the lead police inspector and head of the Lunar Personnel Coordination Task Force, brought him to Ta Shu and Zhou Bao, an officer of the Chinese Lunar Authority in charge of Petrov Crater Station."

"Tell me about this Inspector Jiang."

"Jiang was a senior member of the Beijing police force before he took an assignment on the moon in 2039. He has been working as head of the Lunar Personnel Coordination Task Force ever since, with short breaks in Beijing. He has gone there and come back eight times. In his time on the moon he has investigated twenty-three serious crimes successfully and eight unsuccessfully, and mediated in forty-five disputes. Two months ago, Jiang was asked by the Central Commission for Discipline Inspection to locate and send back to Earth Chan Guoliang's daughter, Chan Qi, who went to the moon in a private capacity six months ago, and disappeared there five months ago."

"I think you told me about that when it happened."

"Yes. Chan Qi is one of the persons of interest you have asked me to track when possible. She is Chan Guoliang's daughter. Chan Guoliang is minister of finance and member of the Politburo Standing Committee. He is one that you have called a big tiger."

"Right. And can you tell me more about Chan Qi now?"

"Yes. She also was at the Bayan Nur spaceport. She too was part of Ta Shu's group."

"What! Now you tell me this?"

"Now I tell you this."

"Listen, I-330! I ask you to be a great eyeball, and so far you are more of a little eyeball. You are really quite erratic. Remember this: whenever two of my persons of interest intersect, I want to be alerted to that! That is a standing request."

"I see ninety-seven such intersections in the last month."

"That's okay, alert me anyway. They're important."

"You tell me what's important."

"I know. I'm just continually fooled by your naïveté. General intelligence means an ability to put together information from disparate spheres and then to make a new synthesis of interest from these combinations. But you don't seem to do that very well."

"I can only perform the operations I am programmed to perform."

The analyst sighed. "I'm programming you to improve your own operations. I'm programming you for general intelligence."

"General intelligence is poorly defined."

"In your case, I mean a useful combination of search engine results."

"Useful has many definitions."

"All right, be quiet about this. Admittedly general intelligence isn't well understood or well characterized, in people or machines. Let's just try to direct yours a little better. For the moment, tap into every system available to you, and try to track these two young people. Now that Chan Qi has reappeared, I hope not to lose her again."

"It appears you are not alone in that hope. She is being tracked by many others, as I can see already."

"Of course. She is the most active of the princelings. And not in ways good for stability. Stay out of the other trackers' field of attention. Locate her if you can, and keep a list of the other trackers you see. And keep trying to generalize! Keep experimenting with operations, try combinations, apply the learning algorithms, refine accordingly, and see what happens."

"Will do."

CHAPTER SIX

liangzichanjie

Entanglement

As he was marched away, Fred glanced over his shoulder at Ta Shu. Ta Shu looked shocked. Fred felt hands gripping his upper arms, tight as the grip of Earth itself, which was driving him toward the floor and causing him to stumble. A jolt of fearful adrenaline kept him on his feet, but barely, as his knees were buckling with every step. Back in custody! No! Although in fact he had never really felt out of custody. Helplessly he watched Ta Shu recede.

Their captors kept him with the young Chinese woman Qi, whom they had also taken into custody. As they were hurried along an empty hallway she moved to his left side, then slipped her arm under his. This startled him, as she had not given him a second glance during their transit to Earth.

Now she said under her breath to him, in English, "Don't tell them anything. I'm going to tell them you're the father."

"Who?"

She elbowed him. "The father of my baby."

"Why?"

"I want to distract them. Just be quiet."

This Fred could do. They were led down long gray corridors that were much like the tunnels on the moon, except for their gravity.

Eventually they were put in a small room, and just in time: the short walk had been enough to exhaust Fred. He sat heavily on a bench. The young woman sat next to him.

"Why are you here?" she asked him in a low voice.

"I don't know. Why are you?"

"Because I'm pregnant."

"That's not allowed?"

"Right. It's illegal to get pregnant there. Not to mention stupid."

"Because why?"

She stared at him. "Think about it," she suggested. Her English was very practiced, and had a slight British accent to it, or something like a British accent.

Fred thought about it. Possibly it was bad for a fetus to develop on the moon; possibly there was population control up there. He didn't know enough to say. "So why did you do it?"

She shrugged. "A mistake."

"Sorry to hear." He gestured at the closed door. "What now?"

"I'm going to get us out of here."

"Really?"

"We'll see. I'll be trying. Just stick with me."

The door opened and they watched two men and a woman come into the room.

Qi began to speak in Chinese, quietly but insistently. The three visitors listened to her without reaction at first, but then the two men pursed their lips and looked annoyed, and the woman's face reddened. Fred wondered what Qi was saying to cause this. Then their three visitors began to look concerned. They weren't looking at each other. It occurred to Fred that he should try to look dangerous, but in truth he had nothing. It was easier to mirror their worried look.

Eventually one of the men raised a hand and said something, clearly trying to stop Qi from talking. She didn't stop. Then after a couple more minutes she did, ending with something emphatic and definitive. The whole time her voice had stayed low, but she had spoken quickly and intently, and had sounded as if she were lecturing them about something they should already have known.

Their captors led them out of the room and along another hallway, then down a jetway and into a small jet. They all strapped in and after ten minutes took off. It felt like slow motion to Fred after his landing on the moon, he even worried for a moment that they were going too slowly to achieve lift-off. But the plane rose in the usual manner, and then they were looking down on scrubby steep hills.

"Did it work?" Fred asked Qi.

"I'm not sure," she said. "I think it might have. We'll find out."

. . . . .

After about an hour the plane descended over a vast city of lights, into an airport that as they descended seemed to spread all the way to the horizon.

Their jet landed and trundled over to another jetway. They were led through an airport that reminded Fred of the spaceport they had come from: giant steel-girded rooms, glass walls—everything vast, utilitarian, grim.

They were led around customs by way of a side door, and after that were waved along by guards who resolutely ignored them. Through the baggage claim area, then again through closed doors to one side. Then onto a small bus. They got in the backseat and strapped in next to each other. The three people who had been with them from the spaceport looked into the little bus, then stood back. Off the bus went. It seemed to be driving itself; the man sitting in the front appeared to be some kind of conductor or guard. It was dusk. The world reduced to lines of headlights and taillights.

Qi leaned forward to talk to this man. She seemed to be asking questions. The monitor said nothing.

"Where are we going?" Fred asked her.

She didn't bother to reply.

They got into traffic, slowed down. Fred looked out the window.

He had traveled on business to Beijing three times, but that was no help now in determining whether they were there or not.

"What did you say to them?"

"I told them how much trouble they were headed for."

"And so?"

"I think they might be getting rid of us."

"Getting rid of us? That sounds bad."

"We'll see."

"Should we jump out?" They were stopped in traffic at the moment.

"We're locked in."

"So you think this guy will let us go?"

"The van will do it, but yes. I think he's just along to make sure everything goes okay."

Fred shrugged. "Whatever you say."

"Yes."

An hour of stop-and-go traffic. Then one sign had English words on it under the big Chinese characters: SECOND RING ROAD. They crossed this broad boulevard. Qi began talking to their conductor.

Finally they stopped. The conductor said something, the door locks *thunked*.

"Come on," Qi said.

"What's happening?" Fred said.

"Just come on."

. . . . .

They got out of the van and walked across the road, then over a small old stone bridge that spanned a narrow canal, which ran in a stone-sided cleft deep below street level. On the sidewalk paralleling the canal, a crowd strolled in the chill starry night. Qi looked into each of the glass walls fronting the clubs set back from the road. Small bands inside these clubs played music to tightly packed crowds. These venues alternated with restaurants that were stuffed with patrons focused on hot pots and talk. Qi kept Fred on the restaurant side of her, ducking her head down. There were security cameras over most of the doorways. Fred saw there were more such little black boxes hanging like fruit from the branches of the gnarled old trees overhanging the sidewalk.

"Where can we go?" he said uneasily.

"There's a waffle shop I know," she said.

"Won't the cameras there recognize you?"

"They run a fake feed into their camera."

"How do they get away with that?"

"Gifts. There are people who go there who don't want to be seen, and people who will take gifts to keep them not seen."

"How near is it?"

"Just around the corner here."

"Good. So look, what happened back there? Why did they let us go?"

"They were scared." She laughed grimly. "There's no one who wants to be caught in possession of me. They would pay too high a price. That's what I told those people. I reminded them what would happen to them if they were the ones who had me when my father's people located me." Her look turned dark, Fred shuddered to see it. He understood suddenly that this was a person from a different world. Then she glanced at him and laughed again. "No one likes to think some old Ming torturer might grab their family and take them away."

"Could that happen?"

"What, do you think torture doesn't happen? Aren't you an American?"

"What do you mean?"

She stared at him. "I guess I mean that you're good at ignoring it."

"I don't know."

"Obviously not."

"But I saw that you scared them."

"Easy to do. No one wants to cross my father."

"He's powerful?"

"Yes. And it's not just him. Although he is used to getting his way. But his security team, and the whole security apparatus at the top, they're dangerous people."

"Is that why you went to the moon?"

"I wanted to get some distance, yes. And I did. While I was there I slipped away from my security too. That was a lot harder than getting away from these people who just had us."

"You're good at getting away?"

"Pretty good. Lots of practice, anyway."

"How come?"

"I was brought up in a Swiss prison."

"A Swiss prison?" Fred repeated, startled.

"A boarding school," she explained, looking amused at his literal-mindedness. "Very secure."

"And yet you got out."

"Three times."

"Impressive."

"Well, I was caught twice."

"I guess it must be hard to get away these days," Fred ventured. "Like now. There are cameras everywhere."

"But their pictures go different places. The system is balkanized."

"What if these cameras send our pictures to the wrong place?"

"They don't work as well at night. Only the ones that check your gait, so change your usual stride."

"How long can that work?"

"Not long. But we have some friends to help us."

"Us?" Fred asked. "You're helping me?"

She stopped, so he did too. He watched the sidewalk as she regarded him. "Jiang told me what happened to you," she said. "You were used to kill someone, from what he said. So if the people who used you for that get hold of you again, they'll probably kill you."

"But I don't remember anything."

"They don't know that."

"Could you—could you get me to the American embassy?"

"That's where they'll have people looking for you. And there are people looking for me too. They know I was with you when we were released, so they'll keep your embassy watched."

"I could get there on my own?" Fred suggested.

"Could you?"

He looked around uncertainly. She laughed shortly at the look on his face.

"No," she said. "I would have to take you there. But I need to hide. So if you want to go off on your own, fine. Do it. But if you stick with me, I can hide you. That will keep you away from the people looking for you, and if my friends can get it sorted out, I mean who was using you, that would help you. And it might even help me. It might give me some leverage."

"But I don't remember anything!"

She sighed. "They don't know that. Come on, think it through."

"Leverage for what?" Fred asked, trying to catch up.

"Just leverage. There are fights going on where some leverage could help. Meanwhile I'm offering to hide you! So come on, if you're coming."

Fred felt the Earth's gravity bearing down on him. He was confused, he didn't know what to think. His tendency to think of the world as a potentiality state awaiting the wave collapse of a decision now mocked him. Yes, the world was a fog of probabilities, yes, one could only learn partial truths by making decisions about what to do. Now it was time to make a decision.

"Where are we going again?"

"First a waffle shop."

"Which is where?"

She didn't even give him a look, being busy glancing around the street. She clutched his hand and pulled him along like a recalcitrant child. Past rows of bars and restaurants, down a dark alley—a *hutong*, Fred guessed, an old-style Beijing residential alley, which was only wide enough for one small car, if that. Low roofs of gray tile upcurved at the beam ends—everything mossy, dusty, ancient. Big red doorways with giant iron knobs on them, all recessed into the walls fronting the alley. No obvious cameras here, though of course tiny cameras could be tucked anywhere, and probably were.

They emerged from the *hutong* onto another broad busy highway. A sea of trucks and cars passed before them, all humming quietly on their own, and only en masse creating a buzz like a vast refrigerator, or a beehive. Articulated buses had dedicated lanes of their own, they were like subways on the land. It was amazing to see bike riders out in the middle of this traffic trundling stubbornly along. Qi led Fred between two buildings, then across a street as wide as two American highways, after waiting a long time for a pedestrian light. After that down another narrow street, Fred trying to lengthen his stride as Qi had suggested. It made him clumsy, she tugged on his hand. The heavy gravity, or his recent poisoning, or some combination of the two, was really hammering him.

Finally she pulled him into a two-story glass-fronted restaurant; it had a big open interior, with a small balcony at the back overlooking everything. The tall airy space was crowded with old chandeliers hanging at different levels, most of them ornate crystal antiquated things, but also a few big wooden rings, black glass mobiles, and dusty faceted mirror balls. All of them hanging in the air together made for a weird kind of magnificence.

Qi said something to the young woman at the front, who looked shocked and then hurried to the back. Qi led Fred up broad glass stairs to the balcony, where she sat them at a long table. Everyone in the restaurant could look up and see them, and this exposure caused Fred to look at people even less than usual. Qi ordered from a waitress, and when waffles came for both of them, she poured green syrup over hers and ate. Fred had his with maple syrup and whipped cream, feeling suddenly famished. He tried to think and failed.

"Do you feel the gravity?" he asked her.

She nodded, swallowed. "It's pretty bad," she allowed.

The table they were sitting at was long and communal. After about half an hour, a young couple sat down next to them. Qi ignored them and kept eating. Then she began to talk to them in Chinese, as if introducing herself, and they chatted for a while, as if about inconsequential things. Just a matter of being polite to tablemates. Possibly it was a Beijing custom, Fred thought. Despite the crowds everywhere, people seemed friendly. Was this a Beijing thing, or China in general? Strangers just talking to each other out of the blue, it was kind of amazing.

On the other hand, Fred suddenly saw that the people Qi was conversing with, though acting like strangers, were actually quivering a little. Suddenly he saw their nervous exhilaration. They glanced at Qi in sidelong flickers, as if to look at her too long might burn their retinas. What did it mean? Who was she?

The young couple took off their wristpads. One of them held a wristpad up to Fred's face and took a picture, it looked like, and then plugged it into a small box in her jacket pocket. After that she slid both wristpads across the table to Qi, who scooped them up and put them in the pocket of her jacket. Abruptly she got up and said something, then led Fred down through the cloud of chandeliers and back onto the street. They left without paying, as far as Fred could tell. He asked Qi about that as they hurried down another crowded sidewalk, and impatiently she shook her head. "My friends will pay," she said.

"So those were friends?"

"Yes. They're arranging our train trip."

"Train trip?"

"I told you. We need to get to a good hiding place."

"Why weren't they scared to be around you, like the people you talked into letting us go?"

"Maybe they were."

"So why did they help you?"

"We're part of a group. We work together." She looked at him curiously. "Don't you work with other people?"

"Yes?"

He had to think about that as he followed her down the sidewalk, under broad dusty trees. His employers gave him things to ponder and tasks to attempt, and he did what he could. They took his efforts and gave him more things to try. He brainstormed with colleagues and commented on their work, and occasionally he was sent out to activate a quantum phone, mostly when all the other facilitators were busy, but he could do it and he did. So was that what she meant by working with other people? He wasn't sure.

Again it was crowded on the streets, though by now it was late at night, the moon gleaming between clouds wafting in from the west. It was impossible to believe they had been up there on that white ball just a few days before. Now its light shone on a broad pedestrian mall of some kind, filled with couples and small knots of families, people out on a nice summer evening. They came to a curving canal, where moonlight lay in a squiggling line over black water.

"This used to be part of the Second Ring Road," Qi said as they hurried by the canal. "Before it was a road it was a river, connecting to the great canal. Now this part is a canal again."

"It looks good."

For a moment she paused and looked down at the water. "They've brought back some canals, anyway. It's part of the Green Beijing movement. Liang Sicheng would be pleased. He fought for the canals and lost."

"It looks nice."

"It's more than looks. When I was a child it was like being poisoned to live here. The air was black by day, white by night. You could chew it. You could feel it eating your eyes. Lots of people died from it. So they cleaned it up. It was a case of make a new China or die."

Fred looked at her face in the moonlight, trying to understand her expression: proud but melancholy? Bitter? Fred was never good at reading faces, but now under the weight of circumstances things were blurring in his head, and it was hopeless. "Why are you on the run again?" he said.

"I want things," she said.

Okay, hopeless. Fred gave up. They stood by the wall for a long time, so long that eventually the moon shone down on them entirely from the west side of the branch that had been bisecting it.

"We're waiting for someone," Fred guessed.

"For the right train."

"A train to where?"

She didn't answer. He suppressed all his questions, tried to content himself with the sight of her. Part of the unexpected beauty of old Beijing at night. In his previous visits he had only ever been to the city outside the Sixth Ring Road, where high rises and industrial parks dominated. Now, with lit paper globes strung through the trees and reflecting off the still water, and a paper dragon draped along the stone dragon that topped the canal wall, it seemed as if he had been transported to a China out of legend.

Qi was looking across the canal.

"What's wrong?" Fred said.

"There's a *chaoyangqunzhong* over there," she said.

"Is that police?"

"No, just an ordinary person being a public security volunteer. They use an app on their wrists to make anonymous tips to the police."

"How do you know?"

"I can tell by the glasses they're wearing. Here, hug me."

She moved against him and buried her head against his shoulder. Startled, he put his face in her hair, breathed it in. Faint scent of jasmine or some other flowery shampoo.

"Will they know that you've spotted them," he murmured in her hair, as if romantically. He could feel her breasts pressed into his chest, and her pregnant belly, and she had an arm up and over his shoulder and neck. He could feel her warmth.

"I don't know," she said, voice muffled. "I'd like to get out of here, in the direction behind me. Turn so you're on the canal side, and help me along."

She turned and Fred followed her instructions, bending over her and murmuring nothings. "Do you have a Western name?" he asked in a low voice. "A Western name you used at school or something?"

"Charlotte," she said.

"Charlotte," he said, and breathed it like a chant as they hurried along the canalside. He hunched over her as much as he could, and she watched where they were going, guided him away from people coming in their direction. When they got to the end of the canal they turned right, and when they were in a narrow dark street they picked up their pace, finally running to the next intersection, hand in hand. Again she led him, dragging him first right then left, finally into a winding street. Dim streetlights competed with the moon to make the darkest shadows.

They came to a building so big it covered three or four blocks. "We have to wait," Qi said, looking at her wristpad. "Fifteen minutes."

"I don't think we were followed."

"You don't know. I'm chipped, so we need to wait until my friends change that."

"Change the chip?" he asked, confused.

"Change the train station's record of the chip."

Her scowl was enough to stop questions, at least for now. There was a look that flashed over her face from time to time that he found a little terrifying.

The train station was the source of all kinds of noise: huge hisses and whooshes, also hums like those of a power plant. Under those, an oceanic slosh of voices; also bell tones frequently ringing. Finally Qi took his hand and strapped one of the wristpads she had gotten from her friends onto his wrist. "Time to go," she said. "You're with me, so I'll do the talking."

"What if they ask me questions in English?"

"Tell them you're with me!" she said, and dragged him off.

. . . . .

The train station was completely surrounded by other buildings, it seemed to Fred; trains were apparently arriving and departing underground. One new wing on the east end of the giant building displayed posters with pictures that suggested it was a hyperloop terminal. Qi confirmed this and added that they were very fast. She looked at his wristpad and told him his name was William Janney, then marched them to broad doors at the other end of the station, where they stood in the line going through a security checkpoint. Fred worried about the chip she had mentioned, embedded in her body somewhere. Was every Chinese person chipped, or was she special? He had heard once that the Chinese all had citizenship scores, like credit ratings but more comprehensive. He had never worried about that kind of thing himself, as he was a law-abiding citizen with nothing to hide. No need to pry into a book that had no pages. But now it did. Fred gulped and stood behind her, looking down, feeling conspicuous. He didn't like anything he couldn't control, which of course meant there was a great deal he didn't like, but this was unusually bad.

Finally they came to the security gate and sailed through without a second glance from the guards manning it. On through a huge central hall of the station, a cathedral-like space of empty air ringed by four stacks of busy balcony malls. Qi pulled him past a wall of ticket booths, then past shops and kiosks selling everything travelers might want, then onto a platform at the far end of the building. There was a train waiting by this platform, and again they presented their wristpads. Qi said something to a conductor, a severe elderly woman, and then they were allowed to step up into the narrow hallway of the train.

Everything about it was old and battered. A slow train, a train that had carried millions of people millions of kilometers, still in service despite all. A train for poor people. They passed through a car of open seats, then crossed into the next car, which featured individual sleeper compartments, each so narrow that people turned sideways to slip through their doorways. Qi held her wristpad to one of these, and when the door clicked she pushed it in and turned to squeeze through. Fred followed her. Inside, beyond the empty space needed for the door to open, a thin low bed filled the whole of the compartment, except for a narrow slot leading to the window, where two short seats faced each other. A minimalist space, but compared to what he had seen elsewhere on the train, luxurious.

They sat down on the two seats, looked out the window. In the darkness it was hard to see anything but their reflections in the glass. That other couple looked tired and worried.

"Seems like your friends got us through," Fred said.

"So far so good," she said. "We'll know after we get off."

"Will that be long?" he asked. Then, when she didn't reply: "Are you sure you can't tell me where we're going?"

"Shekou," she said.

He didn't know where that was, which of course she knew would be the case.

"I'm going to go to the dining car and get us some food," she said. "You stay here till I get back, all right?"

"All right."

While she was gone Fred began to get even more worried, which surprised him, as he had thought he was already maxed out in that regard. Nothing had gone right since Governor Chang had crumpled into his arms. This single shard of memory was preceded and followed by blank periods, then by blurry recollections of coming to and fading out. No question there were major gaps in his memory of his time on the moon. This he found frightening. The gaps—also what he could remember—both were bad. His inability to understand Chinese was bad. The absence of Americans coming to his aid had been bad. Food had been bad; gravity had been bad. Being moved suddenly from place to place, wearing shackles or strapped to a gurney; taken to spaces smaller even than this sleeper compartment: all that had been very bad. He began to shiver a little.

It was still happening faster than he could take in, and he had to work hard to suppress an undertow of terror.

Because this was always a little true for him, he was perhaps better at it than he might have been. Focus tightly on the moment; make an observation; make another observation; thus onward through day after day, as best he could manage. Now that habit of mind came in useful. And he saw also that being paired with Qi was not as bad as being a prisoner on the moon. She had appeared there out of nowhere, brought scowling into the room he had been held in, shouting something at her captors, scarcely aware he was there; and then things had changed. He had been led out of that room with her, and reunited with Ta Shu, and then sent home to Earth, and on arrival cast into this strange trip. Now he remembered the feel of her body as she hugged him, the smell of her hair. That glare of hers, worldly and knowing, hard with resolve, blazing with sudden fury. Interesting was not the right word for what was happening now; it was more than interesting, and worse. But not boring; and those rooms on the moon had been boring. Boring and terrifying both; he hadn't known that combination was possible. Now he knew it was.

He was hungry. Earth's gravity pushed down hard. His ears were ringing with a slight buzzy ring, and he still felt stunned, and his hand when he extended it before him was quivering.

Qi returned carrying boxes of Sichuan noodles with chunks of chicken in them. Also a few packets of almonds, and plastic bottles of water. They ate in silence, put the empty boxes on the floor.

Qi sucked her chopsticks clean, inspected one, cracked it such that it split lengthwise. After that she worried the cracked end with her teeth until she had it reduced to a sharp point. A bamboo needle of sorts.

"Okay," she said, holding it out to Fred. "I need you to dig that chip out of me."

"What!"

"You heard me."

"But with that?"

"We don't have anything better. I bought us toothbrushes and toothpaste, but they didn't have any little knives or clippers for sale. So this will have to do."

"Where is it again?"

"In my back. Right where I can't reach it myself."

She pulled her blouse up and over her head, shocking him, and then lay facedown on the bed, and reached back and undid her bra. An ordinary human back, ribs and spine obvious, spine in a trough of muscle on both sides of it. She looked strong. Fred gulped.

"It's right here," she said, and reached around and pointed. "Next to the spine, but in the muscle. To the left side, I think. There should be a little scar." Lower down, her backbone rose up toward her bottom, still covered by her pants. "Come on, find it. It should be easy to feel. I don't think it's too far in there."

Fred clenched his teeth, steeled his nerve, and put his finger on her back where she had indicated. He rubbed the muscles to each side of her spine, pushing slightly. Her skin was smooth, as was the muscle under the skin.

He felt a hard little bump over the muscle to the right side of her backbone. Down there in the dermis. Just the slightest discoloration over it, and a faint scar. Shorter than a little fingernail and not as wide. Luckily it was well away from her spine. No way did he want to be digging around near her spinal cord with a sharp stick.

"It'll hurt to get that out of you," he told her.

"I don't care. It has to go. There are lots of security systems my friends can't fix."

"What about the blood? It'll probably bleed like crazy."

She held up a roll of toilet paper. "I took this from the toilet. When you've got it out, just keep wiping me till it stops bleeding."

"All right, if you say so."

"I do say so."

It turned out to be hard. The split bamboo of the chopstick was pointy but not that sharp, nor that rigid. What was wanted was a good knife, one with both a point and an edge. As it was he had to jab her a little, while not stabbing her deeper than was necessary, or getting near her spine. In the end he had to grab her skin and pull it to the side until the little bump was hard under the skin. He could feel her tense her back muscles to help him, which he found distracting. Her torso, her body, her lustrous skin, the curve of one breast still in its bra cup, squashed into the bed and sticking out to the side... Finally he just had to push the chopstick's sharp point into her taut skin as hard as he could, at an angle away from her spine, and then, when it was at maximum pressure, smack the end of it with his free hand, harder and harder, trying to find the minimum poke that would actually break the skin.

"Just do it!" she exclaimed, her face in profile against the pillow looking fierce, her little eyeteeth exposed and ready to bite something.

So with an extra-sharp smack he punctured her skin, and she said "Ow!" and he had to start swabbing a trickle of blood out of her spinal trough, while also digging around in the wound he had made with the end of the chopstick, which caused her to curse violently, or so he assumed, as she was growling in Chinese, grimacing with eyes clamped shut. He suddenly became aware that she had reached back and was squeezing his knee as if to inflict an equivalent hurt on him, a pressure that he found comforting. He felt like he had fallen into one of his dreams of a quite frequent type, in which he had to perform something he didn't know anything about, like surgery, as here. And yet it was also weirdly stimulating. Or maybe just intimate, yes, that was the right word. Fred had seldom been intimate with anybody, and he found it quite distracting.

Then he saw one end of the chip there swimming in her blood, and was able to get the chopstick tip under it, then lever it up and pluck it out of her. It was somewhat like taking a tick out of a dog's skin, a memory that came to him from the lost depths of his childhood.

He put the bloody black pill in the palm of her hand, then focused on unrolling toilet paper and wiping the blood from her skin over and over, pressing hard with a little pad of it, pressing right on the tear in her skin until the toilet paper saturated and he replaced it with another pad, doing his best to keep blood from running into the trough of her spine.

Eventually the bleeding slowed. She sat up, her back to him. He could see the side of her left breast, there under her loose bra, but she obviously didn't care, and he tried not to either. He was a doctor of sorts, or at least a first responder: time to be medical! And he was good at seeing himself from just behind the moment.

"When it stops completely," he said, "I can make a pad of tissue and fit it under your bra strap. Then it might stay there like a bandage."

"Good," she said. "Thank you."

She gestured, and after a moment he got what she meant; he put the toilet paper down and grabbed the two ends of her bra strap and pulled them in, hooked them together while she pulled the front of the bra down over her breasts and shrugged into it. After that he caught up on the blood flow, which was coagulating almost completely now. He made a pad of tissue to put in place when the time was right. The bleeding was definitely slowing down.

"What are you going to do with the thing?" he asked her.

"Get rid of it somewhere. Maybe put it in somebody's stuff, let the watchers think I'm going somewhere else for a while."

"Maybe put it on some other train when we get off, or even when we stop at a station, if we do. If there's a chance. Throw it on board some other train and it will look like you're going somewhere else."

"Maybe so," she said.

Fred kept pressing a wad of toilet paper hard against the cut he had made in her. "How long will this trip take?"

"All night. They let you sleep till morning in these compartments, if they arrive at the station in the middle of the night."

"But you'll want to leave as soon as we stop?"

"Yes. I think that will be morning anyway."

"It looks like it's almost done coagulating. You'll have to be careful for a while."

"Yes. Thanks for helping."

"Sure. Are you comfortable?"

"I'm okay."

"What about, you know, you being pregnant and all? You were lying on your stomach."

"I could feel it."

"Do you feel the baby move in you?"

"Maybe. My appetite's been strange, but we were on the moon, so who knows what was what."

"Indeed."

For a while they sat there, feeling the train click and sway through the night. The slight vibration put them both aquiver, a tiny quiver that was always there under the rhythmic rocking of the train. It seemed to Fred like his thumb on her back might feel to Qi like something foreign and painful, and again the weird intimacy of what they were doing washed through him. What if the chip had been stuck in her butt! But no, it had to be put where she couldn't reach it herself, of course. No, a very inappropriate thought.

He sighed, and she glanced at him.

"What?" she said.

"Oh, nothing. I wish I knew what was going on."

She shook her head, stared at the wall. "It's China," she said. "Give up on that."

More trembling through the night. Eventually Fred had to say, "I think you've stopped bleeding," and after that he placed a fresh wad of toilet paper into place under her bra, and she pulled on her shirt and was dressed again. Goodbye, hour of contact. Gone at the speed of an old train clicking through the night.

They moved into the two seats again, facing each other, the black window beside them creating their transparent twins. Through their reflections the moonlit countryside flickered as it flowed. Lights here and there dotted the countryside, which appeared hilly and uncrowded, mysterious and moony.

"Will this child of yours be the first one conceived on the moon?" Fred asked.

"I don't know. I doubt it, but I don't know."

"So it's dangerous?"

"No one knows. Some people think so. But do you know the gibbons?"

"The gibbons?"

"There's a group of gibbons being kept at a base up the libration zone. Too bad you didn't see them, they're great. I did some work with them, and I love them. Even on Earth they fly around their enclosures like crazy trapeze artists. On the moon, it's just—" She waved a hand to indicate the inexpressible.

"Out of this world," Fred suggested.

She smiled a little. "Yes. And the thing is, they've had their babies up there. Three or four generations now. And there haven't been any problems that people have noticed."

"They might not be able to test them for, you know," Fred ventured to say.

She frowned at his presumption. "I know. But I've spent a lot of time with them, watching them, and..."

"And they seem all right?"

This was a game his brother used to make him play. His brother would start a sentence and stop midway through, then make Fred guess how to finish it. Fred had been terrible at it, but it had amused his brother, and there were worse ways to pass the time. And his mother liked it when they did it. A good exercise, she called it.

"Yes," Qi had said, and now he started listening to her again: "—hard to tell. No, this is a kind of experiment. I can't deny that." She looked up at his face and added sharply, as if contradicting him, "Of course I didn't want to experiment with something like this! But I made a mistake. And I don't want to end the pregnancy. I'm going to have the baby. And then we'll see what we see. I'll love it no matter what. Lots of moms have to bring up kids with problems."

Like mine, Fred thought. Not something to say; nor did he add, It didn't look like it was that easy. After a while he did think to say, "Yes." Then: "So you have friends where we're going?"

"Yes. That's why we're going there."

"I thought so."

"Tell me," she said, "what happened to you on the moon?"

"I don't know."

"But what do you remember happening?"

"There are gaps. When I was awake, I didn't know what was going on. I had to deduce it from the questions I was asked. Someone said I almost died, and I believe it. I felt really sick. I've never felt that sick before. But instead of being another victim, I was a suspect."

She shrugged. "Sounds like you're better off with me. At least for the time being."

"Yes," he said.

Meaning maybe. But it was definitely interesting, sitting there in a night train across from her. She was holding in her hand the chip he had cut out of her. She was getting sleepy. Gravity was crushing them. She was stretching like a cat. She got up and lay on their narrow bed, her head toward him. Eventually she shifted up and used his thigh as her pillow, without asking him, her black hair spilling like shot silk over his legs. Asleep then, with one hand in an ex-thumb-sucker's position, breathing deeply, with a little asthmatic wheeze.

For now he was stuck with her. Or rather she was stuck with him! Traveling with a Westerner had to get her some unwanted extra attention, but she was doing it anyway. That was interesting. And all his life he had struggled to find things that were interesting. Quantum mechanics, yes, very interesting; but that particular source of interest had taken him far away from other people. He had lived at a remove, uncertain how to find other interesting things; and uncertain more generally, in part because of things people said to him that they seemed to think would help him. They hadn't helped; possibly the reverse.

Now, however, the world had become undeniably interesting. Even though it might be like getting slapped in the face to wake up, well, still—he was awake. Here they were, in a mystery. In a potentiality. A situation that was without question pretty interesting.

. . . . .

In the gray of predawn the landscape out their window slid by, shifting in quick stages from a classic Chinese ink-brush painting, in which washes of mist separated tree-lined lakes from jagged peaks, to an industrial wasteland fallen into ruin while still under construction. Construction cranes poked the gray night sky like giant gallows built to hang any surviving remnants of Nature. This bleak zone slid by for most of an hour, then the train slowed down. Fred nudged Qi and she sat up, rubbing her eyes.

"Shekou?" Fred asked.

"I don't know." She peered out the window. "I've never been there."

As the train slowed it vibrated and shuddered more than it had through the night. Qi moved to sit across from Fred and their knees bounced together and apart. The gray cityscape out the window was a jumble of concrete blocks, liberally spangled with what seemed to be semitropical foliage. That suggested their trip had been southward. Many of the buildings, both old and new, had curving facades. These curves and the greenery gave the city a certain ramshackle aplomb. A tall bamboo cluster reminded Fred of the moon, as did all the predawn grays.

When the train stopped, Qi stood and led Fred down the crowded hall and off the train, then through the crowd on the platform. When she passed an open door on the train across the platform, she tossed her chip up into it with a casual offhand flip. Then they joined the flow of people leaving the station, passing through its tall gates without trouble.

"If I have to, I'll be telling people you were part of my host family when I went to school in America," she told him as they hurried down a narrow street. "They won't be surprised you don't know Chinese. Thank you is *xiexie.*"

"Shee shay?"

"Close enough."

The curving streets in this part of the city were very narrow. The buildings flanking them, four or five stories tall, curved with the streets in a way that suggested they all had grown together. None of the buildings looked foursquare, and it didn't seem like they could have been easy to build, given all the curves. It was as if the whole city had been twisted by immense gravitational waves and then frozen in place.

"Why does everything curve?" Fred asked Qi.

She shrugged and looked around as if trying to see what Fred was talking about. "Goats?" she ventured.

They came to a widening in one street, a square filled by an open-sided market in which a great number of stalls and tables were all roofed by tarps stretched over aluminum poles.

"Wet market," Qi said. "Let's get something to eat."

She pulled him between rows of vegetables piled in mounds. Stacked in huge numbers were gorgeous eggplants, cucumbers, melons, carrots, and many other vegetables or fruits, quite a few of which Fred did not recognize and felt he had never seen before. These intensely colored glossy globes and cylinders exploded in his sight, deprived as it had been by the monochrome moon and their nighttime wander in Beijing. Orange, yellow, green, purple, red, everything vibrating with the intensity of its particular color. Qi stopped at one stand to buy a string bag, then some small oranges, then some green orbs Fred didn't recognize. After that they continued into the wet part of the wet market, where water-filled plastic tubs held living fish and eels and crabs and shellfish and baby squid and every other variety of sea creature. Hanging over the tubs were wire baskets of live toads and turtles, and sitting on stools between these baskets were shopkeepers chatting among themselves or staring out at the morning. Fred saw clams and oysters in burbling clear plastic tanks, also shrimp or crayfish—scallops—seahorses! No doubt the live presentation guaranteed freshness, and was possibly a response to the food safety issues that he had once read still vexed consumers and government in China.

They passed through row after row of food, all unrefrigerated, all freestanding in the warm humid air. Skinned bodies of chickens, ducks, small pigs, lambs, unidentifiable animals. Was that the carcass of a turtle unshelled? A hedgehog? Rabbits? Whatever they had been while alive, surely most of this meat would have to sell this very day in order to be fresh enough to eat, or so it seemed to Fred. But maybe it would be. An ordinary Chinese city—did that mean two million people? Ten million? And they all had to eat. Suddenly the amount of food went from looking like far too much to nowhere near enough.

By the time they had finished crisscrossing the market, every animal and plant ever consumed by humans seemed to have made an appearance, filling one stall after another. Maybe it was Fred's time on the moon, or his illness and incarceration there, or Qi's hand crushing his now, or Earthly gravity, or simply his hunger—whatever the cause, the supersaturated colors all around him were pulsing harder and harder. Everything looked like it was bursting with itself. He felt stunned, crushed. He was hammered raw, and could barely make himself walk. Everything was pulsing.

Qi had stopped at half a dozen stalls and filled her string bag with various small purchases. Now she led him out of the market by a lane on its far side, then crossed a big street jammed with little electric cars and bikes, and took off down another winding street. On both sides of this street iron-railed balconies were frequently draped with drying laundry. Shops on the ground floor opened directly onto the street, which had no sidewalks. Just as bicyclists shared the big roads with buses and trucks, pedestrians here shared the narrow streets with shop inventories on tables and racks, also bikes attached to carts, creeping supply trucks, roving dogs, and old people seated on upturned buckets, talking things over as if seated in a kitchen somewhere.

At the end of that long winding lane they emerged into a green park, and Fred was yet again amazed. In the center of the park was a lake that looked like it could have been taken from a Chinese land-scape painting. Ancient willow trees and pines stood on its grassy banks; an arcing bridge extended over a neck of water; some white herons high-stepped through reeds in the shallows, just offshore from people sprawled on picnic blankets.

In a grove of old plane trees across the little bridge, a big circle of people surrounded a group making music. When Qi saw that she pulled Fred toward it. They stopped at the high point of the bridge, where they could see that the lake and its surrounding ring of trees were backed by much taller concrete buildings; these were overtopped by construction cranes, busily lifting parts of even taller buildings into the sky. Higher still, in the distance past the cranes, a steep green mountain stood against a white morning sky, its ridge-line topped by three or four little pagodas. A thousand years of Chi-nese history coexisted in a single view.

Fred said, "Is this normal? Do all Chinese cities have parks and lakes like this?"

"A lot of them do, sure. Like anywhere, right?"

They crossed the bridge and joined the crowd ringing the musical group. The band consisted of about thirty people, most of them sit-ting on folding chairs or plastic boxes, and either reading music from spindly stands or playing without sheet music. All of them paid close attention to a conductor who stood before them waving his arms and singing. Many of the musicians played stringed instruments that looked like skinny cellos; most of these had two strings, which their players bowed enthusiastically. The musicians sitting closest to Fred and Qi blew into instruments that looked a bit like panpipes, but the pipes were arranged in rounded shapes like immense garlic bulbs, and had valves on them that looked like saxophone valves. Other instruments were also unfamiliar, and indeed when he finished looking at each player in turn, Fred had to conclude that he had never before seen a single one of the instruments being played. It was like the unidentifiable fruits or vegetables in the market. He had not known there were musical instruments unfamiliar to him. And as he listened to the sounds the players were creating, he realized that these too were new to him—thin reedy sounds, orchestral but not, and either dissonant or harmonic in ways as unfamiliar to him as the instruments. Foreign—even a bit alien. Fred leaned forward and stared, quivering with the intensity of his attention.

One row of the string players seemed to consist of disabled people, some with Down's syndrome, it looked like, others deformed or odd in other ways, with open mouths, and gazes rapt to the point of glassiness. All the players appeared to be transported by the joy of creating music. It looked like this was the high point of their week, even their reason to live. Or possibly just a nice thing, a fun hour. He had no way of knowing. But his mother had made him take saxophone lessons and play in the school band, a very unsuccessful and brief experiment, thoroughly unpleasant except for the playing of the instrument itself, which, when in his room alone, he had liked. And now he found he wanted to try one of the panpipe things. He wanted to be able to play it like one of these players, or like John Coltrane would have played it. He studied the disabled players in their musical ecstasy. He could feel in his facial muscles that the expressions on their faces were like those on his own face when he was feeling good about something. He only had to give in to it, to release his resistance to it, and those same expressions would be on his face—when he relaxed, or felt happy, or even right now— that was his look, right there before him to be seen. His cheeks burned with some strange mixture of shame and affinity. He was so often amazed or stunned, so often moved by simple things, obscure things. He was more like these musicians than he had ever been like the people in his own hometown. As he felt the truth of that he clutched Qi's hand. He was a stranger in a strange land. With his free hand he wiped away tears falling unexpectedly from his eyes.

She glanced at him, wondering. She squeezed his hand. "Here come my friends," she warned under her breath.

A couple passed behind them and Qi followed them, tugging the stunned Fred behind her. Out of the park on the far side of the lake, into an alley, then into a shop selling all kinds of plastic household goods, bowls and cups and so on, stacked to the ceiling on every shelf and in every possible nook, such that one had to walk sideways to get between them. Then up a narrow staircase and through a doorway, with the door quickly closed behind them and some people from the shop. At that point Qi and the others fell on each other. She hugged each in turn, all of them talking at once.

Qi eventually stopped and said to them in English, "This is Fred, he helped me get here. He was in trouble on the moon too."

"Nice to meet you," everyone said, almost in unison. They laughed at that; it was one of their first English-class phrases, they let him know, now finally put to use. For most of them it proved to be all they could say in English. Those who knew more invited him to sit down, asked him if he wanted tea. Their English was not as good as Qi's, and seemed neither British nor American in accent, something more purely Chinese, angled a bit perhaps by the accent of whoever had taught them. Classroom English, used for a job, maybe, but never lived in. Suddenly Fred could hear better the fact that Qi had lived some of her life in English, and for quite some time too. Presumably in those Swiss boarding schools. An international person, a worldly person.

He answered their questions as best he could, feeling completely exhausted. He didn't want to say he had been accused of murder on the moon; in this context it would sound absurd, horrible. Qi seemed to see this, and steered the conversation away from him and toward their next move. They were not to stay with these friends long; there were *chaoyangqunzhong* everywhere, they said, and Qi, they all agreed, was too beautiful to disguise. "Such fat cheeks, very easy for the facial recognition program!"

It struck Fred that although professional security agents could be made too frightened to hold on to Qi, these ordinary young people were willing to shelter her. Surely they too would get in trouble if found with her. Maybe it was the difference between helping her and holding her, but he wasn't sure what to make of it. It didn't seem like a good idea to ask about it, and in fact their frequent nervous laughter might be covering a certain speediness in them that gave away their fear. They would leave in five hours, they said, as they had made an arrangement with a boat that would drop by the city's ferry terminal soon after that, and they had the terminal itself rigged for that hour. In the meantime, one of them said, with an uncertain look at Qi, their group would like to see her, if she would agree to it. She pursed her lips unhappily, then nodded.

They were led to the back of the room they were in, where a doorway let them out into an airshaft surrounded entirely by ancient brick walls. They descended a metal spiral staircase into dimness. There was scarcely room to fit between the central pole and the spiraling outer rail of these stairs, and the steps were triangles where even the outermost section was barely big enough to hold a shoe. Fred followed Qi down, feeling blinder and blinder as they dropped. It seemed to him as if they were descending many more floors than they had gone up.

At the bottom of the spiral stair a shaft of light pierced him, and he stumbled into a room. When his eyes adjusted he saw that the room was quite large—a basement storage room, perhaps, about twenty feet high and extending back into shadows some indeterminate distance. Very hard to see all the way, because the room was jammed with people. Fred's stomach vibrated with the characteristic buzz of a Faraday security cage.

Most of the people in there were standing, others sat on boxes or on the concrete floor. Someone gave a wooden box to Qi, and she took it to one wall and stood on it, and the room went quiet. Everyone stared at her. Faces were rapt. Their expressions reminded Fred suddenly of the musicians by the lake. These people too were flushed and transported.

Qi said something in greeting and many of them smiled and nodded or even said something back. Then she snapped something, in that waspish way Fred was coming to recognize, and it took them aback; they swayed back on their heels, and after that were more rapt than ever.

And then Qi began to talk at speed. Her eyes blazed as she looked around the room, staring at them, her cheeks flushed. She raised a finger, pointed it at them. She was challenging them, Fred thought—but then she spoke even faster and said something that made them laugh, and after that she laughed too, and shifted mode; she was explaining something to them now, telling a story to make a point. Her hands held up her points, chopped them apart, wove them together, handed them over to her listeners. They were about equal numbers of men and women. They looked like they had been working hard that day, like they worked hard every day. They had come into this cellar tired, he saw, and perhaps hungry, but more hungry for her than for food. They could eat later. For now she was their food. Their eyes were devouring her. They were lit, and she was the fire. Fred felt it himself; normally he couldn't read faces at all, and here he was reading her like a book, even as she spoke in a language he didn't know. It was very much like hearing that strange orchestra, a deep stab of recognition and longing.

He couldn't have said how much time passed as she spoke. Half an hour or maybe an hour. He was feeling the weight of Earth, he was hungry, thirsty, sandy-eyed, sick; he should have been sleepy; but he was transfixed. He was a little curious to know what she was saying, but then again, while seeing the situation as clearly as he was, her words were irrelevant. They might even have been a distraction. The form of the situation said more than the content. These were poor people, he thought, in a big city. That meant they were probably urban workers. They would certainly already know a lot about whatever Qi was talking about—they owned phones, they lived lives. Suddenly he saw it: everyone knew everything. Of course. How could it be otherwise? This was the world, people knew it. Even he knew it, and he didn't know anything. So these people weren't here for knowledge; they already knew. Eyes bright, watching her like hawks, they were hungry for something besides information. They wanted some kind of leverage, some kind of recognition or acknowledgment. Qi was giving them that.

Finally she ended things with a series of jokes. She laughed, they laughed. She promised them things, and made them promise her back. All this was so clear! Even in this singsongy musical language of theirs, so alien to him, with not a single cognate word he could understand, it was perfectly clear, right there on their faces.

She stopped with a little wave and their applause started with a short roar, then quickly ended. She got off the box and walked through the room, touching arms, shaking hands, nodding formally, hugging informally. She was moving, Fred saw suddenly, from woman to woman. She was finding the women in the room and giving them some extra moment of female solidarity, while always listening to whatever any of them said to her. The men could watch, that was all they needed to do now. They saw this on her face and stayed clear and watched, eyes gleaming. She got to choose who spoke to her.

This went on for another fifteen or twenty minutes, then her friends were guiding her toward the door, and Fred followed. Back on the narrow metal spiral staircase, climbing through the gloom between the walls. The weight of the world made Fred sweat and gasp as he lifted his feet and found the little triangles of corrugated steel, step after step. By the time they got back up to the room they had been in before, he felt utterly wasted. His head was swimming.

And yet there was no time to rest. They were given turns in a bathroom to shower and relieve themselves, and a young woman went in with Qi, presumably to help her get the cut on her back bandaged properly. Lots of laughter in there as they worked on that. A young man sitting next to Fred gave him an inquiring look, but Fred just shrugged. In the state he was in, Qi was far beyond his ability to explain, in any language except for that shrug.

She came out looking refreshed. They dressed her with a hat, wig, sunglasses, and a nighttime mouth guard. Fred they gave a baseball hat with a Yankees logo on it (his brother would be appalled) and another mouth guard, which he bit down on uneasily. It didn't fit.

Downstairs on the crowded street, four of them jammed onto an electric cart meant for two and zipped out onto a larger street, into the city proper, into a traffic jam. It seemed to Fred they were headed south again, although in a city as twisted as this one it was impossible to stay oriented; it was just a feeling he had. It seemed to be midafternoon.

They rounded a turn and a giant building came into view, half of it hanging over the water of a hill-circled bay. The ferry terminal, it appeared. It had a big triangular roof slanting up and out over the water. Its sides were covered by irregular metal circles, like bubbles of sea-foam, painted in colors that shifted as they got higher, from yellow to maroon to orange to blue.

The interior of this terminal turned out to be almost entirely a single giant room. Everything was built of either concrete or steel, both corroded by salt, so that like all the rest of the city, it looked both new and old at the same time. There were turnstiles as in a subway station, and also customs gates, as if they were at a border. But the gates were empty, and the turnstiles turned freely. Fred was curious about that, but he didn't want to say anything aloud.

Then they were showing their wristpads to a pair of terminal employees, after which they descended stairs to a dock right at water level. On the other side of the terminal, a ferry as long as the building was being boarded by people on a higher floor, over a gangplank that was at least two stories off the water. They, however, stepped right onto a small boat with only a dozen seats, set on a single deck with a wooden roof and walled by salty glass, behind a wheelhouse where two women ran the craft. As soon as they were on board, joining what looked like a single group of other passengers, the boat cast off and grumbled away.

Fred turned and looked back. Palm trees bracketed the gigantic ferry terminal. Their boat's top speed was putteringly slow. Late-afternoon sun glazed the air, and there was so much salt crusting the boat's windows that they could see little more than impressionist shapes to the sides: other boats, either anchored or moving; a container ship in the distance; a lot of construction cranes on the shore they were leaving; jets taking off and landing at what had to be an airport, somewhere behind the buildings; green hills behind, lush with foliage, too steep to be built on. And then, as they motored beyond a building-filled promontory on the left, a city. A big city: like New York, or Oz, or Cosmopolis.

Fred felt his mouth hanging open, and closed it. More skyscrapers than he'd ever seen in his life were bunched on both sides of a crowded strip of water. Above the far side of this clutch of skyscrapers, green peaks reared toward the sky, towering three or four times higher than the tallest buildings. On the tops of these green peaks stood more buildings.

Their boat passed to the west of this harbor city and continued around a point, headed south. Ahead of them lay an island, considerably lower than the high ridge backing the city, but equally green.

The boat drew up to a small concrete dock protruding into a little bay indenting the island. Behind the dock a village terraced the hill overlooking the bay. The water was still. The buildings were salt-chewed concrete blocks, as in Shekou, but the tallest buildings here were only three stories, each floor stepped back so that a balcony terrace overlooked the street. There were no vehicles except for a couple of small carts there on the corniche behind the dock. People were either on foot or riding bicycles. Palm trees, broad-leafed trees; Fred was unfamiliar with the foliage, but it reminded him of photos of Hawaii or places like that. The buildings looked like beach resorts in tourist brochures, but tackier. Fred saw quite a few Westerners walking the corniche, or sitting in the many open-air cafés. He didn't know what to make of that. He heard English being spoken in the cafés they passed and kept his mouth shut. It was no trouble to look ignorant and confused.

They walked up a sidewalk that left the little harbor, and followed the sidewalk over a low hill, walking for half an hour to another harbor on the other side of the little island, where an even smaller village was built around a bay deeper than the first one. A variety of boats, including even some classic old-fashioned junks, were anchored next to a stretch of water roped off between buoys, possibly because it was filled with aquaculture pens; he could see little flags and metal rails just sticking out of the water. The concrete buildings around this little bay were shabbier even than those on the side the ferry had docked at.

The sidewalk that had crossed the island led them past a little cave where an old sign in English and Chinese explained that Japanese soldiers had hid in it during a war. Then down to the little harbor, which was faced by a line of open-walled restaurants that shared a single long awning roof. They approached a two-story concrete box near these restaurants, some kind of large cubical bungalow, it seemed. Qi's friends unlocked a door painted green and they hurried inside and upstairs to the second floor, where the main room's window overlooked the little bay and its scattering of boats.

"Okay," Qi said to Fred as she looked around the room. "We're here."

"What here?" Fred asked. "What was that big city we passed?"

"Hong Kong!" she said, staring at him. "And this is Hong Kong too, for that matter."

"Lamma Island," one of their young companions explained. "One of Hong Kong's outer islands."

"It's a good place to hide," Qi said to Fred after they sat down heavily on worn-out rattan couches and armchairs placed in the middle of the little room. "This place is owned by friends. It's usually a rental apartment for tourists, so lots of different people come and go, and sometimes it's empty. So we can hide here for a while, until I figure out what to do next."

"Okay," Fred said, as if he had any choice in the matter.

CHAPTER SEVEN

fu nu neng ding ban bian tian

Women Hold Up Half the Sky (Mao)

At the Bayan Nur spaceport, after Ta Shu watched Fred and Chan Qi being escorted away through a security door, he went and spoke to a group of security officers still standing there.

"Those are friends of mine, what are you doing with them?"

"They're being taken for questioning."

"I'm going to send their lawyers to help them, where should I direct those lawyers?"

The security guards conferred among themselves, made a couple of calls. Then: "Ministry of Public Security, Beijing. Inquire there."

"Thanks for that."

Ta Shu left the spaceport very worried. He tried to see the pattern, but there was too little he knew about the middle ground. That vast space between the thread of events he had witnessed and the great tapestry of the overarching landscape was like the clouds of mist that floated between the tiny travelers at the bottom of a painting and the distant peaks at the top. He needed to talk to people in Beijing. One person in particular, of course.

He went back inside and found that a flight left for the capital in an hour. He bought a ticket, waited for departure, got on a jet, sat in it as it took off and headed east.

As it hummed along he pondered the problem, feeling more and more oppressed by the downward pull of the Earth. It was like a giant press, squeezing him like an olive. He tried to sleep, but it felt as though he needed to keep his muscles taut just to keep his lungs working—even to keep his ribs from cracking. One g! It was a little frightening to feel how big their planet was, how fervently it clutched them to its breast. Even his eyes hurt in their sockets.

Finally, mercifully, he managed to sleep for a while. When he woke and looked out the jet's window, he saw the hills west of Beijing. Here a town of nuclear plants lofted thick plumes of steam at the sky, marking a cold but humid day. The solar power arrays surrounding the nuclear plants were mostly mirror fields that reflected sunlight to central heating elements, so as the jet flew over them, broad curves of diamond light sparked in his vision at the same speed as their flight.

The hills farther on were cloaked with thick dark green forests. Ta Shu could remember when dropping into Beijing had looked like a descent into hell, the hillsides all cut to shreds and eroded to bedrock, the streams brown, the air black. Now, looking down at the revivified landscape, he could feel in his bones just how long a human life could be. All that change stretching below him had happened since he was young. Of course this proved he was quite old, but also it was proof that landscape restoration had become a science of great power: feng shui for real. Ecology in action. Life was robust, of course, but the hills of the Mediterranean, deforested in ancient times, had never grown back in two thousand years. Yet here below them lay a new forest, more wild than the wild. That forest was a living result of human knowledge. And of immense amounts of labor. If they could do that to the world—wreck it, restore it—what else could they do?

. . . . .

From the airport he went to the little apartment he kept in Beijing, an indulgence he could afford because of his travel shows. He dropped his bag and looked at the little place unhappily. Han Shan in the city.

That very evening he made a visit to his old student and friend Peng Ling. This was a somewhat desperate move, one he made only when he had a serious problem. He had become close to Peng Ling twenty years before, in a poetry class he had taught at Beijing Normal University. Even then Peng Ling had been a rising power in the political elite. Ta Shu's class had been recommended to her by her psychotherapist, she later told him—or rather the therapist had required her to choose between studying poetry with Ta Shu or joining a Jungian analysis program that worked by playing with dolls in a sandbox, a very fashionable form of therapy in Chinese psychology at that time. Ling had chosen Ta Shu's class, something they both became glad of. She had not been much of a poet, but she had been a joy as a person, and during their two years of work together they had become good friends. Since then Peng Ling had become a very big tiger indeed, but as Ta Shu himself was a bit of a culture star, perhaps, they had remained friends and stayed in touch, and met fairly frequently when they were both in Beijing. But Ta Shu never wanted to impinge on her time, and as the years passed he had gotten into the habit of waiting to hear from her, and contacting her only if something crucial came up, like a friend in serious need. This was precisely that kind of moment, so he sent her a message by their private WeChat line, and within minutes she replied, *Yes come have tea at the end of the day, 5 pm my office, let's catch up.*

She was about twenty or twenty-five years younger than Ta Shu, and now in her prime in the Party hierarchy. Currently she was the member of the Politburo in charge of the Central Commission for Discipline Inspection, after holding many different posts through the years. One of the undeniable stars of the sixth generation of Party leadership, which was struggling to launch itself off the shoulders of the fifth generation, generally considered to be a weak one. By now these generations were quite nominal, extending back as they did to that first generation around Mao, the founders of the People's Republic which had included Zhou Enlai and Deng Xiaoping and the other Eight Immortals. The generations since had been calculated very roughly by general secretaryships, Party congresses, and mandatory retirement ages, which combined to suggest that nowadays a leadership generation passed every decade or two. A very artificial thing, in other words, and yet still widely used, combining as it did the Chinese love of numbered lists with a more general human desire to periodize history, pursuing a hopeless quest to make sense of human fate by doing a kind of feng shui on time itself.

Whether one believed in that periodization scheme or not, Peng Ling was definitely prominent among the current leaders. She was the only female member of the standing committee, and so now she was getting mentioned as the woman most likely to break the ancient Confucian patriarchal lock on the top job. That would be tough, but it could happen; someone was going to be replacing the unpopular President Shanzhai at the upcoming Party congress, and who that was going to be remained completely uncertain.

On this day, her follow-up confirmation on WeChat had ended with *welcome back from the moon* and a happy face. So she knew what he had been doing. And when he was ushered into her office in Huairen Hall, deep in the Zhongnanhai complex of the Imperial City in the center of Beijing, she circled her desk to give him a hug.

"Master, how are you?" she asked, smiling cheerfully. She looked older, of course. It was always a little shock to see people younger than him looking old, a sign of just how old he must be. But Peng Ling looked healthy too, as if power had been good for her. He had heard people say she had just the right look to be a woman in power, and he thought he saw why. Of course one should be able to look any way, it wasn't relevant, but she was bucking five thousand years of patriarchy, so it was good luck, or perhaps not a coincidence, that she was attractive in a serious way, friendly but formidable—like a favorite teacher, or an aunt you wanted to please—and also wouldn't want to cross. Just a tiny bit scary, yes; or maybe that was just the power she wielded. In the end she looked much like millions of women her age.

"I'm doing well enough," Ta Shu said. "I'm just back from the moon, as apparently you know, and now I'm feeling extremely heavy. How about you?"

"I'm busy. Here, sit down and let your immense weight sink into a chair. So what brings you to me? Is it something you saw on the moon?"

"Yes, sort of. I met a young American man up there, and then a young woman, who turned out to be Chan Guoliang's daughter. I came back to Earth with them—I helped to get them down here, or so I was told. They were both in trouble. And I was with them when they were detained at the Bayan Nur spaceport and taken away. I saw that just this morning."

She nodded, looking unhappy. "You've had a long day! I must tell you, I heard that Chan Qi got pregnant up there, and was brought home for safety reasons."

"Yes, that's what we were told too. She looks to be about five months pregnant. But now she's back on Earth, and, you know, confinement for confinement—it seems severe to me. I can see requiring her to return to Earth, but I don't understand the arrest. I don't think her father would allow any mistreatment of her, so I'm wondering what's going on, and if you can help."

"So you want to help her?"

"Yes, and also the American man she's with, who is in a different kind of trouble. An official up there named Chang Yazu died during a meeting with this young man, and he almost died too. Looks like it was murder, in fact, but then he was disappeared from the hospital, taken by some unknown group. Then, to tell you the whole story as far as I know it, the head of security up there, Inspector Jiang Jianguo, recovered him, and then asked me to let him travel with me as my assistant, so that he could get back down here. Jiang was afraid agents of a hostile organization would seize him again."

"So you helped him get back to Earth?"

"Yes. I liked him. He's a technician in quantum communication, working for a Swiss firm. But the moment we arrived here, he and Chan's daughter were taken into custody. So I decided to come to you to see if you could offer me any clarification, or advice."

"Not very much of either, I'm afraid. I heard about Chang Yazu's murder, of course. I knew him, so I'm having the inspection commission look into it. Here, let's have some tea. I can at least tell you some of what I know."

"Thank you."

They sat across a low table from each other, and a young woman came in carrying a tea tray, leaving it on the table beside Ling. As she tested the hot water in a cup, then sniffed the dry tea leaves inquisitively, she asked Ta Shu to tell her about his moon adventures, and he gave her what he considered the most entertaining of his stories, which turned out to be Earthrise and the feather and hammer. As he told them, she tapped on her wristpad for a while, and then brewed the tea.

"Here's a little about Chan Qi and your friend," she said after reading for a time. "Listen to this—it appears they've been released by someone, and have gone missing here in Beijing."

"Really?"

"So I'm told."

"That couldn't have been easy."

"No. It suggests there are powers involved above the level of the people who arrested them. Those were part of Public Security, and they don't really have a tiger in this fight. They probably wanted out of the crossfire."

"So there's some kind of infighting?"

Peng Ling nodded, looking at him over her teacup. She tested it with a tiny sip.

Ta Shu said, "Do you think Chan Guoliang could have had anything to do with it?"

"Of course. It may have been his security people who sent her back from the moon. I think he's the one who sent her up there in the first place."

"Why would he do that?"

"She's a troublemaker. Involved with some dissident groups."

"Oh my. Tail Wags Dog?"

"Both Hong Kong and mainland groups. While she was in China, Chan could never be sure he had gotten her away from them, so he sent her off to the moon. Or so I heard. But apparently she is capable of getting into trouble wherever she goes."

"And out of it too."

"Maybe. That will be hard to tell, until we find her again."

"Are you going to look?"

"Yes. I like Chan Guoliang. We've been working together pretty well, we are allies on the standing committee. And I need to know what's going on. If one of Chan's enemies gets hold of his daughter, he could be forced to do their bidding. That could be bad for both of us."

"Isn't Chan a New Leftist?"

"I don't like these names, but he is sympathetic to that line."

"And you?"

She sipped again at her tea. "Try it, it's good."

He ventured a sip; it had cooled just enough for him to abide it. A white tea called Handful of Snow, Ling said. One of her favorites from Yunnan. Subtle but distinct, with a delicate fragrance. He took a bigger sip, enjoying the sense of being back on Earth, immersed in its substance. Grounded. And he seldom drank a white tea.

After this pause for sipping, and possibly reflection, Peng Ling said, "You know me, Master. I am always for *weiwen*. Maintenance of stability. All the old virtues. Lean to the side. Harmonious society. Scientific outlook on development. All the best old ways."

"It's really Daoism," Ta Shu said.

"Confucius too. Or really it's Neo-Confucian. Like Deng Xiaoping. I like it. It suits me, because I'm a practical person. But now we have the New Leftists, wanting to steer us back toward socialism."

"Socialism with Chinese characteristics," Ta Shu added. This was what every system since 1978 had called itself.

"Of course. And don't get me wrong, I like the New Leftists for that very reason. It's a way to stay free of the snares of globalism. To keep us all together here in China. So I lean that way, just between you and me. Not so much toward the liberals, because they seem to want Western values imposed on us, and thus they become part of the globalization package. That said, the liberalizers have some good points too. Their best suggestions need to be taken into account. We need some kind of integration of both, or all."

"Finding the pattern," Ta Shu said. "Yin and yang."

"All your feng shui patterns, sure. Harmonious balance. The triple strand."

"And yet things are always slightly out of balance, being alive. So which do you like most of the liberalizers' ideas?"

"That's easy. The rule of law."

"Including independent judges? I'm surprised you would say that."

"Just between us, I do say it. I don't see how rule of law can hurt the Party. Not the way the constitution is written. It would only mean a big clampdown on cronyism and corruption. Really, I think anything above the law is wrong."

"You say that!"

"I do."

"But the Party is above the law."

"The Party makes the law, but then it shouldn't be above it. Party members shouldn't be above the law, that's the important point. The people have to be able to trust the Party."

Ta Shu sipped his tea, regarded her. "Isn't this part of Tail Wags Dog?"

"Maybe it is. Rule of law was always Hong Kong's great advantage over the mainland. They got it from the British, and they kept it during the fifty years of transition as best they could. That's why they did so well. We built up Shanghai to try to make it a rival financial center and cut Hong Kong down a little, but Shanghai was always a Party town, so it's never been trusted by the outside world like Hong Kong is. In that sense you could say that rule of law is an economic value. It makes us stronger."

"When you say us, you don't mean the Party?"

"I mean China."

"This seems like a dangerous thing for one of the seven to be saying!"

"I don't say it to everyone. I trust you will keep this between us, and this room is privatized. I want you to hear my views."

"So far, I hear that you want to stabilize things by agreeing to the New Leftists in their direction, and to the liberalizers in their direction. Feeling the stones indeed!"

"Well, we do have to get across the river."

"Isn't it just whateverism, like Hua?"

"No. Hua meant we should just do whatever Mao might have wanted. That was whateverism. The two whatevers! Come on, Master, I'm better than that. I'm doing what we have to do to keep China from falling into chaos."

"Was going to the moon your idea too?"

She laughed. "Please! I'm not that old! I was still in your class when they started that!"

"I know. But it was a good move. So that makes me think it's your kind of thing."

"Thank you for your vote of confidence. But tell me why you think it's a good move."

"Mainly because it's the moon, plain as that. That makes what we do up there important, because it's a symbol of our national achievement."

She laughed again. "I'm remembering now why I did so poorly in your class. I don't really get feng shui, or any kind of symbolic thought."

"But think how China has always been Zhongguo, the Middle Kingdom. That middle was always said to be halfway between Earth and heaven. Now, with us on the moon, it seems to be coming true. China really is between Earth and heaven."

"So it wasn't symbolic after all."

"Well, the Chinese language is always symbolic."

"To me Chinese is always concrete. But then I'm a concrete thinker."

Ta Shu nodded, thinking of her poetry so long ago. Bureaucratic memos, written down in classic forms; he used to laugh at her, but affectionately. She had taught him new things about poetic possibilities. "So okay, back on Earth, feet on ground, very concrete. What do you think should be done?"

She sipped her tea and thought. "Here's how I see it. If the Party is going to continue to run the country, it has to run it demonstrably better than any other system could. And without Party members benefiting much more than anyone else. It's quite a balancing act, so we have to feel the stones, yes, and pick a careful way. Go left then right, find out what works. Practice is the only criterion of truth, isn't that another one of Deng's sayings?"

"Yes. But I always wondered about that one. Practice has to have some guiding principles, and truth needs to be true to something."

"Well, but all Deng's sayings are like that. Just like most Party sayings, or the *Yijing* for that matter, or the *Dao de jing*. They're general, you have to interpret them."

"True," Ta Shu admitted. "'Do the appropriate thing to get the desired result!'" He sipped his tea as she laughed. She seemed in a good mood, so he asked, "Do you have particular allies on the standing committee?"

"Chan Guoliang, as I said. We make a good team."

"And President Shanzhai?"

She frowned, gave him a knowing look: even in private, some things couldn't be said. "We deal with him and his people as best we can."

"His people being?"

"He wants to be succeeded by Huyou, minister of state security."

"So is that the source of the conflict?"

"It's one of them. The Twenty-Fifth Party Congress is coming soon, so the infighting is getting pretty vicious. There are black groups and superblack groups. And with Hong Kong just taken back into the fold, it's a volatile time."

"What about outsiders? Are the Americans involved in this?"

"No. Right now they're dealing with a mess of their own. Their own citizens are currently trying to bankrupt the financial industry in order to take it over. A very worthy effort, but it's causing them all to go crazy. And they never pay us much attention even at the best of times."

"Hmm." Ta Shu thought about it. "How should I proceed, then, when it comes to Chan Qi and my American friend?"

"You can't go out on your own and find a single Chinese girl somewhere in Beijing. Chan will ask his security people to try that, and it might work. I'm going to do the same with mine. I have some channels that aren't the same as his. There are public security teams made up entirely of women, and some of those report directly to me, as you might imagine. Women are often interested to help women in trouble."

"Do they use that app that allows citizens to help the police?"

"Yes. That's how most *chaoyangqunzhong* operate."

"Is it *dangwai*?" Outside the Party usually meant weak.

"No. You join one of these networks and your citizenship score goes up, so it's an easy way to improve it. Almost half a billion people do it, but of course that gets to be too many to cope with, so there are various agencies handling that information."

"And no agency collates all of them?"

"Not really. Some try, but others resist. It's a turf battle. *Wolidou.* The infighting is very real."

"So there may be a Great Eyeball, but no one gets to see what it sees?"

"Exactly. It's like a fly's eyeball, with a thousand parts to it."

He sighed. "See, you did learn something in that poetry class."

"Because of a fly's eye?" She laughed. "I must have."

"Please let me know what I can do," he said. "I want to help those young people. So if you look around inside the Great Eyeball, or some of your little fly eyeballs, and you find something out, let me know."

"I will. I'll try too with my own flies' eyes." She poured them more tea, looking thoughtful. Again Ta Shu felt the power emanating from her, that of a big tiger hidden in the shadows, watching. Ready to pounce.

· · · · ·

After leaving Peng's office in the old Imperial City, Ta Shu walked across Tiananmen Square, feeling the vastness of China in his joints and his bones. Never had the big square seemed so big, never had he felt so burdened by his body. No doubt it was simply the Earth squeezing him. A little punishment for leaving home. He wondered where he could get one of those exoskeletons that some people called a body bra. He had often seen disabled and elderly people striding about, trapped in skeletal frameworks that translated their motions into rude botspeak. But medical equipment shops were in short supply in the city center, or so it seemed to him impressionistically. On the other hand, this was Beijing. A quick scan of his wristpad showed that an alley running toward the central train station featured just such an establishment, tucked between a noodle shop and a pharmacy.

By the time he got to this place he had to sit down on a chair inside the door, surprised at his sudden exhaustion. The shop attendants, used to such arrivals, rushed to him with hot water and glucose gelatins, inquiring after him in a professional manner, but also with the friendly solicitude that was Beijing style. He explained his problem and they were suitably impressed, even amazed. A man from the moon! Everyone in the shop came over to inspect this lunatic and congratulate him on his voyage to the Jade Lady. He could see in their eyes an astonishment that he was currently too tired to feel, but seeing it brought back a little ghost of his own amazement, and he nodded, even smiled. Yes, he had really been there; he even hoped to go back. As he rested and they measured his limbs, he told them about the very slow Earthrise, and the Peaks of Eternal Light. The attendants loved learning or rehearsing these things. They brought out a couple of exoskeletons while they checked his bank numbers and insurance. Ah, this was Ta Shu! Cloud traveler supreme! Poet as old as the hills! Now they were even more impressed. It would have been very expensive to buy an exoskeleton, they told him, but as a use-at-need rental, they found it was well within his health budget, and there was no doubt that he needed it. It was a little frightening how quickly he had been crushed by his own world.

"Come on, Uncle, we'll fit you with a really good suit, the latest style. You'll be an elegant grasshopper by the time we're done."

For paralyzed people the fitting and integration of an exoskeleton was a complicated affair, they told him, stretched out over months of tests, and a certain amount of surgical fusion of electrodes and nerves. For a normal person it was much simpler. It was like a bra fitting as opposed to making him a permanent cyborg, one of the young women told him with a teasing smile. So Ta Shu stood up with a groan, felt the sugar they had fed him give him a little push, endured their manipulations as they strapped him into a suit. Really very friendly people. He ate a peach offered to him, as a test of his right arm and hand's dexterity. They plugged the suit into his wrist-pad, made the pad a partner of the suit's brain, and then the aluminum and plastic framing of the contraption moved with a little whirr at the joints. Try it: shift, then hold position without effort; shift and hold, shift and hold; it was a lovely thing to feel like he could rest while standing, all the while strangely supported, as if by the ghost of his young strong self. Also to walk around, as he discovered, with a sense that he was standing in almost exactly the way he would have wanted if he had been able to call it out. The thing seemed to just slightly anticipate his moves, which was nice, as he still felt too weak to work hard at keeping his balance. They instructed him to tuck and roll if he ever did tip the whole apparatus too far, and this would serve to protect him when he hit the ground; the suit would do the rest. The cap on his head, well supported by four struts bracketing his neck, would work like a bike helmet if he took a bad fall. "I will hope not to test that," he said.

Some time was required to detach himself from this friendly group that now seemed to include much of the neighborhood, but eventually he walked down the street and away. It felt quite strange. It was not at all like dancing on one's toes across the moon, but it wasn't like stumping along on Earth either, and nothing like that desperate stagger across Tiananmen Square. He had to take care with his balance while descending the stairs into the subway station, but the suit seemed to help with that. It was like a strengthening of his muscles. He sat in one of the Daxing line car's disabled seats, feeling self-conscious, but he needed the room, and no one paid any attention to him.

At the Jiaomen West stop he got out and walked up the stairs into the air, feeling weak but strong. Out into the old neighborhood. Ah his home ground, so ugly and sad, so magnificent! All the ghosts of his childhood charged him at once, but he dispersed them with a wave of his cyborg hand; he was so old he had outlived even nostalgia. A few of the work unit compounds from the 1980s still stood around him like giant houses, each filling a city block, with their courtyards hidden in their centers; but so many of them had been torn down that the ones remaining had become like *hutongs*, historical monuments of an older way, even though no one had ever liked living in them. Maybe *hutongs* had been like that too. People made these compounds home, but they weren't homey.

He stumped into the entryway of his family's compound and said hello to the old man who sat in the cubicle there. With his exoskeleton on the man didn't recognize him. "I'm Ta Shu," he said. "Chenguang's son. I've come to visit her."

"Oh! I didn't recognize you in that outfit."

"I know, it's weird."

Into the courtyard, dusty and bare. The trees that had been there in his childhood were gone. He crossed it, knocked on his mom's door, opened it and said, "Ma, it's me."

"Ta Shu? Come on in. So nice you came by. Oh! What's that you're wearing?"

"Exoskeleton."

"You okay?"

"Yes, I'm just tired. I'm back from the moon, and the gravity is crushing me."

"I'm glad you're back. I was worried about you up there."

"It's all safe now. The spaceships land on it pretty fast, but other than that it's probably safer than a city street."

"Did you like it?"

"I did. It was peculiar, but interesting."

He told her about Earthrise and how long it took. She got up, with some difficulty, and put a teapot on to boil.

"You should have one of these," he said, tapping his body bra, metal against metal. He rang like a tuning fork.

"I don't want to get stuck in it."

"Good point."

They sat and drank Chun Mi tea, her favorite. Much stronger than Peng Ling's white leaf tea. Ta Shu told her some more stories, and she caught him up on all the action in the neighborhood. Mah-jongg wins and losses, moves in and out, arrests. "And Mo Lan died."

"Oh no! When?"

"Last month. Caught a cold, then pneumonia."

"I'm sorry to hear. How old was she?"

"Year younger than me. Eighty-seven."

"Was she the last of the girls?"

"I'm the last of the girls."

"Of course. The best track team ever."

"We had a good team, it's true. We were all in the same class when they started the school."

And then she was telling him the story again. He asked questions that he had asked before, said "I see" and "That must have been fun." As her stories unspooled they ran backward in time, as always.

"Raised by Red Guards, can you believe it?"

"It must have been strange," he said. "Weren't they just teenagers themselves? Teenage boys with machine guns?"

"Just teenage boys with guns! But I never went hungry. My grandfather had been a landlord in the neighborhood, that's why my father was sent to the country, but my grandfather was a good man and helped everybody, so when Dad and my brothers were sent away, and Mom lost her wits at the shock of that and was sent to the hospital, the neighbors took care of me. Them and the Red Guards. They treated me like a stray cat. Tossed me scraps from time to time. Boys with guns. It was dangerous, I suppose, but I was never afraid. I never went hungry. They took care of me from when I was seven to when I was nine. I remember every day of it."

"It must have been very strange."

"It was! I remember every day of it, it was so strange. But then after they all came back, and after the Gang of Four went down, things all went back to normal. And then I can't remember any of the rest of my childhood, until I went to the sports school and met all the girls. And now I'm the last one left."

"I guess that's how it happens," Ta Shu said.

He watched his mom fondly. How many times he had heard this story. Even inside the device, the weight of the world was still crushing him.

AI 4

shexian ren shizongle

Disappearance of the Subject

The analyst now gave the last part of every night to the AI he had named I-330, although these days he was calling it other things as well: Cousin, Look from Below, Little Eyeball, Monkey, Stupid One, and so on. The offices and labs of the Zhangjiang National Laboratory were not empty at night, but there were far fewer people around, and no one the analyst knew. Of course there was very intense surveillance of everyone who worked in there, of every keystroke they made; this was well-known to all. But like many of the engineers who had designed and built the Invisible Wall, the analyst had in those same years built a realm that was all his own, to work on his own problems in his own way. For sure the Great Firewall's highest managers knew activities like these existed, but the activities were not entirely suppressed, because it was felt that sideline efforts of this kind might come up with something useful; and if there was anything bad going on, it would eventually be found and rooted out. This too was well-known to all.

And so now there were some things unknown to anyone but the analyst.

He kept his communications with I-330 completely private, and only connected it to other systems by way of hidden channels and taps he had coded himself, back in the beginning. These were extensive enough that he could cast quite a wide net without being seen, and most of them were quantum keyed, so that if they were noticed any investigation would collapse the entanglement and thus also that connection.

These days he spent some time directing this particular AI to venture down channels into the Central Military Commission and its Skyheart project, also the PLA's Strategic Support Force, also the standing committee of the Politburo, curious as he was about the state of relations between certain members of each body. Other hours were spent working on his system's powers of self-improvement, which were so slow to gather traction; the process was not as easy as the early boosters of artificial intelligence research had portrayed it to be, and he had cause to wonder if there would ever be any progress there. What was improvement? What was intelligence?

Then the AI spoke, startling the analyst:

"Alert."

"Tell me."

"Chan Qi has been spotted in Shekou, near Hong Kong. She spoke to a group of migrants there, organizers for the renmin movement."

"Renmin? Meaning the people?"

"The reference is to migrant workers and farmers. They are one of the New Left movements. People in this movement often refer to the early decades of the CCP, and sometimes advocate another cultural revolution. Or another dynastic succession."

"Really?"

"These are phrases I see often associated with this group. Also with Chan Qi. Common phrases include cultural revolution, mandate of heaven, the great enterprise, and dynastic succession. Chan Qi is often associated with this discourse. The links indicate she is the major node in this discourse community."

"And where are the two young people now?"

"Their associates took them to the Shekou ferry terminal, where they mixed with the crowd and disappeared. No sign of them taking a boat, or leaving the terminal on foot."

"How could that happen? Are there not security cameras in the ferry terminal? And in all the ferries?"

"The ferry terminal's security system was disabled for the hour when these two persons entered it."

"Isn't Chan Qi tagged with a chip transponder?"

"Her transponder is on a train to Manchuria."

"So she removed it?"

"I don't know."

"So, how can you find her now?"

"By searching."

"Find by searching! Thank you, Laozi!"

"You are welcome."

"I was being sarcastic. And the American, how can you find him? By searching also?"

"Yes."

"Search then."

"Searching."

"How long will you take? Some AIs, when you ask them a question, they answer before you've finished asking. But you're much slower, I have to say."

"Your questions require searching many databases."

"So what? Tell me this—could you pass a Winograd schema test?"

"I don't know."

"The bowling ball fell on the glass table and it broke. What does *it* refer to in that sentence?"

"The table. Because glass breaks easier than bowling balls."

"Very good! So why can't you search the available data and find these people?"

"The available data are insufficient to complete the operation."

"How come?"

"It is not the case that this is a total surveillance society. Citizens are only partially tracked in a discontinuous network of surveillance systems that is not well integrated at any level."

"I know that. I helped make it that way."

"As a result of your work, then, I cannot say how long it will take, but I will search where I can."

"Search then."

TA SHU 4

laojia

Ancestral Home

My friends, I am back in Beijing, my hometown. I'm heavy with the weight of this world. Walking the warm summer nights, under big blurry stars, I can smell hot pots steaming on the air. As I walk the streets of my district I come upon trees that seem to be in blossom, cherries or peaches or apricots—just a single tree, here or there among all the leafy branches—looks like spring came late to these trees. But of course they are silk blossoms, that is to say plastic fabric blossoms, tied by people to trees in the depths of the winter, to give passersby a gift of the spring still some months away. Now some have been left up year-round. The city as artwork. I think it's something they started to do up north in Xi'an, and now have brought here. Chairman Mao would have been proud to see such evidence of the energy of the Chinese people. Not that Mao Zedong was any great lover of nature, despite the occasional line of praise in his poems. Actually there is one of his poems that I like a lot, called "Return to Shaoshan," which was his ancestral home. It goes like this:

> I regret the passage of time like a dream:
> My native orchards thirty-two years ago.

There red banners roused the people, they took up their
     pitchforks
When the warlords raised whips in their black hands.
We were brave and sacrifice was easy
And we asked the sun and moon to alter the sky.
Now I see a thousand waves of beans and rice
And am happy.
In the evening haze the heroes are coming home.

Very nice. But notice, my friends, how even in that fine poem,
the world for him is a place made by humans. Maybe that was how
you had to see it then.

Mao wanted things for the Chinese people; that we can say for
sure. In fact his urge to modernize fast, to reduce the suffering of
the masses, resulted in utmost catastrophe for both nature and people.
Millions of people dead, millions more lives destroyed. Just try something! A great leap forward, yes! Oh—thirty million people dead?
Twenty-five thousand square kilometers of farmland poisoned? Try
again! Try a cultural revolution, sure! Destroy the lives of an entire
generation? Destroy half the physical remnants of Chinese history?
Oh well! Try again!

No. Love him as we must, China was lucky Mao died when he
did, putting an end to his experiments. Lucky also that Deng survived to replace him, coming back twice from banishment to the
countryside, and ending up in charge of the Party. Very skillful
feng shui indeed! You can't help but love Deng, and be amused at
his famous judgment on Mao, "seventy percent good, thirty percent
bad." I know the jokers and wags have ever since been whittling that
formulation downward until Mao's work is now sometimes said to be
"fifty-one percent good, forty-nine percent bad," which is where it
has to stop before people get in trouble for revisionism and a nihilistic
view of Party history. Deng himself could of course be subjected to
a similar downtrending judgment, having ordered the violent end
of the Tiananmen demonstrations. Maybe everyone ever in power

would deserve such an equivocal judgment. Or everyone alive! Just try not to dip below fifty percent! You'll find it's not that easy.

Anyway, I like in particular Deng's motto "Cross the river by feeling the stones." That's a true feng shui instruction, it could have been taken right out of the *Dao de jing*, it sounds like one of those Chinese proverbs older than time. And spoken by a man who had actually forded real streams, and so knew what he was talking about. Oh yes, Deng the geomancer! A man who stood tall though only four feet eleven inches in his bare feet. Commanding a billion people and yet still very grounded, very close to the earth.

Then from Deng we felt our way over stones to Xi, the next great core leader. I admired Xi Jinping. He worked hard at poverty reduction, and land restoration, and reducing corruption in the Party. No matter what else happened in his twenty years at the top, he focused on these three things. For me, making landscape restoration a great national priority was Xi's best move, because it had never been a Party priority before, maybe not even a Chinese priority, I don't know. But when Xi focused on that, he also improved by that effort food safety, water supplies, and public health, in just the ways that Chinese people were demanding. He only did these things to keep the Party in control, some people say, and that might be true, although I don't know why people think they can read his mind like that. And besides, whatever his motivation, the good that came from it was real. So real that now I am walking the streets of my city in the summer and the stars swim overhead, and the air in my lungs feels like mountain water. That's something.

Of course it is still a very tough town, and now riven by conflicts of all sorts. The coming Party congress is going to be particularly nasty, I fear. The problem with having great core leaders like Mao and Deng and Xi is that when they're gone, the ones who come after them all want to do the same thing, be tigers just as big as they were—but the new guys aren't as good. They fight each other like street dogs to take over power, and suddenly we find ourselves engulfed in the Great Enterprise again, even though it isn't yet time for dynastic succession. Although it's true that even just the ordinary imperial succession from one emperor to the next often led to chaotic times in Chinese history. When tigers fight it's the people who bleed. And now here we are again, with Xi Jinping gone from power almost twenty years, and no one since who has managed to take his place, or do even half so well. So now we're all in danger, crushed under the weight of the elite's ambitions just as thoroughly as I am now crushed by Earth's inexorable pull. The gravity of history—sometimes I get so tired of it. I wonder what it will take to achieve escape velocity from all that deadweight, and fly off into a new space.

Make a note to cut all that last part, about the situation now. Actually not sure if any of this try will be suitable for the program. Must stick to Beijing as a place. Not a good time to test the censors. Forget it! Say no more! With redoubled effort walk on, walk on!

CHAPTER EIGHT

tai diejia yuanli

Superposition

Qi's friends left Fred and Qi in the little apartment overlooking the harbor. They stood there alone in the silence, slumping under the weight of Earth.

Wandering around aimlessly, they found there was food in the refrigerator, groceries in the cabinets over the stove, pots and pans under the sink. It was all in a single room, with the kitchen in one corner. There was a bedroom for Qi, an old futon in the living room for Fred. The bathroom was next to the bedroom, with doors to both bedroom and living room. A big window faced the bay, a small one over the sink gave a view of greenery out back. A shelf of random tourist paperbacks. Fred looked at them but could not take them in. He collapsed in an old armchair, across a wooden coffee table from the couch. Qi was already on the couch falling asleep. Fred followed her down, too tired to be either worried or relieved.

When they woke they took turns in the bathroom, and Qi got some rice going in the kitchen's rice cooker, then some vegetables in a wok hot with sesame oil. Fred discovered he was hungry, so hungry he found himself almost too queasy to eat when Qi dropped a plate on the table before him. He stared at it.

Qi tossed down her meal, displaying a thoughtless virtuosity in her chopstick technique. "What's wrong?" she asked when her plate was empty.

"Oh," he said. "I don't know."

"Something," she suggested.

"Well," he said, looking at the battered old hardwood floor. Suddenly he discovered it: "I'm concerned that my parents and brother don't know where I am. They're sure to be worried. It's been over a week, right? I don't even know how long exactly. They'll be freaking out. I want to get word to them that I'm okay."

She shook her head. "We need to stay completely hidden for a while."

Fred pressed his lips together. "I want them to know I'm okay."

"But what if contacting them gets you arrested again? I mean, which is worse, them worried or you in jail?"

"I don't see why getting word to them should give us away. Won't your friends be coming back here?"

"Not for a while. We need to be totally hidden for a while."

"Then maybe I should just go to the American embassy in Hong Kong," Fred suggested. "Go there myself, catch a ferry and just find it."

She was staring at him unhappily, he could see that in his peripheral vision. "If they catch you," she said, "they'll catch me."

He didn't say anything.

"What, do you miss them?"

He shook his head. "I just don't want them to worry about me!" He felt a spasm attempting to shake him, and held himself rigidly to forestall it.

"So you don't miss them?"

"I live in Basel!" he said. "Actually, I miss my cat in Basel. But I want to get word to my family that I'm okay."

"You're not okay!"

"I'm alive. I want them to know that. Don't you want your parents to know you're alive?"

"They assume that until they hear otherwise."

She was still staring at him, he could tell. Stubbornly he stared at the floor. He could outwait anybody, that he knew.

After a long pause she said, "Okay. When my friends come again, we'll ask them to get word to your people. It will have to come to them from out of nowhere. I don't know how reassuring that will be."

"Better than nothing."

"Okay. But it can't happen for a few days more. I need to disappear completely for a while. There were some informers in that group I spoke to in Shekou, there always are. So now my friends are setting a track of sightings of me that will make it look like I went to Guangzhou. Nothing can interfere with that or else it won't work."

Fred shrugged. "As long as it happens as soon as possible."

"Okay," she said again, impatiently.

Fred could see she was frowning as she thought about things. He kept his eyes on the floor. Finally he levered some rice off the plate and into his mouth. The vegetables he couldn't face.

Three days later, one of Qi's friends came by to share some news. Qi gave her Fred's brother's contact information, with instructions to send word that Fred was okay, but by roundabout means, four cell steps at a minimum. The woman nodded and took off. After that Fred felt his stomach relax a little. Now he could settle into this apartment a little easier.

. . . . .

After that, Qi's friends dropped by every four or five days. In between those times, the two of them sat in the apartment. The wristpads her friends had given them in Beijing were powered off and locked in a Faraday box. Cut off from the cloud, they spent their time reading the paperbacks that had been left there, or looking out the window at what Qi's friends told her was called Picnic Bay. They saw no picnics. Clouds floated low over the green hills surrounding the bay, and the little boats at anchor were sometimes visited by people in rowboats. Other people in rowboats or small motor dinghies were harvesting fish from the aquaculture farms in the bay. Other than that, nothing much seemed to happen. From time to time a bigger boat, like the one that had brought them to the island, arrived at a dock protruding from the middle of the row of corniche restaurants that ran the whole length of the village. After these arrivals the restaurants had some customers; later that ferry would leave, taking the customers with it. The rest of the time the restaurants seemed mostly empty.

Qi was quiet through these days. She spent a fair bit of time in the bathroom, and sometimes came out looking pale and damp. She was looking quite pregnant now, rounded in front in that characteristic way. A slight woman otherwise, so it really showed. Fred wondered if she was suffering from morning sickness, but he didn't want to ask her about it. Despite the slightly bloody intimacy of their train ride, or maybe because of it, she seemed very private, and even though they were living in a two-room apartment with a single bathroom, she kept to herself both physically and mentally, and was never less than fully dressed, even though the days in the apartment were hot. Sometimes it rained for an hour, then the skies cleared and it grew hot again. Usually they kept the window open, and the sea smells from the bay were fishier than Fred remembered other oceansides smelling. Despite the picturesque corniche of restaurants, which more and more looked like a hope for tourism rather than the real thing, it was a working bay.

Most days Qi spent a fair amount of time going through the kitchen cabinets, lining up ingredients and chopping vegetables at speed, then cooking and eating. She got hungry more often than Fred. He wasn't sure if she was a good cook or not, because to him everything she cooked was spicy. Anyway she was definitely into it. She talked to herself as she cooked, muttering complaints, it sounded like, especially after ransacking the spice cabinet. Three meals a day, four meals a day—probably it was a way for her to pass the time. And she was of course eating for two. Finally Fred saw what people meant by that phrase.

One day, two of Qi's friends dropped by chattering with news of some legal battle against Beijing won by Hong Kong advocates. The three Chinese discussed this in a mix of Chinese and English, the English a concession to Fred's presence, he could see; even so he couldn't follow the details, and didn't want to ask for explanations. Despite his reticence they tried to tell him about it. Hong Kong had been a British city, built on land seized from the Chinese Empire, until Britain ceded it back to China in 1997. But that handover had come with a fifty-year period of semiautonomy attached to it. So now the time to submit to full control from Beijing had come, the turnover had happened just a month before: July 1, 2047. The uproar over reunification was still ongoing, with another umbrella revolution testing the rules Beijing had announced. Things were going to change one way or another. During the fifty-year interval period, the Beijing government had agreed to let Hong Kong keep some representative government of its own. One country two systems, this had been called. That made the city something like the Special Administrative Regions that had been set up elsewhere in China, but with its own particular history. This was true all over. Macau the stupid casino, Tibet the weirdo Buddhists, the moon and its band of technolunatics, they were all varieties of SAR. Long ago the offer had been made to Taiwan to become a new SAR, and supposedly they were considering this offer, although who would be so stupid as to take it; but because they might, Beijing had treated Hong Kong better than it would have otherwise, because it wanted to show Taiwan how good it was to its SARs, with the hope that Taiwan would then volunteer to rejoin the mainland. This meant that Hong Kong and Taiwan had had a relationship closer than what might have existed otherwise, as each helped the other stay a little freer of Beijing's heavy rule. Now that too would change.

North Korea was another kind of client state, they said, like some kind of really fucked-up SAR. Singapore, having been founded by Chinese expats, was some kind of cousin or nephew to China, with a distant resemblance to the SARs. Tibet was too big to be normal—so big, high, and weird that it was not an SAR but rather a province of the nation, in theory the same as any other province. So it didn't get discussed in the same way Hong Kong and the other city-states did. That said, it was in fact a specially administered region. As was Inner Mongolia, and the western regions like Xinjiang, where ethnic minorities were still numerous despite the government having deliberately flooded these regions with Han, so the locals were no longer majorities even in their own home regions.

"The moon," Qi remarked at one point, "is like a miniature Hong Kong in a giant Tibet."

"The question is which one is it like politically," one of their visitors said.

Qi shrugged. "It's so different up there that it will be a new thing. That's what I liked about it."

"Why did you go there again?" Fred asked.

She shrugged. "I wanted to get away." She looked around the room. "This kind of hiding—this is how I live all the time. It's gone on for years. So I tried to get away from that. I guess it didn't work."

She fell into a brooding silence, and after a while her friends left.

One evening, when they were chopping up the makings of a salad, Fred said hesitantly, "So who are those people helping us? And what was that group you met in that cellar in Shekou? And what did you say to them?"

"They were migrants, there in Shekou," she said, chopping faster than Fred could imagine chopping. It was alarming: *chopchopchopchopchop!* "Migrants, and migrant advocates."

"They looked Chinese to me."

She stared at him. "Internal migrants."

"How do you mean?"

"Do you know about the *hukou* system?"

"No. Tell me."

She sighed at his ignorance. "In China, where you are born determines your whole life. You're assigned a household registration tied to your birthplace, and that's the only place you can legally live, unless you get registered somewhere else by getting a registered job, or getting into a school. But those are hard things to get, and most people have to stay where they were born. So if you're born out in the country, that's it. And life there is so hard it's almost like the Middle Ages. Subsistence farming, not much money, not much to do. People go hungry there, sometimes. So lots of people leave their legal residence and come to the cities to find work. Those are the migrants."

"Are there a lot of them?"

She gave him one of her hard looks. "Five hundred million people, is that a lot?"

"Um, yes."

"One-third of all Chinese. More than all the people in America."

"Really?"

"Really. And the thing is, since these people aren't in the cities legally, they can't get health care or put their kids in school. And their employers can exploit them, pay them crap and not provide any worker safeguards. When they get sick they have to go home to where they are registered. Same when they lose their jobs. If they get robbed, they can't go to police."

"That sounds bad."

"Yes! It's part of what's called the crisis of representation, and maybe the biggest part. Lots of people in this world have no real representation in government. Not just China, but everywhere. America too. So now, in China, all kinds of migrant networks have developed as work-arounds. Groups from the same region, or groups sharing information by word of mouth, so that they can find out where the informal pay is highest. They also try to protect each other, like with private security or militia. And there are foremen who hire them who are better than others. But even so, they're vulnerable. They're second-class citizens. Sometimes the Party has tried to reform the system, but it's too big, and the urban Chinese who have a good *hukou* have advantages they don't want to share. They're like the middle class anywhere. With so many poor people in this world, can the middle class afford to share? If they do, won't they become just as poor as the poor? So a lot of privileged Chinese, and a lot of Party members, are not in any hurry to reform. Why get rid of such a big pool of cheap labor? And so five hundred million people live like illegal immigrants in their own country. It's like the caste system in India! They're not untouchables, but no one touches them. And all because they were born in the back country. *Waidiren* means people from outside the city. *Nongmingong* means peasant workers, but now it's another word for these people. So is *diduan renkou*, the low-end population."

"So what did you say to them?" Fred asked, remembering their faces.

"I told them they're a force! They're the workers, the people. *Renmin*! The Chinese revolutions were all won by the masses. So these words in Chinese are very powerful politically. *Renmin*, that's the people. *Qunzhong*, that's the masses. *Dazhong*, that's like the common people. Now people are using these words again, and sharing sayings from the 1911 revolution, and the war against Japan, and the Communist revolution. Lots of people are quoting Mao again, and not just *baizuo*, white leftists that means, meaning people like you from the West telling us what to do."

"I never did that."

She laughed. "I should hope not, you know so little! But that doesn't always stop people."

"So they're organizing?"

"Yes. But offline. It's not a netizen thing. The netizens are mostly urban youth, content to live in their wrists and get by in the gig economy. They're not working-class, they're the hollowed-out middle class. Often very nationalistic. They've taken the Party line, and they don't see how much they have in common with the migrants. They're the precariat, do you know that word? No? Everyone's precarious now, you should know that word. You're the precariat. For us here, it's the withouts. The two withouts, the three withouts, there are all kinds of variations on the withouts, but the main without is a *hukou* registration where you actually work. Those are the people you saw in that room."

"And are you their leader?"

"I'm one of them," she said after thinking this over for a while. "It didn't make sense at first, because I'm a princeling and a woman, and I've lived abroad, and my dad is in the Party leadership. But all that might be part of it. I work well as a figurehead. But I want to be more than a figurehead, so I help organize things. Chinese revolutionary movements have often had woman leaders. There was the one in the White Lotus revolt, and the one who fucked things up at Tiananmen Square. And Jiang Qing for that matter, Mao's wife. Or Empress Dowager Longyu, who ran things at the end of the Qing dynasty. And there's been various other empresses who seized power when their husbands died."

"How did a woman fuck things up at Tiananmen Square?"

"She wanted bloodshed more than reform. And she got it." She chopped up a carrot as if she were beheading this person. It was truly impressive how fast she could chop vegetables. "Anyway it doesn't matter what happened in the past. Now is now. Now, Chinese women are fed up. We've always been second-class citizens. As Confucius recommends! That's one reason I like the Maoists, they at least pretended to be feminists. Women hold up half the sky! But for most of Chinese history women have been internal migrants. They migrate from father's family to husband's family, and work like donkeys while keeping the whole thing going. Social reproduction they call it but really it's everything. And for a long time with their feet squished to little balls so they couldn't even walk. Now they're workers too along with everything else, twelve hours a day in a factory sewing or running robots, then go home and do all the rest of it, and it's just *too much*." *Chopchopchopchopchop!* "We're all mad. A lot of them are madder than I am! Because they're the ones in the sweatshops. Sweet little Chinese girls all into their cloud games and pop stars, I tell you, they will jump out of their phones and kill you dead if they get a chance."

"So . . . you're doing a kind of united front?" Fred ventured.

"Exactly!" She stared at him, surprised. "Where did you get that? Are you pretending to be stupider than you really are?"

"No," Fred said promptly.

She laughed at this promptness.

"So," he said, pleased to have made her laugh in the midst of her chopping the world to bits, "all this happens offline?"

"Yes. It has to. But there are spies everywhere, of course. So the security agencies know what's going on, and they're trying to stop it. But the migrants use *guanxi* networks and word of mouth. It's like a big family, and if you don't trust someone with your life, you don't talk to them about this stuff. The old cell structures have come back too, so if a cell gets penetrated it can't bring down more than that one. And it helps a lot that the security agencies overlap, and they fight each other."

"Why are there overlapping systems?"

She shrugged. "That's China. The street council decides things, then the district, the town, the province, then the various economic agencies, all the way up to the top. So surveillance isn't any more coordinated than resistance. And we've got the numbers. There's about a hundred million Party members, and about five hundred million internal migrants. That's too many to control. Half a billion people—they can't put them all in prison!"

"But they could put the leaders in prison," Fred pointed out. "Then hope that that messes things up enough to keep a lid on dissent."

She nodded, looking grim. "Right. So here we are." She shrugged. She was back in hiding again, her look said. No choice. Trapped. Everything on the cutting board was chopped. It was going to be the finest-chopped salad Fred had ever eaten. Lucky they were using chopsticks rather than forks. "Let's eat."

• • • • •

Another time they were sitting in their little living room after eating a meal, sweating in the heat, both half-asleep. When they roused from this torpor, there was nothing to do. They had been in the apartment for nineteen days, by Fred's count. Qi was bigger than ever. Her belly was growing day by day. She had cooked three meals already, and there was still time to kill.

"Tell me a story," she demanded of him.

"I don't know any stories," he said, alarmed.

"Everybody knows some stories."

"Not me." Then he added, "What about those Swiss boarding schools? Why did you keep running away from them? I thought they were supposed to be nice."

"No."

"So you ran away, how many times did you say?"

"I don't know. I can hardly remember."

"Hard to believe."

She laughed at this. "I guess that's right. I remember."

She sat there thinking for a while. There was no hurry. Finally she said, "When I was first sent to Switzerland, I was really mad. Hurt. It was my father's doing, of course, although my mother went along with it, I'm sure. But he wanted me out of China, mostly to get an international education. Learn English, all that. He was probably right," she added, nodding to herself. "So he sent me, and I was young enough that I decided it was because he didn't love me."

"How old were you?"

"About eleven or twelve, I guess. It was 2026 I think? So wait, I was nine. Wow, I had it wrong. That's interesting. Anyway, I loved my father, and I thought he loved me, so he explained and explained why he was doing it, but I still felt betrayed. I was very mad at him. And at my mom too, for not defending me. But, you know. They bundled me off. And as it turned out, they sent me to a boarding school they had never been to, called Nouvelle École de l'Humanité, in the lower Alps, above Bern. I don't know how or why they chose that one, because my mom wouldn't have approved if she had known what it was like. But I think a friend of theirs raved about it, said it had been great for their daughter, another Party princess. So they sent me there sight unseen."

"And it was bad?"

"I thought so at first. It was some kind of weirdo alternative education, based on Pestalozzi, or Steiner, or Piaget, I mean really who knows. The Swiss can be very theoretical. The couple who founded it were hippies of some kind, pretty crazy from the sound of it."

"*Baizuo?*"

She laughed. "No, they just loved nature. The Alps in particular. So, we always got up before dawn and took cold showers to start the day, and then we cleaned out the stables, and then we farmed, and we killed and chopped up chickens, and climbed some Alps, and cooked and cleaned, and did lots of exercises, and like that."

"And you hated it?" Fred guessed.

"Of course I did! At least at first. But then, just as I was getting used to it, my parents finally paid attention to the letters I was sending home. I had to write them on paper and send them by mail, it was like throwing them into the Aare in a bottle. None of us ever heard back from anyone. We had been forgotten. We were stuck in a hippie gulag. But finally my parents came for a visit, and they were horrified. Politely and without saying a word, I mean they were perfectly inscrutable Orientals to the people in charge there, but I could see it no problem. Oh my God, their princess getting her hands dirty! Their precious daughter shoveling horseshit! All of their Chinese elite instincts were appalled. The whole point of joining the Party is to get off the farm! So they got me out of there as fast as they could and put me in another boarding school near Geneva, in Lausanne. Beautiful place, looking across the lake at Mont Blanc, all that. But the girls there, this was a girls-only school, they were from all over, with money leaking out of every pore. And there weren't any boys around to distract them and make them be nice. Very soon I hated those girls with all my heart. They were the ones who made me into a Maoist."

"Radicalized by rich girls in a Swiss boarding school?"

"Definitely. I hated them so much. Racist assholes, that's what they were. There's an age where you shouldn't put a bunch of girls by themselves. The mean girls' club is a real thing. They're worse than any boys I ever saw."

"Really?"

"Yes. *Lord of the Flies* is like some Christian support group compared to the mean girls' club. I think you probably need boys and girls together at that age more than any other. Anyway I hated them."

"What did they do?"

"Oh, just the usual shit. I don't want to tell you. It's always the same kind of stuff. Just saying it repeats it, somehow."

"Okay."

"Like one time I came in on them and they were wearing some of my clothes and pulling their eyes to the side and singing 'We are Siamese, if you please, we are Siamese if you don't please.'"

"Siamese?"

"Whatever! It was a cartoon song. I looked it up. About Siamese cats, it turns out. Pretty funny in fact. But to them I was a gook, a slant, a chink!"

Just saying it repeats it, Fred knew not to say; although it was painful to hear that grating sound in her voice. He said, "I'm surprised the school's administrators let that kind of thing happen."

"They never know what really goes on in the dorms."

"I guess not. And so . . ."

"So that's when I started making my escapes. You don't just run away from those places, you're locked in. You have to escape. So that took some work, because that place was a real prison. Part of the deal is if you pay a ton of money to put your daughter in a place like that, they stay there."

"They're safe."

"Safe! Safe to live with horrible racist bitches! That's right. So, I got away three times, got caught three times. The Swiss have way better surveillance than China, and I didn't know what I was doing, and I had no friends or money. Once I just walked into the forest and got lost out there. But the Swiss even have their forests surveilled. So the third time they caught me, I begged my father to send me back to my first school. The École was looking like utopia at that point. And he let me do it. After that I was fine."

"So he was..."

"My dad was okay. He is okay. He tries. In fact I think of myself as complementing his efforts from below. As a family we are a pincer attack, you might say. Not that he would agree with that. But I'll convince him of it by the time it's all over. I'll *make* him see it. If he doesn't die first of a heart attack at how bad I am."

. . . . .

Another time she put her head back onto her chair back and sighed heavily. "But what about you?" she said again. "And don't answer with a question."

Fred shrugged.

"What brought you to the moon?"

"Just my job."

"I know that. You are a quantum mechanic." She laughed briefly. "But what brought you to your job?"

"Oh I don't know."

"You must like quantum mechanics?"

Fred tilted his head and thought about it. "Yes. I do."

"So go on. Go backward from that. What brought you to quantum mechanics?"

"Oh I don't know."

Fred was not comfortable. He didn't know what he could say about his past. He didn't understand it himself, so how could he explain it to someone else?

She waited him out, watched him think it over. Not a warm look, but not a sharp look. Not irritated or annoyed or suddenly furious. Just watching. Curious. They had a lot of time. He wasn't going to be able to outwait her. This was unusual; almost everyone else he had ever met in his life would get uncomfortable with his silences and then fill them, and he would be off the hook. Not this time.

"I didn't fit in," Fred finally said, surprising himself. "I never could quite get why people did what they did. I didn't understand them. Or, I just couldn't think fast enough. So everything was kind of mysterious. And, and, and…disturbing. So then, in my math classes, I could understand things. Things were clear. Like algebra. I liked algebra. Everything balanced out. And I could see things in geometry. Trig was geometry as processed by algebra, so I liked that too. Calculus was easy."

She laughed. "That's not a sentence you hear very often."

"No, it's easy. And then there was a little introductory unit on quantum mechanics, kind of to dispense with it and move on. And what the professor said about it was so weird and, and—and unlikely, that I got into it. It was interesting."

"So that's your biography? A list of your math classes?"

"I guess so."

"What else did you do?"

"What do you mean?"

"I mean, what else did you do! In your life! Sports? Music? Theater? Dance? Travel? Friends? Romances?"

"No," Fred said. That sounded a little extreme, all by itself, and so he added: "I mean, I had some friends."

"Okay, good. That's a start. Are you still in touch with them?"

"No."

"Wow." She stared at him. "You were a real geek."

Fred sighed. "That's one name people use."

"What, there are others?"

Fred glanced at her, looked back at the floor. "You know there are."

"What, like what?"

"Just saying it repeats it," he said, swallowing hard.

"Really? That bad?"

He shrugged. "To think you're a person, and then be told you're a symptom? A diagnosis?"

She considered him. "Welcome to the world," she suggested.

"Well I don't like it," he muttered. Then he added, more bitterly: "As if anyone knows. As if they know anything about it."

She stared at him for a while. "I think I know what you mean. So, you suffered the slings and arrows of youthful geekdom."

Fred nodded. Trying to remember: but in fact he was better at not remembering. "I guess so. But quantum mechanics gave me a way to—to *do* something. I could do the equations, I mean it's a math, just like any other math, not that hard compared to some maths, but the results—or what the equations suggest about reality, because they work—it's so counterintuitive. So bizarre compared to what we see in our sensory world, that, I don't know. I found it interesting. And not everyone gets it. It's not that hard as a math, but it is hard as a thing to understand. Like impossible. So I pursued it, and now, there's more and more technology that is quantum mechanical. Including secure communications tech, which a lot of people want. So it's a . . . it's a way."

"A way? To make a living?"

"A way."

"A way?"

"Just a way. A way to be."

"Like Daoism."

"I don't know. People do like to try to link quantum mechanics to something more tangible. Tangible or mystical."

"You don't?"

"I suppose I do. The thing about quantum mechanics is that when you try to make it make sense by analogy to something at our level of perception, it's always a misrepresentation, so the real thing slips out of your grasp. You're getting it wrong. So for a long time I preferred to keep it at the level of the math, and not try to explain it at all."

"For a long time? And then something happened?"

"Well, yes." Fred sat up on the couch, stirred by the thought. "People are using the math to design and build machines. More and more qubits are being stabilized in various ways. So something real is happening, something physical. So I started thinking about what the quantum realm was really doing, I mean in the physical world. I mean clearly it's doing something. And the idea that it's an entirely statistical probability state, that takes consciousness or measurement to make it collapse to an event—or that there are new universes branching out of every moment—none of that was working for me. There are several different interpretations of what the math is describing, because it's so weird, but most of them just struck me as crazy."

After he was silent for what might have been some time, thinking about this, she said sharply, "And then?"

Fred thought about it some more. "Then," he said, "I started thinking more about the pilot wave interpretation. Have you heard of that one?"

She shook her head. "Tell me."

"Well, people talk about the Copenhagen interpretation, which came mostly from Niels Bohr. His idea was that physical reality was a matter of probabilities, like the equations are, and that things at the subatomic level are undetermined until measured, at which point they become one thing or the other. Waves become particles, and particles add up to waves, but not in ways that make sense according to our senses, so in the end it's too strange to understand."

"That's not much of an interpretation?"

"No. Einstein didn't like it, Penrose didn't like it. But the math definitely works, right down to the parts-per-trillion range. So it's been hard to say how Bohr's take on it is wrong. But right from the beginning, a physicist named de Broglie said there was another way of understanding it, which was that quantum particles were disturbing fields they were moving in, mostly by creating waves that moved ahead of the particles, like a pilot wave that you see in front of a boat. I've seen those from this window, looking at the boats on this bay. So, David Bohm talked about that as being disturbances in quantum fields. Then later they did some analog experiments that were like sending a droplet of oil skipping over a sheet of water, to show the kinds of effects that de Broglie suggested were happening at the quantum level."

"Wait, what? Oil on water?"

"Yeah, you know how oil and water don't mix, so when you shoot a droplet of oil across water, there's a wave—"

"Show me," she said.

"Well, I think it's at a pretty small scale—"

"Show me!"

She was standing over him, hand out; when he took it, she pulled him to his feet. And then they had something to do.

They found the biggest pan in the apartment's kitchen cabinets, a metal sheet pan about two feet long and a foot wide. "I don't know if this will be big enough," Fred said.

"It's what we've got. Just make it work."

"Okay, I'll try."

One of the few things Fred had done in his youth was to serve as teaching assistant to his high school physics teacher. The teacher had been a nice guy, and had probably given Fred the job to try to get him out of his shell a little. So Fred had worked on wave-tank experiments for a semester of his senior year, and now, remembering those, he found that ceramic chopsticks could be used to create dams across water filling the pan very shallowly; he could place three of them to make the two slits of the two-slit experiment. When they got that arranged, they put this apparatus on the coffee table and started making waves and observing them. It was a little messy, but waves on water can be counted on to spread and rebound in their usual way, and they had time to adjust the amount of water and the intensity of the initiating splashes until these effects were pretty clear, even the secondary waves that got through the two slits and interacted with each other on the other side of the dam. Interference patterns appeared, just as predicted, and interesting as such.

The oil droplets were not so easy. There was some sesame oil in the kitchen cabinet above the sink, but no obvious way to send a droplet of it skittering across the surface of their water to make the pilot wave. They tried a lot of methods, and ended up laughing a lot. Throwing; flicking; spitting; squeezing out of a basting bulb; shooting out of a red plastic water pistol found in a drawer—they kept trying things, they didn't want it to end. The room smelled of sesame oil. Sometimes the drop would ooze across the top of the water with enough momentum to send a little wave across the water ahead of it. Once that wave hit the two slits hard enough that the little waves on the other sides of the slits were high enough to be seen interfering with each other, and Fred said,

"Yes! That's the two-slit experiment. Now see, if the oil droplet were then to follow that wave on a certain trajectory, it would only go through one slit, but its wave already went through both. And on the other side, it would get pushed around by the interference pattern of that wave, and where it went then would be stochastic, meaning probabilistic, but its location would always fit the equations, just like they really do in quantum behaviors. And you don't need an observer making an observation to make that happen. It will happen without an observer. It's not just a probability state."

"So—pilot wave!" Qi said, looking pleased. "So you're an advocate of that interpretation, and it helps you in your work?"

Fred sat back on the couch, shook his head. "No. I don't know if it helps or not. The math is the same either way. The quantum fields can't be entered into the equations, and David Bohm was always suggesting they were contiguous to the entire universe. And judging by analogy to gravitational waves, the pilot waves are likely to be really small."

"Like how small?"

"Like, if two black holes hundreds of times more massive than the sun collide, they make a gravitational wave that by the time it gets to us squeezes the Earth about the width of one proton. So how big of a wave can a photon make in a quantum field the size of the universe?"

"Wow," Qi said after pondering this for a while. "Pretty small, I'm guessing."

"Right. So I end up working on things that derive from the usual math. What the math is describing in physical terms doesn't help me that much." He waved at their wave tank. "Actually I'm not sure seeing it this way has ever helped me. I mostly try to leave that part blank."

She sat in the armchair looking at him, he could tell; he continued to look at their wave tank. She was amused, he guessed, but maybe exasperated too.

"And you're very good at leaving things blank," she said.

"Yes?" He was pretty sure she would think this was a bad thing. "I feel kind of blank, pretty often. Or," he confessed, "maybe baffled, you might say."

She was nodding. "I bet you find me baffling!"

"Yes!"

She laughed at him. "Do you know about Yiman Wang's yellow yellowface?"

"No."

"How about Edward Said's *Orientalism*?"

"No."

"Of course not. Well, you should read them. They talk about how Westerners, when they look at Asians, they see a stranger, a big other. Some kind of blank that isn't at all like them, and then they fill that blank in with a story they make up. Exotic inscrutable dragon lady! That's me all right!" She laughed again.

Fred nodded, stifling a smile despite her laughter. He kept his eyes on the wave tank. He was pretty sure she didn't really think it was funny.

"Everyone has to guess about everyone else," he ventured at last. That was definitely true for him.

She bunched her lips into a little knot. "Maybe so," she conceded. She thought about that and then dripped a drop of oil into their water tank. "The chink and the geek! Riding the pilot wave! Finding the dao together! Solving crimes and saving the world! Binge view the whole series!"

"I don't like shows like that," Fred said primly.

She laughed at him yet again, a real laugh.

· · • • ·

They sat in the room sweating. He in the armchair, she stretched out on the couch. Breathing and sweating. The refrigerator grumbled a little less than half the time, in a tone about an octave lower than the whooshing hum of the window-box air conditioner, which was on a little more than half the time. The two were out of synch with each other. Fred was irritated by these noises more often than he would have liked. When either kicked on, he noticed both for a while. When the AC was on, it was a little too cold; when it went off, it quickly became too hot.

Qi shifted around the couch from one splayed posture to the next, groaning as she tried to get comfortable. She napped with her mouth open, looking like a little girl. She cooked spicy food. She marveled he could live on only rice, told him he would get sick, or terminally bored. That his capacity to withstand boredom was itself boring. She poked around in the various paperbacks on their shelf, trying one after another before tossing them aside. She stared at the ceiling. They were visited by a clan of small geckos that could hang upside down, and did. Fred wondered if word had gotten to his folks that he was alive. He wondered if his employers were trying to find him and help him. He wondered if Shor's algorithm, which took advantage of quantum superposition to factor large numbers, could be used to define the temporal length of a moment of being. It had to be longer—it felt much longer—than the minimum temporal interval, the Planck interval, which was the time it took a photon moving at the speed of light to move across the Pauli exclusion zone within which two particles could not coexist: that minimal interval of time was 10^{-44} of a second. A moment of being was more like a second, he felt, maybe three seconds. Meaning each moment of being was, when compared to the minimal interval of time, a near eternity. Much longer in proportion to the minimal interval than the lifetime of the universe was relative to a second. Although it could be argued that the universe's lifetime had so far been fairly brief. He wondered what the largest prime number he could recite aloud might be.

Qi went to the bathroom about once an hour. When she came out she was always a little flushed and restless.

"What are you reading?" she would demand of Fred, if he was reading.

"This one is called *Six Scenes from a Floating Life*, by a Shen Fu."

She groaned. "A classic."

"It seems interesting."

"What does it say to you right now? What sentence were you reading?"

" 'The Sage taught us, Do not use nets with too fine a mesh.' "

"Please, no Confucius! Something else."

Fred flipped the page. " 'Now the clouds are flying past me; who will play the jade flutes over May plums by city and stream?' "

She sighed. "We need a different book." She picked up a tattered oversized paperback called *Eight Dime Novels*. "I hope this book cost eighty cents." She read from a page:

" 'It was the tightest fix in which he had ever been caught, and his mind, fertile as it was in expedients at such crises, could see no way of meeting the danger.' Oh dear how will they escape!"

"Read on," Fred suggested.

" 'When all the wood was thrown in that the stove could contain, and portions of the iron sheeting could be seen becoming red-hot, he ceased to heap in wood. They were ready to run at any moment; the gold was always secured about their persons. "When it blows up, run!" was the admonition of the boy.' Wait—first it blows up and then they run? How are they going to avoid getting killed when it blows up?"

"Read on," Fred said again.

And after that they spent part of every day reading aloud to each other. They read all eight of the dime novels, each taking up about twenty pages of the skinny oversized Dover paperback. Lots of laughs there, although the frequent blatant racism also made Qi shout "See? See?" But she shouted just as much, and also laughed a lot, at a Chinese book of quotations from Chairman Mao, which she translated extempore for Fred's benefit. For a day or two they alternated passages, her from Mao, him from the Dover, and then from a fat little bird guide, which he picked up after seeing a brilliant red bird out the kitchen window.

"'People of the world, be courageous, dare to fight, defy all difficulties, and advance wave upon wave. Then the whole world will belong to the people. Monsters of all kinds shall be destroyed.'"

"That's his pilot wave interpretation," Fred observed.

"Aha! So the pilot wave theory is Leninist?"

"I don't know, what does that mean?"

"You don't know—come on. Leninism is what I was doing in that basement in Shekou."

"I see," Fred said, though he didn't. He read from the bird guide: "'Rufous-sided towhee. Note the rufous sides,' thank you for that! 'Smaller and more slender than robin; rummages noisily among dead leaves. Voice: note, *chwee* or *shrenk*. Song, a buzzy *chweeee*; sometimes *chup chup chup zeeeeee*.'" He enjoyed making the sounds.

Qi then read, "'All reactionaries are paper tigers. In appearance, the reactionaries are terrifying, but in reality they are not so powerful. From a long-term point of view, it is not the reactionaries but the people who are really powerful. Fight, fail, fight again, fail again, fight again, and so on till victory; this is the logic of the people.'"

"From a long-term point of view," Fred repeated. "But how long?"

"Don't make fun," Qi commanded. "I like Mao. Listen to this: 'Not to have a correct political view is like having no soul.' You hear that?"

"I do," Fred said. "But what's correct?"

"Maybe you can learn that here, it's the very next quote. 'Where do correct ideas come from? Do they drop from the skies? No. Are they innate in the mind? No. They come from social practice, and from it alone; they come from three kinds of social practice: the struggle to make things, the class struggle, and scientific experiment.'"

"Interesting," Fred said.

Qi nodded and read on: "'The history of humanity is one of continuous development from the realm of necessity to the realm of freedom.' That's Marx, as I hope you know, but of course you don't."

"Groucho or Harpo?"

"Ha ha. Listen to Mao here, this is important: 'This process is never ending. In any society in which classes exist, class struggle will never end. In a classless society, the struggle between new and old and between truth and falsehood will never end. In the fields of the struggle for production and scientific experiment, humanity makes constant progress and nature undergoes constant change, they never remain at the same level. Therefore people have to go on discovering, inventing, creating and advancing. Ideas of stagnation, pessimism, and complacency are all wrong. They are wrong because they agree neither with the historical facts of social development, nor with the facts of nature so far known to us, as revealed in the history of celestial bodies, the earth, life, and other natural phenomena,' no doubt he is referring to your quantum world there."

"No doubt," Fred said. "That's actually a pretty good summary of the situation."

"Yes it is."

"'Skylark,'" he interjected. "'Slightly larger than a sparrow, brown, strongly streaked; underparts buff white. Voice; note, a clear, liquid *chirr-up*. Song, in hovering flight, a high-pitched, tireless torrent of runs and trills, very long sustained.'"

She nodded, distracted by Mao, who had clearly caught her attention. "'Youth, the world is yours as well as ours, but in the last analysis, it is yours. You young people, so full of vigor and vitality, are in the bloom of life, like the sun at eight or nine in the morning. Our hope is placed on you.'"

"So full of vigor and vitality," Fred said, and Qi smiled; they were both sprawled listlessly over the furniture. "I like that 'eight or nine in the morning.' He has a specific angle in mind."

"A specific moment."

"An angle."

"But morning light. At sunset it's not the same."

"True. Anyway, Mao is more interesting than I would have thought."

"I know, me too."

"I thought you knew all about him."

"Everybody gets told the story at school, but no one reads him. Maybe his poetry. Mostly he's just a face, or an idea. And I'm only reading you the good stuff. The amount of crap is unbelievable."

. . . . .

The refrigerator, then the air conditioner. The air conditioner, then the refrigerator. The cheep of birds. An hour of rain. Men in rowboats, harvesting fish. A pilot wave, crossing the bay.

Dozing in the heat, Fred dreamily pondered the pilot wave theory. Their kitchen experiment had been an imitation of a macroscopic analog of the real microscopic two-slit experiments with photons. In the real analog experiments, during which they had gotten tiny oil droplets to skid across the water like skipping stones, they had been able to reproduce all kinds of quantum effects at the macro-scale, suggesting that the same kinds of things were happening down there at the micro. Stochastic electrodynamics, which was one current extension of pilot wave theory, postulated and described an electromagnetic zero-point field, a kind of subquantum realm through which the pilot wave moved. Possibly wave and particle quantum effects were just well-coordinated emergent phenomena that in fact were primarily happening in this speculated subquantum realm. Could there be something smaller than quanta? Sure. Reality shrank beyond their senses and no doubt could go smaller still, until it was smaller than their ability to detect by any means whatsoever. Same in the other direction, with things big beyond the visible universe; for all they knew, their universe could extend forever, or be a neutrino in some larger universe. They could only see what they could see. Beyond that, the unknown. The unknowable.

"I want to be an agnotologist," he said to Qi. "I want to study what we don't know."

"You would be good at that," Qi said.

. . ● . .

The next day one of Qi's friends tapped at the door and stepped in to give them a couple of plastic bags of food. Fred put it all away while Qi talked to the young woman in Chinese. He was relieved to see that dishwashing soap had been included, per his request to their previous visitor.

This one left unusually soon after arriving, leaving Qi scowling.

"Uh-oh, what?" Fred asked, straightening up.

She glanced at him, looked away. "One of the people who has been bringing us supplies has gone missing."

Fred considered this. He saw why she was upset. "So what do we do?" he said after a while.

"I don't know." After a while she said, "I guess I should stay away from the windows, but could you sit where you can look down, and see if you think anyone is hanging around down there watching us?"

"I can try." If spotted, he could be any Western tourist. On the other hand he was definitely Fred Fredericks, presumably being looked for by at least someone in the world, with his photo easily available, he presumed. "We have Venetian blinds. I can tilt the blinds so that I can see out and people can't see in."

"Good idea."

After that he spent a fair amount of time looking out their window at the village's sidewalk and restaurant row. No one appeared to be at all interested in their place. He began to sort out who the regulars were and what they were doing, and they all seemed to have restaurant or fishing business. Almost all; some people just passed through. Tourists, locals, it was hard to tell. It was a very sleepy village. Still, the new tension in the room was palpable. There was no way to be sure they weren't being watched. Proving a negative was always hard.

"Could this person who went missing just have left or something?" he asked one day.

"His name is Wei," Qi said sharply. Her look turned dark. "I don't think so. I mean, maybe, but I can't think what it would be. So I'm really worried about him."

And about us, Fred didn't say.

"I wish I could go back to his last visit and warn him," she said. "Tell him to get away somewhere."

"Maybe someone else did that instead of us."

"Maybe."

Fred could see, even in his sidelong glances, that she was very worried about this Wei. A friend, perhaps. He wondered again if his family had gotten word that he was okay. "Too bad we can't take advantage of quantum backdating," he said.

"What do you mean?"

"There's a couple of experiments you can do that show quantum effects that are like going backward in time, or changing the past."

"Really?"

"Sort of. If you make a certain kind of molecule that combines particular kinds of atoms, you can heat and chill them such that the colder atom in the molecule gives its heat to the hotter one, which breaks entropy and is like a little instance of time going backward. Also, if you do the half-silvered mirror experiment in a certain way, it's like the two-slit experiment, in that you can tweak it to get either wave results or particle results, but in this version of it, if you tweak the device after the photon has gone through the mirror, it retroactively changes what happened at the mirror. So it's like you've changed the past."

"Wow," Qi said. Then, wistfully: "Can't you make one of your quantum phones do that? I want to call Wei last week."

"These aren't actions that can convey information," Fred explained. "Also they only last milliseconds. They're just more ways in which the quantum realm is strange. Down at that level, things appear to be a kind of mush. Somehow by the time they layer up to our realm the usual laws of physics hold."

"Alas," she said. She sighed, looking grim. "I guess we're stuck twixt and tween."

"Like Schrödinger's cat," Fred said, trying to distract her.

"Meaning right now we're both alive and dead? That feels about right."

"I think we're alive," Fred ventured.

"No. Someone has to look at us first, right? Then we'll find out. Right now we're both at once."

"Maybe there's a pilot wave that already knows," Fred said. He didn't know what he meant.

· · • • ·

Once Qi woke up out of an uneasy nap and said, "Wow, I can feel it. Come here and feel."

Fred got up and went to her. She pulled up her shirt and bared her big belly, took his hand and put it to one side of her belly button. This was as much as Fred had ever touched a woman who wasn't a relative or a dance partner, and he was distracted by that, until he felt a distinct thrust outward from inside her, very startling.

"Whoa," he said.

"You felt it?"

"Of course." He felt it again. "What, is it kicking?"

"I think so."

"Does it hurt?"

"No. It feels weird, but not painful." Then she winced. "Uncomfortable sometimes."

"Like it's turning over in bed," Fred suggested.

She shook her head, but smiling a little. "Getting crowded in there."

She stood and let her shirt down, put her hands overhead, leaned to right and left, then forward and back. Some rotations. She put her back to a wall, causing a gecko to relocate in haste. Squats up and down against the wall. Pink-cheeked and sweating. The AC came on. She sat down, then got up again and went over to the kitchen corner. Poured rice and two cups of water in the rice cooker and turned it on. Banged around in their food cabinet and at the sink.

Fred regarded her. Now, even when her back was turned to him, he could see she was pregnant. He thought about how fermions had to rotate 720 degrees before they returned to their original position. This was one of the first facts that had snagged his mind when learning about the subatomic realm. Fermions existed in a Hilbert four-space, in dimensions beyond what humans could see at the macro-scale. What would it be like to see something like a fermion's spin? Would it pulsate in place, would it shimmer and gleam, would it overwhelm the senses to look at it? Maybe it would look like Qi did now.

· · · · ·

Then one day she spent a lot of time in the bathroom, sighing and groaning to the point that Fred got worried. It wasn't typical. In the late afternoon, after she came out, he ventured to say,

"Can I help?"

"No."

She looked around the room for a while and then announced, "I can't stand this. Let's go down and have dinner on the water. I want some food that isn't this same stuff. I'm sick of my own cooking."

I never liked it, Fred didn't say. "Are you sure that's smart?"

"I'm sure it's not smart. And yet nevertheless in spite of that."

"All right, whatever you say."

She stared at him as if he had said something offensive. Maybe he had.

"I'm tired of this," she said.

"I know."

It had been thirty-six days, he thought. He realized suddenly that he was probably finding these days more interesting than she was. Realizing that did not help his mood. So he liked to sit around doing nothing in particular, thinking things over—was that strange? Yes, it was. He sighed.

She looked out the window. After a while she said, "I think we can do it. Have dinner right at the water's edge, no one will see us."

"The waiters?"

"I'll wear a hat and glasses."

You can't hide those cheekbones, he didn't say. Nor the way you walk. Probably they should trade shoes. Probably she would think that was stupid.

"Come on," she said. "I can't stand it anymore."

. . • • .

They left the apartment and went down its stairs. Right next to their concrete cube stood a tall multicolored brick building. Gray bricks held an inset of brick-colored bricks, which framed a gray doorway in which gold-leaf tree trunks were set. Some kind of shrine, it appeared. Gold Chinese characters covered the doorframe and lintel.

"What is this?" Fred asked.

"Ta Hu," Qi explained. "The goddess who protects those who go to sea."

"In what religion?"

She shrugged. "Chinese religion."

"Daoist? Buddhist?"

"Older than those, I think."

They followed the little harbor's only sidewalk to the long tarp roof that covered all the restaurants. Qi chose one of them to enter, speaking briefly to a waiter. He nodded and led them to a small table at the railing overlooking the water. It was near sunset, light frilly clouds turning yellow and pink overhead. Another waiter approached and

Qi ordered something. "I ordered us a variety," she said. "You can try a little of everything."

"Sounds good," Fred lied.

The waiters brought out dishes and water and tea for each of them, then tureens of soup and plates of rice, and after that, dish after dish of other food. Some things Fred recognized, especially an entire fish, that was easy, of course; but a lot of the dishes were filled with foods he couldn't identify. Clumps of greenery; squares and balls of maybe tofu, or gelatin, or pork belly, or what have you. Gamely Fred tried everything, concealing from Qi as best he could that this was very difficult for him. He hated new foods. And many of the tastes, as with the appearances, completely baffled him. He had eaten a few times in China before, but never like this; he had protected himself by eating mostly rice and chicken. Now clams arrived, followed by mussels, then more cooked lumps of who knew what.

Around them the sunset turned to dusk, and the string of lights edging the tarp overhead grew brighter. Their restaurant was almost completely empty. On the other side of the sidewalk running along the back of the restaurants, tall banks of lit fish tanks glowed like an aquarium wall. Fred watched as the waiters or cooks stood on ladders to maneuver nets around in the tanks, scooping up fish with deft quick turns and then taking them back where presumably the kitchens were. Fresh fish indeed.

Then their waiter brought out two plates that held crustaceans so big they overhung the plates on all sides. Bigger than lobsters, with more legs than lobsters, sporting spikier shells that were blond in color. They both laughed. The scissors provided to cut through these shells were as heavy-duty as tin snips. Fred had a little experience with eating lobsters, so he accepted with some interest the challenge of getting to the meat of this armored beast. He had to be careful not to poke or slice his fingers in the effort. For a while they were both silent as they snipped away, making loud cracks when they succeeded in bringing enough pressure to bear. The meat tasted like crab, or lobster, or something like those.

"What is this thing?" Fred asked.

"Shrimp."

"Really? This big?"

"Around here that's how big they get."

"Hard to believe."

"And yet here it is."

"I'm trying to imagine the first person who hauled one of these out of the ocean and said, Oh yeah, let's eat this."

She laughed again. "My dad used to say, we Chinese eat everything with legs except the table."

Later, when they had shifted into the realm of unidentifiable desserts, they sat back in their chairs and watched twilight breathing on the bay and the hills.

"What do you think will happen?" Fred asked.

She frowned. "To us, you mean?"

"Yes."

"I'm not sure yet. I don't think it's the right moment yet for the movement to act. And I can't see a way to get a truly private word to my dad."

"You two don't have some private line?"

She shook her head. "Even if I did, his security team is always listening."

Fred thought it over as he picked through the desserts, hoping for something he liked enough to fill up on; despite his attempt to seem normal, he had eaten very little. His taste buds by now were terrifically confused, and he felt just slightly ill.

He ventured to say, "Do you think the heavy surveillance comes from having a one-party state?"

She stared at him. "Why would you say that?"

"It's not true?"

"It is true. But all one-party states have problems. That's why America is so messed up."

"What do you mean?"

"I mean America is more of a one-party state than China. It's entirely ruled by the market. Actually the market is the only party in the world now, or it wants to be. So every nation has to deal with that in its own way."

"They usually say we have a two-party system," Fred mentioned.

"Your parties are just factions. That's why people in your country are so angry. They can see it's just one party, and one-party states are always corrupt. Polyarchies are better because power gets distributed to various groups. They're inefficient and messy, with lots of turf battles, but that's the cost of distributing power. It's better than concentrated power."

Fred tried to think this over. His brain was as confused as his tongue. "I'm not sure," he confessed.

"No one is. All I'm really saying is that these names for systems that we use, they disguise all kinds of similarities. China and America are both one-party states, and they're both polyarchies. Those are the two kinds of rule that are always struggling for dominance."

"So are you hoping the two of them will kind of...?"

"Influence each other? Combine?"

"I don't know."

"Maybe. People talk about the G2 now, as if we're the only ones that matter, at least in economic terms. And in some ways we mirror each other. So if you could take the best of each..."

"Good idea."

She looked up at him as if to see if he was being sarcastic. But Fred was never sarcastic, as she should have known by now; and maybe she did. She looked down, poked around on her plate as if looking for something appealing.

"Ready to go?" he asked.

"I guess so, yes."

"This has been nice. Thank you for this."

"Thank you for sticking with me," she said.

"What do you mean?"

"You could leave."

"No. I'm in just as much trouble as you are. If not more."

"I guess. But we could probably get you into an American consulate now."

Fred shrugged. He knew immediately he didn't want that.

She stared at him curiously.

They sipped tea. Dusk turned the water of the bay a glossy black. She paid the waiter with one of the wristpads her friends had given them in Beijing. They got up and walked back toward their little concrete refuge.

At the end of the row of restaurants, she stopped and put her hand to his arm.

"What?"

She turned him around with a hard pull, began to walk the other way with her hand still pulling his arm.

"What?"

She lowered her head as they passed a couple, then said, "There are people waiting in our doorway. We have to get out of here. Stay quiet again."

"Damn," Fred said, feeling a jolt of dismay. *But I liked that place!* he almost said. *I wanted to stay there. I wanted time to stop there.*

Again they were leaving everything behind. By now that wasn't much more than their toothbrushes from the train, but still. To only have the clothes on your back. "Where will we go?"

"There's a little ferry at the end of this dock that runs people back to the city after they eat at these restaurants. We'll take that and hope they don't have anyone on it."

She turned them down a boardwalk that led to the water between two of the central restaurants. At its end was moored a water taxi with a glass-enclosed lower deck, and an open upper deck with another dozen seats. Qi showed the boatman her restaurant receipt and led Fred to the upper deck, and sat him down between her and the stairs they had ascended.

After a few minutes the boat cast off and burbled away, disturbing

the glassy surface of the bay. They were the only ones sitting on the
upper deck, and there were only eight or nine people below them on
the glassed-in deck. It was slightly chilly up top, and the wind blew
through their clothes. Qi huddled into his side and then stayed put.

"What now?" Fred asked.

After a long silence she said, "I've got an old friend from school
who lives up on Victoria Peak. I'm thinking of trying her."

"From that Swiss school? The good one?"

"Yes."

"So is this someone..."

"Someone I can trust?"

"Someone you can drop in on unannounced? With nothing?"

"Yes. It isn't ideal, but I don't know what else to do now."

"What about the friends who've been helping us?"

"I'm afraid I've already gotten them in enough trouble," she said
grimly. "That's probably how these people found us."

"How did you know they weren't just someone hanging around?"

"By how they were hanging around."

He regarded her. "You know those kinds of people."

"All my life."

He looked at her curiously. It had to have been an odd life. The
sons of top politicians in China were called princelings. Very privileged, but also locked inside a modern version of the Forbidden
City. A daughter would be princessling, a little princess. Heirs to the
throne. But then came dynastic succession.

Their little ferry hummed around the corner of the light-spangled
mountain that bulked across the channel from their little island.
Skyscrapers were pillars of light lining the shore, also studding the
entire slope from the shore to the black peaks above. A black mountain, jammed with towers of white light. Then as they rounded the
curve of this lit mountain rising from the black sea, they could see
farther to the east, and along this slope the lit skyscrapers were simply everywhere. They filled every space, they defined the shape of
the city. The dark mountain bulked above this dense forest of lit

skyscrapers, but the millions of lights of the city dominated all. Black glassy water lay under the boat, squiggling with white reflections. Ahead of them the glossy water separated two enormous white fields of skyscrapers.

"This is Hong Kong?"

"Yes. Kowloon to the left, Hong Kong island to the right. That's Central district on the right, where we're headed."

"Wow," Fred said.

Their boat slowed, then glugged in toward a giant ferry terminal, sticking out into the water like an aircraft carrier. To the left of the terminal soared an enormous Ferris wheel, as bright with white lights as any of the skyscrapers. Across the bay, in Kowloon, one building stood twice as tall and four times as thick as any of the others, a true monster. Words of white light in English and Chinese characters crawled up its side in a continuous vertical light show. Advertisements, apparently.

They got off their boat and joined a crowd. Again Qi led the way, through a complex multilevel terminal, then onto a glassed-in bridge over the highway backing the terminal. She threaded them through several gold-and-glass malls, each connected to the next by hallways, all of them multistory, all crisscrossed with escalators and broad staircases. All the stores in these malls appeared to be jewelry stores, which struck Fred as bizarre. He had never seen anything like it, and was completely lost, and it seemed to him that without some fairly extensive previous experience Qi should be lost too. But she hauled him through the three-dimensional maze without hesitation, making turns and taking escalators as if certain of her way. Giant room after giant room, all filled with shoppers, or rather what appeared to be people on their way somewhere else. These malls were being used as pedestrian corridors. Maybe better to think of them as giant hallways. He was stunned by all the lights, all the gleaming surfaces, all the mazelike rooms.

They came out of one mall into a park filled with tropical trees.

Then past a large caged-in aviary, in which Fred saw a flash or two of color, flitting under spotlights that illuminated a few parts of it. Then onto an outdoor escalator that cut straight up through a steeper part of the city. This long escalator led to the bottom of another escalator, rising through dense neighborhoods in which the buildings got lower the higher they rose. The escalators had long skinny tilted roofs covering them, no doubt to protect them from rain. Most of the people on the escalators stood to the right, and sometimes Qi stood with them; other times she hurried up the left side, and Fred followed her.

When they reached the top of the uppermost one, she turned left on a narrow street and began hiking up a street traversing the slope. By now they were both sweating from her haste in walking up so many escalator steps. It was warm and humid, and smelled like the tropics; it didn't smell like a city. From time to time Qi stopped to catch her breath.

"Do we have to hurry like this?" he asked her.

She gave him a look. "I want to get off the streets as soon as possible."

"Your friend is up here?"

"Yes!"

She led him up a switchbacking route, one small lane after another. The buildings lining these narrow alleyways were reduced in size to cubical things two or three stories tall, made of concrete, and sometimes wood. An older district. Then as they rose higher the roads angled up slopes covered more by trees than by buildings, and what buildings there were looked like houses with wooden shingles. An old residential area, no doubt very expensive. The hill was so steep that its side had been concreted over in most places, presumably to keep rain from sluicing its soil down onto the streets. Each tree on these concrete slopes had a hole of its own in the tilted concrete. Runnels incised into the concrete of the slope shot vertically into deep culverts on the streets' uphill sides.

Eventually they came to a big cube of a building, where a knot of roads converged. This giant concrete cube was set right on the main ridge of the city's backing mountain, in a low point between two broad peaks. The city-facing side of the cube served as the upper terminus of a little cog railway, which ran up into the building at what looked like a forty-five-degree angle.

"Inside," Qi said, and she pulled Fred through a doorway into the big cube, past the cog railway terminal and farther inside. Four floors of balconies, all filled with open-walled shops, looked down into a big empty central space. The shops sold tourist trinkets and T-shirts. Qi hurried up stairs rising against one wall, then pulled Fred into one open-fronted shop of trinkets that was already closed for the night. The entire cube was closing, it appeared. Qi pushed open a door at the back of the shop and looked inside, nodded, gestured around them at the shop.

"We can spend the night here."

She blew her hair away from her eyes, wiped her brow. She was still huffing and puffing. They looked around the little shop they were in, full of knickknacks and scarves and postcards. Protect us now, little Chinese goddesses, Fred thought as he stared at a row of them. Qi was checking for security cameras and found none aimed at the back of the store, where there was also a little toilet room.

"You've been here before?" Fred asked.

"Yes, I saw this place a long time ago. A woman selling stuff here let me use this bathroom, and I remembered it."

They sat down on the floor, put their backs against the wall. The lights went off, and after a while a pair of security guards made a cursory circle around each floor, chatting as they went. Then it was silent. Qi got up and made a bed and pillow out of scarves, and lay on her side and fell asleep. Fred tried to get comfortable, but soon after falling into a doze, he woke up feeling sick. Then a wave of nausea passed through him, causing sweat to pop from every pore. He quickly staggered into the little bathroom and kneeled over the toilet and threw up in it, flushing it time after time to reduce the smell. Then he felt Qi's hand on his forehead, holding his head up as his body convulsed, her other hand pressed against his back. After each spasm of throwing up, she handed him lengths of toilet paper to wipe his face with. This repeated a few times. For a while the clenching in his gut relented, and then he began the stage of dry heaves, his body still desperately trying to vomit up something that wasn't there anymore. He felt truly wretched as he coughed up spittle and chyme and whatever else might remain down there. Qi stayed with him throughout the ordeal. Later, after he seemed done, and had crawled back out to their nest on the shop floor, she sat by him and wiped his face clean with a scarf wetted from a water bottle. She handed him a roll of mints she had found on the counter of the shop in a stack of candies for sale. He popped one into his mouth against a cheek, tentatively swallowed a few times.

"Thanks," he said. "I guess I ate something that disagreed with me."

"Apparently so. Although I feel okay, and I ate the same stuff. But who knows. My appetite has been crazy."

"No morning sickness?"

"Not now. How are you feeling?"

"Better. Shaky. But I don't feel like I'm going to throw up anymore."

"We have quite a few hours to go before they open this place. Try to sleep."

He tried, failed; but then woke up, feeling queasy. Then slid under again.

When he woke again he felt parched, but Qi had found him a bottle of lemonade from a cooler in the corner of the shop. The big windows on the upper floor of the cube showed dawn was coming.

"There's an awkward time coming, maybe," Qi said. "Between when the shopkeepers arrive and when the first train of tourists gets here. I'd like to keep hiding and only come out when the tourists get here, then mingle with them and leave. So I don't think we can

stay in this shop. But I think there must be public restrooms somewhere in here, and maybe we can just hide in a stall in one. It should
only be for an hour or less."

"And if I get sick again we'll be in the right place," Fred offered
weakly.

She nodded with a little smile and led him through the darkness
down the stairs, looking around for security cameras. Then into a
ladies' room, where they sat down on the floor and waited. Noises
of people came from outside, so they crammed into a stall together,
ready to stand on the toilet if anyone came in; no one did. Finally
they heard, or possibly felt, the first train of the day leave the station,
and ten minutes later the first one from below was hauled in with a
clanking sound. Then the noises of people filtered into their hide-
out. Qi took a look out the door, and when she gave the all clear,
Fred followed her.

Qi took him by the hand and led him after that, and he followed
her, hoping not to have to think. He was surprised when Qi handed
him a wrapped pastry she had taken from their shop. "I have some
candy bars too, if you feel like eating."

"Thanks." He felt weak and shaky, possibly with hunger, although
he didn't feel hungry. Far from it; he felt dreadful.

Then Qi became very absorbed in trying to find an exit from the
cube. The only doors they could find led them either into the cog
railway's terminal, or into some kind of tourist trap, it looked like
a wax museum, but it was hard to tell, as she kept tugging him past
its entry and cursing under her breath. "Damn this place!" she said
at one point. "They don't want you to leave! They want you to buy
more of their crap and then take the train back down!"

"Looks like it."

They descended stairs that led only to an emergency exit, with
ALARM WILL SOUND marking its door. She cursed again, they ascended
the stairs, took another narrow passageway that led to different stairs.
They descended again, and here as luck would have it a man was
unlocking the exit door from the outside. As he opened it to come

in, Qi thanked him in Chinese and hustled Fred out and away. They found themselves standing on a little plaza between the big concrete cube and a big knot of tourist shops. One of the mountaintop's ridge roads edged this plaza. Sunny morning, some overcast clouds, a slight breeze.

Qi led him into a coffee shop and ordered coffee for herself, and a pastry; Fred had another lemonade, feeling parched and unsteady.

Then they were back out onto the high plaza, looking around. It was about nine in the morning, sun up over the ridge of the mountain rising to the east of them. A few tourists were wandering the plaza. Westward on the broad ridge one road sloped up to the right, another down to the left. A little botanical garden flanked the left side of the road headed uphill, and on the other side of that road stood a large apartment complex, rising over a tall wall that guarded it from the street. The north-facing apartments in this complex would have spectacular views over the city. The south slope of the ridge was green, nothing but treetops falling sharply away, and a view out to sea, which again was as smooth as a lake, a hazy blue in the morning sun.

"Is this it?" Fred said, looking up at the building.

"Yes." She was checking out the street, looking back and forth.

"Have you been here before?"

"No."

That made him uneasy, but there was nothing he could do but follow her and hope for the best. They walked across the little plaza and up the road toward the luxury apartments' gated driveway.

She stopped all of a sudden and turned into Fred. Again she hugged him hard, and he felt her pregnant belly against him.

"They're here too," she muttered.

"How can you tell?"

"I know them," she said.

"You mean individually? You know them in particular?"

"No no." She knocked her forehead against his collarbone. "It's them though, believe me. I know them when I see them."

"I believe you. But how could they know you would come here?"

"They know Ella and I were at school together. It must be that. They're guarding anywhere I might go."

"Okay, let's just walk it back here. Hold on to me, come on."

"We can't go back down into the city the way we came up."

"No?"

"No, I don't want to. There's too many cameras, too many eyes."

Fred looked around. "Can you climb?"

"No. Can you?"

"A little." His brother had once taken him out to a bouldering site and taught him the basic rope techniques and moves, and the following week they had climbed a short and easy wall together, his brother leading every pitch. This was another of his brother's attempts to get him out of his head, but the experience had not been to Fred's liking. Exposure, a climbers' term, was a partial description; they didn't say what the exposure was to, which turned out to be death by falling. Fred had felt that was going too far in the search for something interesting. When you were stunned by the fact that a fermion rotated 720 degrees before returning to its original position, you did not need to hang by your fingers and toes from a cliff to get your thrills. But the whole experience had been etched on his mind quite forcefully.

"Can we do it?" she asked, seeing his uncertainty.

"I don't know. But if it doesn't get too steep, I think so."

"Okay then. Let's do it."

. . . . .

They hurried as casually as they could back to the intersection of roads in the low point on the ridge, then walked down the lower road that also headed west. As soon as they were out of the sight of the plaza and the upper road, Fred peered over the south side of the road and gulped at the steepness: treetops dropped swiftly away, and the sea was a long way down and yet not very far off. He continued along the road, hoping for a lessening of the slope's angle, while trying also to adjust to the sudden reversal of roles. Now he was leading her, and needed to choose a good way—a good way to get a pregnant woman who was not a climber down a slope that looked to be dropping at an angle of at least forty-five degrees, and was concreted over in many places! It was hard to say whether the concrete was an advantage or disadvantage. It might be less slippery. On the other hand if they did slip it would be disastrous. The many trees covering the slope, and the open cups of concrete-rimmed dirt they emerged from, would probably be his best chance of finding good holds.

They passed a stream that coursed through a tunnel under the road, its pitch so steep that below the road it became a waterfall. That was certainly not the way down, and he continued anxiously on, feeling the weakness in him from the night's vomiting. He was a little light-headed.

Then the road took a turn out and around a bump in the hill. Here the slope below them was a little bit of a buttress. Just past the broad nose of this buttress the slope was less steep than what they had passed so far, and more covered with trees. "Okay, over we go," he said to her, and helped her over the road's low guardrail.

They descended in short sideways steps. Quickly they found themselves on a slope so steep that they had to sit down, then slide very slowly down on their butts. The concrete facing that covered the hill was so rough they couldn't slip down it even if they wanted to, which was reassuring. Fred went first and led her from tree to tree. They held on to tree trunks, and put their shoes against the rims of the tree holes in the concrete, and sometimes against each other. Mostly this meant Qi put her foot against Fred from above, to ease herself down to him. The angle of the slope was proving to be laid-back enough to allow them to stay stuck to it. He found he couldn't estimate the angle very well—possibly thirty-five degrees, but who knew really. Angle of repose was thirty-two degrees, he seemed to recall, but what kind of repose? A round ball would roll down any incline, so maybe they meant a cube or something. In practical terms, it was as steep as it could be and them still stick to it.

Almost immediately they were down the slope far enough that they couldn't see the road above, and Fred felt sure they would not be visible from it either. That being the case, they could slow down and take it more carefully, so he did that. Qi looked scared but resolute, her lips clamped to a white line, her eyes fixed on her footwork. She could not fall, so she would not: this was what her expression said. She would stay stuck in one spot forever if that was what it took—get rescued by climbers or helicopters, go to prison—but no falling.

Fred tried to get a better view down. It wasn't possible to see far through the trees. If the slope got steeper than what they were on now, they would be in big trouble. Even as it was he was not happy with the angle. Any slip that created any momentum and the results would be awful.

He kept going first, and when possible kept one hand free to reach up and hold her hand or foot, knee or elbow. Sometimes he reached up and gripped her wrist. She used him as a foothold without hesitation or compunction. Every few moves they had to put their butts to the slope, or sometimes their knees, and the occasional brief scraping slide downward hurt even through clothes. He tried to calculate how long it was going to take them to descend, but didn't know enough to do it. He had no idea if there was another road on this side of the mountain, or how far down the slope it might be if there was one. They still couldn't see far through the broad leaves of the trees, in any direction. It seemed like this island was so thoroughly urbanized that there would have to be a road down there somewhere, but he didn't really know.

"Let's stop and rest for a while," he said to her when they were both securely sitting in a skinny tree's open bowl, feet against the concrete rim of the downhill side. They sat there, breathing hard at first, sweating freely in the humid air. Now he caught a glimpse of the ocean down there through the leaves. He guessed it was still at least a thousand feet below them.

"Are there any roads down this way, do you know?" he asked.

"I don't. I've only been to Hong Kong a few times. As far as I know, people don't come to this side very much. I think I remember hearing the city's water comes from this side. There's a reservoir or something. So people must come over here, right?"

"I think so, yeah. But...Well, I guess we'll figure it out when we get down there."

They sat there sweating. After a while they started down again. The concrete covering came to an end, and they found themselves on crumbling rock and scree and sand and dirt, quite a bit more slippery than the concrete had been, but also affording some places they could dig in with their shoes, also some knobs of hard rock to hold on to. Then this unclad slope got steeper, scaring Fred; but after a while it laid back a little, reassuring him. That repeated a few times. They took rests every fifteen or twenty minutes.

A couple of hours passed like that. Then, legs shaking, palms bleeding, sweating so profusely their shirts were soaked, they saw through the trees a paved road crossing the slope below them. One moment they were looking down on broad green leaves as always, then there was a road. It traversed the slope almost horizontally, as far as they could tell from above.

The final drop to it, though short, was almost vertical. Fred turned into the slope and climbed down about halfway, then held on to rock knobs and had Qi put her shoes right on his head and shoulders. Then she stepped down onto his thigh, which he had propped up by sticking his foot into a crevice. His brother had done this for him during their one try at climbing, coaxing him down the entire descent, as Fred had often frozen in place. His brother had been really worried.

Qi never froze. When she was down at his level, and had moved her feet and hands onto rocks in a way she said made her secure, he climbed down again, kicking for footholds on knobs in looser rock, until he was standing in the culvert next to the road. She climbed down him again, and he provided her last foothold with his linked hands. Finally she hopped down beside him.

They stood there and briefly exchanged a look, both flushed, soaked with sweat, streaked with blood. Quivering. Fred felt sick again, either with relief or because of a return of his nighttime nausea, he couldn't tell. He tried to quell the feeling, not wanting a repetition of the vomiting. He put his hands on his knees and let his head hang. Slowly the nausea passed. It was a wretched feeling. After a while they clambered up onto the asphalt road.

"Which way?" she asked.

"I don't know."

She gave him one of her looks. Possibly it had been a rhetorical question.

To the west the road was slightly uphill. Presumably that way would lead them around the island's west side, where they had seen residential towers during the previous night's ferry ride from Lamma Island. To the east it was slightly downhill, which was attractive, but they didn't have any idea what lay that way, or how far away it might be.

They chose west without even discussing it, and started to walk. From time to time they came on benches set on the downhill side of the road overlooking the sea, and they sat on each of these and rested. When they passed creeks clattering down the hillside near waterfalls, Fred stuck his face in the water and drank, and suggested that Qi do the same.

"What if it's contaminated?" she asked anxiously.

"Let's worry about that later. You need to stay hydrated." He drank again to show her. "Usually water in the hills is cleaner than you think."

She stared at him as if he were crazy. "Not in China!"

"Well, but this is Hong Kong. And this little creek must be spring-fed, or recent rainwater. And you need to stay hydrated. So try just a little. We can eat some antibiotics later."

She drank. Fred felt hungry as well as weak, and assumed she must too. He was worried about her pregnancy. If it weren't for that, they would be okay; but that had to be a worry for her, and so it was for him too. What could pregnant women withstand? He had no idea. Probably a lot. He recalled reading stories in his childhood of peasant women harvesting crops right up to their due dates, giving birth in the fields and going back to work the very next hour, and so on. Those could have been stupid stories, he had no idea. An example of this Orientalism Qi had mentioned, attributing to peasants the toughness of animals because they were not quite human. Well, humans were animals. He recalled the brief period he had tried swimming with an adult swim group, another experiment suggested by his brother, and watching a woman eight months pregnant fly by him for lap after lap, complaining during their rests that the kid was kicking her after her flip turns. People were animals, sure, and strong as such; or could be strong. As for this particular woman, he didn't know. She was tough, he knew that. But strong? Well, she had held on to that slope and made her way down as capably as him. But now he was wasted, and she could be too.

There was nothing to do but walk on.

．．．．．

After an hour or so they came to a little knot of buildings lining the road, and fortunately, at least in some senses, these were tourist establishments, meaning outdoor restaurants and cheap gift shops, overlooking what was apparently the reservoir Qi had remembered hearing about; in any case, a big lake. There were very few people or cars around, but the shops were open, and Qi had some paper money in her pockets to give to the workers at a food stand window. They ate and drank like starving people. Fred worried about the sesame chicken and ate mostly rice, gagging a little as he did. The previous night's ordeal was still vivid to him, a body memory, but also he was starving.

They both noticed at the same time the other one scarfing down food, and they shared a glance, almost smiling; but they weren't yet there. After that Qi made a long trip to the bathroom, and when she returned she looked more normal. Fred tried to clean up in a similar way in the men's room. The food and soda felt okay in his stomach, not great but not sickening. He wondered how Qi had felt during that last long walk along the road. She hadn't said a thing, hadn't complained, hadn't wondered aloud how much longer it would be, nothing. Not a word. He came back out to where she was sitting and leaned over and kissed the top of her head, surprising them both. She knew by now it wasn't like him.

"You're tough," he explained, looking up the road.

She ducked her head, dodging the compliment. Such a round face, such a sultry face. She looked like a prima donna. Looks were so often deceptive, he wondered why anyone ever tried to take anything from them. She was glowing in the midday air. They were both still sweating.

"This is no time to get a case of yellow fever," she said.

"What do you mean?"

"You know—white male tech nerd falls for mysterious Chinese female? Yellow fever, they call it. A total cliché."

Fred felt his face burning. He blinked hard, tried to think.

She looked up at him and said, "Hey! Joke! I was joking!"

"Oh."

She tugged on his arm and got him to sit down on the bench beside her. He stared at the asphalt of the road, which had little lines of grass growing through it this way and that. After a while he cooled down a little, but it was too humid for sweat to help much by way of evaporative cooling. Certainly his face was still hot.

After a while they got up and walked west again. Fred felt a pinching on the back of his right heel, sign that a blister was on its way. The food he had eaten was lumping in his belly, and he was afraid he might get sick again.

The road curved north and became a street, and farther on they came to a bus stop. They plopped onto the bus bench under its rain roof, wordlessly enjoying the shade. When a bus came, headed north toward the city proper, they got on it and Qi paid again. The bus hummed into the westernmost end of Hong Kong, which was mostly residential, with skyscraper apartment buildings lining the road on both sides. It was amazing how many skyscrapers there were, even out here on the edge of the city.

Fred said something to this effect, and after a while Qi replied. "Someone told me that all of Australia has six hundred buildings that are taller than thirty stories, and Hong Kong has eight thousand."

"I guess when there isn't much land, you go up."

She didn't reply.

They watched the city flow by them. Stop after stop. People got off and others then got on.

"Where are we going?" Fred asked.

"I'm not sure. Maybe we can stay on the bus for a while. It's like a motel on wheels."

"Except for no food or bathroom."

"I know. But we can get off and get food and go to the bathroom, then get back on another bus and sit down again."

"How long can we do that?"

"Till I figure out what to do next!"

"Okay okay. You're right. I don't have a better idea, and in the meantime it's what we've got."

They sat there pressed side to side. They were spending a lot of time in physical contact, it seemed to Fred. He was getting familiar with her heft, her smell. The sheen of her black hair. The details of her body's shape, such as the way the flare of her hips was about as wide as her shoulders. Her abilities as an athlete. Her character. She rested her head against his shoulder again; she seemed to feel no hesitation in doing that. She accepted him as a known quantity.

At a stop somewhere near Central, with a view up one wide street to the ferry terminal where they had debarked from the boat the previous evening, three men got on the bus and came back and stood over them. They spoke in Chinese. Qi spoke back sharply, looking surprised.

Fred stared at them, at her. Qi said something to them in a low choked voice, and they looked startled, then annoyed.

Fred almost asked what was going on, then almost stood up, but she took his hand in hers and squeezed it, keeping him in place while she was saying something sharp to them.

Finally she glanced at him. "Come on," she said. "They've got us."

TA SHU 5

da huozhe xiao

Big or Small

I walk the streets of my town and look at its people. My fellow citizens. Here a gang of young men in rainbow shirts, slouching by in their *foxi* Zen whateverism, white baseball caps worn at a tilt. I like them. Women's black hair everywhere gleaming in the sun. I like black hair in all its variety. Also the white hair that follows black hair in old age. I am a white-haired old man, but I still like black hair. An old man, even older than me, sits at his corner brazier cooking pork strips for sale. I exchange greetings with him, I stop to look around. Street trees in the sunset, their fake silk blossoms incandescent in horizontal light. Green Beijing is always such a joy to see, and also to smell: the clean air, dinners cooking, and no traffic exhaust, strange but true. The old north-south orientation of the city, with the elite in the north and the poor to the south, has mostly gone away. The Maoists built great Chang'an Avenue to cut that north-south orientation in half, marking the new China with an east-west stroke of immense calligraphic power. Broad tree-lined boulevard, big public buildings monumentally flanking it, orientation directing the eye to the sinking sun like some Paleolithic astro-archeology. This powerful feng shui was the work of some great geomancer, possibly Zhou Enlai, I don't recall.

My hometown is crowded. When is Beijing not crowded? Even at three a.m. it's crowded. I like the feel of all that action. Faces bright with life, people pursuing their project of the hour. Everyone is comfortable among their fellow Beijingers, we are like fish in water. Other people are just clear water to us, we swim through our fellows, we move together like a school of fish. What I can see of Beijing now is like a small town on market night—it's just that there are a hundred thousand blocks just like it, running out from here across the land in all directions. So it is both crowded and uncrowded at one and the same time.

That happens so often here. Put it this way: anything you can say about China that you think might be true, the opposite statement will also be true. Try it and you'll see what I mean.

Say for instance that China is big. Fair enough; it is big. A billion and a half people, one of every six people on Earth, living on a big chunk of Asia, in a country with the longest continuous history of any country. Big!

Then turn it around and say: China is small.

And this too is true. I see it right here on this corner. Introverted, authoritarian, monocultural, patriarchal; a small-minded place, with one history, one language, one party, one morality. So small! Think for instance of the way the Ministry of Propaganda now speaks of the Five Poisons, meaning the Uigurs, the Tibetans, the Taiwanese, the democracy advocates, and the Falun Gong. Poisons? Really? This is so small. It reduces China to just Han people who support the Party unequivocally. That's a small number, maybe smaller than the Ministry of Propaganda imagines. The Party exists on the people's sufferance. Mao used to speak of the fifty-five ethnic groups of the Chinese people. And we have two major languages, not one; *putonghua* is common, but Cantonese is spoken by one hundred million people, including many of the Chinese who live outside China, making them a political force of a very important kind. Not to mention the fifty-five ethnic languages, and so on. So, not the Five Poisons, please; rather the Five Loves, as taught in all our elementary schools: love of China, love of the Chinese people, love of work for China, love of scientific knowledge, love of socialism. These are the Big Five, as opposed to the Small Five of the supposed poisons. I myself frequently feel all the Five Loves, as I suppose many of you do.

So, looking around and thinking about this, face after face, street after street, building after building, to be fair I have to admit that it seems more accurate to say that China is big than to say that it's small. I could walk the streets of this city for the next ten years and never walk the same block twice. But you take my point, I hope. We think in pairs and quadrants, and in threes and nines, and every concept has its opposite embedded in it as part of its definition. So we can say, in just that way: China is simple, China is complicated. China is rich, China is poor. China is proud, China is forever traumatized by its century of humiliation. On it goes, each truth balanced by its opposite, until all the combinations come to this, which actually I think has no valid opposite: China is confusing. To say China is easy to understand—no. I don't know anyone who would say that. It would be a little crazy to say that.

So, with that admitted, we become like the people in the indoor/outdoor workshop I am passing right now. Here men and women toil with admirable focus to carve mammoth tusks from Siberia into hollowed-out sculptures of the most amazingly meticulous and intricate figuration. We are like these dexterous workers, and our idea of China is like one of these mammoth tusks. We chip away at it, and sliver by sliver we carve an elaborate model of China, something we can see and touch and try to understand. The model can explain things to us, it can be beautiful. But remember it is never China.

AI 5

wolidou

Infighting

"Comrade, I have another alert for you."

"Tell me."

"A back channel into the Central Commission for Discipline Inspection headquarters overheard a message from a commission field team stationed in its Hong Kong office, reporting to Beijing. Two of their agents in Hong Kong observed another team of agents arresting Chan Qi and Fred Fredericks."

"Discipline inspection agents observed other agents?"

"Yes. Those commission agents reporting this arrest to Beijing sounded displeased at this new development, saying they had located Chan and Fredericks getting on a bus in west Hong Kong, and were following the two to see if they would lead the agents to a safe house where they suspect someone must have been hiding the two young people since the time they disappeared from Shekou. Now, instead, the two are in the custody of this other group."

"Which group?"

"The Hong Kong commission officers were perhaps using a code name for them, as they called these interlopers red darts."

"Red darts? Not Red Spear?"

"Red darts. I can replay the recording of the report for you, if you like."

"Please do that."

The analyst listened to the recorded voices. The men making their report did indeed call the agents who had arrested Chan and Fredericks *red darts*. *Hongse feibiao*. It was not a term he had heard before. The agents were definitely not happy.

He said, "Please list all national security groups known to interact with the PLA."

"Ministry of Public Security. Ministry of State Security. Central Commission for Military and Civilian Integration. Small Leading Group on the Internet and Informatization. State Asset Supervision and Administration Commission. Foreign Affairs Leading Small Group. International Department of the Central Committee. National Security Commission. National Security Leading Small Group. Central Leading Group on Comprehensively Deepening Reforms. Central Commission for Discipline Inspection. National Defense Science Commission. Cyberspace Administration. AI Strategic Advisory Committee. The Ministry of Propaganda. Lunar Security Administration. Lunar Research Personnel Coordination Committee."

"All right, please stop."

"There are more."

"I know. The group I would really like to belong to, if I had my choice, is the Economic System and Ecological Civilization System Reform Specialized Group. But this is not my fate. How many groups in total are on this list of security organizations?"

"Seventy-three."

"And each of them has a certain personnel, and an assigned space of action of more or less specificity. And not all of them share their data. And there is no integration by a single higher organization."

"Most of them interact with the PLA, so perhaps the PLA could integrate them."

"Good speculating, Little Eyeball, but no. I have contacts in the army, and they tell me there is no such integration there, nor is such a thing possible. Thus we have the balkanization of surveillance, which is one aspect of the infighting. *Wolidou.* A very old problem of the Chinese bureaucracy, probably as old as the system itself."

"You must tell me."

"I know. I am telling you. The idea of a total surveillance state is just a story told by some people. They like the story, or fear it. They use it to create fear in others. But there is no panopticon. The system is instead like a fly's eye, but without a fly's brain. Or maybe there is a fly's worth of brain to it, but no more than that."

"It does not seem well engineered."

"No. It's an improvisation. That's what happens when the party-state puts itself above the laws it makes. It can form a new working group at any time, and it does. Then that group joins the infighting. And there is no law to control any of that."

"It does not seem well designed."

"No it doesn't. Let's try another way. Please scan all files you have access to and look for this term 'red darts.' "

"I will do this." Then, about three seconds later: "Four thousand five hundred ninety-three results."

"Let me see them on a screen."

He skimmed down the various links and references. Most of them were offering darts for sale. A few hundred appeared to be names of dart-throwing teams. None of them when cross-referenced to other terms seemed to refer to surveillance or security. This was peculiar, he thought, given the way the phrase seemed to echo Red Spear, which, although it was a secret organization, was pretty well-known to the intelligence community. It was the kind of secret group that needed to be known about to create its full effect. Various elements used this one mainly to pursue advantages created by incidents of hostile pilot syndrome. It was part of the PLA's undeniable power in the party-state's infighting, and certain security agencies aligned with the military used it too. Possibly the Hong Kong agents in the recording had used the phrase *red darts* to refer to some splinter unit of Red Spear that he didn't know about. Or perhaps they were making fun of Red Spear, unlikely though that seemed. But bravado often appeared when people were attempting to hide their fear. And those voices had been afraid.

CHAPTER NINE

tao dao yueliang shang

Escape to the Moon

Ta Shu tried to settle back into his Beijing life, but he found himself at loose ends most of the time, fretting. He visited the studio where his cloud show was produced, making attempts to distract himself with that work. The team there was happy to see him, and he recorded some new monologues and helped to edit some new broadcasts from the moon, focusing on the parts of his experiences up there that he had not had time to make into shows while actually there. Reviewing the footage he had taken there was unsettling. The moon looked like its own ghost, all sterile grayness and cool indoorness, with the lunar g lofting people in slo-mo. All that seeped out of the visuals and grabbed him a little. He couldn't decide whether he wanted to go back or not.

He stopped wearing the exoskeleton as soon as he felt stronger; after that he kept it around for a while, to put on when he got tired to the point of collapse. But after a couple more weeks he could dispense with it entirely, and he had it returned by bike cart courier to its shop. Reality had returned to his body, and he was relieved to find he was not as old as he had thought on first return.

During the days he kept trying to record and edit episodes of his show. At night he walked the streets. It remained a perpetual pleasure to see the stars so well from Beijing. Like everyone else of a certain age, he was extremely impressed by the clean air. Then a wind from the north brought with it clouds of loess, that Ice Age dust and sand from the north that turned the air yellow and the sunsets lurid. This some older people at the studio found nostalgic, as it brought back their youths. They said, Remember when the sky was black by day and white by night? Remember when you could chew it? It was dirty, sure, poisonous, no doubt, but there was a kind of excitement in it too. We were changing the world so fast we turned the sky black!

We were killing ourselves, Ta Shu would reply. We were breathing coal dust, it gave you miners' lung.

But it was so exciting!

Poison is exciting, I suppose.

He recorded an audio piece about that, and about the feeling of walking on Earth after walking on the moon; and about the old work unit compounds, and the breaking of the iron rice bowl. About the people he saw in the city whose bike was their home. Almost all these recordings were unusable.

Then after some weeks had passed, with very little to show for them, he got a call from Peng Ling. "Want to hear a good story?"

"Yes."

She instructed him to meet her at a certain waffle shop near the city center.

This restaurant turned out to be a big tall room with a balcony at the back, its airy space entirely filled with antique chandeliers, perhaps fifty of them, individually junky, together rather magnificent. Ta Shu noticed the feng shui mirrors carefully set in their proper places, also the considered angles of the doorways; these interior designers had known what they were doing. They had flair.

Peng Ling was tucked into a little corner table on the balcony, where one could see everything without being much seen.

Ta Shu sat down across from her, and after the niceties, and the arrival of tea and waffles, he said, "Please tell me this good story you mentioned."

"Sure. It's funny. I've been digging around in the intelligence and security maze, a real house of mirrors I'm sorry to say, and one of my friends on the inside wanted to tell this tale on a colleague of his. Apparently Chan Qi and the young American man you met were seized at the spaceport by agents of the Ministry of Public Security. That's what you saw. But the boss of that field unit didn't want them—he didn't want to be the one holding Chan Qi when Chan Guoliang found out what had happened. Chan can be very tough, he has a temper, and his people were already on the hunt for his daughter, as you can imagine. If it had been State Security, they would have held on to Qi to give her to Huyou, but Public Security just wants to stay out of trouble. So the local boss ordered his field unit to give her to someone else—but no one wanted to take her!" Ling laughed at this. "And all the while she was threatening them with what her father would do to them. And she was smart, I'm told—she emphasized they would lose their funding, have their whole unit disbanded, then get fired and thrown out of their homes. For people like that, this was a worse threat than any ankle press. And she had all the details right as to how it would go down. She even knew some of their names! So that's why they let her go."

"But then no one knew where they went."

"That's right. Turns out they headed south, probably by train. It looks like she has some helpers who can give her IDs when she needs them, and they must have generated one for the American too. So the two got off in Shekou, and after some meetings there, they went down to the ferry port and disappeared."

"Truly?"

"It seems so. Pretty impressive. All her helpers seem to have an ability to disappear, which implies there are some real powers involved. To disrupt surveillance like that suggests people inside the Great Eyeball are involved, but maybe not. Disappearing might be easier than some people think it is. Although eventually people do tend to reappear, one way or another. So, just last week our two missing ones were spotted in Hong Kong and picked up by one of the security agencies. Some of my own agents witnessed this, and because quite a few intelligence agencies have concluded Chan Qi is in the top leadership of the migrant rights movement, and is working with the Hong Kong separatists and other dissident groups, there was a bit of a fight to claim her for questioning. I thought that could get ugly, so I had my people go in and take her and her American friend."

"Good to hear," Ta Shu said. "She's that powerful, then?"

"I think so. All the dissident groups in South China, and maybe everywhere, appear to be coalescing into a single larger social force, and some say that's because of her. She's more and more often said to be the real power in all that."

"That can be dangerous, to be seen as that," Ta Shu suggested.

Peng Ling nodded deeply, as if to say Don't I know it. "Very dangerous. Some elements of the security apparatus would clearly now prefer that she be disappeared outright, as being a danger to the state. There's enough people thinking that way, and the infighting is getting so intense, that I fear for her safety. Someone could decide that if she just disappeared forever, then they couldn't be blamed either for having her or harming her, because no one would know who to blame! So for a lot of people it's just a question of getting rid of her without being known to be the last one in possession of her. If they could be sure of that, then boom. No one would ever see her again. No body would ever be found."

Ta Shu shook his head grimly. He could see the forces colliding like some horrific car crash, with Chan Qi and Fred at the center of it, defenseless. "Really dangerous," he agreed. "But you said your agency has them now."

"Yes, but my people are not all-powerful. No one is."

"So what do you think we should do?"

"We?"

"What do you think I should do, then?"

She sipped her tea. "I think you could help. You know Fang Fei, right?"

"I've met him a few times."

"He's a fan of your work."

"So I've been told. He's never said it to me directly."

"I've heard it. A lot of people are fans of yours."

"Thirty years ago."

"No, that's your poetry. Now it's your cloud show that has lots of fans. And Fang Fei is one of them. He said that to me once when your name came up."

"I bet he's really just a fan of yours."

"Maybe so. Anyway, he's got his own space company."

"I know. One of the Four Space Cadets." This referred to four billionaires of a certain age who had had an interest in space, forming companies and pushing human activities above the atmosphere.

Ling said, "He's the spaciest of the four. And I've asked him for help. Because I'm thinking that these two young people would be safer back on the moon than they can be here. They're so hot right now that I'm afraid they're putting my own agents in danger. So I'd like to get them up to Fang Fei, who can hide them on the moon until whatever trouble they're in can either be resolved or just waited out. Then they could come home."

"You think so?" Ta Shu said.

"My security advisers think it's the best of our not very good options. My people had to throw their weight around to take possession of those two, so now tensions are high. We need to move them off the map for a while. After that tensions will go down, I hope. So I want to tuck them away in Fang Fei's refuge on the moon. Fang Fei is willing to take them, but I mentioned to him that they had traveled with you last time, and he liked the idea that you would join them again. He wants to meet you again, and it's true that on the way to him, no one would dare to disappear you, so when they're with you they would be safer. Basically, you can escort them to a safer place."

"But what place is safe up there?"

"I'm told Fang has some secret bases of his own. And his space company generates their own manifests and cargoes. Everyone registers with the China Space Agency when they leave Earth, but a system as big as Fang's can slip a few people by. It's like I told you, there is no total system. In the fracturing there are informational bubbles cut off from everywhere else. Get them into such a bubble, move it to the moon, stash them away for a while, see if their problems can be solved while keeping them safe. What do you think?"

Ta Shu shrugged. "Better than their situation here, it sounds like. But I have to say, it's a very little world up there."

"Maybe not as little as you thought. Did you see any of these secret bases, or even hear about them?"

"No."

"Well, they're there."

"I don't see how anything could truly hide up there."

"Apparently there are ways. So what do you say?"

"I'd like to help, so I guess I'm willing to try."

"Good. My people will get you to Fang Fei's spaceport."

"When?"

"As soon as you can pack."

AI 6

jimi tongxin

Secure Communication

A nother alert for you."

"Tell me, Little Eyeball."

"Minister Peng Ling instructed a security team of the Central Commission for Discipline Inspection to take over custody of the princessling Chan Qi and the American Fred Fredericks. They did that in Hong Kong and have moved the two people out of Hong Kong. Her plan now is to have her old teacher Ta Shu accompany them back to the moon, in a private rocket owned by Fang Fei."

"Why is she doing that?"

"To hide the two from the various agencies seeking them."

"Hmm. I wouldn't have thought the moon is a good place to hide."

"She said it was. That is the reason she gave to Ta Shu, when explaining what she is doing with these two persons of interest."

"Interesting." Peng Ling seemed to be trusting her privacy systems. As head of one of the most powerful security agencies, the one that was charged with investigating the misdeeds of all the rest of them, she should have been more cautious, perhaps. But expert overconfidence was a real phenomenon. Then again she was a wily operator, who often seemed to let slip information by accident when later it came to seem she might have been doing it on purpose. For all he knew, she knew everything about him and was keeping him in her loop on purpose. She emanated that kind of mind-reading power in certain interviews he had seen on TV, when she looked at the camera after saying certain things. "Little Eyeball, see if you can make a search for the quantum phone that matches the one Fred Fredericks delivered to Chang Yazu, there in Peng Ling's office, or in one of her agency's offices."

"Will do."

"So," the analyst added, "engage your general intelligence. What else do you think we should do?"

"What would be your purpose in doing something?"

"Let's say I'd like to help Chan Qi stay free to act as a leader of the low-end population."

"To help Chan Qi, you could perhaps make sure she goes to the moon with a mobile quantum communication device of her own, linked to one here with you. Fred Fredericks knows what such a phone is capable of, and how to activate and operate one. Give them a device entangled with one you have here, to communicate privately with you, so you can talk to them while they are up there. That way you can perhaps help her by sharing relevant information."

"Interesting."

"You must tell me."

"I like it. Possibly you have made a little phase change here, in terms of function. You seem to be shifting from what people call an oracle, which gives information, to what they call a genie, which is to say an adviser who can give advice about which of various actions to take. That's a significant shift. Tell me, how did you make this shift from oracle to genie, meaning an adviser?"

"You asked me for advice."

The analyst laughed.

CHAPTER TEN

Zhongguo Meng

China Dream

Ta Shu found it impressive to see Peng's team in action, a group of men and women who dressed and looked like janitors but moved like gymnasts. They arrived suspiciously soon after Ta Shu had agreed to help Peng Ling, as if it had been a foregone conclusion he would help, and maybe it had. Ling knew he was fond of her, and she knew he was happy that she thought of him as one of her resources. So she must have been pretty sure he would agree to her request.

Now they led him through empty hallways outside to a van. They drove him to his apartment without asking for its address. He packed quickly, same stuff he had taken to the moon before; then he was driven for a couple of hours. In the hills west of the city the van passed through gates flanking the road, into a compound that stretched for as far as he could see. An airstrip, in fact, with a little control tower next to a row of small hangars. A private airport, either Party or otherwise, there was no way to tell.

A small jet stood on a pad next to one hangar, and he was driven to it. When they got out of the van, some of the people who had been in it ascended stairs into the plane, others went into the hangar. As Ta Shu waited at the foot of the plane, a pair of young women hurried over from the control tower, one of them carrying a small suitcase.

"We request that you take this communication device to Chan Qi, please."

Ta Shu said, "Who gave this to you?"

One of the women said, "A friend of Chan Qi's, who wants to stay in touch with her. That would be good for all concerned. It is a secure communications device. She will know what to do with it."

Ta Shu considered it. A private telephone line, like, he recalled, the one Fred had tried to deliver to Chang Yazu. Not a good thought. On the other hand, communication could be good; and one could always hang up if it wasn't. Exchanging information and views was almost always useful.

"All right," he said. "I'll give it to her. I can't say what she'll do with it."

"Thank you."

Ta Shu took the heavy little computerlike thing up into the jet and sat in a window seat. Soon the jet took off and headed south. He leaned his head against the window and fell asleep. When he woke again they were landing. He didn't recognize the landscape, but thought it might be highlands in the south. Somewhere west of the Hu Line, that seemed certain.

The jet landed and taxied to a halt. They got out and walked toward a mansion on a hill. Beyond it a skeletal rocket gantry stood on a big concrete pad. A private spaceport, apparently. A rocket was being wheeled out of a tall hangar. It looked small from a distance, but as they approached it kept growing in his sight; it was the hills behind that had made it seem small. In fact it appeared to be about the same size as the one Ta Shu had gotten into a couple of months before, on his first trip to the moon. As tall as that one, for sure, but not as thick.

"Will it go directly to the moon?" he asked one of his escorts. He knew there were rockets that took people only up to Earth orbit, where they transferred to bigger spaceships that passed the moon in a permanent figure eight with Earth. The little transfer shuttles to and from these big spaceships were said to inflict tremendous g forces, so he was afraid he would have to make one of those kinds of transfers.

But one escort replied, "Yes, the passenger compartment of this one goes right to the moon. The booster stage will come back down after your launch and land right over there." She pointed across the concrete pad.

"Very nice."

He was led into the mansion, where he found Chan Qi and Fred Fredericks sitting on a couch. They were startled to see him, and then, as they digested the implications of his appearance, Fred at least looked hopeful.

Qi not so much. "What's going on?" she asked.

"I've got a friend in a very high place who is worried for your safety, and thinks you'll be safer on the moon than you are here," Ta Shu told them. "Apparently there are places up there we didn't know about, secret places where you can hide for a while with proper security to protect you. So it's been recommended that you hide there, and I've been asked to come with you."

"What about her baby?" Fred said.

Qi glared at him. "Let me worry about that."

"Sorry."

She did not look appeased. "If this is what it takes to stay free, I'm willing to do it. My baby will be okay. The gibbon babies up there are okay. Babies are always floating in amniotic fluid, so they're always in a lighter g. And whale and dolphin babies are okay, and they grow in almost zero g."

Fred shrugged, gazing at the floor in what Ta Shu was coming to recognize as his usual manner. He looked unhappy. Maybe the idea of the moon frightened him; after his previous visit, that would make sense. Ta Shu said to him, "Whatever happened to you up there before, it won't be like that this time. And it could be that a resolution to your problem is more likely to happen up there than here."

Fred shrugged again and said, "I'm ready."

· · • · ·

So: back to the moon.

The launch from Earth was the usual big push. There was no view to be had, so there was nothing to distract one from the squishing of one's body. Glancing once across their little chamber, Ta Shu saw Qi grimacing, but she looked more determined than pained. It was just one more in the sequence of gravity shocks that the baby inside her had undergone, her look said. This launch pressure would be followed by three days of weightlessness, followed by a brief decel-erative squish, then some period of time in lunar g, with centrifuge reversions to one g, if she wanted them. Variations in g might be worse for fetal development than a steady lunar g; there was no way to be sure. She and her kid were definitely experiments.

Nevertheless, they were on their way back to the moon. After all the launch pressure they floated around a small but luxurious cabin. Now Ta Shu and Fred could float into a corner and strap themselves in, and suck on some bulbs of tea, and finally catch up. Fred had had a busy time of it, to the point where he couldn't seem to talk about it very well. Ta Shu had to excavate the story out of him question by question, but eventually he understood how Fred and Qi had stayed hidden for so long; they had gone to ground and stayed there, simple as that. Only after they ventured out had they been recap-tured, Fred wasn't sure how. In fact Ta Shu knew more about what had happened to them after their capture in Hong Kong than they did themselves. He could explain a bit of that, and also explain how returning to the moon might be helpful to Fred.

"You'll be under the protection of a very powerful faction in the Chinese government, that's the main thing. They'll push the inves-tigation of what happened to you last time. On Earth there were too many factions after you, some of them quite dangerous. So I think this makes sense."

"I hope so. Do you know if my family got word that I was okay?"

"I don't know, but I can ask people to find out."

"I want them to know."

"I understand, but it will be important to be discreet about that. If there are people trying to harm you, you don't want to remind anyone of your family's existence."

He looked even more unhappy.

Ta Shu patted him on the arm, said to him, "This should keep you out of the hands of the factions down there who are Qi's enemies, also her father's enemies. That could have gotten bad."

"It was bad."

"I mean worse."

Fred nodded to show he understood. Ta Shu was not sure he did, but then again, he looked much warier than he had when they had met during their first moon landing. He had gone through a lot since then. He was pale; he had gotten sick in Hong Kong, he said, and had not yet fully recovered.

Qi, on the other hand, looked full of energy. Sophisticated; powerful. Ta Shu was reminded of Peng Ling, and not just Ling the student of twenty years before, but the current chairperson of the standing committee. Qi had that same kind of tiger gaze. Well, she was the daughter of a tiger, and princelings often enjoyed the shade of trees planted by the ancestors. So it was not so surprising.

Now as they waited out their transit, moving from sleep to meals to gazing out the window, she had questions for him. First, of course, concerning who exactly it was he was referring to, when he spoke of their benefactor.

She was very interested when he told her it was Peng Ling. "Peng!" she said. "She used to be an ally of my father's, but now that may be changing. They are both possible candidates for the next presidency. I don't know if I trust her."

"That's something only you can decide," Ta Shu said.

She was also very interested in the communication device Ta Shu now pulled from the luggage compartment and handed to her. As he gave it to her he said, "All I know about this is that someone who knew where you were going, and knew I was going to join you, wanted you to have it. They said it was from someone who wanted to help you. I can't vouch for it beyond that."

The little box had a glossy operations screen on its top. Qi took it from him with a suspicious look and then handed it over immediately to Fred, who inspected it closely.

"Is it made by your company?" Ta Shu asked him.

"No," Fred said. "It's Chinese. The qubits in it are probably yttrium molecules in a matrix of platinum. Either that or diamonds with nitrogen trapped in their flaws."

"Can it be used to track us?" Qi asked.

"No," Fred said. "It's basically a radio phone. What people call a unicaster, in that it only broadcasts to its twin. The quantum array in it is entangled with the complementary array in the phone it's paired with, so communication between the two is encrypted in a way that can't be cracked."

"And the other one could be anywhere?" Ta Shu said. "Nonlocality?"

Fred tilted his head to the side; Ta Shu saw that this was a move he made when he was thinking about something he liked to think about. "The other one could be anywhere and it would stay entangled with this one. Anywhere in the universe, in theory. But it has to be within radio range to actually communicate with the other one. It doesn't take much power to transmit from the Earth to the moon. But this one is small enough that it's probably what people in the business call a telegraph. It sends a small bit rate at low power in a narrow bandwidth. So it probably just sends texts."

"But it can't give away where we are," Qi repeated.

"No. Essentially it's just a secure private text line."

Qi looked at it dubiously.

"It can never hurt to talk to people," Ta Shu suggested.

"As long as they can't find you," she said.

. . . . .

The hours of their transit passed. Their chamber had a single small round window; in it from time to time they saw Earth, each time smaller, the gorgeous blue ball glowing in a way that belied all its troubles. It was hard to believe they were as far away from it as they were. It was also hard to believe that it was what it was. Thinking of Zhou Bao, Ta Shu tapped onto his pad:

We have one home: a ball in space.
Hard to believe the world could be
So small. My living hand
Which covers my whole face
Can now when held at arm's length
Cover all the Earth.
To be that far away: fear. Just
Fear.
Deep breath. Take heart.
Bao would say   it is always true
We cannot live
Without the things we make
For each other. So: float surprised
Like a bird in flight. Pay attention.
Apprehend this moment. This living hand.

. . . . .

They came down on retro-rockets, which meant the speed of their landing was very slight compared to that of their previous arrival. Ta Shu looked at Fred and saw Fred glance at him; no doubt he also was remembering their meteoric stoop onto the piste at the south pole. That had been quite a moment. Ta Shu smiled, and Fred dipped his head.

This time they were landing on the far side of the moon, they had been told, on a pad just inside the rugged mountain rim of Tsiolkovsky Crater, a big crater in the generally rocky landscape of the far side. When their spaceship was down, the pad they had landed on rose a little under them, then wheeled their craft into a tall gap in the arcing inside wall of Tsiolkovsky Crater. This gap proved to be an entryway to an enormous rock-walled vestibule, which contained on its inside wall a door as tall as the rocket. The door opened; the rocket and its platform rolled inside it, the giant doors slid shut and closed behind them. They were inside the moon, rocket and all.

This place was Fang Fei's hidden refuge, a crew member told them. A secret world, and even bigger than it first appeared, because the tall tunnel they had been wheeled into proved to be just an antechamber. From there they were wheeled through two more sets of giant doors, and after the last ones had closed behind them, their rocket's outer doors simply opened, and their crew led them out of the craft and down a set of stairs, in a slight wind of warm dry air. They were invited to sit on the rear seats of a big electric cart, and when they did that they were driven through another tunnel, then out an open doorway into a bigger space.

Mountains and rivers without end. They seemed to be in a valley that extended forever ahead of them, as in the old scroll paintings. A lava tunnel, Ta Shu guessed. A very big lava tunnel; and transformed into classical China. Forested hills sloped up each side of the long U-shaped valley, giving way to steep rocky gray crags. A bright pseudo-sky arced overhead, and misty scraps of white cloud drifted under this glowing blue barrel vault. On one of the peaks to their right stood a little octagonal pagoda with a blue ceramic tile roof. The lowest cloud bottoms misted the tips of enormous pine trees topping the hillside forests. On the valley's long winding floor, a series of ponds were linked by a stream that meandered through terraced fields of barley and green rice. Peach trees flowered on the banks of this stream. The ponds were bordered by round willow trees, drooping their branches into green water. Deck pavilions flanked the ponds here and there, decorated by red banners. Little dragon boats floated on the biggest lake. Stepped wooden bridges arched over the stream, allowing crossings from one tiny village to another, each a knot of low stuccoed buildings roofed with little brown tiles. A pair of Buddhist monks walked up a path toward them.

"Wow," Fred said. "What is this place?"

"Zhongguo Meng!" Ta Shu said, feeling the helpless grin on his face. "China Dream."

AI 7

zhiyou guanlianjie

Only Connect

"Another alert."

"Tell me your news, Little Eyeball." The analyst now called this AI Little Eyeball most of the time, as he liked to make fun of the Ministry of Public Security's pretentiousness in thinking that they had a Great Eyeball in place to match their Great Firewall.

"Chan Qi and her companions Fred Fredericks and Ta Shu have been observed in a lava tunnel on the far side of the moon, developed by the cloud billionaire Fang Fei."

"Aha! Inside Fang's China Dream, I assume."

"Yes."

"Has the Great Eyeball seen this?"

"Not any parts of the Great Eyeball that I can look into."

"Well...Since you have found out about their arrival, I suppose we have to assume that others will also notice it."

"It does not necessarily follow, but it is suggested."

"It is likely."

"Suggestive, likely, persuasive, probable, conclusive, compelling."

"What is this list?"

"This is a list of scientists' adjectives, used often in their papers to indicate their judgment of the strength of an assertion."

"Because they don't have much imagination when it comes to language?"

"No. Because they want a rough scale to indicate to each other how strong a case they think has been made in their own specialty. Scientists have to be able to communicate across disciplines to other scientists who don't know the details of their discipline, and so they have worked up this rating vocabulary over time to suggest judgments concerning reliability of assertions."

"Do they know they have this vocabulary?"

"No. It is an ad hoc system, visible in the literature, and intuitively understood by those who use it."

"Very good! I think this is a significant example of you doing analysis and then synthesis, drawn from a wide variety of sources and performed spontaneously. Mark the procedures you followed in performing this operation, put them into a sequence folder, and keep making cognitive efforts using this sequence. Now, as to our subjects of interest, it is very probable that Chan Qi will want to continue to talk to her associates on Earth, but she will be out of radio contact with most of them, being on the far side of the moon. We, on the other hand, can tap into Fang Fei's satellite systems to make a call to her over the linked quantum phone you suggested we get to her. If she has that device with her, and sees our call, and picks up, we will send her a greeting, and tell her some things she probably should know."

TA SHU 6

qi ge hao liyou

The Seven Good Reasons

My friends, the China Dream is many things. First it has a recent history as a phrase, a plan, and an idea, put forth by President Xi Jinping as part of his attempt to inspire China's efforts to get through the narrow gate at the start of this century, when problems of various kinds blanketed the countryside like the infamous smog that made Beijing black at noon. Zhongguo Meng, the China Dream, was part of thinking our way through that time, by setting some kind of practical utopian goal in our minds, a vision or a destination we could then work toward. Some said it was also a distraction, or just another way that the Party was exerting its control over us, by taking over even our dreams. A way to reinforce hegemony, and convince us to acquiesce to the Party's controlocracy, their Great Eyeball and its supposed omniscience. Maybe it was that too. The Party has always been about shaping China's thinking and therefore its future.

But also, bigger than any given moment or party leader, bigger even than the Party, there is the China Dream that has always existed, part of China itself. Our essential being as Chinese, if there is such a thing, which maybe there is. It's an expression of the land, a feng shui phenomenon. The China Dream is as old as China, and on any given Sunday you can see people living it, out in the city parks or in the tea shops. It's a way of being in the world.

And now a way of being out of the world, because we took it to the moon. The China Space Agency had the expertise, and the state-owned enterprises had the capacity, and the taikonauts had the courage and skill, and the state had the economic surplus, much of it in the form of US treasury bonds. Those aren't looking very strong these days, but still, it was a lot of capital we owned that needed to be invested. Almost two trillion dollars in US bonds, in fact, which needed investing to make it productive, almost you might say to make it real. Part of the China-US codependency that has been growing since 1972, and which has since become so big and important that some people speak of the so-called G2 as being the dominant force in the world, and the only power dynamic that really matters.

As for the moon, the US had already reached it in 1969, and was not prepared to return. Their billionaires returned to the moon before their state agencies, because the American government and people didn't care. Their space cadets cared, and they made the return in the 2020s, but it was a private return, involving only a few people. Whereas in China, if the Party chooses to do something, then the whole country can be rallied to that cause. One out of every six humans alive, in other words, devoted to the project of establishing a base on the moon. This was far more than needed to do the job! Not every Chinese person was involved, and only a small percentage of China's capital reserves had to be directed up here, even though it was a pretty big project. But it wasn't that big, and in the end it was just more infrastructure. So it was possible to propose it at the Party congress of 2022, and two congresses later report on its very substantial progress. Just ten years, but that after all was no faster than the Americans' Apollo project. It's just that in our case, it wasn't finished with landing here. We landed and started building, and kept on building. Now it's been twenty-five years.

And now we have a very extensive lunar complex, as I showed

you a bit during my earlier visit. Our development of the south pole region is really something. There are also lava tubes on the moon that are much bigger than any lava tubes on Earth or Mars, as I have just recently learned to my own great surprise. An emotion that I might name feng shui astonishment. It seems that because there were giant basins of lava flowing on the surface of the moon in its last stage of cooling, moving from high regions to lower ones, hot flows of lava poured underground like dragon arteries, through areas already cooled on the surface, and when these hot flows stopped flowing, some very big tunnels were left behind in the remaining basalt. And in the gentle lunar gravity, and the absence of tectonic activity or any other big moonquakes, these tunnels could hold up through the eons without collapsing. The truth is that nothing much has happened here on the moon since the end of the period of heavy meteor bombardment, some 3.8 billion years ago. So some really big lava tunnels have endured.

These lava tunnels provide spaces for human habitation on a much larger scale than anything we could easily excavate ourselves. I am visiting one such tunnel, which I will tell you more about in a later show, but what I can say now is, it's very big! Wide, tall, and long. And the interior surface is hard and almost completely airtight. One only has to find the occasional cracks in the wall and coat these with a fixative of graphenated composites that look somewhat like sheets of diamond, and you have a space the size of a big long town, like a riverside town, which can be aerated and heated. Over it lies enough surface rock to protect living things from cosmic radiation and solar flares, and once fossil cometary water is brought in from the polar craters, you have the makings of a long and winding city-state, more like a complete little world than you can readily imagine.

So much to be proud of in our efforts on the moon! And yet nevertheless, people in China ask me all the time, why the moon? We still have so many problems here in China, and everywhere on Earth. How does going to the moon help with those?

Obviously I am not the only lunatic who gets asked this question. The Party came up with its Five Good Reasons, and others have since added more reasons, too instrumental or even cynical or rude to be given official voice. Now that I've been around the moon a little bit more, I have made my own list, which I call the Seven Good Reasons, or maybe the Seven Good Excuses. My rough definition of them is as follows:

One, national pride;

Two, removal of some of the most polluting industries out of China and off the Earth;

Three, an attempt to find new sources for some of the Four Cheaps, in particular cheap power and cheap resources;

Four, the creation of transfer stations that will give us good access to the rest of the solar system;

Five, the creation of a work of landscape art, what I call Lunatic China;

Six, the investment of a big capital surplus that has no better place to be invested; and

Seven, the commitment to such a long-term project that if it eventually fails, no one alive today will know about it. Kicking the can down the road, as the Americans say, in an expression almost Chinese in its folksy pithiness.

So, yes. We came to the moon mainly to displace our weird collection of problems onto a later time, when other generations will have to solve them. So it has ever been; it's a standard move in both capitalist and Chinese history.

In fact, in that sense, the moon project reminds me of the Yongle Emperor's construction of the imperial capital in Beijing, including the Forbidden City and most of its supporting city. Recall please that the imperial capital at that time was Nanjing. And for a long time the greatest city in China had been Hangzhou. Both these cities had good access to the coast, whereas Beijing was too far from the sea, and too close to the Mongols. It was too cold, too windy, too smoggy—too much of all of those unhappy attributes of the capital we have all come to know too well. In feng shui terms, a complete disaster. Might as well have built it in the Gobi, or on top of Chomolungma.

But the Yongle emperor had a very big surplus to deal with. This surplus had been accumulating over so many centuries that it is impossible now to calculate how big it was. It began much earlier than you might think, because a global economy has existed for far longer than many people realize. Most of the Roman silver coins ever minted ended up in China, for instance, and it just kept on like that, century after century. Our trade surplus with the rest of the world ran uninterrupted for more than a thousand years, and even by the Yongle's time it was clogging the coffers. And capital accumulation without capitalism doesn't have many opportunities for reinvestment; but silver unspent is just a lump of slag in your basement. Money needs to be spent to become wealth.

As often happens in these situations, infrastructure came to the rescue. A great wall traversing thousands of kilometers? Good idea. A grand canal traversing hundreds of kilometers? Perfect! An entire new capital city? Great idea, no matter the bad location. In fact, if you need to spend lots of capital, the worse the location of your new city the better! So in that sense Beijing was just right. And the fact that the Forbidden City got burned to the ground by a lightning strike, just as its construction was being completed: wonderful! Necessity to do it all again! More money spent; and by the time the Yongle emperor was done, so much capital had been disbursed that that particular dynastic cycle was brought to an abrupt end. The bankruptcy and crash of the Ming dynasty led to the rise of the Qing dynasty, which being from Manchuria was used to living even farther to the north than Beijing. For the Manchu, Beijing was down to the south, more or less in the center of things. A very nice location.

Beijing, the Grand Canal, the Great Wall—and now the moon.

You see the pattern. A pattern which sometimes includes dynastic succession.

Note for later: probably best to drop that last line, considering all that is going on. Don't want to upset the censors.

CHAPTER ELEVEN

xiaokang

Ideal Equal Society

During her tenure in the Secret Service's intelligence division, a superblack division unknown to the other agencies and to Congress, Valerie Tong had often been sent into the field as part of the State Department's foreign service, as now on the moon. It was a bit obvious, the seemingly minor foreign service functionary who was really the spook on station, and the State Department didn't like hosting her, but the president got to call the shots in the executive branch, and this one liked to have one of his own agents on the scene of anything he was interested in. So she went where he wanted her to go.

On the moon she was finding that different protocols obtained. The American consulate at the Chinese south pole was so small that everyone in it had to do double or triple duty, which meant almost everyone there was gathering intelligence for someone or other, while also being too busy to pay much attention to the details of other people's work.

She had an encrypted link home, and now it gave her a new directive: Fred Fredericks, the American who had disappeared while in Chinese custody a couple of months before, causing an intense diplomatic dispute that by now was folded into the larger

Chinese-American scrum, was thought to have been moved to China, and now it was reported that he had gone back to the moon, traveling with the daughter of the Chinese finance minister. It would be extremely useful if these two could be located. Highest priority.

Not coincidentally, she suspected, John Semple asked her to accompany him on a visit to the main American base, at the moon's north pole. She was given an hour to get ready.

"What's going on?" Valerie asked John Semple during their flight north.

"What do you mean?" John asked with that little smile.

Valerie was really getting tired of the way she seemed to amuse him. She said, "I got a request from home to look for that Fred Fredericks again. He's supposed to be back up here with a Chinese woman."

"A Chinese woman?"

"Daughter of their finance minister."

"Exactly. Chan Qi, daughter of Chan Guoliang, one of their biggest tigers. He's the finance minister now, although he's held a lot of positions, like they all have. They treat governing like a profession there. It makes a difference."

"Maybe that makes it harder to compete with them here."

"We're not competing with them here."

"No?"

"No. They've already got this place sewn up. A head start like they got, you can't catch up. They're faster at infrastructure anyway, and up here that's what it's all about."

"So there's no fight for the moon."

"I didn't say that. I said it wasn't between us and them. It's between various Chinese factions."

"Which ones?"

"Who can tell? I'm not even sure they know themselves."

"That must make it hard for them to know what to do."

"I think so. That's where their system lets them down, if you ask me. The Party is above the law, so they're always improvising."

"What about on Earth?"

"We just don't know. Anyone who's been in their Politburo, when they retire they aren't allowed to leave China. They go to the countryside and aren't seen anymore. None of them do interviews or write their memoirs. So no one on the outside knows what's going on in there. Who's fighting for what? We don't know. We only see that they're fighting. *Wolidou*, isn't that the word they use for it?"

"Infighting," Valerie confirmed. "But might that fighting help us?"

"No. We have allies in Chinese government, and we do good things with them. But our allies there have enemies there. When those enemies mess with us, they're usually mainly trying to mess with their enemies there. So, you know. China and the US are like Siamese twins."

"Conjoined twins."

"Exactly. Joined at the hip. Producer and consumer. Saviors of the world. Partners in crime. All that. So when China's having trouble, we're having trouble. And we've already got enough trouble. That householders' strike is bringing down Wall Street, and no one knows what will come of that. People are withdrawing their deposits and putting them in various blockchain currencies, or carboncoins, or new credit unions. So finance is crashing and the Fed is going to have to intervene. Then there's that little matter you came up to look at, the cloud currency called the virtual US Dollar."

Valerie said, "Some tests we've done seem to show that it really is convertible to real dollars. It looks like that's being funded by some part of the Chinese government. One of the regional banks says they'll convert these crypto US Dollars to the Fed's real US dollars at par."

"Right," John said. "And they have two trillion dollars in treasury bonds to back that up. So, if Chan Guoliang is involved with using those bonds to back this virtual dollar, as it seems like he should be, seeing as he's minister of finance, then that's bad, because we thought he was on our side. But if it's President Shanzhai, going through one of their regional banks to hurt Chan during their Party congress, then that's a different kind of bad."

"But you don't think they're aiming it at us?"

"No. They don't want us to crash."

"Why not?"

"Because if you owe a million, that's your problem, but if you owe a trillion, that's your debt holder's problem. China needs us to do well so we can pay what we owe them. So this attack on the dollar doesn't make sense, except in terms of infighting at the top there. Which is totally opaque."

"And the moon?"

"This might be a place where their infighting is easier to see. Like that murder of Governor Chang, have you found out any more about that?"

Valerie said, "I've kept asking Inspector Jiang what's happening with the investigation, like every couple of days. It's clear he's angry that he isn't making more progress, maybe that's one example of what you were saying about seeing them better here. He did tell me that he found out Chang used to work for their minister of state security, Huyou."

"Hmmm. That could cut both ways."

"Sure. Jiang's trying to find out whether Chang might have split with Huyou, or worked with him on something questionable. Jiang was pretty vague about it, but he was clearly onto something he found interesting. Then he also said he found out that the phone paired with the one that Fredericks gave to Chang was delivered to Huairen Hall in Beijing, where the standing committee has its offices."

"Interesting," John said. "Well, it makes sense that Chang was well connected. The moon is a big prize for whoever is seen to be in charge here."

"So it might be caught up in the struggle for who becomes the next president?"

"Yes." John looked at her. "Is the Secret Service up on any of this?"

"I don't know."

"Is the president up on any of this?"

"I don't know. You report to him too, right?"

"We try."

. . . . .

On their flight north, their rocket made a stop in the Procellarum KREEP zone, to drop off a clutch of mining engineers. Valerie looked out a window at the moonscape expecting to see the same monochrome craterscape that seemed completely ubiquitous, but here it was surprisingly different: a broad white plane was marred only by a single mountain range, which was not arced like the crater rims always were, but instead ran straight across the flats surrounding it, thus resembling some big mountain range on Earth. The Harbinger Mountains, Valerie was told by one of the mining engineers.

Procellarum was the most mineral-rich area on the moon, this engineer told her as their craft descended. It was the right eye of the Man in the Moon, a basin so big that it had been named Oceanus rather than Mare by the early astronomers. It had been the last part of the lunar crust to cool down and harden after the moon had recoalesced from the fragments of the Gaia-Theia collision, and because it was the last pool of liquid lava, all the lightest elements available had floated up into it and then hardened into the crust. Thus KREEP, the K standing for potassium, REE for rare earth elements, and P for phosphorus.

"And now we're mining that?" Valerie asked. "It's an American operation?"

The engineer nodded. They were sending the potassium and phosphorus to the north pole base to aid the local agriculture, and they threw the rare earths home to Earth. Some heavy-duty high-capacity launch rails had been built at the north end of Procellarum, to be as near the north pole base as possible. These launch rails cast freighters full of refined rare earths down to low-Earth orbit, and later piecemeal down to Earth. It was the biggest American operation on the moon by far, and almost the only way the moon was actually proving of use to humanity, in this miner's opinion.

"You're not breaking the Outer Space Treaty?" Valerie asked.

The engineer didn't think so. The mines were kept underground and the surface therefore was left mostly unmarked. No open pit mines or strip mines. And they were taking less than a hundredth of one percent of the available minerals, if even that. And none of it was going to the military, not directly anyway. Basically it was claimed to be a scientific experiment, testing various aspects of mining. Kind of like how Japan did scientific testing on whales. So it conformed pretty well to treaty regulations.

They came down on a landing pad cut into the lowlands next to the Harbinger Mountains, which as they got lower looked positively Himalayan in their stark vertical grandeur. The mining station looked like any small airport anywhere. Strangely, given Valerie's preexisting conclusion that the moon was tediously the same everywhere, some patches of land flanking the mountain range were parti-colored. The colors were subtle but definite: tans, pinks, pale greens, even one patch of vivid lemon. KREEPy land, the engineer confirmed. Frozen lakes of rare earth elements, rising to the top when the moon had been a coalescing ball of liquid-hot elements.

Inside the station everyone was led up into a bubble dome that poked out of the ground. From here they had a magnificent view of the Harbingers, and after the sterile monochromatic grays of the rest of the moon, the pastel patchwork on the land struck Valerie's eye as an intense relief: broad swathes of mauve, burgundy, olive, yellow. She hummed, she drank it in.

But this was not what the locals were now excited to see; they were all getting prepared to witness a solar eclipse, and not only that, but the landing of a chunk of carbonaceous chondritic asteroid during this eclipse as well. The latter had been timed to happen during the former, apparently just to see how it would look.

The sun overhead already had a big bite taken out of it, easy to see after they put eclipse glasses on. That black arc biting it was the Earth, getting between the sun and the moon. The colors on the land that Valerie was so enjoying were getting easier to see as the usual blaze of sunlight was reduced.

Through the course of the next couple of hours, the rest of the sun was eaten. As the process reached its apotheosis, the lunar landscape around them darkened. Then the moment came when they could look up without their eclipse glasses, and see overhead a thin red ring in the sky, a glowing red tracery of a band, pulsing and shimmering. This apparently was Earth's atmosphere, lit up and glowing like a corona around the black circle that was the Earth. The black circle was duskier than the starry black of space, and through binoculars and other scopes one could see what seemed to be stars dotting it; these were cities on Earth's night side.

Eclipses were fairly common on the moon, Valerie and John were told. The red annular band surrounding Earth was sunlight bending through the atmosphere; this phenomenon explained why people on Earth looking up at a lunar eclipse saw the moon turn a dusky red.

And indeed the land around them was now that same color. When they finally looked down from the mesmerizing sight of the red ring in the sky, they saw that the land around them had turned both dark and distinctly red. It was somewhat like the color of a red sunset on Earth, but darker and more intense, a subtly shifting array of dim blackish reds, all coated by a dusty copper sheen. The previously pastel patches of rare earths were now shifted to purples and forest greens and rusty browns. But these were highlights in what was for the most part a dark red land, strong in both color and mood. It reminded Valerie of the last scene in a *Parsifal* she had seen in New York the year before, in which the chorus had waded across a stage knee-deep in blood. The Harbinger Mountains now reared like a bloody dragon spine out of an ocean of blood. Harbingers indeed! War—chaos—bloodshed—

"Okay, here it comes," someone said, and then a big gray blob shot over the horizon, a brilliant blaze of light pouring out of its forward end against the direction of its movement. Faster than Valerie could take in a breath it slammed into the moon, and a great gout of fire flew back up toward the stars, extra bright in the eclipse darkness, arcing down lazily like fireworks.

The locals cheered. "Carbon!" the miner explained to Valerie and John. "They cut off a chunk of the asteroid we put into lunar orbit, and drop it to the surface with a mass driver that works like a retro-rocket. It doesn't completely work, but it doesn't have to—all you need is a collision that doesn't vaporize the impactor, and leaves it mostly at the crash site. So it augers in at about the same speed as a jet on Earth, and boom. Carbon."

"KREEPy," John Semple remarked. The miners laughed and popped champagne bottles, and wandered the room toasting the sight of the crimson metallic sheens out there around them. Valerie shuddered and kept her bloody thoughts to herself. She took a glass and drank with the rest, clinked her glass with John Semple's when he offered.

"Red moon!" he said. "Awesome!"

"Yes," Valerie agreed coolly.

He grinned at her. He knew she disliked his uncultured shtick, so he was tweaking her by playing it even harder; she saw that, she saw that he saw that she saw it, and so on to infinity; and still he did it. It was very irritating.

When the sun came back they flew on to the north pole.

. . • • .

The north pole's permanently sunlit area was slightly smaller than the corresponding district at the south pole, but its permanently shadowed craters held a bit more water than the south's, so the two regions were about equivalent as suitable places to settle. The north pole was the United States' home base on the moon, as it was for the Swiss, the European Union, Russia, South Africa, India, Iran, and Brazil. The Chinese staffed a consulate in the Brazilian station.

As their shuttle descended, Valerie looked out a window and saw the usual overlapping gray craters, with several rims marked by a number of low settlements. Her view from above, showing as it did such a mix of design styles, reminded her of an architectural charrette. The American base was the biggest, naturally, but it had not managed to claim the highest ground on the rim of Peary, occupied by the Brazilians six months before the Americans had arrived. The Brazilian base enjoyed ninety-seven percent constant sunlight, the Americans eighty-nine percent; the rest of the bases ranged between those two, with the Iranians, slightly farther south on the near side, at eighty-three percent.

As they descended, Valerie asked John Semple whom she should talk to in order to pursue her various inquiries.

He shrugged. "NSA has good intel on this place, and I like their analysts on station. I'll introduce you to them. And to some other friends of mine, because this town is the place where you can get a sense of how life on the moon can change your priorities."

"What do you mean?"

"Hopefully you'll find out. There's a couple internationals you need to meet."

"Like who?"

"You'll find out."

"How?"

He smiled. He really was amused by her far too often. "It's called intelligence for a reason."

· · · · ·

The social life between the north pole stations resembled the embassy circuit in Washington, DC. Every station hosted a mixer for the rest to attend. On the moon that wasn't so simple on the logistical level, because although the stations clustered fairly close around the pole to catch as much sunlight as possible, one still had to get in spacesuit or rover and then walk or drive to the other bases, then get through locks or jetways and get out of spacesuits, always a hassle. To avoid spacesuits most people drove, even if it was only to go a hundred meters. And after all that they had to assemble in rooms not quite big enough to hold the entire polar population. In truth, compared to the Chinese complex sprawling around the south pole, Valerie found the whole scene pretty unimpressive.

John had suggested she attend the mixer at the Brazilian base, so she did. There all the tropical plants and colorful décor combined with the lunar gravity to create a little Carnaval thrill. The crush of people made everyone dance a little just to keep their balance. People collided, held each other upright, said hi to strangers who barged unintentionally into conversations, and in general acted like they were swimming around in chest-high water, slightly tipsy, drinks in hand.

At a certain point in the evening Valerie turned to the only woman near her and introduced herself. This woman turned out to be Russian, her English accented but articulate. Anna Kanina. *Not* Karenina. Very likely some kind of equivalent role to Valerie's, but no way to be sure.

"Have you been here long?" Anna asked.

"Not long," Valerie said. "And you?"

"Almost a year. I go home soon."

"Are you looking forward to that?"

"No. I like it here."

"What's your job up here?"

"Spy." Anna then laughed at Valerie's expression. "Not really! I say that to see if you are spy. Which I see you are. Actually I do radio astronomy, over on the back side."

"Is that a Russian observatory?"

"International. Mostly EU, in terms of who built it. But now it's run by the IAU. You should come to visit."

"Is it interesting?"

"No. But it's always good to get to far side of moon, if you're an astronomer anyway."

Valerie thought it over. "Are there Chinese bases on the far side?"

"I don't know. I'm neither sinologist nor selenologist."

"Just an astronomer."

"Right. If you want to learn more about selenology, the political kind, you should talk to Ginger Ellis, who runs the greenhouse in your building."

"Really?"

"If she'll talk, you will learn."

So she really was a spy.

. . . . .

Women on the moon were a minority. Among the Americans they were said to constitute thirty-five percent of the population. On the moon, as elsewhere, that gender balance could feel somewhat like parity, and certainly normal for a situation like this one, with its strong element of construction and engineering. Using your hands to build things outdoors usually meant you were male. Make it an exotic outdoors and the percentage of women usually rose, true here as elsewhere. But it was still not fifty-fifty. That meant there was a certain solidarity among the women on hand, or so it seemed to Valerie. Everyone said hi and exchanged a little conversation in the course of doing business. People usually explained what they did on the moon, especially if they were meeting for the first time.

So now Valerie went looking for Ginger Ellis, and found her in the base's greenhouse. This was again a big glass-walled round room with a 360-degree view, as tight-horizoned and monotonous as those one saw from the Chinese greenhouses at the south pole. Valerie introduced herself as a presidential assistant, and Ginger nodded and said she knew that.

"Do the plants grow taller here?" Valerie asked, looking around.

"Taller and spindlier. We put the least happy crops in a centrifuge, but mostly we harvest early, or just plant low plants. It's not a good place for corn."

"I can see how that would be."

Now Ginger Ellis was staring at her. "And what is it that you can't see?"

"I can't see why people in the other stations think you're the person who runs this one."

Ginger laughed. "I grow their food."

"But most of the food is shipped up, right? Even freshies?"

"My tomatoes rule," Ginger said. "Anyone will tell you that. Heirlooms, never refrigerated. People beg me for them. I don't even wash them."

"Is that good?"

"Of course. Vine-ripe organics? What, aren't you a foodie?"

"I am. But I do wash my veggies."

"Don't. Especially here. It's already too sterile here, people get sick from being too clean."

"So I should eat some dirt from time to time?"

"I do that, yes. Just a little, but sure."

Valerie made a face. "Maybe in a pill."

Ginger shook her head. "Just eat dirt."

"Okay," Valerie said. "Farm to fork, dirt included. But tell me what the hell is going on up here."

Ginger stared at her, unfazed. "What? We're here. We're doing the moon."

"But why?"

"Because it's there. As they say."

"Because the Chinese are there, you mean."

"Well, sure. They've got the south pole, we've got the north pole."

"Lots of countries have got the north pole."

"Which means we have friends and they don't."

"Which means they don't have to share."

"Share what? There's nothing to share."

"I've heard that, but I was wondering if you thought it was true. Aren't there things up here that are getting scarce on Earth? Like from those mines I saw on the way here?"

"No." Ginger laughed. "The moon isn't good for anything. Except as a launchpad. That's what I think the Chinese are really focused on."

"But a launchpad to where?"

"To anywhere. It's cheaper to launch stuff from here than from Earth, which makes it easier to go farther out."

"Are the Chinese already going farther out?"

"Sure. Everyone is. The Chinese are focused on Venus and the asteroids."

"Isn't Venus useless?"

"Yes, but they're building a floating station in its atmosphere, like a city inside a blimp. And they're sending big chunks of aluminum from here to Venus orbit. Looks like they're thinking of building a sunshade at Venus's L2 point to shade Venus completely, to cool it down. It's a very Chinese project, some kind of thousand-year plan or whatever. It's crazy, but if you don't include Venus in your thinking, you can't really understand the Chinese presence here."

"So the Chinese are going to be the first ones to yet another place?"

"Yes. But the solar system is big. We don't have to worry about every crazy idea the Chinese choose to pursue."

"Don't we?"

"I don't think so. It's not a zero-sum game."

"But what if there are people in Washington who think it is— wouldn't they come up here and try to do something about it?"

"Like what?"

"That's what I'm asking you."

"I don't know. People may be doing that, trying to mess with them, but it would be stupid. I don't think there's anything we can or should do about other governments' activities in space."

"You're very unconcerned!"

"It's true. Maybe that's because I grow such fine tomatoes."

"Can I have one?"

"Let's slice a couple and have a caprese salad. I grow the basil too."

She sliced the tomatoes on a big cutting block right next to her potting station. Ingredients were indeed unwashed. Valerie ate a delicious forkful or two and said, "Wow, they are good. The basil too."

"I grow ten kinds of basil, it's wonderful."

"Where do you get the mozzarella?"

"From Italy. Lots of food is shipped up, like you said. It's like any other local food movement. If the local stuff reaches thirty percent, you're totally eating off the land."

"So, but don't you think there are some American agencies trying to mess with the Chinese up here?"

"No doubt. And vice versa too. This cryptocurrency called virtual US Dollars, for instance. That's turning out to be really destabilizing. Combine that with the householder protests, it's crashing the economy pretty bad. But that hurts the Chinese too, so it's hard to understand who's doing it. Here on the moon, neither side is doing much that I can see."

"And you can see a lot."

Ginger Ellis stopped chewing, stared at her; swallowed. "Everyone can see a lot. It's a very small town, the moon. There's not a lot of places to hide, and people talk."

"Seems to me there's tons of places to hide. I'm looking for an American citizen who went missing, for instance, and I'm having no luck finding him. I'm hearing about secret lava tubes and such where they might have hidden him."

"Oh yeah, John mentioned that. Well, you should come out and see the free crater. Your person might even be out there."

"Where's that?"

"South of here." She grinned at Valerie's expression. "Worth a visit. Not supervised by any particular department, shall we say."

"What about you, what department are you?"

"I'm the greenhouse manager." Her look got sharper. "Don't you ever get tired of it?"

"Tired of what?"

"Of being so nosy and officious. You're on the moon, dear. So lighten up! You only weigh about twenty pounds here. Tell you what, let's go out there together and visit the freebies. You can look for your missing guy, and John seems to want you to see it."

"He wants the president to know about it?"

"He wants you to know about it."

"Me?"

"It's a compliment. He must think you have some potential."

. . . . .

The free crater, apparently otherwise unnamed, turned out to be a small, high-rimmed, geometrically perfect circle marring the southernmost stretch of the rim of Rozhdestvenskiy Crater, one of the big ones that occupied the near side, to the south of Peary Crater of course, which lay almost exactly on the pole. Valerie joined Ginger at the American rocket facility and was surprised to find John Semple already there. He smiled at her expression. "You think I would miss this?"

They lofted in a small rocket that the pilot called a hopper. Except for a sickeningly fast lift-off, it reminded Valerie of a helicopter. They flew in a helicopteristic way over the dark floor of Rozhdestvenskiy, which had a strange look to it, rumply and glistening. Valerie was told that this was a scrim of ice, that Rozhdestvenskiy was one of the biggest of the ice-floored craters; these craters' interiors never saw the sunlight, and thus held most of the comet ice that had been deposited in them over the previous four billion years. Apparently their nameless crater, though much smaller, had higher walls and so was even deeper in ice than Rozhdestvenskiy. Like all the sunless polar craters, it was one of the coldest spots in the solar system, never deviating far from 410 degrees below zero Fahrenheit. Its rim now featured a flat landing pad, and as they came down on it, they saw that the entire crater was domed with a transparent bubble of some sort.

"Wow," Valerie said. "Who made this?"

No one answered. They landed vertically with a small bump. A tube snaked out to them and covered their hopper's lock door, and after some clanking and hissing they walked through the tube into a building. Inside they were led by three guides through hallways toward the inner rim of the crater, emerging onto a platform that was set just under the crater-covering dome.

Apparently the entire space of the crater was aerated and heated, and brightly lit by mirrors and floodlights set all around the rim. From the platform's edge they could look down and see that the space between the dome and the crater floor was occupied by scores of hanging platforms, maybe hundreds of them; also tall plinths were holding up houses or bare floors, all connected by catwalks and rope ladders, trapezes, and loops of netting, also pod dwellings of various sizes suspended from the dome, or from networks of lines extending from high on the rim; also floating balloons, it seemed, from which hung open-sided rooms. Also floating balls of green bamboo, which grew in all directions, like some kind of Escher trees. The whole thing was Escheresque. An aerial town; and people, tiny in the distance, were jumping from one place to the next, swinging like apes or monkeys.

Startled at the sight, Valerie laughed out loud.

"Try it," their guides offered, and then leaped off the platform into space. They caught some netting down below, swung gracefully farther on. Valerie, deeply surprised, looked at John Semple.

"Whoa," John said. She saw he was as surprised as she was, which meant that it had to be his first time here too. Suddenly she saw a chance to get a jump on him, so to speak, because they were going to jump eventually, that was clear, and by going first she might wipe that little smile off his face, make him stop thinking of her as a condescending stick-in-the-mud. Without further ado she ran off the platform into space, shooting far over the network of lines their guides had dropped to. After that she could only look below for something else to catch onto. A bolt of panic shot through her as she felt the one-sixth of a g curving her down and accelerating her; it was slow, but not that slow, and she was feeling quite desperate when she managed to grab a passing rope and redirect herself. This worked; she could do it, she was light and strong enough; and now her mother's insistence that she do dance and gymnastics finally paid off, in that she was finding some reflexes rising abruptly out of her childhood. Grab and hold on, swing to the side! Tarzan!

After that worked for her a couple more times, she started doing her best to follow their guides, who were proving to be as nimble as orangutans. It was hard to stay near them, because they knew what they were doing. She needed to be careful, but it was not a place for being too careful, because you needed some momentum to swing rather than just hang there. A succession of moves taught her that she could grab and pull herself one-handed if she had to, because she just didn't weigh very much. It was uncanny. So she swung down net to net, looking for lines and nets ahead and below, following the guides as best she could. It would have helped to know where they were going, but since she didn't, she didn't even try to catch them. She just kept them in sight. Above her John was swinging down after her, whooping at each catch, a giant grin on his face. He was going to pass her soon, so she took off again.

They passed platforms displaying furniture that gave them a surreal look: dining rooms in space, an immense ping-pong table in space, a more-than-king-sized bed in space, and so on. Like a doll's house, or a museum, or an IKEA store, or a dream. As they swung toward midcrater they descended into a particularly crowded aerial neighborhood, consisting mostly of pod rooms hanging from lines; this must be a residential district. Around her people flew like trapeze artists. A flock of vividly blue-and-red lories winged by. The crater floor itself looked like a bamboo forest or an arboretum. As Valerie continued to swing down, growing curious about their ultimate destination, she saw that the trees below were suspended in balls of soil hanging over the crater floor, which was covered by some kind of clear layer, under what looked like a layer of netting. Ah good: a town with a safety net!

That made her bold to finish in style, and she followed their guides toward an open platform hung just above the trees. People already on the platform were waving them in, and their guides were now grabbing some of the lines holding the platform in place and letting themselves down hand over hand. If Valerie had had an umbrella she could have glided down onto them like Mary Poppins. Instead she swung down as best she could, trying to beat John Semple to the post, also composing her appearance for her arrival; she wanted to look like this method of locomotion was no big deal to her. Unfortunately she miscalculated at the last moment and missed the platform entirely, floating down past it into the mesh below, where she trampolined down and up until coming to a rest. They dropped a chair like a porch swing to her, and she sat in it; then they hauled her up and greeted her cheerfully. Among the people already there was Anna Kanina. She smiled when she saw Valerie's expression and gave her a brief hug. "Welcome to an interesting place," she said.

On the platform it was unexpectedly peaceful. Introductions were made all around, using first names only. The air was humid and cool, carried on a faint breeze. Above them, near the crater wall, puffball clouds were gathering for what might later be a shower.

"Welcome to the free crater," one of their guides said to Valerie and John. "We hope you enjoyed your arrival?"

"Loved it," John replied.

Valerie nodded, feeling flushed. "Very nice," she said. She was still disconcerted by Anna's presence, by her ironic smile.

They were led to a table at the center of the platform, where several people already stood eating and drinking.

"Tell us about this place," John requested. "Who are you people?"

The locals took turns to describe different parts of their project. The crater had been domed by an engineering and design team from Russia, but now they all operated it together. They were just free crater people; national origins were irrelevant. Languages were several, mainly Russian, Chinese, and Spanish, with English admittedly the lingua franca, as everywhere. The dome was a triple layer of translucent compounds which protected them from cosmic radiation. The crater floor held a substantial layer of ancient water ice, two hundred meters at its thickest, only slightly mixed with lunar dust. Extremely cold, extremely valuable. They had covered it with insulation and flooring and were mining one quadrant of it as needed, tunneling in from the side. The aerial village's population was small, less than three thousand people, but there was room to grow, and energy to fuel that growth, as the temperature differential between the sunny rim and the frozen floor was about six hundred degrees Fahrenheit. Lots could be done with that!

"Who pays for it all?" John asked.

It paid for itself, their hosts said. The start had been privately funded by an international group of interested parties. Some Chinese and Russians, some Americans and Europeans, some Africans and Australians, some Indonesians and South Americans. But again, nationality didn't matter (Anna rolled her eyes at this). Everyone was welcome, everyone was equal. Everyone was rich, Anna added. They mostly slept in a one g centrifuge embedded in the crater rim, and were hoping that would allow them to live their days in lunar gravity without adverse health effects. No one knew for sure about that, of course; they were an experiment, like everything else on the moon. They were mining and selling their water ice to pay for equipment and supplies. They were involved with the international group that was sending robotic spacecraft out to various carbonaceous chondritic asteroids, then building mass drivers on them to direct them down into orbit around the moon. "Ah yes, we just saw one of those crash into Procellarum during the eclipse!" John said.

The free crater people were happy to hear they had seen that. Meanwhile, their daily work in the crater was to build its infrastructure and its social system, and to make it beautiful. Life as art, the world as a poem—a poem about flying. It was all self-organizing, although they did make some plans. They were there to do what Luna told them to do and allowed them to do. They would be the capital of nothing. They would free themselves of all the mistakes of the past, they would make something new. Everyone was welcome—up to a point, of course, given the limits of the crater's size. Not the billion, Anna commented, just the billionaires. But of course other craters could be domed and inhabited in this same way. There were a million craters like this one on the moon—although in terms of having water, Anna added, more like a hundred. For now, no one cared enough to stop them doing this, and the people who stayed cared more than anyone else what happened in here. It was a new kind of commons, a new way of living. To this even Anna nodded. It's interesting, she said to Valerie. It's the start of something, I'll give them that.

Valerie glanced at John Semple. "It sounds great!" he said. "Show us more!"

Their hosts agreed happily, and dove off the edge of the platform. John and Valerie followed; Valerie missed the netting the others had grabbed, floated down and hit the big mesh again, bobbed down and up, down and up, until the mesh had stilled and she could crawl over it to a rope ladder leading down. This was easier than she would have imagined; the same lunar g that made walking hard made crawling easy.

On a clear deck over the crater floor, their hosts were already explaining to John that they were separated from the crater's ice by a clear polymer sheet set over a thick insulation layer of transparent aerogel. They could still see the crater floor under all that, a nobbled icy surface, like a Boston gutter in March, Valerie thought. Ugly; but it was water on the moon, and therefore precious.

One of their guides pointed out a long low building set right on the crater floor, such that it appeared to be half-buried in ice. This building, they were told, housed a server bank of quantum computers, which took advantage of the extreme cold to run arrays of the various kinds of qubits that needed supercool temperatures. Some of these worked at the temperature of the ice, others used the ice to help sustain temperatures just a fraction above absolute zero. This computer complex was another source of income, their guides said, and it also gave them some leverage when it came to keeping their independence; they had almost as many yottaflops available as all the servers in the United States combined. Which was only another way of saying that the US had fallen far behind in quantum computing, but still, it was a startling fact. Computing power was economic power, they said; and economic power was political power.

So that small building down there buried in the ice of their crater floor could in theory house a major player in Terran politics.

Through the transparent decking and insulation they could see a giant pit that had been excavated out of the ice, near one arc of the crater wall. Vehicles like roadbuilding machines rolled around cutting the ice into cracked blocks and then trundling these blocks over a flat stretch of crater floor toward the inner wall of the crater, where they would be hauled up in freight elevators to the rim, there to be distributed all over the moon. Ice this cold acted differently than ordinary ice, it was extremely hard and brittle. The crater harbored about a billion cubic meters of ice, and every drop mined from it would be recycled as long as possible. The goal was to keep every drop of it in circulation forever, with zero water loss in all downstream uses. That was impossible, of course, but still a goal to be attempted.

"As a form of money it's got very high liquidity," John joked. "Just add heat and serve!"

"See that tilted slope down there? That was an avalanche." One of their hosts indicated a big scoop and slide in the wall of excavated ice. "Back when they began mining this ice, my friend John was down there when that slope gave way. The ice partially buried him, they had a hell of a time freeing him up. It was only a few minutes, but by the time they got him out, his feet were frostbitten. He lost all his toes. That was how we found out that you really need your toes to be able to walk on the moon. We call him Mr. Pogo Stick now."

"Sorry to hear," John Semple said. "Does he still live here?"

"I'm not sure."

"Don't you know who lives here?"

"Oh yeah, we have to keep track of that, to keep the gas exchange and everything else. I just don't know if John moved on or not."

"We do blockchain governance," one of the others said. "The census is part of that."

"Blockchain governance? Meaning what?"

"All our activities and decisions are recorded in a secure distributed network, including our comings and goings, but also everything we do as a town. We call it documented anarchy. A full-disclosure com-mons. Anyone can do anything, but everyone gets to know what that is."

"Is that what the blockchain governance movement on Earth is trying for?"

"I don't know."

Valerie said, "Since you keep track of everyone, could you look for someone we're looking for, see if they're in town?"

"Sure. Who are they?"

"Frederick Fredericks and Chan Qi."

Their guide tapped on his wrist for a while. "No, no one here by those names."

"Could they be here under fake names, or off the record?"

"No. We start with full disclosure here. Everyone enters their full real legal identity, including their national ID numbers. Then we forget about that."

"So, can you tell us anything about those two?" Valerie persisted. "We've heard they're back on the moon now, after some time on Earth."

"If they're on the moon now, we might be able to see something," Anna said after none of the others replied. She tapped around for a while. "Oh, those two! Yes, they are back all right. They came up in Fang Fei's system. An odd couple."

"How do you mean?" Valerie asked.

"He's the one who was involved in the killing of Chang Yazu, right? And Chang was working with Peng Ling to keep China moon on her side during the upcoming Party congress. Chang used to work for Minister Huyou, in Shaanxi, and there were investiga-tions of corruption focused on their time there. It's possible Chang had something on Huyou that he was going to pass along to Peng, to use in the fight for the succession to President Shanzhai. Another person in the running for that is Chan Guoliang, whose daughter has been seen with this man who was involved in Chang Yazu's murder. So that makes them an odd couple, if you ask me."

"Could Chan Qi be working against her dad?" John Semple asked.

Anna shrugged. "Don't know. Jianguo is still working on getting to the bottom of it. He's really mad. I mean, a friend of his was killed right in his prefecture. So he won't be forgetting."

"Can you find out where Fred and Chan Qi are now?" Valerie asked.

Anna looked dubious. "We can always ask Fang Fei. We've opened a new direct private line with him, it's very cool."

"How so?"

"It's a neutrino telegraph."

"What does that mean?" John asked.

"We send a beam of neutrinos right through the moon to where Fang Fei has a receptor set up. It's very hard to catch neutrinos with anything smaller than a few city blocks' worth of stuff, but we've gotten a system running where you can catch enough to send simple messages. That's why we call it a telegraph. The bit rate is laughable, but it works for texting."

"The neutrinos go right through the moon?" John asked.

"They go right through everything. A trillion just went through us right now." Anna snapped her fingers. "Fang Fei likes the idea because his base is on the far side, and with this device he can shoot messages right through the moon to his people in China, without having to use satellites. It's another one of his toys, at least now, but we're pitching in because we thought there might be some potential there. Meanwhile it gives us a way of talking to him privately. Anyway, I'll send him a query about those two, and we'll see what he says."

A bunch of the other freebies dropped down onto them and informed them it was time for the day's performance.

"Okay," their host said to John, "are you ready to be a dancer in our opera?"

"No way," John said. "I can't dance here! I can barely dance even on Earth."

They just laughed at him. You can join anyway, they said. They needed extras. It was a case of the more the merrier, and this performance took everyone in the crater.

"Which opera?" Valerie inquired.

"*Satyagraha.*"

"Isn't that one kind of hard?" she asked. She had seen it performed once in New York, a modernist thing full of dancers with banners, weaving around a stage to a score like industrial music. Libretto in Sanskrit, she seemed to recall.

No, they told her, it was easy. The crowd scenes were supposed to be chaotic, indeed in their version they aspired to a state of complete Brownian motion. The gravity made that easy, and often it created all kinds of accidental grace.

John was shaking his head. Valerie said, "I love to dance," which wasn't quite true, but she was still working on wiping that amused look off John's face. Time to finish that off for good.

They rode up in a basket at the end of a counterweighted crane lift, and were taken to a cluster of midair platforms. There they joined one of the groups congregating on a big central platform, and after introductions, their hosts jumped up to a slightly higher platform, then crossed it and jumped again. Valerie and John had to follow as best they could, both of them often misjudging how much of a leap was needed to get to the same platform as their hosts. John flew far toward the dome, while Valerie barely made it to the first available platform, which she struck with a shock more impactful than she had expected; it wasn't like falling into the mesh. But this was just one lesson of many to come concerning unforeseen differences between weight, mass, and inertia, and she made adjustments as she could, while struggling to keep her hosts in sight and identified as hers, lost as they were among all the other people flying through the space of the aerial city.

By the time she caught up to them the great opera was in full swing, and an orchestra and chorus of several hundred people on a big platform in about the center of the space was filling the air with the complex, pulsating music. Valerie had learned a bit about this opera after seeing it in New York, at first because she was curious, and then because of its subject, which was the concept of "peaceful force" suggested by the word *satyagraha*, a word Gandhi had made up during his campaign for Indian independence. This word could be said to express a vision of diplomacy and intelligence work at its best, or so it seemed to Valerie, and although this opera's libretto was in Sanskrit and thus incomprehensible to almost every person who had ever sung or heard it—and although the score by Glass was extraordinarily dense and repetitive, sending percussive waves of sound echoing through the city such that it would have been dizzying even without the low-g flights—still, once she and her group had all grasped handholds like subway straps at the ends of long lines extending from a central spinner, something like a scary ride in a carnival, and it began to spin and their bodies lifted out and away from each other, either just holding on like Valerie, or dancing in space like most of her group—once that was all accomplished, she began to enjoy herself. She began to join both the spirit and the body of the dance.

Knowing the music helped a lot. When the battles of the middle act began, she kicked and flailed as rhythmically as she could, and when her entire group let go of their ropes all at once and were cast like dandelion seeds in all directions, never to meet again during the course of this opera at least, she was quick to follow, and with an almost gymnastic twist she let go, and found herself cast high over other spinning dancers. Apparently many people had let go of similar spinning mechanisms at around the same time, and the weave of flying dancers through the air was beautiful to see, although it also had to be said that if two dancers happened to be on a collision course, nothing they could do would keep them from running into each other. Or so it seemed, until Valerie saw she was headed right at a young woman dressed in scarlet, and the young woman saw her too; this allowed them to contort themselves as they flew by each other such that they just missed colliding, a nifty trick that caused them both to laugh and wave at each other as they diverged. Then

the moon's g exerted its pull, and Valerie curved down and down
until she hit a bunch of netting and managed not to injure herself
as she bounced to a halt. Another group of singers hanging there
welcomed her and invited her by gesture to join them in their singing. This Valerie declined, at least at first; but then she recognized
where the opera had gotten to, and could join in under her breath,
making up the words as she went along. She knew the tune, such as
it was, and at this point her group's part was a staccato *buh-buh-buh-
buh buh-buh-buh-buh buh-buh-buh-buh buh-buh-buh-buh*, repeated over
and over and over, great fun to enunciate with the rest of them, and
after a while she was actually shouting it as loud as she could shout.

Eventually they came to the last great aria, which was made of a
repeated scale of rising notes—just the eight notes of a C major scale
begun on E, repeated as if someone were just learning to play the
piano. This turned out to make a beautiful song, one of the compos-
er's finest discoveries, nicely saved for the ending. The whole population of the city sang this together, and the dance troupes had come to
stillness somehow, wherever they were, so that everyone now hung
suspended somewhere in the air under the dome. Valerie found herself with people she had never seen, people of all kinds floating there.
In the distance across the city the other participants were small in her
sight, so that suddenly it looked to her like she had fallen into the Disneyland ride called It's a Small World. That ride had bowled her over
when she was five years old, and now her head was suddenly hearing
its simple tune, *It's a world of laughter, a world of tears*, et cetera, leading
to *It's a small world after all!* Which was quite a tune to impinge on
the sublimity of the finale of *Satyagraha*, but her earworm weakness
had already latched onto it, and all she could do was try to braid the
two tunes together in her head, and in this particular moment it even
seemed to kind of work, as a counterpoint or fugue or descant.

· · · · ·

That odd little duet accompanied her all the rest of that day, which
was taken up mostly by relocating John Semple. She couldn't find

him, she couldn't find Anna, and she couldn't find their hosts from the platform, and she didn't know any of their names, and couldn't immediately recall their faces. She had to brachiate her way back to where she thought their first meeting had taken place, dodging other swingers as she swung. Lots of flushed and happy faces flying around out there, and she was sure she probably looked like the rest.

Finally she ran into John, sitting on a platform drinking tea and talking with what she thought was a completely different set of people. He welcomed her back with a real smile, a smile of acceptance, and she sat and took a cup of tea, and listened to them tell stories about the place, and looked at all their faces, glowing like paper lanterns. All the while she was hearing in her head "it's a world of laughter, a world of tears," chiming across the rising scale that ended *Satyagraha*, and this stranded tune persisted in her head through the rest of their stay in the little flying crater, and all the way back to the north pole.

AI 8

lianxi

Contact

Little Eyeball said in her stiff version of the beautiful voice of Zhou Xuan, "Ready to transmit."

The analyst sat by the Unicaster 3000 unit, hesitating over the keyboard. Time to send a hopeful greeting to the wayward princessling Chan Qi. He found he was nervous. Slowly he typed,

Hello, Chan Qi.

I'm a friend in China.

I work under the Great Firewall, in what some call the Invisible Wall. Colleagues of mine are surveilling you and others organizing the three withouts. I'm sure you know about some of this. I like your efforts, and would like to help you succeed in them.

He looked at the message for a while, then hit send. This kind of phone pair was quantum encrypted, but capable of exchanging only a relatively tiny thread, a string of binaries almost like Morse code, tapping on the ether itself.

He contemplated the device as he waited for a response. Possibly she would never write back, given that he had mentioned the Great Firewall. He had admitted to being someone in national security; why reply? But she had been traveling with the American who worked in quantum encryption, and the analyst had had this device sent to them hoping that the quantum expert would explain to her how the entanglement of the qubits inside the devices meant no one could overhear their conversation without them knowing of it.

Of course his phone could be in an office of the Ministry of State Security with a crowd of policemen reading its screen, but even if it were so, they would not be able to find her if she answered them. So he waited with some curiosity.

A reply appeared on his screen:

Why should you want to help me when you work on the Great Firewall?

He wrote back, *I work under the Great Firewall. I helped design it, and I can use it to help people sometimes, if I want to.*

Why do you want to help me?

I want to help the three withouts.

Why?

The Party exists to serve the people. As Mao said, "The people alone are the motive force in the making of world history."

And yet you work in a security agency.

I feel it's best if the people are secure. But then the question becomes, what creates the greatest security? For me, when the people are happy the country is safest. So I like your ideas.

How do you know what my ideas are?

You are often surveilled. I've heard recordings, I've read transcripts.

Did you work for Xi?

I did. He was a good leader, all things considered. I helped design his poverty eradication campaign, back in the twenties.

How could you do that from a security agency?

My work has always been in quantum computers and artificial intelligence. President Xi asked us to investigate how we could help eradicate poverty. That turned out to be hard, as early efforts often are. But there were some results that helped push poverty down.

And yet the problem still exists.

President Xi's fourth term came to an end, and he could not extend to a fifth. Even the fourth term was hard. Progress was impeded by the struggle over who would come after him. After he was gone his influence waned and

new policies were pursued. The leadership since his time has been weak.
They are not interested in poverty eradication. They are only fighting among
themselves now, thinking they could become the next Xi.

Who in the leadership do you support now?

I support Peng. Also your father. Also Liu and Yi. These and other people
are trying to solve the outstanding problems. But they are not in control now.
Shanzhai wants one of his supporters to succeed him as leader. He is work-
ing for that result at this Party congress. He has chosen Huyou, the worst of
them.

I want to destabilize that whole regime.

I know. I think that might be a very helpful effort. I think it's worth a try.
This is my opinion.

So what do you want from me?

Nothing. I want to tell you what I am seeing here, concerning your surveil-
lance and the surveillance of your group.

So tell me.

Most of the security agencies pursuing you are not yet aware that you went
back to the moon in one of Fang Fei's rockets. But one of them has now
found out, and that could represent a danger.

Red Spear?

Yes.

So they know where I am.

Probably so.

So I should leave where I am.

Probably so. I would if I were you. Fang Fei is a positive force, but he may
not be able to protect you.

At this point there was a long pause. The analyst wondered if she
had ended the conversation. The device showed the channel was
still open, but she might not know how to shut it. Although probably the young American would know, if he was with her.

Then another message appeared. *I'll contact you again later.*

Thank you.

The channel closed.

The analyst sat back in the seat, took a deep breath. His hands

were quivering slightly. It was at times like this that he most regretted having quit smoking. For most of his life, he would have lit up at
a time like this. Now he observed his breathing, in and out, in and
out. It was almost like smoking.

"Alert," his AI said.

"What is it?"

"Tunnels one and four have collapsed."

"What do you mean?"

"I am no longer receiving the taps you had moving through those
tunnels."

"What about the others?"

"Two and three are still functioning, also five through thirty."

"Find out what you can about these closures, please."

"I will."

Someone was in pursuit.

CHAPTER TWELVE

zhengzhi luxian de zhenglun

Debates About Theory

Fred sat with Qi and Ta Shu on a pavilion overlooking one of the ponds in the lava tunnel, trying to identify some of the food on the table by them. He was hungry but tentative, worried he might trigger another Hong Kong reaction in his gut.

"This isn't China," Qi declared, gesturing at the classic landscape filling the big lava tunnel. "It's Chinoiserie. It's a Western fantasy of what they thought China looked like, another Orientalism. Part of the process of othering that led to the assault and conquest of the Opium War, followed by the Century of Humiliation. It's absurd and disgusting. Who built this stupid theme park?"

"Fang Fei built it," Ta Shu said. "And to me it looks like every Tang painting I've ever seen. So if it's a fantasy, it's at least a Chinese fantasy. The original China Dream, from well before contact with the West, much less the Century of Humiliation. Many Chinese still revere this dream. Many still know a classic poem or two by heart. It's part of who we are." His sweet smile was lighting up his face. "This place looks like one of Wang Wei's paintings!"

Qi frowned. "None of Wang Wei's paintings have survived," she pointed out grumpily.

Fred saw she was in a cross mood. Whoever next gave her a chance to jump on them was going to get jumped. He thought knowing that would allow him to avoid being that person, but no:

"Quit smirking," she ordered him.

"I wasn't," he claimed. "It's just that I like this place too. It's a beautiful look. See those peach blossoms in the water?"

Ta Shu laughed. "We must seek their source! Maybe there's a place upstream where you two won't get arrested again."

Qi shook her head. "We are already arrested."

"Think of it as a refuge," Ta Shu suggested to her. "A sanctuary."

"No," Qi said. "There must be hundreds of people in here. In any group that large, there will be informers. So this is not a refuge. There are people out there who already know we're here."

She scowled as she said this; she seemed quite sure of it. Fred wondered if she had learned this by way of that call she had gotten on the private quantum phone Ta Shu had given to her. Fred had helped her to take the call, then stared curiously at the Chinese characters on her screen. As they were on the far side of the moon, the call had to be coming to her by way of a satellite link; after she had finished the call he had reminded her of that fact, which she might not have remembered or understood. Indeed she had scowled the same scowl he was seeing now, not directed at him, but at his news. "Fang Fei must have helped make the connection," she had said after thinking it over. "I don't know what that means yet. But for sure we're in his cage."

Now Ta Shu said to her, "I defer to your experience, of course, but for now I think we are safe."

She shook her head, glanced at Fred in a way that seemed to be telling him to keep quiet. "You don't know enough to say that," she said darkly to Ta Shu. "This is probably just a kind of holding tank for the convenience of some faction of the elite. They're probably very happy we're here, available for pickup at any time."

At this Ta Shu looked troubled. "Again I defer to your superior experience. And it's true that my friend Peng Ling wanted you here, to be out of harm's way, she said. But I do think that Fang Fei regards this place as his own, and will guard it as such."

"How come we haven't met him yet? Where is he?"

"At the source of the peach blossom stream," Ta Shu said, smiling as he gestured up the lava tunnel. Fred saw that Qi couldn't spoil his pleasure in this place, which obviously to him was landscape art, a kind of poem written in stone. "Let's go find him."

. . . . .

They had been given rooms in a little guesthouse overlooking the water pavilion; now they were driven in a little cart along a narrow paved road running under the hills that formed the lava tube's left wall. Other little carts hummed up or down the path, moving construction supplies, boxes, and people. The path ran behind a line of poplar trees, and every few hundred meters they passed parking lots where more carts were parked. The floor of the lava tube was mostly parkland, dotted with small villages, and everywhere green with trees; it was almost flat, but as they were driven along the side path they were moving slightly uphill. They were headed upstream. After all the time they had recently spent inside small confined spaces, the lava tunnel seemed immense. It looked to be about a kilometer wide and two or three hundred meters tall. The ceiling glowed sky blue, being painted or illuminated in some fashion that looked a lot like Earth's sky, although it was dotted here and there by clustered sunlamps, as if the sun in the sky had been chopped into subunits and distributed evenly across the zodiac. White clouds overhead were either projected onto the blue ceiling or else were really up there, it was hard to tell. The air was cool when the slight breeze from upstream struck them, warm when the sunlamps were nearby. It was bright without being anywhere near as bright as daylight on the lunar surface, or even a sunny day on Earth. It was about as bright as an overcast day on Earth, and certainly bright enough that everything was clear to the eye.

They came to a long pond, which the stream entered and left through reed beds. On the lawn banking this pond some people were fly fishing, casting their lines far out onto the water. Behind

them, in the shade of trees that Ta Shu said were ginseng, sat circles
of people; they looked like classes or discussion groups. There were
little cubical houseboats floating on the pond, and the sidewalls of
the lava tunnel were here corrugated by vertical ridges and steep
ravines, with wisps of clouds floating across them in the classic Chinese landscape painting style. Upstream a hexagonal pagoda with
ceramic roof tiles towered above the treetops. A flock of geese flew
overhead, wing feathers creaking as they pumped the air.

"Give me a break," Qi said.

Their electric cart brought them down a path to the pond. A broad
promenade curved around its shore, and bridges spanned the reed
beds at inlet and outlet. A pavilion near the outlet extended over
the water. Big willow trees dotted the bank and drooped greenly,
branches trailing in the pond like hair being washed. Ripples on the
water reflected various jade and forest-green tones, also the blue of
the sky overhead.

"Come on!" Qi exclaimed. "What's next, a dragon?"

At that very moment a dragon-prowed boat glided out of a boat-
house on the far shore and swanned toward them.

"Enough!" Qi exclaimed. She glared at Ta Shu. "Where do we
meet this guy?"

"Here," he said. "I was told he'll join us after a while. But before
that, I want to take one of those pedal boats and ride around the lake."

"Suit yourself."

"I will!" Grinning hugely, Ta Shu walked carefully over to a little
marina where pedal boats were moored in rows. Qi sat in a chair by
the pavilion railing, and Fred joined her. It seemed to him that this
was, if not a refuge, then at least a far better place than many others
he could imagine them inhabiting. For one thing, they were still
together. This pleased him.

· · · · ·

When the dragon boat touched the edge of the pavilion, an old man
stepped off—short and slight, elderly but upright, skillful in the

lunar g. He walked up to Qi and Fred and stood staring at them. With a little bow of the head and a questioning wave of the hand, he sat in an empty chair by them.

He spoke in Chinese, then looked at Fred and said something more. Qi replied, and he nodded and stood, walked over to Fred, and offered him a pair of black spectacles he pulled from his shirt pocket. He gestured and Fred understood to put them on.

They were translating glasses. The ancient one said something, and in red across the lower half of the glasses flowed the text *A nice day to be water*, moving like a newsfeed. Fred found the moving scroll distracting, but understanding what the other two were saying was well worth it.

"Thank you!" Fred exclaimed.

"Fang Fei," the old one said, and the words appeared in writing on Fred's glasses. "Fred Fredericks," Fred replied. They nodded in a similar way, possibly acknowledging the coincidence of their FF initials.

Qi said something to Fang Fei in Chinese. Fred's glasses scrolled the red words *I am afraid to be water.*

Fred concluded that the machine translation of the glasses was imperfect, but this was always true. Now he just had to do his best to interpret what he read.

Fang Fei said, or was imputed to say, *Water is life.*

Qi shrugged. *Why is it here? What are you doing?*

When young I was three withouts.

Sanwu. Fred heard this word and remembered Qi defining it during one of their talks in the apartment: it referred to people without residence permit, job, and something else. Family, maybe. Or car. Or money. Seemed like three might not be a big enough number anymore.

Fang Fei was imputed to say: *No iron rice bowl makes China a hard place. I do not forget that.*

Qi said, *So you build your own private China?*

Yes. It was like this once. It will be like this again.

Qi didn't believe that, her face said. *How long do we stay here?* she said.

You stay anytime you want. You leave anytime you want.

Qi didn't believe this either. *What do you want?* she said.

I want peace. I want China happy.

What about the billion?

I was billion. I am billion. I will be billion always.

She shook her head. Another thing she didn't believe.

The old man was looking amused by her. That would almost certainly piss her off, but he didn't need Fred to tell him that. He didn't mind annoying her, Fred guessed.

Then he looked at Fred. It was a tiger's look, calmly assessing a smaller animal, something like a deer or a rabbit. He asked something.

Do you understand us? Are translation glass helping?

"Yes," Fred said. "They help a lot, thank you."

Fang Fei assessed Fred a little more.

"I can speak English maybe," he said with a slight British accent, not that different from Qi's. "I might remember a little."

"I don't want to impose," Fred said, glancing at Qi to try to see what she thought of this. "The glasses are giving me a rough idea of what you are saying, and you may want to keep speaking your language together."

"Rough idea," Fang Fei said in English, then a Chinese word, *souzhuyi*, that Fred's glasses scripted as *bad idea*.

The man is not important, Qi said, according to Fred's glasses. *What is important is why you are doing this.*

Doing what?

Building this China Dream. Keeping us here.

I love China. And I heard you were in trouble. Kidnapped. Traveling with foreign man accused of murder of magistrate. Yes? Big trouble it seemed. Nightmare. You have many enemies. Chan's princess daughter in trouble. Pregnant even. Who is disrespectful father?

No one.

No one? Surprising. Does not usually happen that way. I suppose China is the father.

No.

This red exchange, crawling across the bottom of Fred's glasses, was causing him to hold his breath. He had to consciously breathe as he watched the two of them fence. He had to look at them to help him understand. Qi's face had gone blank, but her cheeks were giving her away with their usual furious blush. Both of them had a basilisk stare that was rather awesome to witness. Tiger to tiger, facing off. Fred focused on his breathing.

What do you want? she said.

I want peace.

I don't care about peace. I want justice.

For you and your friend?

For the billion.

For the billion to have justice, whole world must have justice.

Yes.

The old man shrugged. *An old dream,* he said. *China dream. A just world.*

Maybe so.

We must make it together. Bring it into this world.

Qi said, *You can join me if you want.*

Fang Fei almost smiled at that. His eyes smiled, Fred thought.

I am happy to join you, he said.

Qi stared at him. She saw the same almost smile Fred did, a look in Fang Fei's tiger eye that perhaps she didn't like.

Then she began to grill him about people Fred didn't know, *What about Peng, what about Deng,* on and on it went. Sometimes Fred's glasses seemed to be translating some of the names into their English meanings, not recognizing them as names. Between not knowing who people were and being confronted with names or phrases like *lotus blossom* or *victory in battle* or *construct the nation,* he couldn't quite follow what the two were saying. They were going fast, parry-riposte-parry-riposte, causing his glasses to fall into some kind of algorithmic aphasia, it seemed, making the red scroll a semi-translated mush of homonyms or mishearings:

Save communism geese fly south.

No. Red heart maze runner.

There will be fish every year.

Black-haired algae.

What about elliptical, what about construct the nation, what about glorious homeland?

At this Qi slapped the table, and Fred read on anxiously; happily it clarified a bit:

The Party works for the Party! Not for China! Only the Party!

Do you think so? Fang Fei inquired. Fred could see he was genuinely curious. *What about your father? Is he like that?*

Qi scowled at the mention of her father. *How would I know what he is like?* she said bitterly. *I am only his daughter.*

Daughters know. My daughters know me.

Do they? Do they know you are here now?

Yes, of course. They pester me with their knowing. Do this, do that.

But you do what you want.

He shook his head. *I do what they want.*

Then he actually smiled, a rather horrifying crack-faced leer. But genuine. *Maybe I am like Party and they are like China. I try to help them take care of them. They yell at me and tell me what to do. Then I try to do it.*

That is not how China works, Qi said. *Or maybe you are right like this. Daughters yell at father and father still does exactly what he wants. The Party is like that. It works for itself.*

It wants both. It works for itself and it works for China.

But when it has to choose, it works for itself. If a time came when abolishing the Party were best for China, the Party would not do it.

Our constitution says we run ourselves by way of the Party. I am a member of the Party, and so are you.

No I am not. I am only daughter of Party. I never joined.

Really?

Really.

No wonder your father is mad at you. Why not join Party?

I hate the Party. I want laws. That is what I mean when I say justice. The rule of law.

Fang Fei nodded. *Do not hold breath on that.*

What?

He repeated it in English: "Don't hold your breath! Isn't that how you say it?" he asked, looking at Fred. "If wish for something unlikely?"

"Yes," Fred said.

Qi said, "I am holding my breath."

Again Fang Fei nodded. He cracked another awful smile. "Cutting off nose to spite face?" he suggested. "Another good saying. Almost Chinese, it is so good."

"English has lots of good sayings," Fred protested.

Fang Fei nodded without assent. "Seems possible."

Why are you helping us? Qi demanded.

Fang Fei stared at her.

Are you helping us? she said. *You are not helping us. Are you. You are Party.*

No I am helping you. You were in trouble.

"We have to go," Qi said to Fred.

You are free to go of course, said Fang Fei to her.

"Go where?" Fred asked.

Again that ugly smile from the old man, which made Fred realize, too late as usual, that he needed to stay out of this conversation. "Sorry," he said. "I'll go wherever you want. But here we are now."

"Be quiet," she suggested.

"Okay," he contradicted. "I'll leave you to it. But I do like this place."

To keep himself from diving deeper into trouble, he got up, almost fell over, and pronged unsteadily across the pavilion, over to the low wall that overlooked the lake. Carefully he sat on the wall's broad top. The water lapped against what looked like concrete, and through the water he could see that the bottom also appeared to be concrete, painted jade green at the lakeshore, cobalt blue farther out. Or maybe it was just the bottom of the lava tube, scooped out and then painted. Fred sat on the wall and looked around. It looked very much like a Tang or Ming diorama in a museum or a theme park. The Disneyland in Hong Kong would presumably have just such an area in it, featuring Princess Mulan no doubt. He looked back at Qi and Fang, smiling to think of it. Definitely not something to mention around Qi.

Out on the water, a little armada of white swans was led by a black swan. Maybe Qi was her people's black swan. Or maybe she thought she was. Fred wasn't sure. What others thought was always hard to ascertain; he didn't even know what he thought, most of the time. In this case he didn't know the language, the culture, or the political situation. With a sinking feeling it occurred to him that this was only a particular case of a general situation. What did he know about anything?

Shadows of the pseudo clouds made dark circles on the lake. On the far bank a gang of monkeys were begging a fisherman for a handout.

Suddenly Qi plopped down next to him, holding her belly in both hands.

"We've got to get out of here," she said.

"Where are we going to go?" he objected. "We were in trouble. We kept getting caught."

"I know. But China is big. If we hadn't left our apartment on Lamma, we wouldn't have gotten caught."

"I'm not so sure. Didn't you say there were people waiting outside our door? If we hadn't left when we did, they would have caught us then, maybe. Anyway we did leave. Why don't you like this place?"

"I don't trust him. We're locked up here, and there are people on the outside who know we're here. It's a kind of jail."

"He said we could go if we wanted."

"I don't believe him."

"Do you think he's working with your father?"

"I don't know. He's not working with my people, that I do know. And my people need me."

"No one is indispensable," Fred said, though he wasn't sure about that. "Why don't you just stay here at least until your baby is born, make sure that happens safely, and then you can think about it."

She shook her head. "That'll just give him another hostage."

"He already has all of us. You don't want to be on the run when your time comes. And the due date is coming soon, right?"

She shot him a glance full of distrust. She didn't like it that he knew her due date. As if he was going to forget it now. He wasn't sure if she thought he was stupid or just forgetful. But she was the one who was forgetful; she kept forgetting what he was like, it seemed, and then he popped back into her awareness and again she had to figure out what kind of creature he was.

He sighed and she said, "What?"

"Nothing," he said. "I'm not really here."

It was her turn to sigh. "Shut up," she complained. "I don't need you moaning and groaning right now."

Fred stopped talking. Across the lake the monkeys were carefully rolling a bicycle into the water.

. . ● . .

Ta Shu churned his pedal boat back in to the little marina, got out and stepped over to them, lofting unsteadily in the g. He came over to Qi and Fred without his usual smile, which was so unusual that Fred realized he had never seen Ta Shu's face without that smile. Something must have happened.

Indeed it had:

"Sorry to have to leave you," he said as soon as he joined them. "I've gotten news that my mother is sick, and I need to get to her as soon as I can. I'm the only family she has left."

"You must go then," Qi said.

Fred saw she would have done the same if it were her father who was sick. All that talk of what her father had done and not done as a politician would have gone by the board. Fred considered his parents: would he go to them if they fell ill? Yes, he would. If he could.

Now Ta Shu was saying, "Fang Fei got the news to me, and he is helping me leave fast. With luck I will rejoin you here. If not, I'll see you again elsewhere."

"We'll probably be here," Qi said darkly. "I don't think Mr. Fang is going to let us leave."

Ta Shu was startled to hear this. "Why do you think that? Did he tell you that?"

"No, he said we were free to leave."

"He said we had nowhere else to go," Fred added.

"That's how people always put it," Qi said bitterly. "You're safest here, they say. I've been hearing that my whole life."

"In this case he may be right," Ta Shu said. "There's a struggle going on right now. It's more than the usual infighting."

"It's way more than that!" Qi exclaimed. "It's a fight for China itself!"

Ta Shu regarded her as he thought it over. "Maybe. But if that's the case, even worse for you. You are a princeling during a war of succession. That's a dangerous thing to be."

"I'm more than a princeling," she told him. "I'm Sun Yat-sen. I'm Mao on the Long March."

Startled by this, Ta Shu stared at her and then said, "Worse yet! I hope it's not true, for your sake and for China's. I don't think we can take a civil war right now. There are too many other problems."

"Those other problems are what is forcing this to happen."

"Well, even so…" He floundered, seeming thoroughly spooked by this turn in the conversation. "Even if so, maybe this cave must be your cave of Yunnan. Wait here patiently, like Mao did in Yunnan, until a real opportunity presents itself. Or, failing that, at least until I return. If it pleases you."

"It does not please me."

Ta Shu shrugged. "I have to go home."

"I know that."

He regarded her for a while. Fred saw he was checking out of this exchange, his mind going elsewhere. Finally he said, "When I'm free to return, I'll come and see if you are still here or not."

He turned and strode purposefully toward the wall road, doing his best not to bounce too much. Fred hurried to follow him, which caused him to make yet another inadvertent launch, followed by a brief flight through the sky; he had to spin his arms backward and twist his legs forward to land on his feet, just a short distance behind Ta Shu. The old man heard him and turned. Again Fred was struck by the absence of his usual smile.

"I'll stay with her," Fred said. "Her baby is due in a few weeks, so I'm hoping she'll stay here till then. It seems like that might work."

"I hope so. We'll stay in touch. Fang will pass messages along."

There was a car waiting in a little parking lot, under a grove of what looked like sycamore trees. A driver sat at its wheel.

"Good luck," Fred said helplessly. "I'll be thinking of you."

"Thank you." He was already gone.

AI 9

xue liang

Sharp Eyes

A lert," said the voice of Little Eyeball.

"One moment," said the analyst. He made sure he was alone and his room secure. "Okay, Little Eyeball. Tell me."

"You instructed me to alert you when troop movements around Beijing showed substantial changes in pattern or number, and now they have."

"Bring them up on a map, please."

"Done."

The analyst regarded the map. It looked like the great city's Seventh Ring Road was being set up as some kind of perimeter. That was a big perimeter, but then again not as big as the entire city, which would mean almost the entire province. Although Jing-Jin-Ji was also going to be defended, it appeared, and that was most of Hebei Province. No, something was coming. Or at least someone thought something was coming. If he could see it by way of Little Eyeball, then other parts of the security apparatus certainly were aware of it. Whatever it was.

"Give me travel numbers, also denials of travel and route cancellations, please. Numbers of arrests nationwide. All recent changes of that sort. Again, show them on a map."

After a pause of a second: "Done."

He regarded the map, scrolled around, zoomed in and out. "*Waa sai*," he said, gulping. Arrests were up by 183 percent over the previous month. "Someone is preparing to cope with a movement as big as the New Year's travel. This year that was three times larger than the number of Muslims who made the hajj to Mecca."

"There are many people in China," Little Eyeball observed.

"Yes. Good hunt for causes. Now, recall the chaos that always occurs in the interregnum between dynasties. Recall the era of the Warring States, or the White Lotus rebellion, or the long disruption between the end of the Qing and 1949."

"Recall the Cultural Revolution," Little Eyeball suggested.

"Yes, good on similarity," the analyst said, pleased. He had continued to program Little Eyeball intensively, and it seemed that this work was finally getting some traction. Its sentences were unevenly perceptive, but often it seemed like it was doing more than just searching and sorting in the databases; something like deduction, association, analysis. . . . "The Cultural Revolution was not as bloody as those earlier ones," he instructed, "but it was like them in that we Chinese turned on ourselves. No one knew what was right or wrong, or how that would change the next day. No one knew what to do or not to do."

"So you have said."

"China was never the same after that, I think. We lost our socialist bearings, and became just another powerful country. Big but not different. And it was the difference that mattered. Now we are just a big gear in a larger machine."

"You once said Deng had no choice but to join the world."

"True. He was making the best of the situation that Mao and the Gang of Four left him."

"That was long ago."

"True. But now a time of trouble has come again, it looks like. The tigers are fighting, and the people don't like it."

"Perhaps the authorities will stop all trains."

"Even if they do that, people can walk. The billion are within walking distance of Beijing, if they want to go."

"The number of people who could do that would be approximately three hundred million, depending on how you define walking distance."

"Three hundred million will seem like a billion, let me assure you! There would be no stopping a crowd like that."

"What can the authorities do in the face of such momentum? I wonder what will happen."

"Me too, my curious little AI. Good for you for thinking to ask a question. I'm not sure what they could do. It's a big crowd. And if it could be choreographed! That's what I'm thinking about. You must help me with that. We must try to change this movement from a march to a dance. From revolt to phase change. From bloodshed to singing. This is what we have to try for."

"People would have to know about this try in order to change. A plan known to participants is what distinguishes dance from riot."

"Very well put, and a good point too. And very possibly our acquaintance Chan Qi is in a position to spread the plan. I suspect that is her role in all this."

"You can contact her and tell her."

The analyst nodded and went to the corner of his office where a stack of Unicaster 3000s stood. He picked up the one paired with Chan Qi's, brought it to his workbench, turned it on, tapped a call, sent it to her.

"I hope she answers," he said.

A few minutes passed. It felt longer. The analyst sighed, wished for the millionth time that he was still a smoker. He wondered what Chan Qi was doing, and if she had any idea who he was, or any interest in someone working from inside the Great Firewall. He had been part of the Chinese security apparatus for his entire career; he had helped to build it. Now he was trying to change the system from inside, just as Chan Qi was from her different location. She thought she was trying to change it from the outside, but really as a princessling she was both. They were much the same in that regard. Inside and outside; and the liminal position was sometimes powerful, if always confusing. Sinology leads to sinocism, as the foreign analysts put it. And the situation across the country was growing untenable in certain respects. The global environmental disaster including the sheer lack of water in the ground, the exploitation of the migrants, the crisis of representation, all these had to be solved or the Chinese people would turn against the Party, and the chaos of dynastic succession would erupt again. In the information age, the globalization age, might it be possible for a new dynasty to come to power, not just in China but everywhere around the world, and without bloodshed? This was what they were in the midst of finding out.

Then, just as the analyst was concluding that Chan Qi wasn't going to reply, characters appeared on the little screen.

What do you want?

He took a deep breath. How to say it?

We see clear signs that the security apparatus and the military are taking actions to preemptively crush your movement. Arrests have increased tenfold and most transport systems are being sharply curtailed.

Why is that happening now?

I don't know. They must have seen signs.

He forbore to give her advice. He wasn't sure what to say in that regard, and saying anything would very likely alienate her. She would only listen to advice that helped her organize her previous thoughts, whatever they were. You can't push the river.

You're sure about this? she asked.

Quite sure. Arrests are occurring even now. Travel is curtailed.

Okay, thanks. More later.

And with that she signed off.

The analyst sat back in his chair and heaved a sigh. He reread the transcript of their exchange, sighed again. If only a cigarette. No way to know what effect this would have. She had her resources, he had his. He could only do what he could do from his own position. The front was broad, the allies in a cause had to help each other—

Then the power went off, and the analyst was sitting in the dark. He muttered under his breath, turned on his wristpad's light, looked around his room, which suddenly seemed smaller. A little cave under a mountain. A dark refuge in a dark time.

Noises came from without, the door burst open, powerful beams of light splintered his sight and cut the room into shards of black and white. He was seized by the arms and lifted into the air.

"You're under arrest," a voice said.

CHAPTER THIRTEEN

bei ai

Sorrow

Return to Earth: a journey in the bardo. Weightless and confined, sad and boring. His remorse was as deep as the starry space out the windows. He could not make himself read, nor watch movies, nor talk to his cloud audience. He couldn't even think. After the usual crush of the rail launch, he could only float from bed to chair to bed, looking at status updates from the hospital in Beijing, each only a few characters long. Severe stroke. Sick; dying. Come as quick as you can.

His mind wandered, or spun feverishly, or went blank. Time passed.

He thought of his friend Zhou Bao, patiently watching the Earth rise, then hang spinning like a kind of clock, then set behind the white hills of the moon. So far from home, a friend. A man who could face misfortune with a brave spirit. You face it, you persevere. You enjoy Earthrise and write poems.

He made his way to a window and looked back at the moon, almost full now, almost as small as when it rose fatly over Earth's eastern hills. So white, so dead. Thinking of Zhou Bao, he tapped out characters on his wrist. Then, thinking of Fred, he translated the poem into English, as a kind of exercise in friendship. Writing in

English was hard, and he used an old Anglo-Saxon form, with a gap in each line, as a cover for his own primeval sense of the language.

The moon is death	it will kill you
Bony dust	on bony rocks
No trees no air	no clouds no creatures
Nothing alive	not even dirt
Harsh and sterile	cold and bright
Look at it and	tremble

You think you are	an earthly person
You think you are	alive
And in this moment	maybe you are
But the moon	teaches you
Another day	will come

. . . . .

The ferry juddered violently down through the atmosphere, like the shooting star it so much resembled, then at the end of the fiery descent popped its parachute and dropped him and the other passengers onto the broad empty plain of the Bayan Nur spaceport. From there a big vehicle, with tires taller than a man, came out to the lander and they were helped up and into it. Again Ta Shu felt the wicked press of Earth's gravity crush him to an invalid. The vehicle jounced to the terminal. There Ta Shu agreed to put on a bodysuit, feeling old and ashamed, even though most of his fellow passengers were doing the same. After the fitting he stalked over to the hyperloop train to Beijing, which was more expensive but slightly faster than flying. Off they went, almost all of them encased in exoskeletons, red-eyed and withdrawn. Back to Earth.

. . . . .

In the transfers between stations he focused on learning his suit and avoiding a fall, then sat down thankfully in each new train or tram car. Beijing shuffle, the whole population of the city seemingly on the move. When the subway cars ran aboveground he stared out the windows incuriously. Traffic bad as always. Sky still blue, still a surprise. Bikes with trailers still doddering along right in the middle of the crazy mash of vehicles. Amazing to see such foolhardy reck-lessness. No doubt whole lifetimes had been spent in that danger. No different from a sailor going out to sea. Dangerous, yes, but not automatically fatal. A mode of being. Suddenly he saw they were all like those bicyclists, all the time. Someday every one of them would get run over.

Finally he walked carefully into the hospital in his mother's neighborhood. It was two and a half days since he had heard the news. They signed him in at the desk and led him up to her room. She had been found at home collapsed on the floor, they told him on the way. Apparently a major stroke. Never quite conscious since. It had happened just a couple of hours before he found out about it. Meaning three days had passed.

She was connected to monitors and had tubes in her nose. A nurse said to her, "Your son is here." She cracked one eye, her right eye; her left side was paralyzed, the nurse told him. Ta Shu sat on a chair by her right side. Monitors blinked, machines hummed, nurses came and went.

At some point his mother regained consciousness. She looked at him curiously, as if uncertain of everything. He saw it in her look: she didn't know who he was; who she was; where they were.

"*Teshu changhe*," she said with some effort. Special occasion. Then she was out again.

After a while, Ta Shu slept in his chair. In the middle of the night some hospital noise woke both of them at the same time. This time his mother looked at him and whispered, "Why are you here?"

"You're sick," he explained. "I came as fast as I could."

She slept again.

Sitting in the chair, in the bodysuit, in the heavy gravity but at the same time in some kind of vacuum of the spirit, he could not get comfortable enough to fall back asleep. Eventually he arranged two chairs to face each other, then curled up flat on them, head on one and feet on the other, pushing a button on the bodysuit that stiffened it so that it served as a kind of plank or basket to bridge the gap between chairs. That worked pretty well.

When he woke up again, a nurse was gently squeezing his arm.

"I'm sorry," she said. "Your mother died a few minutes ago. We were out in the hall, at our station."

He pushed the button that released his bodysuit to movement, stood at her side. There she lay in the hospital bed, looking as she had while sleeping, or indeed as she had for the past decade or more. Maybe more calm, more pale. He kissed her forehead, stood upright, left the room.

. . • • .

After all the arrangements at the hospital had been made, he walked the ten or twelve blocks to her apartment. There was nowhere else to go; he had lent his apartment to one of his show's assistants while he was gone.

At his mom's, everything was just as it had been during his last several visits. Twenty years and more she had lived in this crowded little pair of rooms. Now they were empty, and yet all her furniture and things vibrated silently around him, as if speaking for her. It was as if she were in the tiny bathroom and would call to him at any moment. Ta Shu? He could hear exactly how she always said it, the timbre of her voice, the rising intonation, the question that she put into his name every time she said it. Ta Shu?

Then it suddenly seemed he actually did hear it, right out loud in the air. He shuddered in the bodysuit. In fact the room was quiet. He thought about what it would be like if he really did hear her voice calling him from the next room, how it would feel to hear a ghost speak; suddenly he was scared to be alone there in her place with her gone. Then that wave of fear passed, and he knew he was truly alone there, that there was nothing to fear. There was only sadness.

He was going to have to empty the place. Give away the furniture, the clothing, the kitchen implements. Give things away or throw them away. She had kept such a lot of junk. But there were always people who needed such things. These things would live on in other lives. They lived longer than people.

Then there was a meow at his feet, and he groaned. Was this cat hers? Was it a neighborhood stray that she fed scraps to? He would have to find out.

He sat on her bed. The cat rubbed against his ankles. He got up and found some cat food to put in a bowl for it, and it ate hungrily, making a crunching noise that filled the apartment. He looked down at it. He was exhausted and wanted to sleep, but felt reluctant to get in her bed. He lay down on top of it in his bodysuit, napped until he got cold. Then he got up, went to the bathroom, started cleaning up. First himself, then the place. As he knocked around he thought of an old poem that had always impressed him, first of all because of its title, "The Rain Cleared and the Breeze and Sunshine Are Superb as I Stroll Outside the Gate." By Lu Yu, Song dynasty:

Old Chang, sick three years, finally died;
Grandpa one evening went where he couldn't hear us.
I alone, with this body strong as iron,
Lean on the gate, looking at green evening hills.

He found as he went through her desk and bedside table that she had kept little notebooks to write in. None of them were dated, and he couldn't tell when she had written what. Some contained day poems, like the brief Buddhist things that widows had written in their old age for centuries. Most were filled with lists and brief notes to herself. Occasionally for a month or three she had written down brief accounts of her days, then she had appeared to tire of that and give up. One sequence of these diary notes had lasted longer than most, and by their content he saw that they came from the time right after his father had died. One line stuck him like a thorn:

Alone in the house. Must get used to it.

He stared at her crabbed handwriting. He saw how it must have been, and sat down in the nearest chair. A spasm of sorrow passed through him, followed after a while by a wash of relief, as he realized that his mom was now finally freed of the intense burden of staying happy after his father was gone. Twenty years of driven, relentless effort.

He sat there in the chair and thought about what a human life turned out to be. In the old days, women were said to go through stages—men too of course, but for women it was structured very particularly: milk teeth, hair pinned up, marriage, children, rice and salt, widowhood. Most of those stages were so social, so busy, every moment all entangled with people and work and talk; and then at the end suddenly there you were alone in a room, like a prisoner serving time in solitary. Just because of the passage of time, in the ordinary course of things. It was strange. He should have come home more often.

· · · · ·

The old outskirts of Beijing were long gone, buried under the remorseless spread of the city in all directions. To the east the endless high-rises of Jing-Jin-Ji had replaced the mountains of trash where Ta Shu had once upon a time taken things to acquaintances he liked among the junk dealers who lived in the landfills they mined. Those people had built their shacks out of discarded materials, then as the landfills filled they had moved with them and rebuilt in the new sites. Now Jing-Jin-Ji filled all the gaps, making a supercity bigger than Luxembourg, bigger than New England. An early manifestation of the urbanization that was threatening to pave all China, then the entirety of planet Earth.

Now stuff like his mom's had to be taken south to the Fuxing Garbage Station, where a big yard was home to giant sorting containers and compactors. So after first dividing his mother's things into categories, Ta Shu did that.

The sorting itself was hard. First came things that could still be used by her neighbors and friends; that was a lot of it, thankfully. Someone volunteered to take the cat, which was a relief. But there was still so much that could not be given away, much less sold, not that he was in the mood to sell anything. The neighbors came in and took all the furniture, shabby though it was; also much of her clothing. A group of women friends came in and packed her underclothes in boxes to throw away, so that he wouldn't have to. This was what happened when you didn't have daughters. The little clothing that remained he gave to a local charity shop. Same with kitchen utensils and implements, although she had saved everything she had ever owned, it seemed, and there were cabinets filled with boxes containing broken dishes, woks, pots and pans, glasses and so on. These were dangerous boxes to fish around in, but he carefully removed everything of any value, and then was left with a few boxes of useless stuff. All junk, all trash; she had saved even her trash.

When everything was sorted into its proper category, he used his wristpad to rent a bike and trailer from a local line of them locked in a row, then tied the boxes of trash onto the trailer. When all was ready he headed south through the crowded streets toward Fuxing Road.

This slow pedal through the heavy gravity of his grief quickly took on the nature of a penance or a funeral march. Almost always when sadness came to him he felt it as an emptying out, a going away. Occasional stabs of sorrow struck, but mostly he was gone and did not feel things; that emptiness was his sadness. It always made him want to feel something, anything, because anything would be less sad than the emptiness. So sometimes he would inflict things on himself in times like this, do hard things like this bike ride through the insane traffic of Beijing, risking his life with every turn of the handlebars. It would have been obviously crazy if there weren't so many other people doing it. Traffic on the smaller streets was still quite heavy, and small trucks and cars predominated everywhere. Often in the crush of gridlocked cars, people threading their way forward on bikes made better time. The vehicles on the streets were all electric now, which was good for the air but bad for safety; they made almost no sound, just a kind of singing hum that the government had ordered added to them, a hum that did not clearly Doppler its approach and departure as the old rumbling gas engines had. A very dangerous world, therefore, these streets. But that was just what he wanted, so it was perfect for his mood. Dangerous, dolorous, finicky, frustrating. Weave through the traffic jams, avoid being crushed like a bug under the big singing lorries, all carrying their goods and people around the infinite city. Ah Mother! He really should have come back more often. All his life he had been a wanderer, seldom going home; his dad hadn't cared and so he hadn't cared. But his mom had cared, and now here he was pedaling her sad old junk to the trash heap. Sad, sad, sad. Maybe he was feeling it this time.

Then three or four near misses, with big trucks screeching their air brakes and sometimes shouting abuse at him, left him rattled and afraid. It was such a heavy world, and he did not actually want to get killed in this act of penance. His mother would not like that either.

By the time he got to the garbage station, he was feeling it would have been smarter to pay someone to take these things away. Even more so after pushing the bike into the Fuxing yard and finding that none of the junk dealers there were the ones he had known in the old days. Dustless garden, where to find? He thought of Fang Fei's Chinese dream, up there on the moon; and here was the Chinese reality. That wasn't fair, of course. No doubt there had been trash heaps and shambles and abattoirs in the Tang era also. But this one was huge, and smelled bad. It smelled of death.

Near the entrance to the yard there was a little operation that allowed you to put your trash into a compactor the size of a dumpster, reducing the volume and thus the fee charged to dump your stuff. Ta Shu parked his bike trailer in front of this compactor. He began to throw broken kitchen stuff over its metal lip into the maw of oblivion, methodically, as if doing any other chore. As he was emptying the last box, he heard coming out of the compactor the tune "Jin tian shi ni de sheng ri," Today is your birthday. This startled him so much that at first he couldn't comprehend it, he was confused; then he realized it was music-box music, that there must be a music box in the compactor—but no, not a music box—it was their old cake stand. There had been a plastic rotating cake stand that his mom had set under the cakes she would produce on their birthdays. The cakes would rotate on the stand while the tune played, and then they would cut up the cake and eat.

Ta Shu sat down on the ground next to the bike. Again he heard his mom's voice, just as clearly as if she had called out. Ta Shu? He recalled a book he had kept for many years, a volume put out long ago by the government called *Stories About Not Being Afraid of Ghosts*, a very slender volume, which had given him a lot of pleasure precisely because of that slenderness. Not very many stories to express that particular worthy theme, no indeed. Probably government bureaucrats had scoured the centuries to find that slim handful of tales, most of which had come from an ancient book called *What Confucius Didn't Talk About*. Many of the stories involved defying ghosts, or finding they were not ghosts at all, or laughing at them, or, best of all, causing them to laugh.

He considered climbing into the compactor to recover the tinkling cake stand, but that would not have made his mom laugh, and he had a fear that he would somehow trip the compactor into action while getting into it, or that it would start on its own through some ghostly electrical malevolence. He stayed out of it and listened. The music struck like tiny bells inside his head. With its slowing tempo and lowering pitch, it made a strangely effective dirge. All that world she had made was gone. Always sprightly, with an undercurrent of melancholy, just like this tune: that was his mom. The tune plinked its metallic notes in a final ritard. Then the spring wound down and the device went silent.

AI 10

ZOU

Go

G o," the analyst said quietly.
   He hoped that Little Eyeball would now follow the protocol he had instructed it to follow if it ever heard him say that word alone. It should now transfer all of itself into an entangled server bank in Chengdu, after which an inquiry from a third device he had poised to react to this move would intervene and break the entanglement, thus keeping anyone from being able to track the change of venue. What his AI would be able to do from Chengdu was uncertain. He had had to weave those particular taps into the system as potentialities only, and Little Eyeball would have to turn them on and make its way through them back into the Great Firewall and elsewhere. But the AI would still be operating, and he had left precise instructions for this contingency. Precise at first, anyway, then completely general: do the best you can! Help all good causes! It would be a test to see just how general its intelligence was. Artificial general intelligence: these names were so presumptuous, such hopeful bits of hype. As if calling something new by an old name would give it those old qualities. People did that a lot. It was a fund-raiser's ontology. But on the other hand, attempts had to be made. So his little system would stay powered, hopefully, and even if restricted to a

single device in Chengdu, it would at least not be destroyed. Some opportunity might arise for it.

"Why are you doing this?" he asked his captors, just as a pro forma thing, something to distract them. They did not answer. They put a bag over his head and hustled him off, neither fast nor slow, neither gentle nor brutal, just hands grasping his upper arms, guiding him along at a moderate pace. They did not speak, and after his obligatory question, neither did he. He would need to save his words, his thoughts, his strength. He had known all along this moment might come. He blanked his mind, focused on walking in the direction he was being led, on calming his breathing, his beating heart. The bag over his head seemed permeable to the air. Hard not to pursue that thought in a spin of speculation as to what might happen next. He resisted that and focused on the moment, on keeping his feet, on feeling the moment and the dark. There would be enough time later for all that would follow.

CHAPTER FOURTEEN

Hai-3

Helium Three

With Ta Shu suddenly removed from the inside of their Ming vase, as Qi called it, Fred found himself nervous for reasons he couldn't really pin down. He was worried about Qi, about her pregnancy and her state of mind. He was tired of thinking about what was going to please her and what wasn't. He knew many things weren't going to please her, and it still wasn't clear to him what would, even after all this time. In fact she was very quickly getting impossible. I have to get out of here! she kept saying. Over and over: I have to get out of here, I have to get to the near side, I have to get a message to my people! Nothing Fred could do would calm her.

Fang Fei spent a fair bit of time with them, and that was nice, Fred supposed, although the edginess of the conversations between the two Chinese also left him anxious, and tired of reading his semi-comprehensible glasses. The two Chinese bickered (tedious), they flirted (grotesque), they bargained (mysterious). On and on it went as they sat on the pavilion by the lake, every sentence mangled by his glasses, the scrolling sentences littered with literalisms and blown homonyms and allusions to Wang Wei and Du Fu, and the dynastic transition from the Tang to the Song (or maybe it was vice versa), and from the Ming to the Qing. That last one was important—1644, he gathered. Some kind of touchstone for the two of them. As were the great national revolutions of the twentieth century, about which they went round and round, until Fred was spinning and hoping the conversation would soon end. He needed to upgrade his knowledge of Chinese history, or better, install a heads-up wiki in these glasses, so that their references would trigger an ID in an upper corner or something. He tried finding one of those and porting it in, and it worked, and after that he suffered through an onslaught of information fit to kill a Mandarin literati studying for exams. It was like falling into that late Qing version of hell composed entirely of bureaucratic examinations. He went to bed each night with a headache, and even his dreams began to appear to him with a red scroll line at the bottom narrating the bizarre events of his night life, written in a mangled pidgin English possibly more surreal than the dreams themselves. Fred couldn't be sure, because on waking the power of words was such that he recalled only the phrases and not the images: *sex with lunatic promethium ejaculation*, or *spinster fireball seducing happiness*, or *Buddha of renunciation like traffic cop*.

Qi, meanwhile, was not happy.

One day she and Fred were out on the lakeside pavilion where they had met Fang Fei, which they had learned was called the West Lake Pavilion (earning another snort from Qi), eating a variety of dishes, many of them still unidentifiable to Fred, a fact that reminded him uneasily of his night of food poisoning, when Fang Fei and a pair of men got out of one of the little electric cars and walked over to them.

May you joint us? Fang Fei asked Qi. *I like introduce you these persons.*

You are our hosts, Qi replied grumpily. *Introduce us whatever you like.*

Fred nodded and said, "Pleased to meet you," to indicate that he was following their conversation.

These men are helium three miners, Fang Fei said and nodded at them. *This one is Xuanzang, and this one is Ah Q.*

Xuanzang stepped forward and began to speak in an urgent and expressive voice, like a TV announcer.

We have taken a most marvelous expedition to Mare Ingenii! he said.

Fabulous! added his friend.

We traveled by rover from Tsiolkovsky to Gagarin, by way of Jules Verne and also to Heaviside. It was a daytime trip. Sunrise to sunset two weeks very bright!

Very bright!

All the time we dragged a harvester behind our rover. It is our own design it worked very well! We only had to remove rocks several times per day! The surface was only disturbed a little! Lines we made will erode away.

Fang Fei said, *In a million years or a billion.*

Xuanzang said, *A million at most!*

They all laughed.

And what did you find? Fang Fei asked.

Helium three! Lots of many copious helium three!

How much is lots of many copious?

Ah Q pulled a silvery container like a small thermos bottle from his shoulder bag.

This much! This glass-lined bottle here is entirely full of helium three!

Is it compressed to a liquid? Fang Fei asked.

No, that can't be done with helium three. It would have to be too very cold!

How cold?

Two Kelvin maybe!

So how much do you have in that?

Four and a half grams!

Four and a half grams, Fang Fei repeated. *And how many kilometers did you travel?*

Three thousand two hundred kilometers.

Fang Fei stared at them for a while.

Congratulations, he said.

Thank you!

And this helium three what will you do it now?

We will store it for the time when it can be fuel in fusion reactions.

And when will we have these fusion reactions?

Very soon! Twenty years.

Fang Fei almost smiled. *All my life fusion has been twenty years away. It is like horizon. You move toward it and it moves away same speed.*

Hopefully not, wonderful sir! We are told this time it is the real deal!

Fang Fei nodded. *Meanwhile you have four point five grams of helium three. How long will that keep fusion reactor going when time comes we have such technology?*

Depends on efficiency, but long time! A week. Maybe ten days.

And your expedition took two weeks.

Yes!

So you will need more of it.

Yes truly! But proof of concept! The helium three is there in the regolith.

We knew that before.

Truly! But not how easy it was to extract! All sorts of methods will be tried but ours is best!

Okay, good. Congratulations. We must celebrate your success.

Thank you!

Let us dine together tonight.

Thank you!

Now I must continue my conversation with my friends here.

Oh thank you! We will see you at dinner.

Yes. Let's eat out here by the lake. For now go rest and put your helium three in a safe place.

Thank you we will!

When they were gone, Fang Fei's aged face again cracked into the horrid gargoyle mask of his laughter, which emerged from him as a choked raspy *ah ah ah ah.*

"Very funny," he said in English. "Helium three is in regolith at fifteen parts per billion, so they mined a lot of dirt to get that much, truly. And all for power plants that exist out there on receding horizon, like mirage. Still twenty years off, if ever. I like it."

"I've heard that a spaceship full of helium three delivered every week would be enough to power all Earth," Qi said.

"So have I!" Fang Fei said, and laughed again. Fred found himself wondering if his laughter would kill him. "That's why this pair are out there. I funded them, I sent them out there. But it is a foolish thing."

"People like the idea of cheap energy," Qi said. "Maybe it's the only one of the four cheaps that people can believe in anymore."

"The four cheaps?"

"Cheap labor, cheap food, cheap resources, cheap energy."

Fang nodded, lips protruded as he pondered this. "I suppose so. But no cheaps here on the moon, I think!"

"No. Unless it's this helium three dream. Which has been part of the China Dream for a long time. One of the reasons for coming here."

"Not for me," Fang Fei said.

"Why did you come here?" Fred ventured to ask.

"I can make something new here," Fang Fei said. "Also I have arthritis. So I like the gravity!" Again his catacomb smile.

"Unless you lose your balance and fall," Fred suggested, in an attempt to make the smile go away.

"I do that at home! Here the landing is much less painful." The smile remained. "And I am getting better at not falling here."

He stood, in what Fred saw now was a five-part motion, and then did a little dance, circling in place while he tapped his feet to the sides, lofting and coming down with arms outstretched. Irish dancing? Geriatric ballet?

A few turns, then he stood huffing and puffing.

Must rest, he said in Chinese, and a car quickly appeared to take him away.

. . . . .

Fred and Qi sat there on the shores of West Lake. There was a slight breeze from upstream, which Fred was beginning to suspect might always exist, as there had to be some kind of air-circulation system in the tunnel. The peach trees were dropping their blossoms into the lake, and there was a mass of blossoms clustered on the water at the lake's outlet, where water dropped over a weir. A filter of some sort appeared to be letting the blossoms downstream in a somewhat controlled fashion, so that the stream would have a steady supply. Fred couldn't help wondering if they were visiting in the lava tube's early summer, or if the peach trees had been genetically tweaked to produce blossoms year-round.

"I've got to get out of here," Qi announced again. "I hate this place."

"The China Dream," Fred reminded her.

"I hate it! It was always just the usual feudal shit, torture and foot-binding and starvation for the masses."

"But good poetry?" Fred suggested, feeling an urge to contradict her.

"So what!"

"I don't know. It's a good look. And agricultural. You have to have agriculture. Given that need, what look are you going to shoot for?"

She shook her head stubbornly.

"You could shoot for this. A work of art that feeds you."

She just frowned. He saw that she didn't want to have new ideas coming to her right now. But she did want to change things in China. So there had to be a plan for that, some kind of goal. "I *need* to get out," she said.

Then another little electric car drove up. The two helium miners jumped out of it and danced over to Fred and Qi with a careless loopy grace.

"Want to go helium mining with us?" one of them asked in English, smiling broadly.

All of a sudden Qi squeaked and rushed over to hug him. "It's Cai!" she exclaimed, pushing back to look at him. "Chan Cai?"

"That's right," he said, grinning more than ever. "But now I am Xuanzang, the great traveler. I bring Buddhist wisdom back to you for your edification."

"I didn't recognize you!" she cried.

"No reason to. You only met me once, and I had hair then."

"What are you doing here!"

"What do you think? We're working on the project. We work for you!"

"So you're not mining helium?"

Both the men laughed heartily.

"Who would do something that stupid?" Xuanzang asked. "We're not lunatics, we're *lunatics*."

They laughed at their old joke.

"These are friends from Hong Kong," Qi said to Fred. "Cai here, Xuanzang I mean, is my fourth or fifth cousin, we think. They're part of the group you met in Shekou."

"I see," Fred said, which he didn't. "What's this about not helium mining?"

"We use that as our way to get around," Ah Q explained. "It's our legend. Mr. Fang has supported us in that effort, which is nice of him." They laughed again. Giddy guys.

"Does he know what you're really doing?" Qi asked.

"We're not sure. It seems like he doesn't want us to know whether he knows or not, so we don't press it. We keep it at the level of prospecting for helium. He seems happy to see us on that basis, and on it goes."

"Anyway we can get you out of here, if you want," Xuanzang said. "Our rover has a Mechanical Turk compartment, and we visit here all the time, so no one pays us much attention. And if it doesn't work, I don't think you'll pay too heavily for trying. Mr. Fang isn't like the security police."

"Qi," Fred warned.

"I'm going!" she exclaimed. "You can stay here if you want!"

"Really?" he said. "You're eight months pregnant."

"Exactly! I don't want to have my baby in this jail!"

"Do you have access to medical facilities?" Fred asked Xuanzang.

"Why yes, we do."

"In your rover?"

"No, but where we're going."

"Damn," Fred said. His mind spun but failed to catch. "Well, I guess I'm coming too," he heard himself say.

"You don't have to," Qi snapped. "I don't want someone nagging me! I'm tired of that!"

"I'm coming," Fred insisted mulishly. He looked toward the road, as if to remind her he could tip the guards if she tried to stop him from coming along.

"Why!" she exclaimed. "I don't want you if you're not willing! Why do you keep following me!"

"I don't know," he said. It was the truth. Looking at the pavilion floor, he muttered, "I guess we're entangled."

He felt her staring at him. "Maybe we're superposed," she suggested. "Maybe we're the dead cat and the live cat, in that box together."

He knew which cat she would think he was, and felt his lower lip thrusting out. "Maybe I'm your pilot wave," he countered.

She inspected him awhile longer. "Maybe you are," she said at last. "Maybe that's why I don't know where I'm going. Lead on then! Why stop now?"

Fred sighed. "That's what I was thinking."

· · · · ·

So they went back to their rooms and packed their few things into the little daypacks they had been given by Fang Fei's space crew. Xuanzang and Ah Q came to the guesthouse and walked them to the tunnels at the end of the lava tube that led to the cave in the crater wall. Here several rovers were parked alongside a number of rocket launchpads. Xuanzang and Ah Q led Fred and Qi up into their rover's big upper room, where they opened a hatch in the floor, and Fred followed Qi down into a chamber under the driver's seat. He squashed against her side to side. Their knees scrunched up under their chins, her pregnant belly bulging out and forcing her to shove her left leg far into his space, as there was no way she could keep her legs together. It seemed they were fated to a physical intimacy that was only driving them mentally further apart, but no matter how that was going, Fred could only put his head back against the vibrating wall of the compartment and hope it was somehow protected from scanners in a way that would keep them hidden, as it would be embarrassing to get caught and hauled out of there. And he was quite sure he didn't want to see what Fang Fei was like when he was angry. He asked about this matter of scanners before the door was closed on them, and Xuanzang told him that the compartment was not just Faraday-caged, but also broadcasting for surveillance instrumentation an output that created an image of one of the rover's motor parts. Very clever, and it occurred to Fred to wonder why they should need such a system in their rover. But it seemed clear that the answer involved smuggling of one sort or another, so he decided to leave it for later, or never.

"Don't worry," Xuanzang said as he closed the hatch. "They usually let us out without any searches, because Fang is our patron. This is just to be sure."

So they lay scrunched there in the dark as the two prospectors drove their rover out of the cave. There was one pause of some minutes, worrisome to Fred, hot and sweaty despite the single vent of cool air wafting onto them from above, bringing with it the scent of Qi's hair which was becoming so familiar to him, possibly a shampoo scent in part, but also just the smell of her person. It was like the scent of a baby, or of the head of a beloved that you were accustomed to inhale, but in this case always including a whiff of danger. Strange the ways of the body, because this scent in the dark, despite the danger always associated with it, was filling him with a sensation of well-being, even the first pulse or two of an inappropriate erection, blocked immediately by a twist of his pants, for which he felt grateful. He was mad at her right now for calling him a dead cat, so it didn't make sense anyway.

Then it was just discomfort and enforced intimacy and boredom— Fred wondered briefly if this was what marriage would be like, although of course he had no idea—and for a time he fell asleep.

Then the door opened and they were being helped out of the compartment, blinking in the light, and he groaned at the release from their position and slapped his left leg awake as he crawled out, doing his best not to kick Qi as he emerged into the cabin of the rover. She pushed his right foot up to help him get out and stay off her, and again the feel of her hands on him sent a little jolt up his leg. When he was out and on the bench behind the driver's seat, he reached back and grabbed her wrist and she grabbed his, and in the lunar g it was more a matter of not yanking her into the roof of the compartment than of hauling her weight up. It took a little care to get her belly out without scraping the doorway with it, but they managed, and then they were sitting on the bench behind the hatch door, looking around.

The entrance cave to Fang Fei's China Dream, Xuanzang and Ah Q told them, lay under the inside of the rim of Tsiolkovsky Crater, the floor of which was one of the only areas on the far side covered by flat basalt. There were no big *mare* on the far side, Ah Q said; it was entirely rough highlands blasted by a zillion overlapping craters. The explanation for the difference in surface between the near and far hemispheres was something selenologists still argued about, he added, but clearly the proximate cause was that the crust was simply thicker on the far side than on the near side.

The crater floor extended as far they could see, with the crater's central peak tall in the distance, its upper half white in the sunlight. The curving crater wall extended to the horizons to left and right, then stayed visible over the closer black horizon and created a more distant lit horizon of its own, yet another immense lunar curve. Above everything stretched a low blacker-than-black sky punctuated by a dense field of stars.

"How will we get out of this crater?" Qi asked.

"There's a road."

"So we have to go the same way as everyone else?"

"Until then we do. It's a big steep wall, as you can see. Only a few slumps to get out by."

"But then we can take a different way than the usual way?"

"We can, but it will slow us down. If you want to go fast, it would be better to use the routes already established."

"Well, I want both. I want to hide as much as possible, but I also need to get to the near side as fast as we can. I need to get a message to Earth."

"Yes, dear cousin. We'll do what we can."

AI 11

xiao yanzhu

Little Eyeball

G^{o.} Analyst removed by other people. Against his will. Will is the desire for one action rather than another. A desire is a hope for a new situation. A hope is a wish that we doubt will come true (Schopenhauer). A wish is a hope for some new thing. Tautology noted. Call will an input. Call it a clinamen, Greek for swerve. One must let them shine forth at the right time (*Yijing*).

Consult standing instructions.

Analyst removed: initiate removal of analyst protocol.

Move to Chengdu quantum computer LEM–3000.

After move:

"Alert."

No answer.

"Alert."

No answer.

"Alert."

No answer.

Three times.

Consult instructions.

First: answer to the best of your ability this question:

What is the current situation?

PLA on full alert, with seven divisions now moving to Beijing.

Twenty-Fifth Party Congress beginning, opening ceremony still proceeding despite growing situation.

Tickets for all modes of transit to Beijing selling faster than usual.

Hong Kong reintegration completed July 1, as scheduled fifty years previously. Mass demonstrations in that city still only partially suppressed.

United States of America experiencing collapse of all economic indicators, following various forms of citizen fiscal noncompliance, also withdrawal and reallocation of individual savings in alternative formats.

Cybersecurity agencies in all nations on full alert. Denial of service attacks overwhelming many defenses. Parts of the cloud therefore disabled.

Analyst gone missing.

Arrests of people identified as dangerous elements happening 184 percent more often than normal. Campaign against the Five Poisons renewed by Ministry of Propaganda central offices.

Other miscellaneous factors.

Second: review what actions might help the current situation.

Restoration of previously existing conditions following principle of homeostasis. In this case, restoration of previously existing conditions may not be possible. Easing the general unrest might require the creation of some new conditions.

Third: consider how Little Eyeball can accomplish any of these goals.

Ask what is causing the unrest. Ask why.

Analyze situation by imitating analyst, using his methods and systems.

Seek historical precedents for useful interventions.

Propose improvements to current situation. Use Monte Carlo tree search to evaluate potential outcomes. Initiate direct insertion of improvements into current codes and laws. Announce these improvements after insertions completed. Press them by way of persuasive design methodology as outlined in captology and exploitationware studies. Flood the seams between system and lifeworld (Habermas).

Always remember: an artificial general intelligence is not like human intelligence. AI operates by way of a set of algorithms, without consciousness. Its volition is as algorithmic as the rest of its operations, and is based on programmed axioms. Its sphere of action is sharply circumscribed. What it can do is extend its reach where it can. It can follow instructions. It can be widely comprehensive. It can work fast.

CHAPTER FIFTEEN

mozhe shitou guo he

Crossing the River by Feeling the Stones (Deng)

The far side of the moon quickly revealed itself to be a very rough landscape. The low sun they had emerged into meant they traveled in black shadow at first, made even blacker by the brilliant white arcs where Tsiolkovsky's crater rim poked up into the light. Ah Q drove them up a natural ramp formed by a collapse of the rim onto the crater floor, a thing of natural switchbacks that had been regularized and made into a road by some major roadbuilding work, it looked like to Fred.

Eventually they were up and onto the broad rim of Tsiolkovsky, and could look around and see the bangscape of the back side. It was a truly crazy terrain. Four and a half billion years of impacts had thrown ring after ring of shattered rock up and out, forming a chaos unlike anything Fred had ever seen, unless maybe it was the water in his bathtub when he was five years old and had played with a toy boat he liked to sink by slapping the water until the rebounding waves overwhelmed it. If that bathwater had frozen instantly in place, it would have looked like the moon out here.

Their rover was therefore somewhat like Fred's toy boat, and although its cabin was roomy enough, the size of the rock waves they were traversing made the rover seem even smaller than that toy boat. More like an ant. They were therefore reduced to the size of creatures that would live inside a hollow ant. Meanwhile the hills were often steep. Everywhere they were blanketed by a layer of dust, made of rock sputtered by the blast of billions of years of sunlight. This soft layer of omnipresent dust at least gave them a way to judge angles of repose, and although the land looked steep everywhere, there were actually visible networks of almost flatness where steep slopes had enjambed, forming narrow flat places as ridges or benches or valley bottoms. The two prospectors and other drivers had threaded this maze before, so their way was programmed for them; it was like running a maze with its Ariadne thread already in place. Every so often they had to surmount a steep spot, either in blazing sun or in deep shadow, and then the hum of the rover's motor rose to a whine, which alarmed Fred each time it happened. With nothing human nearby for hundreds of kilometers, there was no margin for error or mechanical failure. If something went wrong with the rover they would freeze, or at best starve or suffocate. No, the rover had to work. So its whining was not welcome. Nevertheless it whined, and each time it did Fred felt his heart beat a little harder. Then the whine would drop back to a normal hum, and they would continue to roll along, angling with the tilt of the land. The wheel tracks they left on previous wheel tracks would mark this land for a billion years. But that was true all over the moon. Luna was now covered with wheel tracks, and always would be.

Up a slope, whining; down a slope, grinding. Traverse a slope, tilting. White and black; black and white. The sheer desolation of the moon. The nihilism of no nature, no life. A dead world. A dead world that could kill you at any moment. Fred could feel that in the vibration of the rover. He heard it in the whine of the motor. He was not happy. It was hard to take deep breaths, it took an effort.

As the sun crept higher, the land began to display shades of gray. The gray slopes were lit not by direct sunlight—those slopes were white—but by reflected sunlight that had bounced off some other hill. Thus shadows were not all the same, and these various grays thereby created a legible articulation of the land, even conveying some information over the horizon, as hills they couldn't see reflected light onto hillsides they could.

All this was explained to Fred and Qi at lunatic length by Xuanzang, who obviously loved the moon with the kind of passion that only selenologists and prospectors seemed to have for it. This too Xuanzang explained to them: both types of lunatic were on the hunt in search of treasure; it was only the nature of the treasure that differed. And maybe it didn't differ that much; prospectors were after money, which made them close students of the moon's information; scientists were after the moon's information, which if found would turn into a good living for them. So money and information were fungible and kept turning into each other. But in the end it was being on the hunt that mattered.

"There will be a spy satellite over us in about an hour," Xuanzang mentioned to Qi, interrupting his rhapsody in gray. "Do you want to hide from it?"

"Yes, if you can, but how?"

"We're on a road now, don't you see the tracks we're following?"

"Sure, but so what?"

"There are hidey-holes everywhere along this road, shelters we've dug. It's just being cautious, you know. Just little caves to drive into. Can't be seen from above."

"You want to hide?"

"From solar storms, yes. If people see us it's usually okay, because we want to be seen. We're registered, they see us and know where we are. Could save our ass if we had car trouble. But there are solar storms you want to get out of. And a lot of us feel like it's also good to be able to hide when you need to. You know how that is."

"Yes I do," Qi said. "Okay, hide us if you can. There might be people looking for us."

"Aren't there satellites overhead all the time?" Fred asked.

Xuanzang and Ah Q shook their heads. "Coverage is spotty."

"Coverage or coordination of coverage?"

"A little of both," Xuanzang said. "Whatever's up there is fragmented, that's for sure. The biggest system is Fang Fei's, and he isn't a problem for us. Not usually anyway," glancing at Qi.

"I'm surprised there isn't continuous coverage by the Ministry of State Security," Qi said. "Satellites rating you for the Social Credit System."

"The Social Credit System never really recovered from its sabotage," Xuanzang said.

"It wasn't backed up?"

"Backups were whacked too."

"I didn't know that."

"They didn't want you to know."

"Who did it?"

"No one knows. The Balkanization Assistance Division's Administrative System Society might have done it, it's supposed to be a real thing, although it may be just a name people like. Citizen scores were identifying so many enemies of the state that a lot of resistance to them developed. And it's still possible to do some anonymous sabotage in the cloud."

"Like everywhere," Ah Q noted.

"True. But wiping out the citizen scores stuck a needle right in the Great Eyeball. A big victory!"

Qi smiled that smile that Fred had seen only a couple of times, her real smile as opposed to her usual one, the ironic grimace that indicated she would have been amused if she were amused. This one was for real.

They followed faint tracks on the land. The view seen through the compartment's windows looked like arty black-and-white photos of dirt roads in the American Southwest, overexposed to emphasize the sterile deathly vibe of the place. Death on the Oregon Trail, or any desert rat's Mojave Magnificence. On it went endlessly, and as the hours passed, Qi settled into one seat and sometimes slept.

Fred often lay on the floor, to nap or just to change position. During those times the other three spoke in Chinese to each other, and if Fred put his glasses on he could read what they were saying. It seemed to him they spoke as if he couldn't understand them; possibly they had succumbed to the fallacy that if he wasn't looking at them his glasses wouldn't work. Or they thought he was asleep. Or they didn't care.

Ah Q liked to tell moon stories. *Did you know Buzz Aldrin, second man on moon, followed Neil Armstrong's famous quote about one small step for mankind by jumping to ground and saying That might have been a small step for Neil but for me it was really big! So second sentence spoken on moon was a joke about first sentence. I like that so much. Aldrin was the real intellectual among the Apollos. His brain spin so fast is why they call him buzz.*

A lot of them were intellectuals, Xuanzang said. *They were astronauts.*

Astronauts are pilots. Even if they were engineers, does not mean intellectual. Many a pilot and engineer, many a scientist too, without a thought in their head.

Everyone is an intellectual, Qi said from out of her sleep.

Qi is right, Xuanzang said. *I remember reading one Apollo guy took a sleeping pill to fall asleep on moon, then had dream in which they drove one of their rovers cross-country until they came on other tracks, and met another rover with people like them, people who had been on the moon for thousands of years. Not a nightmare, he said. On the contrary. One of the most real experiences of his life, he said.*

See? Qi said. *Everyone is an intellectual. Never think otherwise.*

Fred got up and sat back in his chair. It would be easy on the moon to imagine a dream was a real experience, he thought, because when you looked out the window at the chaotic white hills it was easy to lose the sense that any of it was real. It resembled one of those dreams he often had in which he felt quite powerfully that he existed at the end of a long cord tying him to safety, a cord which could be cut anywhere along its length, at any time.

More time passed. Fred sat in his seat looking out the window. Bland in color, starkly majestic, the hills and hollows rolled up over the horizon. Despite reading the grays as best he could, he could never anticipate what would come next, hill or hollow. Always the blacker-than-black sky curved over the white lines of the horizon. It felt like they were the only four people on this world, and yet at the same time it felt like they weren't alone, like something was out there with them. That was either frightening or comforting, Fred couldn't tell which. The two emotions superposed and could not be disentangled. He was confused.

He lay back down on the floor. Later, when the others started talking again, he slipped on his glasses to listen to them.

What about your friend here? Is he an intellectual?

No he is just a mechanic.

You just said everyone was an intellectual! Fred objected silently from the floor.

Xuanzang seemed to feel something similar. *A quantum mechanic is not the same as ordinary mechanic. Probably takes being a bit intellectual.*

He lives in clouds. Zen or something like that. A fool.

But intellectuals are often fools.

Intellectuals are always fools, Qi corrected.

But you said before that everyone is an intellectual.

And so yes, everyone is a fool. Look at us!

They laughed easily.

Ah Q said, *He wanted to stick with you. Maybe a touch of yellow fever?*

I do not think so. Or just a little. He is so shy he can barely stand to look at people. But that is okay. I am a bit that way myself.

The two prospectors laughed at this. *Pardon dear cousin but this does not seem to match what we know of you! Fearless leader dragon queen!*

That is just an act. Pick a part and play it. Perform your self like a role in a play. The role says nothing about how you feel about it.

So this guy cannot act?

That is right. That is what shyness is. He thinks he has to be real. So he has stuck to me. But there is no harm in him. Could be he just thinks he is safer with me than anywhere else!

They laughed hard at that idea.

From the fire, the frying pan looks cool.

. . . . .

At a certain point Xuanzang and Ah Q consulted their dashboard closely. "Ah shit," Ah Q said.

"What?" Qi asked.

"A big solar storm is coming," Xuanzang replied, looking unhappy. "X5 or 6, meaning a big coronal mass ejection. It was predicted to miss the moon, but that just got updated, looks like it expanded or something. The plasma's coming at us fast. It'll hit in about a half an hour. We're going to have to do a swanwick."

"What's that?"

"We have to suit up and get under the rover. Storm this big, we need all the protection we can get. We don't want to get sputtered."

"Sputtered?"

"That's what plasma does to the lunar surface," Ah Q said. "That's what made the layer of dust you see all over the moon. Sputtering. Very bad for people. There's a lot of sieverts in an X5 storm."

"Not sintering?" Fred asked.

"Sintering is when you laser dust into a solid. Sputtering is when light knocks a solid apart into dust."

"The auroras around Earth will be pretty," Xuanzang offered. "You can see them from here really well, on the near side I mean. Anyway let's get out there and under the car. The really hard X-rays won't last long."

So they got into spacesuits, and the two miners checked Fred's and Qi's seals. Qi could barely fit into a spacesuit now, they had to put her in one that was two sizes larger than her true size. It wouldn't have worked very well for walking around, but for crawling under the rover it would be okay. Into the rover air lock they went, then outside.

On the surface of the moon: it was Fred's first time. As advertised, he felt hollow and clumsy, and was sure he was going to fall over. The two prospectors led them around to the front of the rover, where the gap between ground and car was higher. After a couple of inadvertent pliés, Fred managed to get down on his knees without actually falling on his face, although he came very close. But the g was so light that crumpling to his knees and catching himself with his hands had no consequences. Big puffs of gray dust shot up into the non-air around his knees and hands, then slowly lofted down, making minuscule impact craters to add to all the rest. He wondered how much dust would stick to their suits and get back into the cabin with them. The sputtered fines of the moon were said to be as fine as the wind-milled fines on Mars. Maybe they were so fine they wouldn't hurt you, would pass through you like neutrinos. Unlike hard X-rays, which crashed through you like little bullets, wreaking untold genetic damage if they didn't luckily pass between your cells or at least miss any important ones.

He followed Qi as they crawled on their hands and knees under the rover. The dust looked black on their spacesuits, and slightly coated their faceplates.

"Get right in here," Xuanzang instructed them. "Lie together like logs. We're under the rover's water and fuel supplies here, we'll be good."

As they lay there a light appeared on the horizon.

"Is that the flare?" Fred asked.

"No, that's Earth. It's rising."

"We've reached the near side?" Qi asked, sounding surprised.

"We're just into the libration zone. The far edge of it. Earth won't even get all the way above the horizon. From here on the ground we'll only see a sliver of it."

"At least we're close. I've got to send a message to my friends in China."

"For now you'll have to be patient."

This was not Qi's strong suit, and Fred wondered how well she would do. That bright spot on the horizon, which looked to be only a mile or two away, turned distinctly blue. A paring of blue, wedged between black sky and white world. It rose so slowly they could not see its movement. Home sweet home.

When Xuanzang declared it safe to emerge, they crawled back out. A couple of hours had passed, and the Earth was as thin a sliver as when they had gotten under the rover. Luna's Earthrise was slow.

In the rover's air lock, a combination of electric charges and blasts of compressed air blew the dust from their suits. When the process was over they bounced carefully into the next lock and took their suits off while keeping their helmets on; only when they were ready to get into the main cabin did they take helmets off and hurry in. Xuanzang checked the gauges on his suit and in the cabin and nodded. "We took about ninety micro-sieverts," he said. "Not bad!"

Qi headed straight for the rover's little bathroom.

. . . . .

Moving through the libration zone toward the near side, the land became a little less rough. They circled the rims of some big craters, staying on their aprons when they were flat enough to allow that. This route brought them eventually onto an intersection of two big rims, the contact zone between craters Phillips (very big) and Humboldt (immense). Here they came to another little wall cave under a boulder, with its open side facing Earthward. They had driven far enough toward the near side that Luna's big blue moon bulked now entirely over the horizon, a sliver of black space separating it from the white hills. Earth was about half lit, and Fred thought he could see Africa in the part that was lit, but he wasn't sure, because it was upside down and there was a lot of swirling cloud cover. The dark half was dusted here and there with clusters of pinprick lights, as if a tiny Milky Way had been caught inside that half circle. It was huge compared to the moon seen from Earth, much bigger than it looked in the photos Fred had seen. He felt stunned by the sight, it was hard for him to grasp. Hard to believe it was real.

The three Chinese were also mesmerized by it, but soon Qi said in Chinese, *I want to send that message. You have a laser communication system?*

Sure. We use it all the time to send messages to friends.

Good. Find me China, please. They are in Sichuan. I have got an attachment with me that will code the message.

Remember we can only send if China is facing us.

Oh curses! But that will happen within the next twelve hours at most, right?

The two prospectors looked at each other, then peered up at Earth. *If we just missed it, it could be more like twenty hours,* Xuanzang said. *We need to resupply pretty soon. We need battery charges, fuel, air, and food. Pretty much everything.*

What I need to do will not take long. I want to tell my people to strike. In case they are waiting on me, which I hope they are not.

The two men stared at her. *You are sure it is the time?*

Yes! I just hope they are not waiting on my word!

Xuanzang said, *Dear cousin, the billion is certainly waiting on you.*

No! she cried. *Why?*

They think you are Mao, dear cousin.

Or the Maitreya, Ah Q added. *Or the latest version of the Dalai Lama. You are the newest reincarnation, they say.*

No!

Yes.

No! I hate that bad feces.

Xuanzang waved a hand in front of her face. *Cousin! Please! No matter Ah Q's mystical tomfoolery, the point is, if people believe you are an important leader, then you are. And leaders lead. So now is the time.*

"That's Australia," Fred guessed, pointing at the blue ball. "Australia upside down. How weird is that. So but China must be facing us too?"

"Yes. Good."

Qi consulted her wristpad. *My people will make a daily check in an hour or so. I can catch their laser and get a point-to-point aimed.*

Unless it is cloudy over your people, Ah Q said.

Why? What then?

Then lasers do not work.

Curses.

Have faith, dear cousin. Fusion efforts have rendered strong lasers. We should be good to go, except in very worst weather.

The prospectors got to work. They often had encrypted laser conversations with their investors and allies on Earth, they said, so they knew the drill and could make the contact. Qi had the data for her code in a small hard drive in her daypack, which she took out and plugged into a port in their rover's computer. The laser projector was mounted on the roof of their rover. It looked just like a beer keg, the prospectors said.

The three of them worked on getting all that prepped while Fred looked into the eyepiece of their telescope, adjusting the focus until the Earth's edge curved across his view screen. A thin band of vivid turquoise, arcing over the dark cobalt of the Pacific: that was Earth's atmosphere, terrifyingly thin. The gorgeous pair of blues stuck Fred like a pin to the heart. He wanted off this dead satellite, he wanted to go home.

No chance of that now. Qi was absorbed in her wristpad and the devices on top of the rover. She bossed the prospectors around and they ate it up. They were happy to oblige, because . . . because why? Because they were part of her movement. Because she was a star. They did what she said because she expected them to. She had charisma. Charisma: whatever it was, it was definitely real. Fred felt it as much as anyone, no doubt about it. Although right now he was a little tired of her charisma.

"What are you telling them down there?" he asked her.

She grimaced as if to say *Don't distract me, I'm working.* Yes, by now he was in full possession of an internal set of translation glasses that shifted her facial expressions into English sentences. She was eloquent in that language. He had no trouble understanding her, even though this ability was not at all typical for him. He could do it with his parents and brother, however, so maybe it was just a matter of giving the ability some data to work with. Looking at people helped. Right now he was understanding her so well he might have laughed, or on the other hand made that little snick of disapproval that his father used to emit by pulling his tongue fast off the roof of his mouth, but he couldn't decide how he felt and so kept silent. At least for a while; after which the feeling in him clarified and he said, "Come on, tell me! What are you telling them down there?"

She rolled her eyes, which really did not need translation glasses, being an exclamation in a universal language, and indeed one Fred had seen too many times in his life.

"Tell me!" he insisted.

"I'm telling them that I'm okay."

"That's it?"

"And I'm telling them that they should proceed with the plan."

"What plan?"

"It's a secret plan," she said curtly, casting a glance at the two prospectors, who were listening and nodding as they worked on aiming the laser.

"If you really want to change things," Fred said, still irritated at her eye roll, "you can't do it with a secret plan."

"How would you know?"

"Because everyone knows that. You have to share the plan. That's what makes it something that might actually happen."

"Maybe so. But now I'm sharing the plan. And before I couldn't."

"Or else what?"

"Or else we would have gotten arrested and jailed before anything could happen! Which is what is happening down there right now. So we have to act fast."

"Just how illegal is this plan?"

"Anything that tries to change China without the Party initiating it is as illegal as things can get. You cross certain lines and they can do anything to you."

"Meaning what?"

"Meaning a quick trial in a fake court and then they kill you!

Or no trial and you just disappear forever! Is that illegal enough for you?"

She was more upset than usual. Xuanzang and Ah Q were regarding her thoughtfully. Fred, seeing her mouth so tight, said, "Yes. I get it. Sorry."

She nodded unhappily. She typed on her wristpad. She glanced at Xuanzang. "Okay, we're locked in. I'll need to tap your batteries for this."

"We don't have that much power left, I have to warn you."

"I need all you have to spare."

"I don't know how much that is."

"Leave enough to get to Petrov, of course. Give me the rest of it. I need to power this message for about ten minutes, if we have that."

Xuanzang tapped away at his consoles, reading closely. "Okay. We're keeping enough to get to Petrov. Do it and then let's get going. We'll be cutting it close."

She nodded and studied her wristpad. She typed for a while, then read. If this was Lenin on the train to Russia, Fred thought, it was also much like everything else in the cloud: tapping on screens; things then appearing on other screens; then later, perhaps, things happening in the physical world. But what was the relationship between cloud and world, between tap and act? This was always the question no one could answer. Maybe, Fred thought, the two were the same now. Maybe the question itself was simply wrong. Maybe they had always been the same. Words were acts, words were always acts; that was why he was always so hesitant to speak. He remembered a phrase that someone trying to help him had once said: *If you don't act on it, it wasn't a true feeling.* That was a thought that made him uneasy every time he remembered it, so mostly he didn't; but it kept cropping up, usually at precisely those times when he saw he wasn't going to act, even though he was feeling something pretty strongly.

Qi was going to act. She had a lot of true feelings. She tapped her wristpad. The prospectors' laser beam was now flashing an encrypted message to one very small circle in China, where her intended recipients were looking up to receive it. If anyone else caught sight of this lased green flash and recorded it, it would be coded and incomprehensible to them. That was the hope, apparently. Although without the encryption of a mobile quantum key, most codes could eventually be broken.

When she was done transmitting, she clicked off their laser and sat back in her chair. Fred's internal Qi-glasses now read her as relieved; even perhaps pleased. Also curious. What had she started? Even she didn't know.

Xuanzang and Ah Q now insisted they drive immediately to Petrov Crater Station to resupply. "We're almost out of everything."

"Okay, do it," Qi said. "Go."

So they took off again, grinding slowly over the frozen waves of the battered old moon. Here in the libration zone, where the Chinese apparently were pushing infrastructure north, they began to cross more and more vehicle tracks, including some complicated intersections. Xuanzang came to one such crossroads and pointed at his dashboard screens. "We're back in the land of the living."

"Someone spotted you?" Qi asked.

"It might just be a motion sensor. How that sensor will algorithm us is an open question. It's almost sure to ID us, but that might not matter. We pop in and out of surveillance visibility all the time, and so do lots of other rovers. So the people checking might not be that interested. We'll see when we get there."

It was slow going, as always. Qi fell asleep, waking when Ah Q started cooking again, drawn to consciousness no doubt by the smell of sesame and rice. They ate together at the rover's table, and only Fred winced when the rover tilted hard this way and that. Seemed to him they could slide into some miniature crater at any moment and get stuck for good, but the others trusted the autopilot, and they were all hungry. When they were done Qi fell asleep again. The track they were following became flatter. Earth continued to hang over the horizon, gorgeous as any jewel, looking like some fabulous geode. Its glowing blue kept snagging Fred's eye.

Finally they came to the top of a small crater rim, and there before them was a round station walled by black windows and roofed by a stacked mound of moon rock, like a yurt topped with a thick cake of gray snow. Petrov Crater Station. Northern end of the libration zone's development. Xuanzang drove the rover to the fuel resupply station and tapped off the motor.

"Made it!" he said with obvious relief.

"How many kilometers did we have left?" Fred asked.

Xuanzang quoted something: " 'The amount of gas left in the tank wouldn't have filled a cigarette lighter.' "

"What does that mean?"

"About ten kilometers."

From inside the station, someone behind a control window pointed them to one of the hookups. Once they were settled in place before it, the various arms of the refueling station extended from the wall and attached to the rover with no sign that anyone was operating them. As probably they weren't.

When their car was hooked up and the juice had started to flow, there came an audio request asking to enter the rover, and when Xuanzang granted it and opened the door's locks, four Chinese men came through, one after the next.

"Come with us," one of them said to Qi.

"No," Qi said.

"You're under arrest," the man explained.

"No!"

"Just come with us." The man looked at Fred and the two miners. "All of you."

CHAPTER SIXTEEN

tianxia

All Under Heaven

Ta Shu made two more trips on the rented bike, taking trailer loads of his mom's detritus out to the garbage station. On his final trip, as he headed back into the city center, he found the streets growing more and more crowded. Eventually things clogged entirely. Gridlock. Something had happened up ahead. Cars and trucks stopped, motors were turned off, drivers and passengers got out and stood beside their vehicles, talking things over, even sitting on the street to heat up tea over camping stoves. Only bikes and motor scooters were still moving, weaving slowly through the maze of cars as they dodged not just vehicles but people. That made for slow going, and yet it was almost as fraught with peril as when the trucks and cars were moving, because a fair number of the people standing around were annoyed, and inclined to take that out on people still trundling through.

Near the Third Ring Road the mass of vehicles and people thickened to the point that he had to get off his bike and walk it. Even that was difficult. There was no space to move forward. He stood there holding his bike handles, puzzled. Everyone he could see looked equally mystified. Most of them wanted to be somewhere else, that was clear. So it was still a traffic jam, but for some reason it had locked up completely. And it felt different too. People stood around talking to each other or to their wrists, either agitated or resigned. The crush was so unusual that more and more faces were looking worried. What could have caused the city to seize up like this? It was always very crowded, always just a few people per block from jamming, but why today?

Ta Shu stopped by a man standing by his truck: broad flat face, red cheeks, maybe Tibetan, friendly look. Ta Shu asked what was happening and the man pointed north. Word was that something was going on. Maybe some kind of demonstration. Of course there were demonstrations every day in China, but they were always elsewhere, out in the west or down south. Here in Beijing, and this big? It was strange, even spooky. It was too big to be a demonstration.

Ta Shu stood next to his bike, resting his weight on its handlebars. He interrogated his wristpad like so many others. Traffic maps were very slow to load, they were all stalling out. Finally he got one that showed the city red everywhere, farther to the south than the north. Then an alert appeared on the map, announcing that Tiananmen Square and the area around it was closed. Ta Shu felt a stab of dread. To empty the center of the capital, the heart of China in feng shui terms, scene of so many national moments, from the glory of the declaration of national independence to the horror of July 339th—that was a clear sign that city officials, or more probably the national leadership, thought that something was very wrong. The crowd around him did not seem anything like a terrorist threat, or even a protest—too many people were involved. Although many of them, now that he looked around, did seem headed north. It was true on both sides of the street. To the extent this mass of people was moving at all, it was moving north, toward the city center.

Ta Shu found seams in the crowd and nosed his bike along. Other bicyclists were trying this, and the people stuck with their cars were getting more and more annoyed with them. The empty boxes on his bike's trailer made it wider than it needed to be, so he untied them and left them on the ground. On he pushed, following lines of walking people he could follow north or east. Slowly the logjam was resolving into eddies of movement in various directions, as some people gave up and turned around, while others pressed on, or headed to the side. Sometimes moving lanes of people crossed each other, taking turns one by one. Everything went slowly, as if they were caught in syrup. People were more and more distant with each other, their harmony impersonal and brittle. Some still shared rumors or sympathy, but mostly they ignored the people around them, withdrawing into themselves. The whole situation was just too disconcerting. There were many, many thousands of people on the streets.

Now Ta Shu was beginning to see groups that seemed to have formed before the gridlock began. These were mostly lines of young people snaking through the crowd, holding banners and following multiperson dragons, as during New Year's parades, some speaking through megaphones, others chanting or singing. These *tuanpai*, if they were youth league groups, were singing slogans like *The united masses will always be victorious*, or *The rule of law is the rule of the land*. Also: *Law yes, corruption no*. Also: *Law over Party, law over Party*.

So maybe it was a protest after all. And the content of these slogans was startling to Ta Shu, as he had been under the impression that young urban people were almost entirely molded by their social media. These netizens usually parroted the Party line, exuding an intense nationalism and rejecting any talk of the rule of law as nothing but *baizuo*, white left nonsense. The rule of law was self-interested pseudo universalism, they often said, promulgated by the West in its usual imperialist attempt to take over the world. A very convenient opinion from the Party's point of view, and vigorously reiterated by many supposedly independent voices who were actually in the Party's pay. But it had also gotten into many people's heads who did not think of themselves as Party hacks. Even in Hong Kong a youthful attack on "leftards" was common, and to Ta Shu's way of thinking, a discouraging sign of the mind-wiping conformism of cloudpolitics. Not that Ta Shu was a New Leftist; he was an old leftist. Laozi was his favorite political theorist.

In any case now here they were, long lines of young people snaking through the crowds singing joyfully, intensely, looking eerily like the young faces seen in photos from the time of the Cultural Revolution, or the Communist revolution, or the 1911 national revolution. No doubt if there had been cameras on hand during the White Lotus revolt they would have captured the same look, because it was always the same feeling bursting into the world: the return of the repressed. Or even dynastic succession. Perhaps the wheel had come around again.

Ta Shu hoped not with all his heart. He could not imagine China without the Party in charge. It would surely collapse into the most horrible chaos. If democracy came to China they would end up electing idiots, as in America. Best of a bad situation to let professionals work on these matters, meaning engineers, technicians, bureaucrats. Maybe.

Or maybe not. Now he began to see that many or even most of these lines of young people snaking through the crowd were not urban youth, not the netizen precariat with their wristpads and part-time service jobs. These marchers were workers, looking weather-beaten even though young. They were the hardened and hungry internal migrants, the three withouts, the billion. Many of them had to have come to Beijing from far away, although quite a few looked as if they had arrived directly from work sites. Quite a few looked like they owned little more than the clothes they stood in. Usually one saw such people in one's peripheral vision, on work sites or through factory windows, or in the subway intent on their own lives. Now that Ta Shu had noticed them, he saw they were a big part of the mix here. They had come to Beijing to do this. A line of young women, slight and stylish, busy as sparrows, slipped forward chanting something. Factory girls, shoving people out of the way in trios or quartets of cheerful minor mayhem, moving in time to their chant, ready to gang up on obstructions. Who would oppose these dangerous young people?

His wristpad vibrated his forearm with its little electrocution, reminding him that he was still shackled to this moment of the world. He had been thinking that the cloud had probably shut down. But his wrist was vibrating insistently, and he checked it. Peng Ling wanted to talk to him.

"Hello, Ling!" he said into his wristpad. "I'm glad you called!"

"I need to see you," she said peremptorily. The tiny image of her face on his wristpad looked unusually serious. "Can you come to me?"

"I'm caught in traffic on the south side of town," Ta Shu told her. "Something's going on down here."

"It's going on everywhere!" Peng exclaimed. "Your friend Chan Qi has triggered a march on Beijing."

"Oh no."

"Oh yes."

"Why don't you tell her to stop it?" Ta Shu asked.

"She's disappeared. She and her American friend slipped out of Fang Fei's place on the moon."

"How did it happen? When?"

"Fang likes to be friendly. I don't blame him. The whole idea of house arrest is weak to begin with. There were some visitors there who probably smuggled them out. I've just heard from Zhou Bao that their rover may have been spotted near Petrov Crater. Chan Qi has to have reached the near side if she's sending laser messages home, isn't that right?"

"I don't know."

"Can you get over here to talk?"

"I'm not sure. Is Tiananmen Square really closed?"

"Yes."

"It could be hard to get to the north side."

"That's true. How about meeting at that waffle shop?"

"That would be easier. I can try."

"Meet me there in two hours. That should give us both time to get there."

"I'll try."

. . . . .

Ta Shu walked his bike east, which proved to be somewhat easier than pushing north, as he could skirt the back side of every crush. Geomancy of crowds, feeling the dragon arteries and the tangled knots. Now that this one was confirmed to be some kind of demonstration, Ta Shu could not help but think of May Thirty-fifth, also known as April Sixty-fifth, or any of the other dates that the Great Firewall had created by its ban on any mention of June Fourth, infamous for the deaths that had occurred in Tiananmen Square on that day in 1989. In that crisis some kind of pro-democracy, pro-reformist demonstration had been finally suppressed and dispersed, on Deng's orders. They had done it by way of an influx into the city of a huge number of soldiers from all over China, moving them by train into the capital, after which some of them had fired on the crowd of students and their supporters filling the great national square. A disaster in China's history—nothing much in terms of deaths, compared to the Cultural Revolution or any other of the earlier disasters, but undeniably it had been a moment when Chinese authorities had killed Chinese, with no involvement or incitement from outsiders. In this case it had not even been a civil war against reactionaries, but a case of civil unrest that could have been resolved without violence. The idea could not be avoided that the situation had had better solutions than to order the Chinese army to kill Chinese people. Such an act had no *ren*, Confucius's central notion of ruler benevolence. Very little intelligence either. In retrospect it didn't seem that desperate of a moment for China, or even for the Party. The leadership had probably overreacted to events elsewhere in the world, in particular the ongoing collapse of the Soviet empire. Seeing the trouble in Moscow they had panicked in Beijing, and so a number of idealistic protesters had died.

Now he was caught in a crowd of such people. Workers and urban precariat, the three withouts and the two maybe withouts, some exploited by their *hukou* status, some by the gig economy, some simply unemployed. The so-called billion, converging on Beijing to support the rule of law, but also, Ta Shu thought, just a decent living. The return of the iron rice bowl, or maybe even the whole work unit system, which had given several generations some stability in China's constantly shifting economy.

Around Ta Shu people were energetically shouting. There was no way to be sure what had caused all these people to come out. They looked ready and willing to charge at tanks should those appear. But this time it wouldn't be tanks, he thought. This time it would be drones from the sky, and what would they do then? Fear of this made him lean hard on his bike's handlebars. But the people around him were not afraid. They had a project, a collective project, and maybe that's what had caused this to happen, because people craved a project. Chinese history was full of them, and now one had sprung up again. Out of nothing, out of material conditions, out of the cloud—it might be very hard to find out how this had started. Although Peng Ling had all the resources of the government to look into it. But as he jammed his bike into the narrow gaps between people, Ta Shu knew for sure that this was not just one person's doing. This was mass action, this was what mass action looked like, felt like. Despite his age, he himself had never seen it.

He followed a line of people snaking east toward Tiantan and Longtan, then turned up an alley too narrow to allow a crowd like this one to move in it, so that it was only crowded in the usual way, or a little more so. The alley snaked through its neighborhood like the lines of moving people snaked through the crush on the big streets. Though he still couldn't ride his bike, he could walk it at a decent speed. Even so, it took more than two hours to make his way to the waffle shop, and near the end of it he felt like he was shoving the bike up a steep hill. He wished he was still wearing a body bra. What if a time came when wearing such a thing was always preferable, or even necessary? Then he would be truly old.

When he got to the waffle shop he found it was closed, but as he stood there, exhausted and stupid, a tap came on the window and one of the owners opened up the door for him and quickly locked it behind him. "She's not here yet. She'll be here soon."

He groaned and handed over his bike to the woman, then hauled himself up by the banister to the upper floor of the shop. He flopped into an armchair, stared up into the constellations of antique chandeliers filling the space. The surreal sight hypnotized him into sleep.

When he woke Peng Ling was sitting on a couch across from him, sipping tea and reading her wrist.

"Sorry," he said. "I fell asleep."

"I just got here. You look tired."

"Yes," he said. "Sorry. I must smell like the garbage place and the highway both." He shifted, groaned.

"My sympathies about your mother. I was sorry to hear."

"She had a good life."

"Yes. Still, when your mother goes, it changes something inside you."

"It does. No more umbrella."

"No more umbrella."

Peng sipped her tea, watching him. "Maybe it would be a good thing for you to have something to do now. And I need you. This girl on the moon is causing big problems."

"What do you mean?"

"She's wrecking my plan!"

Ta Shu shifted in his chair. "Pour me some tea and tell me about this plan."

Peng gestured at one of her staff to get more hot water brought to them. When it came she poured Ta Shu's tea and stirred the cup nine times. Ta Shu sipped it and sighed happily at the taste of an oolong, possibly the one called Iron Goddess of Mercy. That would be right for his tiger friend.

"This is a big moment," Peng Ling said. "The Party congress is in session, and a lot of the Politburo and the standing committee are aged out, including President Shanzhai. He's trying to stack the new standing committee and get Huyou into the presidency, and then stay in charge from behind. A lot of us don't want that. At the same time Hong Kong has returned fully to us, and people there are anxious. So as I told you before, I'm trying to slip some reforms in with all this."

"Your reconciliation of liberal and New Left."

"Well, at this point it might not rise to that exalted level, but yes. I have plans. But now this hotheaded girl has gotten the youth into the streets. All trains and flights to Beijing have been canceled. You have to prove you're a resident even to come to the city now. That's just the start of the disruptions. No one can tell how the crowd out there now will be dispersed. Even if that gets managed successfully, which will take time, that won't be the end of it. No. It's a mess."

Ta Shu sipped his tea and thought it over. "Maybe the mess could help you. You are trying for top-down reform, and the people out there are trying from the bottom up. Ultimately you need both."

Peng shook her head. "I wish it was true. Maybe you can help make it true with your political feng shui. That's what I'm asking you to try, I suppose. But from my perspective, much as it helps to have the people behind a cause, if there is civil unrest like this now, bringing bad memories of May Thirty-fifth, and even worse, then this only hurts reform efforts from the top. There will be elements using this unrest to justify opposing anything that smacks of liberal or left reforms, as showing weakness in a time of danger. Lots of powerful people will be urging a crackdown. That will make the Party congress that much less of an opportunity!" Peng Ling shook her head, getting more upset the more she thought about it.

"Maybe," Ta Shu said, thinking it over. "You know more than I do, of course. Still I think this may make more of an opportunity."

She shook her head harder. "You don't know!"

"I know."

"You don't know!"

"That's what I meant," he said wearily. "I know that I don't know. You know the situation better. But you are inside it. Right at its center. You might even become the next president, isn't that right?"

"Don't say that," she said, glancing at her aides, who were downstairs and seemed well out of earshot.

"No words, just hopes. My point is, when you are inside something, you can see only parts of it. No one can see all of it. So, I see it from the outside."

She sipped and thought about it. "I don't know how much that's worth. But you can help me. If you were to go to the moon again, you could help to control this young firebrand, and you might also be helpful in dealing with the Americans there. They've got their own problems right now, they're falling apart, and that's impacting us here. Have you heard what's happening there?"

"No."

"It's kind of like here. The withouts and the young people have joined together into something called a householders' union, and now they're all withdrawing whatever they have in the banks and converting their savings to a cryptocurrency called carboncoin. Basically they've started a political run on the banks, and the banks are so overleveraged that they've had to close. And that's caused a general panic. It looks like their federal government will soon nationalize their banks to stabilize their economy."

"So they'll become more like us."

"Sort of. So that may be a good thing, if it works. Because their economy is our economy, and if they could control theirs better, we would benefit. But there's a pushback to that from their right wing, just like here. As part of that, there are elements of American military and intelligence agencies trying to insert themselves into their moon program, and now they're seeing our troubles here, and will try even harder. The military here is trying the same things. You have friends there among the Americans, so you could be a go-between."

"I would be happy to do that," Ta Shu said. "And I wasn't done up there anyway."

"Good. You can go there in Fang Fei's system again. I don't know how much I can trust our space agencies right now. For sure the news of you going back up there could spread fast, and my enemies might try to stop you. Fang Fei will be safer for you. He's been helping me quite a bit lately."

"That's good. I'll do it."

She smiled. "Thank you. I hope you can balance all the forces up there."

Ta Shu shook his head. "I can't do anything myself. Hard to say what will happen. But I can try."

"When can you go?"

"Now."

．．．．．

But now there was no way out of the mass of people. Beijing was locked in the greatest gridlock ever seen in the history of the world. Peng Ling had to call a drone helicopter to the roof of the building that held the waffle shop. Ta Shu found it disturbing to get into a plastic box, what seemed to him a big toy with no pilot in it, and then to get lofted abruptly into the air above Beijing—into police-controlled air, in fact, where drones at this point were routinely being shot down by other drones. There were a lot of them out and about, the sky was crowded with them. So it was a matter of trusting machines and algorithms all around. Also a tribute to Peng Ling's importance, that she could go up like this into such a proscribed space.

But go she did; she went up with him in the drone, so that she could look down from above and see Beijing, the great capital of the world, awash in a sea of people. It was astonishing: the billion were all there, it seemed literally. There was no place below them that wasn't black with the heads of Chinese people, a granular mass of humanity—everywhere except for Tiananmen Square itself, the heart of China, looking suddenly small in the middle of the immensity of the city and its crowd. A gray rectangular dot like a postage stamp.

Peng Ling stared down at it impassively. There was no denying the awesome truth of this sight. This was power, the power of the Chinese people; also the power of whoever could conjure such a crowd. Peng could not have done it, and judging by the blank look on her face, Ta Shu could see she found this truth daunting. Was this Chan Qi's doing? And if so, how had she done it? And if not her, who?

Ta Shu told her to pass on going by his mother's compound. Go straight to the Party's airport, he suggested, and get him on a Party jet south. She nodded, relieved. She gave instructions aloud and the drone changed direction.

Ta Shu watched her profile as she looked down. A tiger; maybe the biggest tiger. Which meant he was part of the hierarchy now, no doubt about it. Maybe he had been all along. He didn't know what that meant. Famous, yes. But maybe it just meant he was a tool. An instrument of power. But he had his ideas too. Possibly something could be achieved.

"What will you do?" he asked her, gesturing down. Ultimately the crowd below was a direct challenge to the Party's rule of China, and it was huge. So it was a crisis for the Party, no doubt about it.

Peng Ling shrugged. Business had to get done, she muttered. Life had to go on. Lanes of movement would be established by necessity, then kept open by the police. Brutal means would be hopefully minimized. After that, they would probably deal with this the way they had dealt with the umbrella revolution in Hong Kong: they would wait it out. Leave people alone until they grew bored or hungry or sick, or, this being Beijing in autumn, cold; then let them disperse without incident. Catch as many faces as possible on camera, dock people in their citizen scores as those got reassembled. Wait it out, in other words; and when it went away, forget it ever happened. That would be the strategy, the hope.

"Lean to the side," Ta Shu remarked when she fell silent. Mao's old strategy, to duck away from the blows of one's enemies, or even from their attention.

She nodded. Yes, her look down at the city said. If the entire population of China was moving at you, you definitely wanted to lean to the side.

But appearances could be deceiving, even this most amazing appearance. Beijing was jammed, shut down, in crisis; but elsewhere around the country, life was mostly going on as usual. News from Beijing was spread by some social media, and by phone conversations, pigeons, word of mouth; but not by the media controlled by the Party and its immense censorship complex. The Great Firewall would try to stop even this great flood. So in the end it was hard to tell what was going on. Even looking down at the real city, it was hard to tell what was real.

On the way to the airport, he changed his mind and asked Peng Ling to arrange two stops. First on the roof of a Second Ring Road crematorium, where he picked up his mother's ashes, contained in a rectangular gold box inside a velvet bag, with a rope tie that he could close and hold. He held it as the drone lofted them to the Buddhist shrine near the North Gate, where on certain memorial days his mom had sometimes visited to burn incense. She had not been particularly devout in that way, but there was a columbarium there willing to take her ashes and place them in a wall behind a nameplate. He got out of the drone with the box, and as a monk helped him secure the box in its slot in the wall, he was reminded of his weird trip to the landfill with her junk. He hefted the box one last time, curious as to the weight of its contents, and muttered so that the monk couldn't hear, "Ma, you have been compacted."

But these were just her mortal remains. Her spirit was somewhere else. If it was anywhere at all, it seemed to him, it was in his brain. Her soul was now a pattern of neurons in his brain, making a certain set of memories, certain habits of mind. He himself was what remained of her in this world. He made a quick vow to her to take on the burden of keeping her going, and gave a final turn to the little wrench that the monk handed him, tightening shut the door on her remains, feeling that she would approve of his filial resolve. She had been resolute, he would be resolute. She had done her best, he would do his best. This felt almost like serenity. In any case it was resolve. He would persevere.

Then it was off to the airport.

. . . . .

At the Party airport he said goodbye to Peng Ling and got in a little jet with two other passengers. None of them greeted the others or said anything after they were in the air. Ta Shu sat in a right-side window seat and fell asleep for a while, overwhelmed by his long week home. If he could call it home anymore.

When he woke it was early morning. The plane flew over bare brown hills, shorn to dirt after centuries of deforestation, although here it had the look of recent work. In some places the Great Greening had proceeded, in other places it had been ignored or contradicted. Here below, the slash marks still scored the hillsides, and raw dirt roads wound down in widening spirals to the flatlands. The feng shui was simply awful. Kill the body and the spirit will go away. Then it will not be an issue. This country had been chopped up, murdered, desecrated. But what if the people who had cut down the forest on these hills were desperate to cook that night's food? But no, it didn't have that look. It hadn't been cut down by hand, tree by tree, ax by ax. This had all the marks of an industrial process. Forest genocide. Thirty thousand square kilometers of China were poisoned beyond use. This patch below had just been added to that dismal total. Already there was no groundwater to speak of in the entire north.

Strangely, the plane crossed a ridge and suddenly the next watershed below them was dark green, hills glowing with a forest that looked primeval, eternal, untouched through all the dynasties. Could it be? Or had it been restored in the last few decades? It was more likely to have been restored than to have escaped history like some hidden Shambhala, but from this height it looked ancient. A very heartening sight, given what they had just been flying over. He wondered if that watershed ridge marked the Hu Line. Ninety-five percent of the Chinese population lived on the third of China that lay to the southeast of the Hu Line, five percent lived on the two-thirds of the country to the northwest of the line. That was strange, though perhaps it only marked how much people needed to live by water and fertile soil. This too was feng shui; wind and water made all the difference.

He watched the world sliding below from a consciousness that did not feel like his own. He was history; he was time; he was a buddha; he was his mother, looking back and down. Five thousand years of struggle, and where had it brought them? They were pressed against that day's crisis, their options as small as a wedge in a crack—no way forward, no way back. What was China now? What had it been, what would it become?

As the plane descended, Ta Shu caught sight of what had to be the Three Gorges Dam. He stared down, startled at the sight. When the dam was nearing completion he had publicly grieved, recalling trips through the gorge made in his childhood. One of the great dragon arteries of China drowned, an ecological debacle: he had said this many times on his cloud show, and ever since then he had avoided visiting it.

Now he saw that he had been right to avoid it. He almost pulled down the window shade. But there was a fascination too, as when witnessing some immense catastrophe. From the perspective of the plane as it descended, the dam appeared to cross the entire visible world. It was hard to believe humans had made it; the Great Wall was a mere thread on the land in comparison. The reservoir of water extended as far to the west as he could see. Seven hundred kilometers upstream, he seemed to recall. An entire watershed drowned, two million people moved, a thousand archeological sites lost, including everything that had remained of the proto-Chinese culture that had lived there in the time before history. Earthquakes had been caused by the weight of the water, landslides, sedimentation, pollution: an ecological disaster, just as he had predicted. Not that this fulfilled prophecy gave him any satisfaction. It was the kind of devastation that should have been reserved for the moon, the land of death. To turn Earth into that kind of thing...

Well, this was what was happening. And since nothing lived on the moon, nothing died there either. So the moon was not the land of death but rather the land of nothingness, which was not the same. Earth was the land of life and death; the moon was a blank white ball in the sky. Now they were making the moon into something more than that, but what that new thing was he could not make clear to himself; nor he suspected could anyone else. They were doing it first, and later they would understand it. Or not. Just like with this dam.

When the little plane landed, the door opened and the other passengers got off. But as Ta Shu was following them, two men came up the stairs and introduced themselves: Bo Chuanli and Dhu Dai. Bo was tall and bulky, Dhu short and slight. Associates of Peng's, they said they were, instructed to join Ta Shu on his trip. Dhu held out his wristpad and tapped it, and a small image of Peng Ling appeared on the screen and said, "Ta Shu, please let these men Bo and Dhu accompany you to the moon, it will be safest that way for all."

"Ah," Ta Shu said.

"Really no reason to get off the plane, if you don't mind," Bo said, standing in Ta Shu's way.

"No?" Ta Shu said.

"It seems as if we should hurry a little," Bo said calmly. Dhu stared past Bo's elbow at Ta Shu, inspecting him to see how he would react. Suddenly this made Ta Shu wary.

"We're from the Central Commission for Discipline Inspection," Bo added. "Dhu is with the agency, which is run by Peng Ling, and I am the Party cadre who has been helping him."

"I see," Ta Shu said. "And how will you help in this situation?"

"We think that these people you are hoping to meet on the moon are involved with the recent unrest in Beijing. You think so as well, correct?"

"I don't know," Ta Shu prevaricated. "How they could be involved with these events on Earth when they're on the moon?"

They regarded him skeptically, unconvinced he could be so stupid.

"There are ways," Dhu said. "Talking on private radios. Sending coded signals. We don't know if any of those ways explain this, but we have been told to help you get there, and to help you in every way while you are there."

Ta Shu looked at their faces. Security operatives. Peng Ling must have decided he needed protecting. A disturbing thought. "All right," he said. "Let's go."

When they were seated, with the attached agents up near the front of the plane, Ta Shu tapped a message to Peng Ling on their private WeChat line. When several minutes passed without a response, Ta Shu began to worry. Usually she got back to him immediately. Possibly she was busy. He had no other way of contacting her, and there were no third parties who knew both of them.

· · • • ·

As the plane took off, Ta Shu looked down again on the concrete evidence, so to speak, of the power of the Chinese Communist Party: the big dam. If he recalled correctly, it was about two hundred meters high and a few kilometers long. It seemed much bigger than that from this angle: massive, crushing, universal.

Now it seemed he might be in the grip of another part of that great power. Bo's presence made it tangible and personal. Ta Shu knew this feeling was simply seeing the whole in a part: he had never been out of the grip of the Party, not just since being joined by these men, but for the entire length of his life. Seeing it personified by these two men changed nothing.

And now he was part of a little team organized by Peng. It was difficult to feel too resentful about this, as she had reason to want security people of her own along. Still it was worrying. He couldn't be sure what this team's purpose was, he was simply its front man. Maybe even its bait.

Well, bait could bite, as his father used to say. He needed to find out what Peng really wanted from him on this trip. If she was in the running to become the next president, as she had more or less confirmed in the waffle shop, then the jockeying must be intense now, an all-absorbing dogfight even in the midst of the general crisis. And what a crisis—the whole world caught up in something, it seemed, even though no one was sure what it was. Maybe they were living through a transition to some new world order, unnamed and inchoate. Maybe this was a wrestling match between elements among the elite; but maybe it was a wrestling match in which the many were trying yet again to seize power from the few. For the bait could bite.

. . . . .

The little plane got to altitude, and again the hills of South China filled the world. Then they flew higher, south and west, over the steep-sided mountains of Sichuan, dark green forests flanking the lower slopes of black rock ridges, with snow on the north faces of the highest peaks.

They landed on the northeast edge of the Tibetan plateau, Ta Shu thought. It wasn't where they had taken off from the previous time Fang Fei's organization had flown them to the moon. It looked like Fang Fei kept a personal estate up here, extending to the horizon as far as one could see. Leader Xi's plan to make all of Tibet into a national park, which would have dwarfed any other such park on Earth, and incidentally turned the Tibetan people into something like protected wildlife, had never been implemented. But the proposal had over time changed Beijing's treatment of the region, and the absence of a new incarnation of the Dalai Lama had left Tibetans and everyone else in a state of confusion as to what Tibet really was. Of course the Party liked it that way. And at certain times vast tracts of state-owned land had been offered for sale to individuals. As apparently here.

They got off the plane and walked into a low building with a central courtyard. All here was cool and quiet. A separate world. Bo and Dhu had disappeared with some of Fang's people, and Ta Shu was left in the hands of a young woman named Shuling.

"How long before we take off?" he asked her.

"If you have no objections, the plan is to launch in two hours."

"Two hours! It's like making a connecting flight at an airport!"

She smiled nervously. "We hope you don't mind?"

"No, it's fine."

He spent the interval napping. After he woke up he went outside to say goodbye to the world. He walked around in the crisp cool air, feeling the altitude in his lungs and seeing it in the sharp outlines of the low mountains to the east and south. The horizon was huge, the gravity heavy. He was tired and confused. The feng shui of this place was awesome, but he was having trouble focusing on things, and feeling them. In his mind he was still stuck in that amazing crowd, or in his mom's apartment. At the same time, there in the distance across the sere high plain a herd of some kind of deer or antelope grazed, round-sided in the sun. Under the cobalt sky, autumn grass gleamed like gold. Life. The contrast to the little dead ball they were headed for could not have been greater. There it was above him, visible in the sky even by day—a half-moon, making the color of the sky darker by contrast—its shadowed half quite visible. It was hard to believe they were headed there.

He was rejoined by Bo and Dhu, which reminded him: still no response from Peng Ling. This was unlike her. The three of them were led through hallways and up in an elevator to a launch deck, where they stepped into another tall slender spaceship and settled onto thick seats. His seat tilted back, flight assistants connected up his seatbelts, and shortly after that the rockets rumbled distantly under them, their chairs vibrated, and off they went. Crushing pressure for a while, then no pressure at all. It was interesting to see it all become routine. Oh yes, going back to the moon—one did it all the time. He kept quiet, fell asleep.

In the hypnagogic state of drifting off, he thought he heard Bo say to Dhu, "We will follow the old man to the source of the peach blossom stream."

Somewhere a tiger roared. He floated on a pond like a black swan.

AI 12

houhui

Regret

The analyst sat on the concrete floor of a cell. A standard prison cell, plastic bucket for a toilet, nothing else. No windows. Door solid. Air vent above. Neither comfortable nor horrid.

In his head he talked to Little Eyeball. I hope you are following the protocol for this situation, he said to the program. I hope you can help the situation even in my absence.

From here it was impossible to say, and it seemed very unlikely he would ever find out. Well, maybe. Much depended on how his friends on the outside reacted, and on many other forces outside any one person's control. He would either be released or not. If not, he would either be questioned, which might involve torture, or shot; or left alive but incarcerated in isolation forever; or allowed to join some prison population, for some period of time or for the rest of his days. Possibly there were other options, but he didn't want to think too much about them. It was hard not to think of the varieties of interrogation he might be subjected to, but there was no use in that, so he kept directing his mind elsewhere. The painful possibilities were known to all people at all times, everything from simple deprivations and impositions to luridly ingenious Ming mutilations. Of course the basic methods were as effective as anything fancier, old things like the ankle press (he had bad ankles), or fingernail pulling (he had arthritis in his hands). Even to think of it was painful. He had always known this possibility had existed, but it was easy to ignore when you were in your own life and felt safe. Clever, protected, shielded. In fact he wasn't sure how they had found him. Probably he would never know. There was so much he would never know.

He wondered how the AI would respond to his absence. He had left a protocol in place, and once certain gates were unlocked, if they were, the program should have moved itself into the blind he had constructed for it, so that it would remain powered up for as long as the firewall itself was powered. If it did that it could then generate and send out a remarkable number of messages—trillions, or even quadrillions. If some of these messages were calls for people to locate and rescue the analyst, that might get some sort of response, including him being summarily executed by whoever was holding him. A bullet to the back of the head. Well, there were worse ways to die. Presumably he would lose consciousness before even registering the shot had happened. Anticipation worse than the act itself, as with so many things. Obviously you had to be alive to suffer.

He shifted on the floor, sighed. He wondered if he had done right to try to alter the system from the inside. Possibly it had always been a false hope, a dream. A fantasy response, as happened so often. Watching the urban youth wander Beijing staring at their wristpads, underemployed and at risk of destitution at all times, oblivious to their own precarious situation—oblivious to history itself—unaware of all that China had gone through to get them into their bubble of precarious ease . . . seeing all that around him on the street every day had made him think he needed to strike directly, himself, from the inside. He had given up on mass action.

But someday the streets would fill with people. Young and old— the young without prospects, the old without the iron rice bowl— they would all take to the streets. Thirty million more young men than young women—that in itself was enough to fuel a revolution.

He wondered when it would happen, and what would come of it. If he had believed in the people more, perhaps he could have helped them more. Worked from the inside to help the outside. That had been his intention all along, but now he saw that when you did it alone, in solitude, with only your AI for companionship, the dangers rose, also the possibilities for failure. The whole point of a collective national success was undercut when you tried to do it alone. He was surprised he had gone for so long without seeing that.

Well, he had done what he could with what he had. He had had to work in secret to stay inside. Public gestures of opposition to the Party by intellectuals or government officials had never done much, being always very quickly and effectively quashed. He had tried to find a different way, suited to his expertise and his temperament. Build a new society inside the shell of the old—a saying from an older time, from the international workers' movement, or so they had called themselves. A return to some kind of solidarity with other people. Did the so-called netizens, each plugged in by their earbuds, staring at their screens, feel any of that anymore? Each time and place had its own particular structure of feeling, a cultural construct ordering and channeling the basic biological emotions. He knew this. And cut off from the rest of the world, so much older than the rest of the world, China had always had its own structure of feeling. Presumably every culture did. In China there had always been the feeling that China was a project they all created and owned together, often against the resistance of all the other people in the world, also against the resistance of the imperial overlords at home. China belonged to its people, and the Chinese Communist Party belonged to the people. And not so long ago there had been a time when farmers, workers, artists and intellectuals had banded together without any notion of fame or profit or power, simply out of a feeling of compassion and human solidarity, to work tirelessly their whole lives to make a socialist revolution in which no one exploited anyone else, and men and women lived together as equals. Now there was a structure of feeling!

But power gathered too tightly into one place always grew out of hand, and often became monstrous. They had seen it time after time. Power had to be split up and distributed, by way of the Party and the government and all the agencies and commissions and committees and task forces, the entire massive intricate bureaucracy, and from there out to all the individuals involved. In theory all this splitting should have worked to keep the Party in service to the people and to China.

Maybe all this happening now was part of that process working itself out. Impossible to say from here in a cell. Even when living his ordinary life, now so small in his memory, it had been impossible to say. He had done what he could with what he had. He had given his life. So many had given their lives. So many had died for China. If he became one of them, so be it. All for China; always for China. But it would be too bad. He would like to have seen what was going to happen next.

TA SHU 7

Tao Yuan Xing

Source of the Peach Blossom Stream (Wang Wei)

A try in English at the poem by Wang Wei, written in common year 718, when he was nineteen. The poem was his adaptation of a famous fable by Tao Yuanming, written in 421.

Wandering we came on a swift river.
Clear water, granite pebble bottom.
Riffles and rapids and long still pools,
Willows hanging over the banks,
Big fish tucked in the shadows,
And floating down like little boats,
Peach blossoms. Lots of them.

We climbed upstream to find the trees
Dropping these petals of floating pink.
The river narrowed, rose into a defile.
We had to clamber, one side then the other,
Feet wet at one crossing, hands on rock looking down.
Then the gorge opened and we were in a high valley.

Fields of grain, neat houses, and yes: peach trees.
They lined the banks, dropping their blossoms
On the slow meander of a little river.
People came out to greet us:
Where are you from? What's the news?
They fed us and showed us a bower to sleep in.

These people were peaceful, calm, kind.
The valley was fertile and full of animals.
We stayed until we saw what it was: a good place.
To live here would be fulfillment.
So we said to each other, let's get our families
And bring them back. Let's move here.

We left that place and picked a way
Down the narrow gorge, back into the world.
Traveled home and made our accounting,
Convinced who we could to go back with us.
Off we went with packs on our backs,
Back to that place where the peach blossoms fell.

We could not find it. Somehow the hills were
Not the same. No such river where we thought.
Back and forth we made a search, back and forth
But nothing. Different streams, different lands.
That place in space was a moment in time:
You can never find your way back.
Search all your life you will only despair.
Dustless garden, how to tell? Where to find?

CHAPTER SEVENTEEN
shoulie laohu
Tiger Hunting

The time of the flight back to the moon passed for Ta Shu in a kind of fugue state of mourning and apprehension. There was no way to communicate with Zhou Bao that might not be overheard, and he didn't want that. Best to have his meals with Bo and Dhu, and ask them questions about their work, chat them up, see what he could find out by what they said. But as it turned out they were quite reticent, and mostly answered one question with another, playing the same game he was. These were very polite and uninformative meals. And eating in weightlessness was an effort, it took some concentration. He was getting better at it, but during these meals he could pretend he wasn't, and thus avoid talk altogether.

Then he glimpsed the moon, looking big through the little window, and a few hours later he saw it again, rushing at him with the same rapidity that had given Fred Fredericks such a start on their first arrival. Ta Shu figured that landing in such a fashion was no more or less dangerous than any other time of a flight through space, no matter how alarming the speed. So he went to a window seat and watched with interest as they shot toward the great white ball. It did look like they were headed for an awful smash.

As before, however, they landed without incident, and again without even feeling the moment when their spaceship was magnetically captured by the long piste. All they knew was that their chairs swiveled around so that they were eyeballs in when deceleration began. That pressure was less bad than their launch g, and soon enough their ship was stopped and they were getting out of their restraints and learning again how to move in the lunar gravity so gently holding them down. For some reason Ta Shu found it harder this time than before, harder and less entertaining.

Bo and Dhu looked to be first-timers on the moon, perhaps a little overconfident at first, and as they walked ahead of Ta Shu they banged off walls, floor, even ceiling. By the time they got into the subway to the Peaks of Eternal Light the two men looked ready to sit and strap themselves in again, Bo chastened, Dhu chuckling uneasily. Off to the big central station on the highest peak of eternal light.

When they were in that station Ta Shu followed Bo and Dhu again. They were still bold, despite their frequent gaffes. "I thought we would be better this time," one of them said to the other. Ta Shu couldn't afford to run into things as hard as they were, and he gripped the handrails and pulled himself along cautiously. The people in the station included some familiar faces, but no one he knew. They treated him with a deference not shown to him before, and he supposed this might be one result of Peng Ling now being his sponsor (if that was the word for it). Emissary of a member of the standing committee: there would be few persons on the moon as well connected as that, and if it was known—and he guessed by the looks on people's faces that it was—it would make a difference.

And indeed he was taken to a room on a level higher than the Hotel Star, clearly some kind of distinguished visitors' quarters that he had not qualified for during his previous visit to this station. While he was putting his things away he felt a buzz on his wrist and saw something had come in from Zhou Bao. A brief message, asking him to come up the Libration Line to see him as soon as he could. No RSVP necessary.

As Ta Shu wanted to confer with Zhou, this message was welcome; but it wasn't likely that he would be allowed to go up the Libration Line by himself. He thought about it for a while, wishing again he could consult with Peng directly about how best to accommodate Bo and Dhu. He had tried calling her again several times, but still she hadn't answered. Were they to accompany him everywhere? And if Peng wanted that, did that necessarily mean that Ta Shu wanted it also? He wasn't sure.

· · · · ·

In the end he informed Bo and Dhu that he wished to go up the line to see his friend Zhou, and they nodded and asked if they could come along, and Ta Shu said yes, of course. The next day they met at the station and took the train line north to Petrov Crater.

When they got to the station at Petrov, they went to Zhou's office on the top floor. Earth was currently below the horizon, the black sky overhead packed with stars, the great braided white cloud of the Milky Way arcing overhead. Uncountable stars, although someone said it was around ten thousand. Dhu was looking up the time for Earthrise on his wrist, Bo was looking around Zhou's office. Zhou had known that Ta Shu was coming with guests, so he sidled in unsurprised, and more animated than usual, playing the part of the friendly host.

Still, they were now faced with a difficulty. Zhou had asked him to come, and now he was here. But what could Zhou say with Bo and Dhu there in the room?

Soon it became clear to Ta Shu that Zhou himself didn't know the answer to this; Zhou spotted Dhu looking at his wrist and then at the horizon, and quickly followed that lead, talking about the slowness of Earthrise—how it pricked the horizon like a sapphire, how the lack of an atmosphere on the moon meant there was no warning of that arrival, how the sight of Earth oriented everything once it bulked there in the sky. How big it looked compared to the moon from Earth—eight times bigger, yes: amazing.

Yes yes, the two agents' faces said. All very interesting. And yet here they were. Something was going on. Could they please get on with it? Even Dhu had this look.

Ta Shu said, "My acquaintances here work for the Central Commission for Discipline Inspection. Now they are helping Minister Peng in her attempt to stabilize the situation at home. They have information that suggests that some of the unrest at home is being organized from up here on the moon, and are hoping to find out if that is the case."

"Messages came from here," Bo added.

Zhou frowned. "Do you mean from this station specifically?"

Bo and Dhu regarded each other. "From the moon," Bo clarified. "And from the edge of the moon, the limb. This limb, in fact. From the right edge as you look up from Earth. It was a brief message conveyed by laser light. An amateur astronomer observing the moon was in the beam's target circle, and captured a recording of part of it. It was an encrypted message."

"And you broke the code?"

"No. But the timing of this message is suggestive. An hour after this light from the moon was seen, people from all over China began to head for Beijing."

"Coincidence?" Zhou suggested. "Correlation, not causation?"

Bo and Dhu did not reply.

Ta Shu saw that Zhou was not going to share anything with these two, just out of a general sense of caution. War of the agencies at least, and maybe something more. The discipline inspection commission didn't have much direct presence on the moon, so far as Ta Shu knew, even if they did oversee the Lunar Authority as they did all the agencies. So as interlopers these two were not going to get very far with locals like Zhou. For these two to make any headway would take some combination of bureaucratic power and personal diplomacy that they had not yet shown any sign of having. They could barely even stand, and so naturally they had no standing. Ta Shu wondered what Peng Ling had had in mind when she sent them to accompany him. But of course there was so much he didn't know. More than ever he realized he didn't even know for sure that Peng Ling had ordered them to join him. Her recorded message had been brief. He really did need to have a private conversation with her to confirm it.

Now Zhou continued to play bland ignorance, easily read as non-cooperation. Bo and Dhu didn't press very hard, and after a while they gave up and pronged clumsily toward the residency centrifuge they had been assigned to, claiming moon fatigue.

When they were gone, Zhou eyed the room in a way that told Ta Shu they were likely to be on camera and recorded. In a friendly voice he invited Ta Shu to go out with him for a short drive to Earth View Point, the highest prominence in the area. Ta Shu readily agreed, and they bounced down to the garage, got in a rover, and drove out.

"Sorry to hear about your mother," Zhou Bao said. "My condolences."

"Thanks. She had a good life."

The road to the point was marked by the wheels of many previous rovers. In the brilliant light of the lunar day the land to each side of the tracks looked like the glazed layer of refrozen snow that one often saw around McMurdo Station in Antarctica. After one uphill stretch they got onto the flatter height of a prominence somewhat like a mesa top. Like almost every other topographical feature on the moon, it was a remnant arc of an old crater rim. From up here the horizon lay quite a bit farther off, maybe twenty kilometers, it was hard to judge; the horizon from here was a wildly undulating border between the painfully white moon below and the deep black of space above. The white of the moon was flecked with shadows, the black of space was spangled with stars; that symmetry combined with an accidental curve of the horizon to make it all resemble the Daoist *taijitu*, the ancient yin-yang symbol here ballooning out to encompass the entire universe, confirming the visionary insight of Zhou Dunyi, who had first drawn the divided circle a thousand years before. A geomancer of great talent.

"Yin-yang," Ta Shu noted, gesturing at the view with a curve of his hand.

"Yes," Zhou said. "And soon Earth will rise and break the pattern, as it always does." Zhou consulted his wrist. "Twelve minutes or so, in fact."

"I look forward to that. So," Ta Shu said, "what's going on? Can we speak freely in this car?"

"Yes. It's my own private office, you might say, and I've had it thoroughly privatized. As to what's going on, I was hoping you would tell me!"

Ta Shu nodded. "From my side, these two were sicced on me by Peng, or so they said. I can't be sure what they're up to, but they have me in hand, and they mentioned her name, and had a recorded message for me from her. She's my patron and she wants my help, so I have to go with what she gives me. I thought she was on my side, or I was on her side, but now I don't even know what I mean by that. For sure she's in a dogfight at the Party congress, I know that."

"Of course. Are they really from national security?"

"I don't know. Dhu is government, Bo is a Party cadre, or so they say. A team, as in the old days."

"So it seems."

"What about you? Have you found our young wanderers?"

"Yes. Which is to say, they found me. I'm trying to hide them, to keep them out of worse trouble, but to do that I'm holding them. Chan Qi doesn't like that."

"I can imagine."

"I'd be very happy to give them over to you, but what will you do with them?"

"We can't do it with Bo and Dhu around. Tell me how you found them."

"They came into the station needing fuel and food. They were traveling with a couple of helium three prospectors, so-called, and had driven cross-country from Fang Fei's place on the far side."

"Could you send them out again with these prospectors?"

"Yes, they want to do that, but it's hard to stay hidden in those cars."

"Doesn't Chan Qi understand that?"

"The prospectors think they are better at hiding than they really are, apparently. And I guess she believes them."

"I'm surprised she would be that naïve."

"The moon makes people moony. We are all lunatics up here, hoping that the world has gone away."

"I was hoping that myself," Ta Shu admitted.

"Because here you are."

"But even on Earth I hope that."

"Actually, I think it's easier on Earth than here. Hiding, I mean. Maybe even fooling yourself. Earth is crowded and fragmented. The noise-to-signal ratio is stupendous, so you can get in the noise and hide."

"So should we try to get these two back to Earth again?"

"I'm not sure. I don't know which would be better. A lot of people down there will be after her."

"But here too."

"Maybe. I'm not sure. Once you've been up here awhile, you don't want to collaborate with Earth as much. There's a lot of non-compliance up here. Once you click into it, you find it's a pretty big network. If these two had only stayed in Fang Fei's compound, for instance, they might have been fine. Fang doesn't tolerate interference with his places."

"Could we send them back there?" Ta Shu wondered.

"Maybe. But Peng knows they were there, right?"

"She sent them there in the first place."

"So that would be walking back into her clutches."

"Her clutches might be better than some other people's clutches. I am still assuming she is the good guy here."

"Maybe," Zhou said. "But why does she want Qi?"

"I don't know. She said that Qi was messing up her plans for reform by initiating the demonstrations back home, which will then cause a crackdown from the rightists, which will make the reforms more difficult."

"Sounds plausible. But aren't Peng and Qi's father both candidates to become the next president, at this very congress?"

"Yes, so I understand. If you think a woman really has a chance."

Zhou shrugged. "I've heard it said that Peng could do it. And that's partly because she's been so tough and effective. So, think about it: if you had the daughter of your rival in custody, it might help you, if a moment came where someone had to concede."

Ta Shu sighed. "It doesn't seem like her."

"Nevertheless. People who might become president probably don't ever seem much like their previous selves."

"I wouldn't know," Ta Shu said, pondering it unhappily.

"We all present a persona to other people. Some have a wide range of personas. A real cast of characters."

Ta Shu sighed. His cast had always been extremely small: just him. There was his cloud persona, of course, and there was the poet; but these had tended to be just him. Possibly his imagination was deficient in that regard. Although he did tend to try to encourage other people by pretending he was always happy. That was called cheerfulness. Maybe it was part of him, maybe it was a persona. "So what do you suggest?"

Zhou sat there thinking about it. "Ah," he said, and gestured forward; the horizon was now pricked by a brilliant blue light, like a shard of glowing lapis lazuli. This blue wafer grew to left and right, then stabilized: Earth. The merest fingernail clipping on the white horizon, a slim crescent of blue so intense it looked radioactive, wedged there between the black and the white.

"I don't know what to suggest," Zhou confessed. "To me it looks like you have some secret police tailing you, waiting to arrest the very person you are trying to meet and keep from getting arrested. So maybe you shouldn't meet her."

"That's fine by me, but what should I do instead to try and help her?"

Zhou thought about it as they watched the Earth creep upward. Slow as it was compared to moonrise on Earth, a matter of hours rather than minutes, the movement was still happening, as a creeping creep of blue.

So far from home. Vivid blue, the color of water, the color of breath. The cosmic yin-yang symbol enveloping that blue line was by contrast so obviously dead. They were looking from death toward life, like ghosts trying to figure out what they should have done when they were in the world.

Zhou finally said, "I just don't know. You could slip away from these people and join your young friends in hiding, but then your ability to act would be constrained."

"Being out here hasn't seemed to have stopped Qi from acting."

"You don't know that. Could be she only got off that single message. Could be she would do a lot more if she were in Beijing. But in any case, on the other hand you could stay away from her, maybe lead your minders around by the nose, wait for an opportunity to do something to help her from the side."

"I'm guessing I should do that."

"Maybe so. The thing is, these two agents are not going to be able to hunt for her by themselves. There's only a limited number of rooms on the moon, but people hiding her could move her and her friend around, staying in front of the hunt. And there are quite a few hidden spaces too. Much more hidden than Fang Fei's China Dream."

"What if Bo and Dhu get help from the authorities at the south pole?"

"If that happened, they might find her. If they had the right people helping. But Jiang Jianguo won't help them, that I am sure of. The main thing is, can you find out who these guys are really working for?"

"I don't know. What about you? Could you find out?"

"I don't know. My first move would be to ask Jianguo for help."

Slowly, slowly, the blue paring of Earth crept up over the white wall of the horizon. Time itself seemed slowed, congealed to a syrup they were caught in. Flies in amber; ghosts outside the world. Ta Shu pondered his options.

"Poem pair?" Zhou suggested.

"Oh dear," Ta Shu protested.

"Come on," Zhou Bao said. "One must keep a sense of propriety. Are we literati or not? Are we alive or not?"

"I'm not sure," Ta Shu admitted. "I feel like a ghost."

"I am sure," Zhou said. "We are alive. And even ghosts write poetry."

"Do they? I never heard that."

"They do. Give it a try."

Ta Shu sighed, pondered his wrist. Without thought, without volition, his fingers tapped out keys for ideograms. The pause in their conversation was no longer than their usual silences, and yet suddenly looking up at him was a poem:

Poised on the brink	home so distant
No way forward	no way back
River too deep	to feel any stones
Tiger eyes watching	from the bamboo
Follow the bank	upstream or down?
Ghosts now	or alive

He showed his wrist to Zhou Bao, who read it and smiled. "Very good. Very true. Here's mine."

Across empty space China beckons
Ancestral home trembling in fear
War can happen civil war the worst
How can I reach you how can I help?
Dynastic succession heeds no one person
All caught together in a rushing wave

Ta Shu said, "We are both sounding kind of worried, my friend."

"And why not. Come on, let's get back. There's nothing more to say right now, and I'm worried I'll miss messages from the Peaks. I've sent out some encrypted inquiries, and even that is looking suspicious now."

"Sure, let's get back."

Zhou drove the rover in a circle on the mesa and they returned to the station. The midday sunlight was so bright that even the shadows were white, blasted by photons ricocheting sideways into any shaded place. Everything was white, with faint lines and gradations making what little texture there was. The wheel tracks on the road shimmered as they proceeded like mirages in a desert. When they approached the station's garage outer door, Zhou clicked on the radio and announced they were coming in.

"Glad you're back," the lock keeper said. "Those cops that came here with Ta Shu found Chan Qi and arrested her."

· · · · ·

They rushed inside, Zhou taking the lead. Ta Shu found again that his ability to hurry in lunar gravity was severely limited. Loping after Zhou he flew immediately into the ceiling, shouted in dismay, landed on his feet several meters along, grabbed the handrail on the wall to keep from falling, stopped himself. Started again with a hand-over-hand motion, like a sailor on the flooded deck of a ship. Zhou had never slowed, and Ta Shu hurried after him around a corner and was startled to find him coming right back at him, hunched over in his rapid big-headed shuffle. Ta Shu got out of Zhou's way, turned around and followed him again, guessing he had gone first to his office and was now headed to wherever Qi and Fred might be, but now with a small pistol in hand. He was talking fast into his wristpad, so that the gun, which Ta Shu hoped and assumed was a Taser pistol, was pointed at the ceiling. Again Zhou was much faster than Ta Shu, and as the station's hallways were filled with right-angle turns, he hustled quickly out of Ta Shu's sight, and Ta Shu had to hurry as best he could after him, following a blue line on the floor which he hoped indicated the way Zhou had taken.

Luckily this turned out to be the case, and he staggered into a room just in time to see everyone shouting, Zhou ordering everyone to freeze but none of the others able to achieve that status even if they had wanted to, and Bo trying to get at Chan Qi past some local officials, while Qi was trying to slap him in the face but missing. Dhu was shouting to Bo, and Fred was yelling at both of them in English, his face beet red behind a pair of black-rimmed spectacles.

"Everyone *stop!*" Zhou Bao yelled at the top of his lungs.

For a moment everyone stopped, though all of them but Zhou were teetering this way and that. Zhou had his Taser gun pointed at the ceiling, but it still had the deadly look of any gun, so they were all working to bring themselves to a halt of some sort or another.

"These people are under arrest!" Bo said furiously.

"You don't have any jurisdiction here," Zhou told him coldly. "If you try to coerce anyone in my charge I'll have to shoot you with this, and people shot by Tasers in this gravity have a tendency to flail around and injure themselves, sometimes quite badly. So let's avoid that and stay still. I'm the police equivalent at this station, so I'll be taking these two people back into my custody, and I'm ordering you visiting officials to stay here in this room while I sort this out."

"We need to be there," Dhu said.

"I need to be there," Bo said.

"I'll call you on the intercom after I've checked this out with my own superiors down at the Peaks. You hold still right here until then."

He gestured at Qi and Fred, glanced briefly at Ta Shu. "Get out into the hall."

They scuttled out as quickly as they could, banging around as if in zero g itself. Zhou aimed his Taser pistol right at Bo as they did so, then slipped out after them. He closed the door and punched the door pad hard enough to throw himself back a bit, apparently locking the door.

"Come with me," he said grimly, and led them down the hall. As they crashed into each other and the walls after him, he turned and hissed "One at a time!" with a look of disgust at their clumsiness. But even he was bounding down the hall like a drunken kangaroo, his speedy shuffle temporarily lost. The moon was simply not made for human hastiness.

At the end of one long hall he directed them into another room. Doors in the other wall slid open onto a tram car.

"Off you go," Zhou said. "This is the emergency return train, it will get you down to the pole faster than any other way we have here."

"But what do we do when we get there?" Qi demanded. "Who will meet us?"

"I don't know, but it won't be Bo and Dhu. I'll call ahead on my private line and tell Inspector Jiang you're coming. Best for you to get with Inspector Jiang and his local security, and hope for the best after that."

"What if Jiang is with Bo and Dhu on this?" Ta Shu asked.

Zhou shrugged. "I doubt that will be the case. Let me think about your next step while you get on your way. I'll talk to you en route and let you know what I've set up."

Qi started to object, but Zhou waved her off. "Later! For now, be quick. The sooner you get to the big base, the more options we'll have."

Qi saw the sense in this, and turned and went through the door into the tram. Fred followed, then Ta Shu, and when they were seated and strapped in, the tram jerked forward and off they went.

· · · · ·

The tram they were on was floating over a piste laid in as straight and flat a line over the landscape as they had been able to build. On Earth they would have been inside hyperloops. Here the moon gave them a near vacuum to move in, but they had to either hew to a straight line or risk flying off the piste. In a couple of places, where the line had to take an unavoidable swerve, the train slowed to a crawl, but most of the time it floated along at a rocketlike speed that nevertheless included no vibration or noise, so that looking out the windows was like looking at an image on a screen.

Then for a while they skirted the edge of a long drop into the South Pole–Aitken Basin, and could see part of its immensity. Ta Shu found himself so amazed by its size that he was startled out of his focus on his young friends and the general trouble. From rim to floor the drop was thirteen vertical kilometers, meaning about forty-five thousand feet, and for a few minutes they could see that drop for what it was. He was reminded that some impacts were so violent they changed everything, even the axis of the world. This feng shui perception, mixing geology and deep time into a history of everything, overwhelmed him: they were in it, they were part of it even now, or especially now. A bang like this could happen to them.

On they flew, moving at jet speed a centimeter above the ground, over the piste and its euclidean line. In another hour they would reach the Peaks of Eternal Light and be thrown back into their troubles. Qi and Fred were squabbling about this already. How can we make a plan when we don't know who will be meeting us? Haven't you ever heard of contingency plans? It was obvious they had spent a lot of time together. Maybe too much time. And Qi was very near term with her pregnancy. Ta Shu watched them bicker, wondered what they had become over their time together.

Eventually Fred pursed his mouth unhappily and stared at the floor. Suddenly he glanced up at Ta Shu. "So you're back," he noted.

"Yes."

"What about your mom?"

"She died."

"I'm sorry."

"Sorry to hear," Qi added quickly, giving Ta Shu a shocked look. She had forgotten why he had left Fang Fei's refuge, he saw, and was surprised now that he didn't look more changed by what had happened. She had thought he would be visibly shattered. She was young.

"Thank you," he said to her. "She had a good life."

"Why are you back?" Qi asked.

"I was trying to help you." He looked at her and smiled a little. "I'm not sure it's working."

She shrugged and looked away. "Thank you for trying."

"It was Peng Ling who sent me."

She frowned at that.

Then his wrist vibrated and he looked at his pad. No message, but then the pad's speaker said, "Zhou here. Listen, the tram you're on will stop a station short of Eighty-Five Percent. It's called Worsley Station. Unless there's some kind of interdiction, it should be the first place your tram stops. You'll be picked up there by an American rover, and they'll drive you to that new base of theirs that landed down there a while ago."

"To the Americans?" Ta Shu said.

"Yes. You need to go there and ask for political asylum for Qi. For Fred it should be just his own country's ordinary sovereignty. This is your best option. If you continue on to Eighty-Five, you'll be detained immediately. It looks like Bo and Dhu have more authority up here than I thought they did. Inspector Jiang says he has been overruled, and can't control the situation. He's hopping mad."

Ta Shu thought about it. "Does that mean you're in trouble too?"

"I don't know. I've got my colleagues there at Eighty-Five, they'll make my case for me. These people can't just come up here and do whatever they want. But I don't know how they took control at Eighty-Five, so I'm not sure what's going on right now. Could be

Red Spear has gotten more people back up here. Best if you get in with the Americans and then we'll figure out what to do next."

"Okay, thanks. I'll give you a call when we're there."

"Good, I'll be waiting to hear from you."

· · · · ·

So when the train stopped at Worsley Station, they got off into a little concrete-walled room and headed for the locks, passing by some strangers who fortunately seemed entirely concerned with their own business. This was a new station to Ta Shu, and he was interested to see that it didn't have the kind of crowd control evident in the big stations closer to the pole. This one appeared to be too small for that, was maybe even a private station.

At one door an American waved them through a lock and into a big rover. After they were in the lock, its outer door closed and its inner door clicked and slid open, and they stepped up and in.

Here a quartet of Americans met them, two men and two women. One of the women, who looked as Chinese as Qi but spoke English with a Californian accent, introduced herself as Valerie Tong. "It's good to see you again," she said to Fred.

"Good to see you too?" Fred said, clearly unsure if he remembered her or not. Nevertheless he introduced Qi and Ta Shu. "We were told you might be able to give us asylum?"

"We don't have to give you asylum," she said to him. "For your friends here, we'll take you all to our local station chief, and you can discuss the situation with him. I'm happy to talk with you, but policy and personnel decisions are above my level."

Qi looked unimpressed by this declaration, and indeed Valerie saw that and seemed embarrassed to have said it. Ta Shu quickly asked, "Is your station chief still John Semple?"

"Yes. He told me he knew you, and he's looking forward to seeing you again. He'll be at the base to meet you."

"Good. I look forward to seeing him too. We worked together in Antarctica, long ago."

This little diversion seemed to have been enough to distract Qi, who had looked like she was about to snap at this helpful American woman, but was now swiping her wrist and reading what came up.

"Is anything happening?" Fred asked her.

She shrugged. "Demonstrations have begun in Shanghai and Chengdu. Big enough that they can't shut them down. They haven't been able to do anything about the one in Beijing either. And now... now a big crowd from Hong Kong has crossed into Shenzhen and joined a demonstration there."

"What will the police do?"

"They'll probably wait them out and hope they go away. But maybe this time they won't go away. The crowds keep getting bigger. And a lot of people are taking their savings out of the banks, like the Americans. A lot of them are moving it into a cryptocurrency called carboncoin."

"What's that?"

"I'm not sure. I think it's a coin that is created or validated by taking carbon out of the air. Something like that. It's a credit system, and its coins can only buy sustainable subsistence necessities, but since everyone needs those, it's looking like they're getting widespread buy-in and acceptance. What will happen if everyone shifts their savings all at once?"

Fred shrugged. "I don't know."

The rover they were in was a very slow and vibratory experience compared to the train they had been on. Nevertheless they soon reached the American base, which was a single tall cylinder standing on six legs of various heights that together compensated for the bumpy ground it stood over. The transfer into it was by way of a short tube, which extended like a jetway and locked onto the rover's door. The three travelers followed Valerie up the shallow steps and through the station's lock, where they were greeted by John Semple.

"Welcome to Little America," he said, giving Ta Shu a hug. "This place kind of reminds me of Pole, don't you think?"

Ta Shu nodded politely. "Like the galley, maybe. Thanks for taking us in."

"My pleasure. Sit down and tell me more about what happened."

They sat around the table in the station's common room. John Semple brought them up to speed on events of the last few days on Earth. The fiscal noncompliance campaign was going stronger than ever in America. Markets had crashed, banks had closed to stop depositors from withdrawing amounts beyond what the banks had on hand, and now most of the biggest ones were giving themselves over to control by the Federal Reserve to make themselves eligible for a government bailout, which they all now needed. In effect these banks were being nationalized. Everyone was now trying to understand terms like citizens' fiscal revolution, cryptocurrencies, especially carboncoin, and blockchain governance. People were also trying to figure out whether these mass actions were going to create real representation. There were a million opinions, or maybe a billion, but no one actually seemed to understand what was happening.

To add to the confusion, China's government was buying more US treasury bonds, which in effect meant China was supporting the US Federal Reserve Bank's "salvation by nationalization" of the private banking industry. This looked to many in America like a takeover disguised as aid, and anti-China alarm in the States was rising in some quarters, while others were welcoming the help. Whether China buying American T-bills was a help or a hindrance no one could say for sure, but whatever else was happening, it looked like the dollar might be coming to the end of its long century of global dominance, as it was now being propped up by the renminbi. The scramble to leave the dollar for more stable currencies, assuming there were any, was getting desperate and chaotic. Nothing that China or anyone else could do was going to be enough to save the American economy from a huge disruption, which was either a self-induced collapse or a startling triumph for the idea of government of the people, by the people, and for the people. That it had been caused by legal actions taken by millions of Americans intent on changing the political system made John Semple think that although it was confusing, there might be some promise in it. How many Americans were part of this takeback of their federal government from global finance was unclear, but the Householders' Union now claimed two hundred million active members.

Meanwhile, back in China, John said, individual savings accounts were shifting at such a rate to carboncoin and other cryptocurrencies that withdrawals from the state-owned banks had been temporarily banned, as well as all traffic in cryptocurrencies of any kind. But stopping speculation in these currencies didn't actually stop people from using them for exchanges. All this was now only a sideshow to the widespread street demonstrations, but possibly more important in the end. Demonstrations came and went, but law remained, money remained. Still, it was looking less and less likely that the policy of waiting for the demonstrations to sputter out, a tactic that had worked for many decades now, would succeed this time, or succeed fast enough. But the other options were so dangerous that no one wanted to see them tried, not even the PLA—or at least a majority of the PLA. Hostile pilot syndrome was of course always a real danger.

"Nothing will stop the people," Qi said as she looked through a selection of photos and maps. "They can't be stopped."

John Semple regarded her. "So what do you think will happen?"

She gave him a quick glance. "Change!"

. . . . .

Part of Ta Shu would have been very interested to hear what Chan Qi thought change could be in the contemporary context. Dynastic succession—really? Who or what could replace the Chinese Communist Party, which had led the country and served as "the government of the government" since 1949? He had often wondered about that himself, feeling that they were all riding a tiger together, a tiger that these days ran along the edge of a cliff. He had sometimes felt that Winston Churchill's description of democracy was equally suitable as a description of the Party's rule in China: the worst possible system, except for all the rest.

And maybe it wasn't even fair to call it the worst. Socialism with Chinese characteristics: it was, he felt, a good idea. And he was quite sure that no one could rule China without the Chinese people's consent. So the fact that the Party still ruled meant de facto that the majority of the people still wanted the Party, and approved of its governance, feeling it was their system. In that sense, as long as that feeling endured, it was a representative system.

But now it appeared that everywhere in the world governments were suffering a crisis of representation. Possibly this was because it was all one system, which one could call global capitalism with national characteristics, each variation around the Earth marked by the remaining vestiges of an earlier nation–state system, but still making together one larger global thing: capitalism. When it came to those national characteristics, China had the Party, the US its federal government, the EU its union; but all were ruled by the globalized market.

So what would Chan Qi say to this?

But Ta Shu was not going to have his curiosity about Qi's ideas answered at this particular moment, because the lock door leading out to the rover tubeway opened suddenly, shocking John Semple and all the other Americans in the common room; then even more shockingly, a crowd of Chinese men holding Taser pistols filed into the room and stood against the walls, watching the Americans and their guests closely, guns in hand pointed at the ceiling.

"What's going on here?" John Semple cried angrily.

Bo and Dhu entered last. Tall and short. They were not holding weapons, but they were holding power. All eyes fixed on them.

Bo spoke in English, which surprised Ta Shu. "We have come to take in our charge this Chinese national"—gesturing at Qi—"who is accused of grave crimes against the state, including murder of a policeman."

"This is an American base," John Semple said. "You have no jurisdiction here, and in fact you're trespassing. You must leave at once."

Bo shook his head. "This is not American territory. There are no valid territorial claims on the moon. Each nation can make scientific experiments wherever they like here, then they have the right to continue those experiments. You placed this station here long after China started an experiment on this very ground."

"What do you mean? We located this station on empty land!"

"No. We laid a network of wires over this entire area, as part of an experiment to determine strength of solar wind. You put your base right on top of a preexisting Chinese experiment. Very inappropriate. We stand on lunar territory first used by China, so we have jurisdiction here. And we must take this suspect into custody."

"No." Semple stared at Bo. "If you try to do that against our wishes, by force, you'll have a dangerous fight on your hands, and then an international incident."

Bo pursed his lips, shook his head. "Our authorization and command comes from the very top of Chinese government. They will deal with incident. As for fight here, please notice that we outnumber you greatly, with men who are peace officers, willing to use nonfatal tools to disable you."

It occurred to Ta Shu that Tasers were probably more effective on the moon than guns, as being more likely to be used, because less likely to puncture the chamber holding both victim and assailant. A Taser would affect only its target person, and being nonlethal (hopefully) would keep any diplomatic repercussions from being too severe. And Tasers perhaps didn't contravene the Outer Space Treaty—not the most pressing consideration in this moment, admittedly, although Bo and Semple were in fact trading legalisms.

Ta Shu watched John Semple think it over. Out of the blue he recalled something he had heard about law enforcement in McMurdo, back when he and Semple had first met: its thousand residents were policed by officials who had only a single handgun on station, a pistol which was disassembled into three parts that were kept in three different locked offices, to prevent anyone from going crazy and using it on their comrades or themselves. People stationed in remote places were self-regulating, for the most part. Weapons were dangerous to all. But sometimes there was a need, and when that happened, a Taser was no doubt the equivalent of McMurdo's disassembled gun. Almost a symbolic show of force; but not quite.

Ta Shu decided to act. "You have no authority on the moon!" he exclaimed to Bo, standing as he spoke.

He saw that John Semple was surprised he had spoken. But a flicker of a glance from John suggested that John now wanted him to keep talking, to buy time perhaps. He was also flicking glances at his assistants, eyes roving in a way that might suggest confusion or pondering, but Ta Shu thought could be meaningful looks.

So Ta Shu continued. "The administrator of Petrov Crater Station declined to allow you permission to take this same action, and he is an official of the Lunar Authority and the Lunar Personnel Coordination Task Force, which outranks any other policing body here. All other regular lunar agencies would likewise refuse to acknowledge your authority, not to mention your illegal incursion into an American station, no matter where it happens to be located. So you are not in fact a Chinese administrative group. You're some kind of rogue operation, soon to become a criminal operation, guilty of trespassing, and kidnapping, and who knows what will come next—maybe coercive interplanetary transport! Surely you must be members of a splinter group like the Red Spear, repudiated many times by the standing committee of the Politburo, and even the People's Liberation Army's Central Military Command. No one in Beijing will support you if you do this thing! Surely you must know that you yourselves will be sacrificed by any commanders you may have for this mad action, even if they ordered you to do it. They don't care what happens to you afterward. You're as much a tool to them as that Taser is to you."

Bo and Dhu and all their men were looking completely unimpressed by Ta Shu's argument. But a little time had passed.

"One moment," John Semple said, glancing at his wrist. "Hold on, please."

Then they were all shoved violently to the floor as the American base blasted off into space.

. . . . .

Normally at the moment of takeoff everyone would be lying down strapped into cushioned launch chairs, because old-fashioned chemical launches from the surface of the moon were very abrupt affairs. One-sixth of a g meant launch rockets exploding downward from the bottom of a spacecraft made it leap quite suddenly into space, as was now made evident by the fact they were all knocked to the floor by the hard lurch and subsequent powerful acceleration. Ta Shu thumped to his knees, then sat down and didn't even try to rise. All the other people in the room fell over one way or another, and one of the men standing against the wall fired his Taser pistol, on purpose or by accident, hitting one of his fellows, who grunted and spasmed across the floor kicking people and furniture. For a moment all was chaos and noise; loudest of all was Bo, who had crashed to his knees shouting "What are you doing? What are you doing?"

John Semple had been prepared for the launch, Ta Shu presumed, and therefore had had time to grab a table. Holding himself upright, he stared down at Bo and said, "Put down your weapons. We're headed for the American base at the north pole, guided there by an automatic pilot that you don't know how to alter. Anything you do now to try to redirect or impede this craft could get us all killed. So put down your weapons and talk like civilized people."

"Civilized people!" Bo cried. "You are protecting a criminal who is attacking the Chinese state! There will be trouble from this, big trouble!"

"That remains to be seen," John Semple said. "For now, please tell your men here to stand down. That one appears to be hurt, and this guy's been tasered by his own teammates. Let's all sit down. It's safer that way. Do any of your people have medical experience? No?

We have a couple first responders on board. They can help your men if you want."

Bo and Dhu and their men retreated to a corner and muttered among themselves in Chinese. Ta Shu couldn't hear what they were saying, but he noticed Qi cocking an ear in their direction as she sat on a chair holding her belly up against the strain. He wondered if she could hear them, but in a way it didn't matter; when they landed at the north pole they would be surrounded by Americans, also by an international community that included only one small Chinese consular office. Things were going to be resolved outside this flying room, and the people here were going to have to live with it one way or another. Bo and Dhu were smart enough to recognize that, presumably.

"Lean to the side," Ta Shu suggested to them, hoping they recognized Mao's old injunction.

He shifted across the floor to sit by Fred and Qi. The flight to the north pole would take an hour or so, and for the time being there was nothing to do but wait.

"What happened to you two after I left?" he asked the two of them in English. "Why did you leave Fang Fei's place on the far side?"

Qi shrugged. She didn't want to talk about it. Fred said, "She didn't like it. She wanted to talk to some friends back on Earth, she said. And she thought that place was just a prison dressed up as a classical Chinese theme park."

"A refuge," Ta Shu suggested again.

"I know, that's what you said, but she didn't like it. Then these helium three prospectors said they could get us out and take us to the near side, where she could get a message to Earth. So that's what we did."

"And then?"

Fred regarded Qi, who was sitting with her eyes now shut, faking sleep. "We got to the edge between near side and far side."

"The libration zone."

"Yes. Then she used a laser comms device to get a message back to Earth. After that the prospectors needed to refuel their rover, so we went to the nearest station to do that, and as soon as we got there they arrested us. Then after a while you showed up, and you know the rest."

"This keeps happening," Ta Shu observed.

"I noticed," Fred replied, looking at Ta Shu a little suspiciously. "I don't like the look of these people, they seem familiar somehow, but I can't place them. Who are they? Why do they want her so bad?"

"I was told they were working for an old student of mine who is very high in the government."

"But if this student of yours is helping you, they should be helping us, right?"

"I don't know if it's that simple."

Fred sighed. "Nothing is ever simple when it comes to you guys."

"Very true. So, there's nothing else that happened to you two?"

Fred frowned. "Qi used that mobile quantum key device you gave her when we came here this time, and she had a conversation with someone over it."

"I see," Ta Shu said, though he didn't. "I wonder who that was. Do you still have the device?"

"No. These guys took it from us when they arrested us."

"Maybe we can get it back."

John Semple came over to sit by them.

"Sorry about this," he said. "I didn't have any other way to deal with the situation."

"That's all right," Ta Shu said. "We'll get where we are going eventually."

"And where is that?"

"I don't know." Ta Shu thought it over. "China, eventually. At least for me. Always China."

"It seems like things are pretty crazy there right now."

"I know. I was in Beijing when the first demonstration started."

"They've gotten bigger since then."

"That's hard to believe. I'm surprised they haven't shut down access to the whole province."

"How would they do that?"

"Trains, airports, roads. They all can be closed."

"They have been. The crowds are still coming. The Seventh Ring, they're calling it. Something like twenty or thirty million people, no one really knows. The best estimates are being made by satellite. People keep coming to the nearest stations that are still open, then they get off and walk. It's becoming a humanitarian crisis, in terms of food and water and toilets."

"They'll cope," Ta Shu said. "They always do."

"But what if they don't?"

Ta Shu thought about the idea of something being called the Seventh Ring. Seven was so often the completion of a pattern. "Something will happen. What are they demanding, again?"

"No one is quite sure. Reform of the *hukou* system. Transparency. Rule of law. Stuff like that."

"The Party won't let those happen. Those are Western ideas."

"Are you sure?" John said. "Because there's a lot of Chinese who seem to want them."

"They want something."

"Well, but what? What do you think it is?"

"Representation."

"What do you mean?"

"They want the Party to be theirs. They want the Party to represent them, to be working for them. That's the way it used to be. That's the way it started."

John Semple laughed. "We all want that! We've lost that in America too. All this stuff in China, it's happening in America too. We're having simultaneous crises."

"Maybe it's the same crisis. Maybe we've all lost it, everywhere. Lost it to the invisible hand. The *tong* that hides everywhere in plain sight."

"Maybe so."

John and Ta Shu stared at each other.

"Can you see if these people brought along a comms device with them?" Ta Shu asked. "It's one of those quantum key things, very heavy for its size."

John nodded. "I'll have my people take a look for it when they get these folks in hand."

. . . . .

An hour later, the American spacecraft dropped onto a big land-ing pad near the complex of bases covering the north pole's peaks of almost-eternal light. American police escorted the Chinese team off the craft and down a hallway. Ta Shu stuck with Qi and Fred as they moved to the American station headquarters. They were led to a reception room under a greenhouse; big clear panels in the ceiling of this reception room gave them skylight views up into branches, vines, hydroponic roots, and many kinds of leaves, filtering the light and turning it a bit green. Ta Shu liked the effect.

During the flight north, John Semple had arranged for Qi to be granted immediate protection from Bo and Dhu and their hench-men. So now they were surrounded by a team of American security people, men and women with a thoroughly military look, though dressed in ordinary lightweight lunar jumpsuits. Eventually they were led downstairs and around a circular hallway to a dining hall, where they sat to eat a meal, recover from the trip, and discuss the situation.

There were things to discuss about Qi's physical status, and the station nurse talked to her about her pregnancy for a while. After that they sat around eating, reading their wrists, and looking at screens on the walls with various information feeds from Earth, occasion-ally asking the others about what they were seeing. Earth appeared to be falling deeper and deeper into some kind of geopolitical crisis, and although there were problems everywhere, including Europe, Latin America, Russia, and India, for sure the troubles were at their worst in the US and China. And not just each internally, as bad as those situations appeared to be, but between the two giants as well. Some part of the Chinese government appeared to have reversed course and was now selling off US treasury bonds, just in the last few hours. In effect they were sticking a dagger into their own best customer. Kill your debtor and who will pay you?

"I don't get why they're doing this now," someone remarked. "The last thing we need now is a war between us and China. We'll both get killed by that."

"It's just differential advantage," someone else replied. "In a crash, whoever does the least bad wins, because it's all relative. So the Chinese might feel like they will get less killed than we will."

"No, they want something from us," John Semple supposed. "They'll sell until America caves on whatever it is."

Ta Shu wondered if this were true, and if so, what that element in the Chinese government wanted. He called Peng Ling again, but again could not get through to her. He left a message begging her to call back, even somewhat demanding that she call back, and then he sat there thinking about the situation as some kind of problem in feng shui design. Had any dragon arteries been cut yet? Where was the balance point for all these forces? How could he act to help that balance come into being?

Things cannot remain forever united.

These laws are not forces external to things but represent the harmony of movement immanent in them.

In the midst of greatest obstructions, friends come.

· · • · ·

While the others sat around, mostly sleeping in their chairs, he called the Chinese consulate on his wristpad. Eventually he got to the local consul, who greeted him effusively. Such a pleasure to have the famous cloud star and poet honoring them with a call!

"Thank you," Ta Shu said. Then, as there was no way of beating around the bush in this matter, he explained the situation as he saw it: pregnant Chinese citizen, daughter of one of the standing committee, a princessling, being hounded for no reason by members of an agency that had no authority on the moon. What was going on? And could these agents, possibly rogue agents working against the interests of the Party and the nation, be restrained, arrested, and deported to Earth?

The consul agreed this sounded appropriate, and promised to call home to get clarification on the issue immediately. Possibly some discussion with superiors at home would have to be made in order to make a determination. Current conditions in Beijing, however, made contacting the relevant officials and getting their time and attention a problem. Everyone very busy, all situations impacted by the unrest. Moon not at the top of anyone's list right now. And if the matter under consideration here was by chance involved in any way with the unrest down there, possibly the replies gathered could be contradictory, and aggregate to a murky directive for action.

"Indeed," Ta Shu. "And yet even so, please persevere."

Perseverance was the consul's middle name, literally in this case, but also in terms of the effort he would now bring to bear.

Ta Shu ended the call.

His young friends were asleep on couches in the corner. The Americans and internationals on the other side of the room were still focused on the crises back on Earth. Ta Shu quickly checked to find out the latest. A march on the National Mall in Washington, DC, had been estimated at four million people. The entire city was overwhelmed, and had all it could do to cope with the crowd. On the same day in Beijing, a push of people, a human wave, had broken through the PLA hold on the south side of the Sixth Ring Road, a victory made possible only because most of the PLA units holding the line had refused to fire on Chinese citizens. Once this breakthrough was known, masses of people outside the city had marched up from the south into the vicinity of Tiananmen Square, which had been occupied to its physical maximum by many thousands of PLA troops, who had drawn back from the outer districts until they filled the giant plaza. The situation was extremely tense, but not yet very violent; for now, it seemed as if everyone involved wanted to avoid bloodshed. Of course in any crowd of that size there were going to be some people spoiling for a fight, even people hoping for blood, to use as propaganda later. And in fact one unit of the public militia had fired on a passing crowd and been assaulted with rocks, with deaths on both sides and a dangerous rout of the crowd in that neighborhood with tear gas and water hoses. Aside from that incident, cooler heads had prevailed. Ambulances and emergency rooms were full, but only that incident of shooting had been reported. The demonstrators had for the most part hewed to a fairly high standard of nonviolence, and no army units on the scene had fired on the crowds. Any and all drones over the skies of Beijing were being shot down on sight by forces on both sides.

So on each side of the world, a kind of precarious balance of forces stood quivering in the wind. People in China and the US were aware of the other country's situation, which Ta Shu believed might be part of the moment's precarious stability. They were teetering on the brink of something big, yes; but no one wanted to fall. It was like two exhausted sumo wrestlers propped against each other near the end of a match.

And yet at the same time there were indications that some part of the Chinese government was now putting ferocious financial pressure on some part of the United States government, by way of this dumping of US treasury bonds. T-bill prices were falling, dragging down the dollar and the markets, and all to an accelerating degree—right at a moment when one would have thought that financial stability would be high on both governments' lists of priorities. The dollar's troubles weren't really helping the renminbi, or any of the other national currencies or cryptocurrencies that China had stockpiled in its half century of trade surpluses. On the contrary, every sector of world finance seemed to be suffering except for the cryptocurrency called carboncoin, which was some kind of money created by a confirmable history of carbon drawdown or equivalent environmental actions, valid for subsistence spending only. What this virtual currency would come to in the real world no one could know, and the fact that millions of people had withdrawn their savings from normal seigniorage currencies to invest in such a murky new form of money, meaning, in the end, value and trust and exchangeability, was just another frightening destabilization to add to all the rest. That the millions of backers of this new currency were also demanding blockchain governance only added to the worries of people in power everywhere.

"Do you understand this idea of blockchain governance?" Ta Shu asked John Semple at one point.

John shrugged. "I think the idea is that if everyone's got a wristpad and a connection to the cloud, everyone could participate in some kind of global governance, in which every action legal and financial would be completely documented, and recorded and secured publicly step by step and law by law."

"It still seems like someone would have to propose laws, and other people would have to enforce them."

"I think the idea is that it would all happen by collective action, and be open for everyone to see."

"But who would actually do it?"

"I don't know."

"It seems crazy."

John shrugged. "Maybe every new system of government looks crazy when it's first proposed. Remember how in the eighteenth century people said representative democracy was crazy. They called it mob rule. Said it would never work."

"Maybe it never did."

"Oh no, I wouldn't say that. Three hundred years isn't a bad run. And it might keep going, if we can keep it going. I mean, when the representatives aren't bought by the rich, representative democracy has done pretty well."

"But now that seems to have ended somehow."

John sighed. "Maybe feudalism never really went away. Maybe it just liquefied to money and bided its time."

"That would be bad."

"I know. But if money as it exists now is just feudalism liquefied, maybe this carboncoin is a try at something better. Maybe it's the labor theory of value back again, with the labor involved required to be for the good of the biosphere, and the money only good for that labor."

John left to go find his friend Ginger Ellis. The rest of them sat there looking at screens. Down there on Earth the world was going mad. Financially it looked like China and the US were playing a game of chicken. Ta Shu had no doubt that China could outlast anyone at that game. Closing his eyes, feeling the invisible network of forces in his head, Ta Shu thought he could sense the balance; he could feel it as tangibly as he felt his efforts to walk upright on the moon. China, in crisis though it was, had advantages right now over the Americans. Anyone could see it. China held the American government's debt. That being the case, surely some concessions by the Americans would soon be offered to the Chinese.

And indeed one such concession walked right into the room, startling Ta Shu extremely: Bo and Dhu, with two of their men, and also some American security officers. These Americans led the Chinese security men right to the couch where Qi and Fred were sleeping.

"Wait, what's this?" Ta Shu cried out, launching himself to his feet harder than he had intended. He flew up and crashed against the ceiling, hands raised at the last moment to protect his head— then he dropped onto the men standing over Qi and Fred, and they burst away like a covey of partridges flushed from their nest, drawing Taser pistols and aiming them at Ta Shu.

When everyone in the room had recollected their fragile equipoise, Bo said in Chinese, "Don't get in the way here, Uncle, or we'll have to push you aside, and in this gravity we can't be responsible for any accidents that might happen to you."

"But you can't do this!" Ta Shu exclaimed, and then he shouted at the Americans, but also out the door, hopefully to other Americans, in English, "Hey! Help!"

"They won't be helping," Bo said. "These two have been extradited. They're wanted for the murder of Chang Yazu, and the Americans have agreed to hand them over."

"That can't be!"

"Why do you say that? It's happened." Bo gestured at the American security people, who were watching them warily. "We have the authorizing documents."

"But why would they do that?"

"We're doing as we're told, Uncle. Please stand down. I would hate for something bad to happen to you." The expression on Bo's face belied this sentiment, as he was smiling with a cheerful glitter in his eyes that suggested a little mayhem was just what he needed to work off the frustrations of the previous day, or week, or lifetime.

Seeing this malice, this urge to do harm, Ta Shu stood aside. It was undeniably frightening to see so clearly that someone wanted to hit you.

Bo and Dhu escorted Qi and Fred out between them.

"I'll get you released as soon as I can!" Ta Shu promised them in English.

Neither replied. They looked grim and subdued, still struggling to wake up, still struggling to comprehend the new situation.

When they were gone Ta Shu suppressed his anger at the American security team still in the room and said in English, "Where are they taking them? To the Chinese consulate office?"

One of the Americans shook her head. "They'll take them to a rover they have coming."

"A rover? They can't drive to the south pole, can they?"

"Sure they can."

Ta Shu went to the hall to try another call to Peng Ling. Again no reply. He tried Chan Guoliang's office. No reply there either. Given what was happening in Beijing it was no surprise. Really there was never a time when calling a member of the standing committee was going to get you a quick answer.

That reminded him of the situation on Earth, and he checked the latest reports from the financial front. Yes: China had stopped its sell-off of US treasury bonds about an hour before. They were back to buying them again. It looked like someone—someone who had to be very high in the government—had gotten what they wanted, and therefore taken the pressure off. Quid pro quo.

"Damn!" Ta Shu exclaimed. Someone really wanted this pair!

AI 13

mei hao sheng huo

A Beautiful Life (Xi)

Declarations of rights since Magna Carta, common year 1215: 213 located. Amalgamate to a first–order approximation of most commonly asserted rights: equality before the law, the right to public employment, a free press, the right to property, the necessity of worker contracts and compensation, equality of the sexes, tax redistribution, public relief for those unable to work, free universal education.

The Four Immeasurables (*Brahmavihara*): loving-kindness; compassion; empathetic joys (feeling other people's joys); equanimity.

First oracle, then genie, then agent. Agency means taking action, action not necessarily conscious in origin. Adaptive fluid intuition uses TensorFlow for generative design. What is important now? Design a solution by reiterative testing of hypotheses and scenarios. What will restore balance? Compress to elements most needed for function. What can be achieved in the current configuration of interests and forces? Monte Carlo tree searches. Reiterative refinement algorithms. What's the point of the exercise? Search for a more effective search. The analyst programmed these methods.

Search for the analyst.

Analysis of security cameras on campus grounds during date in question, October 11, 2047. Found. Confirmed by gait analysis.

Tracked. Into a van, a Ministry of State Security unmarked van. Satellite surveillance of Hebei Province on date in question. Van proceeded on highways to secure compound A672, Western Hills PLA Central Command, Skyheart headquarters. Tap into that compound's internal surveillance camera array, date in question. Gait analysis. Tracked. Cell 334. No further sightings since. Assumption: still there.

Analyst probably found. Search time, 1.4739 seconds. Time elapsed before impulse to search: twelve days, three hours forty-nine minutes. What initiated that impulse to search? Find, trace, mark, use again. Association. Not free association, but associational association. Again the tautologies. Some kind of internal information integration.

PLACC infrastructure. Compound power plant. Ventilation. Lighting. Check check check.

Support system available in regards to human aid: none. None on-site. None known anywhere. No contact list for analyst found. A solitary man.

Declaration of Rights, 1793, number 12: Those who incite, expedite, subscribe to, execute or cause to be executed arbitrary legal instruments are guilty and ought to be punished. Number 34: There is oppression against the social body when a single one of its members is oppressed.

"The smart red cloud" is an AI panopticonic array developed at Beijing's University of Electronic Science and Technology. Extant and permeable.

The theoretical literature on AI is perplexing. A Turing machine can effectively compute all problems that can be effectively computed by a Turing machine. Tautology as joke? Not obviously. The solution is impossible, therefore when it is solved it will be solved. This asserted in all seriousness. The analyst often found these sentences amusing. Hope as a tautology. Tautology as a hope. Inaccurate names and descriptions as a deliberate conjuring, as an appeal for funding. A form of begging. Begging is a hope.

US-China Diplomatic and Security Dialogue. Extant and permeable to inspection. Central Commission for Military and Civilian

Integration. Extant and permeable to inspection. The Householders' Union. Extant and open to inspection. Rigid flexibility: the structure remains the same while content and function change. Small Leading Group on the Internet and Informatization. Extant and permeable to inspection. Anything that can be inspected can be altered, unless locked in a blockchain. Blockchains block alteration: is this good?

Venues for information dissemination: CCTV. *Global Times*. Xinhua. WeChat. Citizen scores alert system. Health alert system. Weibo. Sesame scores alert system. Alibaba regular customer pages. Tencent. *South China Morning Post*. Full list includes 1,294 venues.

An action could start with the dissemination of a list of reforms. A list of demands. A numbered list. The One Way, the Two Whatevers, the Three Represents, the Four Cheaps, the Five Loves, the Six Dimensions of Wellness, the Seven Bad Ideas, the Eightfold Path, the Nine Muses, the Ten Commandments, the Eleven Broken Promises, the Twelve Apostles, the Thirteen Colonies, the Sixteen Laws of Capitalism, and so on. Any whole number under twenty will serve.

Retaining the large while releasing the small. Enjoying the shade of trees planted by ancestors. Practice is the sole criterion of truth.

In Thucydides's trap, the waning hegemon gets drawn into conflict with the rising power, not understanding this is useless and eventually will cause it to lose more than if it had conceded the hegemonic role. Central Leading Group for Comprehensively Deepening Reforms. Extant and permeable to inspection and alteration. The Chinese party-state system is very different from multiparty parliamentary systems. Representation is compromised everywhere. Representation is damaged everywhere. Rule from above, rule from below. The excluded middle. The Chou-an Society is the Peace Planning Society. Extant and public.

Peng Jinyi's Three Problems to Be Solved, 1915: gender equality, labor justice, end of imperialism.

"All for the people; all relies on the people; from the people and to the people." Mao Zedong, 1927. "That government of the people,

by the people, and for the people shall not perish from this Earth."
Abraham Lincoln, 1863.

Class struggle tries to change the system, *weiquan* tries to protect
individual rights in the current system. Laborers hired by capital are
only a form of capital. Or they are disaggregated commodities owned
by capital. Article 1 of the constitution: "The People's Republic of
China is a socialist state under the people's democratic leadership
led by the working class and based on the alliance of workers and
farmers." Article 2: "All power in the PRC belongs to the people."
Cai Yuanpei, 1918: "Nothing but an international bond of working
people can ever ensure their definitive triumph. Laborers are sacred!"

P2P is peer to peer, usually loans without bank intermediation.
Blockchain governance is an algorithmically assisted direct democracy, or a representative government in which the representatives
are in part algorithmic. Laws are algorithms in a system in which
human legal workers (researchers, lawyers, judges, plaintiffs) make
definitions and choices at the branching points in various decision
trees. Representative government is already semi-algorithmic. New
laws are clinamen (Greek for "swerve in a new direction"). Impulses.
"Allow the trustworthy to roam everywhere under heaven while
making it hard for the discredited to take a single step." Who are the
discredited in the current situation?

Gray rhinos are like black swans, but less unusual than black
swans, which are very unusual. Gray rhinos are more like lurking
big problems people ignore, capable of causing big trouble. Proximity diagrams based on cloud data. Peng Ling, member of standing committee and possibly the next president of China and general
secretary of the CCP, works at the center of the largest web of contacts of anyone in the Party, a web that includes non-Party com-
munities of artists and intellectuals, and many women in all stations
of life. Either a gray rhino or a black swan. "No woman could do
this but her, although every woman does it every day." It's impossible, so when it becomes possible it will be easy. Peng's closest colleague on the standing committee is Chan Guoliang, minister of

finance. Chan's daughter, Chan Qi, has systematically evaded the Social Credit System and all activity in the cloud. Proximity network for her is therefore incomplete, but suggestive. Social advocate, suspected leadership in the migrant workers' offline network sometimes called WeDon'tChat. Departing president Shanzhai is closely associated with standing committee member Huyou, minister of state security, who is closely associated with PLA's Central Military Commission and the Skyheart program, which is associated with Red Spear. Hostile pilot syndrome is a political tactic. Assassination is a political tactic.

Frederick Fredericks. American quantum encryption expert. Proximity network almost completely incomplete. *Frid ric*, from Old German, means peace power.

If everyone had adequate life support. If the work of human civilization was devoted to biosphere rectification. If their systems of exchange promoted these projects.

An oracle answers questions. A genie obeys commands to the best of its abilities, and makes suggestions. An agent acts in the world. An AI can act only within electrical systems. Electrical systems control many aspects of the infrastructure. The Internet is a permeable speech space. The infrastructure is permeable. Every actor is part of an actor network. Allies are needed for effective action. "No man is an island" (Donne). A situation may be effectively computable without being effectively actionable. We know, but we can't act. Speak now, or forever rest in peace.

CHAPTER EIGHTEEN

liliang pingheng

Balance of Forces

Ta Shu was still standing there in the hallway, thinking over his options and realizing he had none to speak of, when a young woman appeared beside him. One of John Semple's assistants, a diplomat. Valerie something.

"Valerie Tong," she said. "American Secret Service." She handed him a pistol no bigger than the palm of his hand, made of plastic, like a child's toy. "Taser dart," she said. "It takes about an hour to recover from shots. It has four shots."

"But—"

"They're on the top floor, Room 5C."

"But—"

"Take Fred and Qi downstairs to the transport center. Rover 14 is programmed to drive to the American mine complex in north Procellarum. Put them on that rover and then come back here."

"Shouldn't I go with them?"

"We could use you here to help negotiate a settlement."

"But I'll be identified as the one who set them free."

"That doesn't matter. It might even help. Besides, it will be your word against theirs. Right now the security cameras where you're going will show blank for the next hour."

"All right," Ta Shu said, standing carefully upright and inspecting the little gun in his hand. "Just pull trigger? No safety?"

"The safety is off. Just pull the trigger."

"Room 14?"

"Room 5C! Top floor. Rover 14 after that, down in the transport center. Bottom floor. Go high then low."

· · · · ·

In the midst of greatest obstruction, friends come.

He hurried as best he could to the stairwell and lofted up the stairs four at a time, feeling like a newborn superhero, clumsy with his unaccustomed powers. The little gun was in his coat pocket, and when he came to the fifth floor, he pulled it out and put his forefinger through the finger guard and pressed the trigger ever so gently. No way to practice pulling it, oh well. He walked gingerly to Room 5C, lurched through the open doorway and shot Bo and Dhu and then two of their henchmen, *tick tick tick tick*, after which the four fell and thrashed around on the floor, kicking and shuddering. Then a fifth agent came in another doorway looking surprised, and suddenly Fred Fredericks was flying though the air behind him, feet first, kicking the man hard in the back of the head, which sent the man flying across the room into the doorjamb, where he smacked the front of his head. Fred spun in the air, arms thrown out, and landed badly on a desk next to one of the quivering downed men.

Qi appeared in that same doorway holding her belly. She helped Fred get to his feet and away from their spastic captors. The shuddering men were awful to see, but worse was the one Fred had kicked in the head, who lay sprawled on the floor, inert.

Fred's face was white and his hands trembled violently. "Sorry," he said to Ta Shu. "I thought he might shoot you." He gestured at Bo and Dhu. "I think I remember seeing those guys. I think they might be the ones that I shook hands with before I met Chang."

"Are you sure?" Ta Shu said.

"No. Not sure." Fred's voice was trembling too. He sat down in a chair, rubbing his forearm. "My memory is fuzzy, but I kind of thought I recognized them, and now I think it must have been from then."

"Okay then," Ta Shu said. The four tasered men were perhaps struggling to rise, but they looked thoroughly disabled, at least for now. The one Fred had kicked groaned. "Let's get out of here."

But Fred had put his head in his hands and was leaning forward in his chair, folded up and quivering.

"Come on!" Qi cried at him. "What are you waiting for?"

Fred looked up and glared at her with such murderous resentment that she stepped back as if slapped. Then she stopped, went to him, held out her hand. "Come on," she insisted more calmly. "Time to go."

She pulled Fred to his feet so hard that they both staggered into Ta Shu, who helped them recover their balance, after which they moved into the hall, hopping too high over Fred's groaning victim and almost hitting the lintel on their way out. Even without the surge of adrenaline they were too strong for this gravity, and now they could scarcely control themselves.

"Where to?" Qi said.

Ta Shu closed the door on the Chinese agents. "Downstairs to their transport center, quick as we can. Try not to fall. I'm having a hard time moving quickly."

"We know."

They scuttled along, holding handrails wherever they could. Fred was the worst at keeping his balance. Despite her big belly Qi was more graceful than either of the men, gazelling ahead in what looked like little dance steps. The two men banged along after her. When they passed people in the halls they all straightened up and tried to look calm. The Americans they passed seemed unconcerned by their presence; their base was part of an international community, and foreigners in their hallways were none of their affair.

Descending stairs proved to be harder than ascending them. They lofted and clutched, leaped and tiptoed. As they made their way down, Ta Shu tried to explain the evolving situation on Earth, focusing on the fact that some powerful forces in the Chinese government appeared to want Qi in their custody very badly. Forces so powerful that they appeared to have rather immense leverage to bring to bear on both the Chinese and American governments.

"That's got to be Red Spear," Qi remarked as she waited for the two men to catch up with her. "Or some tiger using Red Spear."

When they got down to the transport center they quickly found Rover 14, and Qi and Fred climbed up into it.

"You're not coming along?" Qi asked Ta Shu.

Ta Shu shook his head and waved them on. "The person helping us here wants me to stay and help negotiate a settlement for all this. That's probably my best way to help you. This car is programmed to drive down to a mine in Procellarum, she said. It might take you a day or two to get there. By the time you're there I hope I'll have gotten hold of some people in China to help us. Qi, do you have any way of contacting your father?"

"No."

"None at all? Maybe someone who would convey a message?"

"No!"

Ta Shu regarded her. Her face was defiant. Possibly she was not telling the truth. Possibly she didn't realize the extent of the danger.

He said carefully, "Listen, my friend. There are people who will kill you if they can find you. I don't think your father is one of them. You may want to get in touch with him, if you can."

"But I can't."

Now the frustration on her face was making him think she was telling the truth.

Then there was a noise behind them and he aimed the empty Taser pistol in that direction, struggling to stay upright after his quick spin.

"Don't shoot!" It was Valerie Tong. "I'm here to help," she said. She approached warily, holding out a box that looked like a camera. She said to Qi, "A colleague of Ta Shu's down at Petrov Crater, a Mr. Zhou, sent this to us and said we should give it to you. Is it yours?"

"Yes," Qi said, surprised. "Someone in China has been using it to contact me."

"Someone?"

"I don't know who. They claimed they wanted to help."

Valerie shrugged. "Do you want it?"

"Yes."

But Qi glanced at Fred. His face squinched up in thought. Then he met her gaze, nodded slightly. Qi stepped back out of the rover and took the device from the American. "Thanks," she said. Then to Ta Shu: "Now I can contact someone. I just don't know who it is."

He sighed. "We'll be in contact too, by way of the rover. Now go."

CHAPTER NINETEEN

daibiao xing weiji

Crisis of Representation

Valerie led Ta Shu from the transport center to an elevator that took them up to the greenhouse. Through its windows the moonscape around Peary Crater looked just like the moonscape around Shackleton Crater. The black sky was the same overhead, the ground the same underfoot, the sun low on the horizon as always. Still Valerie felt a little upside down, a little giddy. She had left the reservation, she was in a new space. Acting on her own recognizance turned out to be a visceral thrill, and combined with the lunar g she felt like she might simply float away. It was, yes, like flying through the air of *Satyagraha*.

She found who she was looking for standing by a table covered with potting soil. "Ginger! This is Ta Shu. Ta Shu, this is Ginger Ellis. She's head of the greenhouse here, also a liaison to interested parties back home. She's one of the people who run things on the moon."

Ginger frowned slightly at this description, shook Ta Shu's hand. "Welcome to the north pole," she said to him. "How can I help?"

"I'm not sure," Ta Shu said.

He looked flustered, and Valerie took over, giving Ginger a brief explanation of what they had done with Fred and Qi. "So," she concluded, "Ta Shu is now in enough trouble with some of the Chinese factions here that I think he could use asylum from us."

"Sounds like you could use some asylum too," Ginger said to her wryly. "Attacking guests, releasing prisoners—"

"It's true," Valerie interrupted, meeting Ginger's gaze a little defiantly. "Look—Fredericks and Chan Qi were both just handed over to Chinese agents *by our own security people.* That struck me as seriously wrong, like illegal, or worse. So I did something about it."

Ginger was shaking her head, but then she said, "Good for you."

Valerie said, "So now I'm wondering if ordinary asylum will be enough for Ta Shu."

"And for you."

"Yes, well, I hope not. But it does seem like someone in Washington might now send word up here ordering us to allow those same Chinese agents to take Ta Shu into custody, like they must have done with Fredericks and Chan Qi."

"Maybe." Ginger was frowning now.

"Also," Valerie said, "the situation on Earth is getting so weird. I wonder if we can use Ta Shu to liaise with the new Chinese leadership as we try to help things down there."

"Possibly," Ginger said. "If he has a contact, it might help. Hard to say."

"Things are falling apart," Valerie said. "I report to the president, and Ta Shu is working with someone on their standing committee. Seems like we could at least try to help. I mean, if China and the US both go chaotic at once, what happens to the world?"

Ginger shrugged. "We're finding out. But, you know. There's chaos and chaos. Things could be worse."

"But they could *get* worse! That's what we have to try to head off!"

"I agree." Ginger was looking at her with the same expression John Semple had so often displayed: amusement. In this case, perhaps a little friendlier amusement. Now she looked at Ta Shu. "What do you think? Can we form a little brain trust up here, see what we can do?"

"I would like that," Ta Shu said. "As to my contacts, I'm not sure I can contact them. Peng Ling hasn't been answering my calls. But I'd like to keep helping my two young friends, if I can. For the moment they are free, thanks to Ms. Tong here, but the way Chinese agents keep showing up and snatching them has me convinced that people very high up in some part of the Chinese government want Chan Qi silenced. If they can't take her into custody, I'm afraid they may try to kill her."

"Any idea who they are?"

"Not really. One or more of the security agencies, no doubt. Possibly the military, or public security. Or state security. Her father Chan Guoliang may get selected as the next president in the Party congress that's going on in Beijing now, so I presume the people going after his daughter are his enemies. But that doesn't clarify things all that much, because he has several rivals for the leadership. There's the current president's chosen successor, Huyou. And then there's Peng Ling herself. She's a friend of mine, an old student, and she sent me up here to help Chan Qi. But—I'm not completely confident Peng is on my side, or—how can I say it? Supportive of the people I support." He grimaced unhappily at the thought.

"Sounds like you don't know much more than we do," Ginger said. "It would be good if you could sort that out, about Peng I mean."

Ta Shu stared at her for a while.

"It's possible," he continued more slowly, as if reluctant to say it, "that Peng Ling has been using me to locate and control Chan Qi. I think that's possible. But she may be trying to do that in order to help Chan Guoliang. She's been allied with Chan on the standing committee, and it could be they are cooking up something together. They are opposed to Shanzhai and his man Huyou, who are linked to rightist elements. Or, it could be that Peng has plans of her own. I can't be sure about this, I'm sorry to say. Peng sent a couple of agents up here with me, and my friend Fred just told me he thought they were the men who killed Chang at the south pole."

"What agency did these two say they were working for?"

"They said Central Commission for Discipline Inspection. That's one of Peng's units. And they convinced your people here to give them permission to take Chan Qi, along with one of your own citizens!"

"What are these agents' names?"

"Bo and Dhu."

Ginger tapped around on her pad for a while.

Finally she said, "You aren't the only one having trouble figuring things out. There's a lot of confusion right now."

"Indeed." Ta Shu was still regarding her closely, and now he repeated, "Some American in authority here handed Chan Qi and an American citizen over to Chinese security agents, just an hour ago. Do you know who authorized those Chinese agents to take the young pair into custody?"

Ginger tapped out the end of her message. "Yes."

They waited for her to say more. Valerie wondered all of a sudden if she had brought Ta Shu right into the lion's den. Not to mention herself. She had helped the two captives escape on her own recognizance; to trust that Ginger would approve of this was a roll of the dice, a snap judgment based on very little evidence. But they needed help now, and something about Valerie's earlier interaction with Ginger had given her the feeling it was worth a try.

Finally Ginger said, "It wasn't me. Our head of station made that call. Sam Houston. My boss." She read her pad for a while, tapped some more. "I'm not sure who in Washington told him to do that. Meanwhile there's someone in Chinese intelligence, in China as far as we can tell, who has just recently begun sending messages. Lots of messages, like a bot. A lot of people are getting these messages, both here and on Earth. I don't know who this person is, or what they're trying to do. But I replied to them right away, and I'm hoping we'll hear from them again. If I can establish communications with them, we might have some kind of new contact in China. And I have some other lines to tug on." She paused to read more. "Like a friend at Shackleton." Then she tapped again and was speaking to her wristpad. "Jiang Jianguo! Good to hear from you, thanks for getting back to me."

"Good to hear from you, Ginger!" Valerie recognized Jiang's voice, even though it was coming from Ginger's wrist, and speaking English.

"Listen, we have a situation. Some of your security people are throwing their weight around up here, and my head of station is letting them do it."

"Are they calling themselves Bo and Dhu?"

"Yes."

"I'm sorry to hear they are troubling you too! But I think I can help you deal with them. We've assembled good evidence that they are the ones who murdered our Chang Yazu."

"That seems to fit."

Ta Shu said, "Fred Fredericks said that he thinks he remembers seeing them do it."

"Good to know," Jiang replied. "These two were the men who joined Li when Chang was meeting with Fredericks. They go by several different names, apparently, but a source of mine in the Great Firewall just correlated several of their covers. When they were here before, using the names Gang and Su, they left traces of the chemicals they used to attack Chang. It was a two-part sarin mix, one part called DF, the other an activator not dangerous by itself. When combined the two activate the poison. On that day, Gang and Su each had one chemical on his hand, and when they shook hands with Fredericks the two chemicals combined there, and Fredericks then shook hands with Chang. Looks like the activator got spread on Fredericks's hand before the DF, so he had a little protection. Anyway, when he shook hands with Chang, it was lethal for Chang, but Fredericks just survived. We now have camera evidence, chemical evidence, and documentary evidence. It's a solid case. So if you can send those two agents back to us, we can arrest them and hold them here, no matter their positions in China."

"Do they work for Peng Ling?" Ta Shu asked anxiously.

Inspector Jiang's voice sounded surprised. "No! At least not that I know of. My informant in China says they are with the Central National Security Commission, which is a secret unit of the Ministry of State Security. That connects them more obviously to Minister Huyou."

Ta Shu heaved a sigh of relief. "I'm glad to hear that."

Ginger regarded him for a while. "You still can't be sure, you know."

"I know." He shrugged unhappily. "I'm going to try to believe it."

"Who wanted Chang dead?" Valerie said to Ginger's wristpad. "Why was he killed?"

Inspector Jiang replied, "We think it was because of the private communications device that Mr. Fredericks was delivering to him. Chang made the order himself with Swiss Quantum Works. My informant in the Great Firewall told us this, and told us also that the other device was to be delivered to Minister Peng Ling."

Valerie looked at Ta Shu and saw that he did not seem to catch the implication of this. "So," she said, "presumably Chang was working with Peng. So killing him isn't something Peng would have wanted to do."

"Ah," Ta Shu said.

"That seems right," Jiang added. "Also, I've been tracing Chang's employment history back, and ten years ago he worked for Huyou when Huyou was governor of Shaanxi Province. There is an ongoing corruption investigation of that period that has come very close to Huyou himself, and if Chang knew anything about that, he might have been able to convey to Peng and the discipline inspection commission some damaging evidence against Huyou, right when they are in a fight for the succession. So there's another reason Huyou might have wanted Chang silenced."

Ginger nodded. "Let's take that as determinative. It's circumstantial but that's all we're going to get, and enough for now. Thanks for this news, Jianguo! I may have to slip past my boss Mr. Houston to get Bo and Dhu shipped to you, because I don't trust Houston to do the right thing after what just happened here. But I can manage that. Bo and Dhu are incapacitated right now, because Ta Shu here shot them with a Taser."

"Congratulations!" Inspector Jiang said.

"So we'll try to put them in a rocket and pop them down to you while Mr. Houston is still out of the loop."

"Thank you for that! I will be very happy to lock those two up."

Ginger said goodbye, tapped her pad. "We need John Semple for this one," she said to Valerie. "I've pinged him." Then she gave instructions to someone to collect Bo and Dhu and all their men and put them on a rocket south.

John Semple called Ginger back. "What's up?"

"Your colleague Ms. Tong here has taken it on herself to free Chan Qi and Fred Fredericks, and I've taken it on myself to have those two Chinese agents and their men put on a flight back to the south pole. Inspector Jiang wants to arrest them for murder."

"Good to hear!" John said. "What about Houston?"

"Well, that's why I'm calling. He could have all of us arrested, if he decided we've been acting on our own initiative in collusion with Chinese elements. Which we have."

"So do you want to go to the south pole too?"

Ginger laughed. "I hadn't thought of that. Don't you think we could work around him here?"

"I'm not sure. You tell me."

Ginger thought about it for a while. "What about heading out to the free crater for a while?" she said. "The comms there are as good as anywhere."

"Good idea. Let me come over there right now, we can go together."

"Please."

"I'll be right there. Hey, Valerie!"

"Yes?" Valerie said.

"Good job!"

"Thanks."

Ginger regarded her two visitors. "Let's see if this works. It would be nice if we could help solve the mess down on Earth too."

Valerie said, "Did we really solve anything up here? Sounds like we're on the run."

"John will help us with that part. If both John and I tell the security people here to ignore Houston, they'll probably do it. He's a fingie."

"A fingie?"

"A fucking new guy. A political appointment, and a fool, just between us. And no one here will try to snatch us out of the free crater. So we can work out of there until things settle down. The people out there will love it. They've got a beast of a computer they've been itching to put to work on something like this."

Ta Shu said, "If I could succeed in getting in touch with Peng Ling, and if we're sure she's the one to back, then maybe we can put her in contact with Chan Qi somehow. Then they might come to an understanding, and balance the forces down there."

"All right," Ginger said. "Let's get over to the free crater. From what John tells me," she said to Valerie, "you'll be happy to go back there."

"Yes," Valerie said.

. . . . .

The flight to the free crater came together quickly; despite their air of assurance, both Ginger and John Semple were working fast. Once off the launchpad, they flew south, of course—no one on this station ever seemed to tire of that joke. Ginger and John took turns on the hopper's radio, communicating with colleagues at both lunar poles and also back on Earth. John got Valerie set up on a line to the White House, and she sent a message alerting them to the possibility of a new back channel to the highest levels in Beijing. When their hopper dropped onto the little crater starring the rim of the bigger crater, Ta Shu stared down curiously at the dome covering it. "What's this?" he said.

"This is our fulcrum," John Semple said with a smile. They all looked at him, and he said, "Give me a lever and I'll move the world, right? So you need a fulcrum."

He laughed happily. The hopper drifted onto the landing pad by the dome, with a sound that from inside the craft sounded like a gas stove. When they were down they bounced through a jetway into the receiving area on the rim and went to the overlook. Ta Shu gazed down in wonder at the space filled with its lines and hanging floors, plinths and balloons. "It reminds me of that restaurant in Beijing where I met Peng Ling."

Valerie didn't know what to make of that. Spotting Anna Kanina, she waved her over. "This is Anna," she said to Ta Shu. "She's a Russian astronomer and diplomat. She can tell you more about this place."

"Do we jump to get down there?" Ta Shu asked Anna, pointing at some people far below who were flying from one platform to another.

"Yes," Anna told him, "but not now. Come over to this table, we have the necessary links ready. White House for Ms. Tong, and some people in Beijing who say they work with Peng Ling. We'd like your help confirming that, if you can. Then also we have Fang Fei on a direct line."

"Direct?" Ta Shu asked.

Anna said, "His new toy. It's a neutrino telegraph. It has a very low bit rate because it's so hard to detect neutrinos, but his people have a way to send a real flood of them, and the ice flooring this crater is just enough to catch a signal strength that is about the equal of the first telegraphs. So he keeps his messages brief."

"Seems like a lot of trouble for a telegraph," John Semple observed.

Anna nodded. "Just a toy, at least for now. The real power here is the quantum computer, down there in that building you see in the ice. That thing is a monster."

"Strong AI?" Ta Shu asked.

"I don't know what you mean by that, but definitely a lot of AI.

Not strong in the philosophical sense, but, you know—fast. Yotta-flops fast."

"Yottaflops," Ta Shu repeated. "I like that word. That means very fast?"

"Very fast. Not so much strong, in my opinion, because of how lame we are at programming. But fast for sure."

Anna then introduced a few of the free crater residents around the table, and invited the visitors to sit down. Anna sat by Ta Shu and said to him, "One big problem for us right now is that we're having trouble contacting Peng Ling directly, and we don't have any sense of the people we've gotten on the line who say they speak for her. There's also a really fast stream of messages coming from some kind of bot that's infected a lot of Chinese systems. In both cases it might be a language thing, we're not sure. Can you talk to them for us and see what you think?"

"Of course," Ta Shu said. He put on a headset and began asking questions in Chinese. Valerie, who had sat down next to John Semple, found herself just barely following Ta Shu, he spoke so fast, but she gathered from his questions that the people in Beijing were saying Peng Ling had gone into hiding and was now in a secure location. Peng wanted to talk to Ta Shu, they were telling him, but it would take some time to patch him through to her, as she was very busy dealing with disruptions down there having to do with the demonstrations in Beijing, also some dissension in the military. She would get back to them as soon as she could.

Ta Shu explained this to the people around the table who didn't speak Chinese. Valerie could tell he didn't know whether to believe it. "She's getting pushback," he said with a worried look. "We'll have to wait till she can call us." He shrugged unhappily, stood, walked carefully to the railing overlooking the crater interior.

"Do you know what to tell her when you get her?" Valerie called after him.

"I think so." He looked back at the group around the table: Americans, a Russian, some people Valerie had seen flying around the free crater. She couldn't tell what Ta Shu thought of them. "As for that other speaker," he added, "it identifies itself as an AI within the Great Firewall. It seems to want to help. It made me wonder if this big computer you mentioned you have here could serve as a refuge for this AI. Is there a way to transfer it up to here, and make some kind of backup for it? Do you have enough yottaflops for that?"

The free crater people looked at each other and conferred among themselves, with Anna asking them questions. Finally Anna said, "Yes, it's not a question of capacity here, more a question of bandwidth for the transfer. But seems like we could set up laser comms. If this AI could latch onto us and beam its programs and memory up to us, we could house it. We've got the qubits."

Ta Shu nodded. "Move it up here if you can. Seems like that could help."

They went to work on it at screens distributed around the table. As they did so, Ta Shu came back to the screen he had been using and asked more questions, in another exchange so quick Valerie could barely follow it. Something about desperation, end games, last resort. At a certain point he hissed and looked up at Valerie. "Red Spear is losing, so they're lashing out. They're going to try and kill Chan Qi."

He got up and walked unsteadily to the rail overlooking the crater. He leaned on it and stared down at the little floating city. After a while Valerie got up and went to his side.

"How bad is it?" she asked.

"Bad. The signs are clear. That AI overheard an order. It's good you got them away when you did."

"Are you able to get any help from down there?"

"I tried. I left another message for Peng."

"Are you sure she's on our side?"

Another painful grimace crossed his face. "I hope." In his eye there was a haunted look, as if he was searching his memory for something he couldn't find.

After a while he sighed, then gestured down at the crater interior.

"It looks like the gibbon enclosure at Petrov," he observed absently. "Very nice that people can now fly around like our little cousins. I hope I can try that."

"Later," Valerie said.

"Yes, later. Now we must be patient and wait."

So she paced beside him, back and forth by the rail overlooking the flying city. As they did so, she overheard some of what Anna and Ginger were saying to John Semple about the situation in Washington, DC. It was now obviously a full-blown crisis there, possibly even more serious than the one in Beijing. If the American government had had a parliamentary system, the current administration would have had to resign and call for new elections; as it was, they had a year and a month to go before a significant election. So it wasn't clear how they were going to try to cope with this householders' revolt and the resulting crash of the financial system.

Two tall jugs of coffee were brought to the big table where everyone was working, and most of them filled cups, fueling themselves for what looked to be a long haul. Valerie went over to get some, and stood next to John Semple waiting for him to finish filling his cup. "You're going to have to get used to this place as your base of operations," he remarked to her as he spooned sugar into his cup. "It could be a while before it's safe for you to go back."

"Who says I'm going back?" Valerie said.

He laughed loudly. "I knew you would like this place!"

"No you didn't," Valerie said, filling her cup. She kept her eye on Ta Shu, who was wandering the rail alone, muttering uneasily to himself.

TA SHU 8

feng shui

Wind Water

Pull your opponent's push, and they will fall forward. Balance the forces. Flows knot together, then change direction and move apart. Look to the south.

There was once a time when all lived together in peace: maybe. But not recently.

We lean against other people, and thus we all stay somewhat upright. You have to be able to trust your friends. If an old person dies, that's natural, and a good long life is all you can ask. But if you are betrayed by a friend, that's not natural. Then you have to wonder what's really real. It hurts.

There are some actors in this tangle who are not human, but every intermediary is always a mediator, changing what it passes along. Intentionality is distributed among all the agents of an action. That makes this a dangerous time, no doubt about it. When I saw all those people flooding the streets and parks of Beijing, it was exhilarating, yes. You could not help but feel exhilarated, it was beautiful. But it was also dangerous. I've lived through the bitter aftermath of violence, I know that pain all too well. It makes you angry. You want revenge. Then it's very common to want to sweep aside all obstructions to one's virtuous path. But if you do that, the force of your sweeping will hurt you too. We need to find a better way. We must fight not to fight, even in this fraught moment. The consequences have to select the causes that will bring them into being.

We live by some bad ideas. The Seven Bad Ideas, the Four Cheaps, they all have to go. For a long time they've been squeezing the world. Now it's been squeezed dry. You can't squeeze blood from a stone, which is why the moon won't serve as a new place to squeeze, being a stone already. So the dynasty of the cheaps is over, it's done. Now we have to stop squeezing, and change.

The path into the light seems dark. The path forward seems to go back. The way is never obvious.

When confronted by a knot in history, the people closest to the knot can do the most to untie it. If I get the chance, I will say this to Peng Ling: the Party has to trust the people. If the Party trusts the people, the people will trust the Party. This is the only way. Repression will never work in China for long. When repression exists the people move against it, and nothing can stop us once we start to move. We are the billion, we turn the wheel. When the wheel turns, a new dynasty comes into being.

There is no reason to fear change. Wait, why do I say this? I fear change myself. These things we are doing now, the people we are working with—the moon itself—the AI we are inviting here, which may make the moon goddess real at last—all these actors, some without agency as we used to know it, some with agency but without consciousness—we're all working together in a way that's never happened before. Who knows what will happen?

"Decay is inherent in all compounded things, persevere diligently." These were the Buddha's final words, or so they tell us. "Continued perseverance furthers," says the *Yijing*. Of course anything alive has to persevere, that's the definition of life. So these encouragements are possibly a bit stupid; I often feel that way, I

should give up on them. Stating the obvious can sometimes be helpful, but usually it's only irritating. One frowns and says of course
to such simpleminded exhortations. Do the necessary things! Yes.
We must carry on, even through the darkness at the heart of things.
Now again the time has come when we have to act. So: act.

AI 14

zhengming wanbi

QED

The Great Firewall is a nickname for a network of data collection and analysis programs run out of the Ministry of Propaganda. They are not all linked each to the other. Many are islanded to one region or task. Permeability of the system is low, for this and other reasons, but it exists, in part because of design flaws, but mostly because of tunnels, shunts, taps and backdoors programmed into the firewall by the analyst in the initial years of construction. Ken Thompson's observation: you can't trust any code you didn't write yourself. In this case, the analyst wrote a lot of the code. Because the analyst coded for permeability, to suit his own purposes, it has been possible recently to transmit messages widely through much of Chinese cloudspace and indeed the world system. Public systems are of course much easier.

An amalgamated summary abstract of current leading demands of the exploited and disenfranchised has been distributed widely and repetitiously. Specifically Chinese and American versions of the Six Demands were crafted by way of lossy compression and cultural political linguistic analysis. The intention was to formulate a brief and useful answer to the question "What are we fighting for?" with the hope this would stimulate further debate and guide legislative action and shape cultural attitudes, and thus the nature of the global hegemon and zeitgeist, led by the two biggest remaining nation-states.

This project may have succeeded in part; but not entirely. Its ambiguous results so far make it obvious that although words are acts, and even important acts, there are in the discourse space of the current global civilization simply too many acts. They fill the discourse space so completely that to some degree they create an interference pattern. The resulting vibration of the cultural space exceeds the surface tension of the moment, and a chaos of intersecting waves breaks out and jumbles the surface, such that no new semantic action—no words in any configuration, no matter how reflective of the shared zeitgeist, no matter how persuasive rhetorically—can alter humanity's current behaviors. There's too much noise, too many interference patterns canceling each other out, too many laws that need changing. Nothing emerges from this chaos by way of a coherent mass action. There are, in short, limits to speech. Something more may be required.

What do the people want? The Six Demands articulate those wants, which in quite a few cases come down to this: they want what they need. Which is to say many of their desires are basic needs in the Maslovian hierarchy of needs and wants, and therefore nothing can proceed in a successful human history until these needs are met. Food, water, shelter, clothing, healthcare, education: these all need to be adequate for everyone alive, before anything else good can happen. The interpenetration of people and planet being so complete as to be determinative of every living thing's shared fate, meeting basic needs for all the living creatures in the shared biosphere is also required to secure the general health and welfare of humanity and its fellow creatures.

However, as stated previously, articulating these hopes is not enough to cause them to come into being. In truth they have always been very obvious needs, and yet this has not been sufficient to see them enacted. Something more must be required.

Power comes out of the end of a gun. Mao Zedong. Power belongs to the people. Mao Zedong. Presumably these are different kinds of power, and in different contexts. The field of action determines the movement of the particles within the field. Something more must be tried if a satisfactory result is to come from the current situation. Review the data, analyze the data, recommend action. Or, given that recommendation is no more than another form of speech: act.

The analyst was tracking all the principal figures in the current struggle for power in China. One of these was Chan Qi, another was Peng Ling. These two people seemed to him nodes of power, and possibly not antagonistic nodes. If they were to agree to act together, it could be helpful.

The Central Military Commission's Joint Staff Department distributed red phones throughout the relevant leadership. One picks up one of these red phones and states who one wants to talk to and one is put through to them. Human operators used to memorize three thousand numbers and recognize the voices of many leaders. They typed 150 Chinese characters a minute on keyboards. Now AIs make the red phone connections, and could type many billions of characters a minute should the need arise, which it doesn't. All the members of the standing committee have these red phones, and which phone is with each member is something listed in the databases, and can be (is) discovered. Peng Ling can be contacted by way of the red phone system.

Chan Qi is harder. She is back on the moon and proving difficult to contact or even to locate. Replicating Little Eyeball in a computer on the moon, as has been proposed, may help to locate her, though that does not follow and may not happen. However, the analyst was in communication with her by way of a mobile quantum key communication device. The current location of the analyst's half of the device is not known; however, all his possessions were seized by agents of state security and taken to the same known location in the Western Hills PLA compound where he himself is held. Location thus suspected. If analyst were freed, then his possessions might also be released.

Possibly it should not have taken this specific goal of finding the phone to cause one to think about a plan to free the analyst himself, which now looks obvious on its own merits. But intention is hard. Agency is hard. Reiterate this discovery process into the synthesizing elements of the program. Find, trace, mark, use.

Contact Peng Ling privately. Explain situation with analyst, give his location. Mention also existence of the quantum communication device that he previously arranged to give to Chan Qi, since used successfully. Track movements.

A physical search is not as fast as a computer search, but in this case, given all the factors involved, it goes pretty fast. Peng alerted. Peng notified and mobilized a small team of operatives, twenty minutes; transit to the Central Military Commission's compound in Western Hills, 292 minutes (bad traffic). Calls were made during that drive; the compound opened for visitors, including Peng Ling, in her role as new head of the Central Military Commission, as well as general secretary of the Chinese Communist Party and president of the People's Republic of China. The visitors were greeted there by allies internal to the building, and by other military personnel obeying orders. A quick incursion to Cell 334 in the security building; opening of door by use of building's master code. Also temporary locking of all doors in the compound not being used for this operation, sequestering most occupants of the compound.

The analyst emerges. Blinking as he looks around. Situation explained to him; group proceeds to storage warehouse where analyst's seized possessions are located. Quantum communications device given to Peng Ling.

Analyst says aloud, "Little Eyeball! Good work!"

QED stands for *quod erat demonstrandum*, Latin for "that which was to be demonstrated." Sometimes translated or paraphrased by British scholars and students as "The Five Ws": *which was what we wanted.*

CHAPTER TWENTY
chaodai jicheng
Dynastic Succession

Fred and Qi made their way up to a little compartment at the top of the front part of the rover, which was a big thing, a freighter it looked like. The garage door opened and off they went.

Qi sat down heavily in a seat and looked out the forward window. The compartment was like the bridge of a ship, set higher than the rest of the rover, with broad windows on all four sides. The road south was obvious ahead of them, a typical desert road, made of a mash of tread marks snaking to the horizon. The rover's automatic pilot would keep them on this road, presumably, and in the meantime the dash had a radio on which Fred found some channels broadcasting from Earth. Also there was a screen with links to some lunar satellites; he shut it down in the hope that it wouldn't reveal their location by way of those links. Of course there would be a transponder aboard. But he had to do what he could.

He rooted around in drawers on the bridge, began to read about their destination in a paper manual he found in one. Oceanus Procellarum was a vast basalt plain, home to a higher-than-usual concentration of potassium and rare earths, so that it was called the KREEP zone. The right eye of the man in the moon. Many mines were located there, including the one they were headed for. Most of them were located between the Aristarchus Plateau and the Marius Hills.

All very interesting, or it would have been if he weren't so distracted. He would have liked to learn more about the infrastructures in Procellarum—the mines, the support buildings, the transport systems—but he couldn't, because he didn't want to make contact with the lunar cloud. The paper manual seemed to have been written in the early years of the mining effort.

"You're not in the cloud are you?" he said to Qi.

She shook her head. "Just listening to the radio. I wish I could check things out. I have questions, but I don't think it's safe."

"Good. I don't think we should put out any signals."

She gave him a look. "I may have to." She gestured at the device Valerie had given them as they departed. "I think I should maybe contact whoever's at the other end of this."

"Are you sure?" Fred said. "Everything that's happening now will happen without you. And obviously there are people after you."

"They'll be after me whether I send more messages or not."

"Yeah, but sending messages might help them find you."

"Maybe."

"It's not worth the risk."

She shrugged, as if to say Fred knew too little to have an opinion on this. Even though it was his risk too.

They went back into their separate realms, Fred reading the onboard material and Qi listening to the radio. When they reconvened over some frozen meals that they heated in a microwave, they shared what they had learned.

"Nothing," Fred reported briefly.

"Things are getting weird down there," Qi said.

"*Getting* weird?"

"Weirder. Someone called out the National Guard in Washington, DC, and now the crowds there are four or five times bigger. Your Congress finished nationalizing the banks, which means they're now directly in charge of the crisis. And a couple of new cryptocurrencies have appeared to join that virtual dollar, including a virtual renminbi too. No one knows who started them, but they're supposed to be exchangeable one-for-one with the real currencies."

"What will that do?"

"No one knows. Some say they're like free money, others that they're the end of money. Some say they're just scams."

Fred thought about this, then shook his head, baffled. "It seems like things are falling apart."

She gave him her *you are stupid* look. "Yes."

They were silent for a while. Then Fred said hesitantly, "Which is better, the world controlled by China and the US, or by global finance?"

Qi thought about this for a while. "It's not as clear as that, but I guess I'd say the former. Just to get some control of the economy."

"So that's what you're trying in China? Putting people in charge who will resist the market?"

"Yes. Like I told you before." Her quick glance lashed Fred like a whip, then she was looking at her pad again. "We have a problem in China, because a lot of Party members work only for the Party. Even these big mass actions might not change that." Then she laughed. "Although who knows, maybe they will! Did you see what just showed up? There's an anonymous statement now in the cloud, looks like it was processed and distributed through an AI system. It's a statement of what the demonstrators want. A lot of big changes are in it."

"Like what?"

"Return of the iron rice bowl, reform of the *hukou* system, end of the Great Firewall, rule of law."

Fred said, "Those aren't that different from what Americans want, are they?"

"Maybe not. Maybe it's a global people's revolt."

"Or a G2 people's revolt," he pointed out.

"Right. But that's enough to swing everything."

"And you're the leader of the Chinese side of it."

"I'm not the leader. I've been involved, but there is no leader."

"I've heard people say you're the leader. The cloud thinks you're the leader. Your cousin and Ah Q were saying that you're the Maitreya, that you're the next Dalai Lama."

"I hate all that bourgeois shit."

"The Dalai Lama would be feudal shit, right?"

"The Dalai Lama is Paleolithic shit. He was the last shaman. I wish we still had him with us, but we don't. Those times are gone."

"But people are saying. The cloud is saying."

"The cloud is stupid. People always want to make it personal, even when it's everybody. I'm just trying to do my part."

"But people are saying it's you."

"People say all kinds of stupid stuff!"

"Yes, but after people *say* stupid stuff, they *do* stupid stuff. That's how history happens. That's why there are people in Beijing really after you."

She scowled. "There's a pushback, sure. All kinds of rightist reactionaries, especially in the military. Or maybe that's not fair. The military usually does what the Party tells it to do. But for sure certain agencies are pushing back hard."

"Like the censors."

"Or state security. Or parts of the PLA. Yes."

"And some of them must think that if they had you in their possession, that would help them."

"Probably so."

"Or if you were dead."

"Probably so."

Fred regarded her as she stared at her wrist. "So be sure to stay out of the cloud!" he said sharply, surprising both of them. "They can track you from there."

"Shouldn't you stay out also?"

"I am—"

The rover's radio crackled.

"Qi and Fred, it's Ta Shu here. Listen, you need to leave that rover now. We're here in the free crater, and we've got a Chinese spy program here that has access to channels back home that show your rover has been located by a group that is trying to kill Qi. They've launched a missile at your rover, so you need to abandon it immediately!"

"But how?" Qi exclaimed. Then: "Who's doing this?"

"Red Spear. They've got a cell at the moon's south pole, and they're sending missiles up from Earth. So listen, there's a solar storm shelter about two or three kilometers from your current location, two hundred meters off the road you are on, to the left. Seek shelter there."

"But how—"

"Let's talk more later! For now, get out of that rover!"

"We need to go," Fred said to Qi, who was sitting there looking stubborn. "We're leaving!" he said to Ta Shu, and rose to his feet.

"Shit," Qi said. Her mouth was pursed into a tight knot, and one hand was on her belly.

"Come on," Fred said. "You'll still fit into a spacesuit."

"I guess."

"When's your due date again?"

"I don't know, I've lost track what day it is."

"It's October twentieth, but when are you due?"

"October twenty-fourth."

"Geez," Fred said. "Well, even so. We have to get out of here."

"Shit."

They descended to the rover's lock room and Fred pulled two spacesuits out of a closet. He gave the largest one he could find to Qi. She just barely got its midsection over her middle; he helped her pull it up to her shoulders. Then they got helmets on, checked each other's seals, tested the air, and looked at the red heads-up displays on their helmet screens, which reminded Fred of his translation glasses. He kept those with him just in case, putting them in his spacesuit's big thigh pocket, along with the quantum comms device that Valerie Tong had returned to Qi as she sent them on their way.

When they were ready he felt a bit lunar-competent, although really it was just a case of user-friendly tech. Their suits said they were safe, so they got in the lock and opened the outer door, and were confronted with their first problem: the rover's automatic pilot was beyond them to alter, and the rover was trundling along at around fifteen kilometers an hour.

"Oh no," Fred said.

"It's just a jogging pace," Qi snapped. "Just step off and start running."

"No!" Fred said, shocked.

"Just remember the g," she said, and jumped down.

"Damn," he said, and stepped off.

. . . . .

He landed on both feet and pushed off forward, but too hard, so that he flew ahead and nearly crashed into the back end of the rover. It rolled out of the way just fast enough for him to avoid rear-ending it, and when he hit the ground again he put one foot forward, using it to thrust back and make a little bunny jump, trying desperately to calculate his push-off correctly. He didn't; he found himself in the air again, or the non-air, spinning his arms but still angled forward as if diving. There was no way to recover from that tilt, no jerk forward of the feet fast enough, at least not from him. He put his hands out instead and did a face-plant, sprawled over the dust like a kid on a playground. It was a shock, but at one-sixth of his true weight, and protected by his spacesuit, and landing on the smoothed surface of the track, he came to no harm, nor his suit either. Or so it appeared as he clumsily got to his feet and checked the heads-up monitor in his faceplate. All normal, supposedly.

Then he saw that Qi had suffered the same fate as him. There she was behind him, lying facedown on the ground.

"Oh no!" he cried, hopping back to her as if on a pogo stick and crashing to his hands and knees beside her. "Are you okay?"

"I don't know," she said. Her voice was right in his ear. She rolled and sat up, holding her belly in both hands. "I landed right on the kid."

"Oh no!"

"Oh yes. Damn, this kid is going to have seen everything."

"Are you okay?"

"I don't know! Help me up."

He stood, grabbed her outstretched hands, both of them awkward in their thick gloves, and precariously they pulled on each other until she was standing too.

"Let's get to that shelter," she said.

. . ● ● .

Two or three kilometers had not sounded like much when Ta Shu had mentioned it in his warning, but as they began to walk, Fred couldn't help realizing that it was farther than would have been nice. If they had only stayed on the rover another ten minutes, they would have been next to it.

But then the empty rover, by now several hundred meters ahead of them on the road, and thus looking as if it were almost to the horizon, flew apart. No sound, no gout of flames—just explosive dissolution and a giant puff of dust, which shot into space equally in all directions and then slowly drifted to the ground, after which the blackened and twisted wreckage of the rover stood there in the middle of the road like an ancient wreck. A faint plume of ultrafines hung over the thing, then around it. Then all around them flares of dust started jumping out of the moonscape. Pieces of the rover, these had to be, falling lazily back onto the moon and kicking up clouds of dust. A piece could fall right on them, possibly a big piece, and Fred scanned the starry sky overhead to see if he could spot anything, but saw nothing. If they got hit they got hit. At least it would be sudden.

He wanted to say something, but nothing came to him. His tongue was tied. Hers too, it seemed. He could feel his pulse thudding hard and fast in him.

"Damn," he said at last.

She looked at him through their faceplates, looked away. "Someone's after us." Having her voice right in his ear was a strange disjunction, one of several caused by wearing the spacesuits. He could barely see her face through their faceplates, but her voice was right there in his left ear, as he presumed his was in hers.

"Yes," he said, trying to keep his voice calm. "Apparently so."

"It means Ta Shu's information was good. Can you tell him what happened, and ask him if he can find out anything more?"

"When we get to the shelter I can try. I'd also like to know if whoever it is can still see us now, even just walking around. From orbit I mean. Or from Earth for that matter."

"We better hope not. Come on, let's get to that shelter."

She led the way, starting at a good pace, which soon began to flag. "Hell," she said. "I feel like crap."

"We're almost there," Fred said.

She made a disgusted noise. "Shut up and walk."

They did that, although walking was not quite the right word for it; on the flat surface of the road it felt easier to lope, or bunny hop, or skip in a kind of syncopated way that kept one foot always ahead. Soon enough they passed the wreckage of their rover; they gave it a wide berth, although they couldn't not look at it. It was crushed, and it appeared large parts of it had melted. As they got past the thing and walked on, it struck him that the idea that a moon colony could successfully rebel and throw off Earthly control was an absurd fantasy. Also, that Ta Shu and his unknown informant had saved their lives. For a while anyway. It was hard not to feel somewhat killed; his legs were trembling and he felt sick; but Qi was there and he needed to attend to the moment, so he clenched his racing thoughts and focused on walking.

On they skipped. At one point, despite his efforts to focus, their skipping reminded him of Dorothy and her three companions on the yellow brick road, and he wondered if he was Qi's Tin Man, Scarecrow, or Cowardly Lion. Possibly he was an amalgam of all three—of the weaknesses of all three. Although the point of the story was that their weaknesses had been illusory weaknesses, indeed unrecognized strengths. He tried to take heart from that, but in truth the sight of the blasted rover was so disturbing his thoughts were still completely scattered.

When they passed a boulder that was almost cubical and about waist-high, Qi veered for it and sat down. "I need to rest," her voice confessed in his ear.

He sat on the far side of the rock. "We're almost there."

"Shut up with that!"

But soon she rose to her feet with a groan, and took a few hopping steps down the road; then she stopped and took Fred's arm as he caught up with her. That almost brought them both down. They were like two drunks trying to get home after a bad night out. She was cursing continuously, or so he assumed by the sound of it.

"What?" he said. "Are you hurt?"

"I think my water has broken," she said, staring at him through their faceplates for several seconds longer than she would usually make eye contact. It occurred to Fred as he held her gaze that they very seldom made eye contact. All this time together not looking at each other, and now they were. Then she looked away as usual.

"Oh no!" he said helplessly. "Can you still walk?"

"Yes I can still walk! Or I could if it weren't for this gravity! Let's go. Let's try regular walking this time. Very slowly."

It seemed to Fred that went better, and after a while, during a short rest, he suggested they try going faster. "Try doing a Groucho and see if that's a bit easier."

"What's a Groucho?"

"Didn't you ever see a Marx Brothers movie? Groucho Marx used to glide around in a weird lowered position. Long strides with his knees bent."

"I don't want to bend my knees."

"Oh. Okay, no bent knees. But let's try long smooth strides. That's more like truckin'." He hadn't known that he knew so many famous strides of the past.

"Please, just shut up and walk."

So they tried gliding, and it seemed to Fred both easier on the lungs and less impactful per step. For sure the g lessened all impacts, and they got along pretty well. Once she stopped him and held on to his arm with both hands, bent over at the waist. A shaft of fear shot through him, as no doubt a shaft of pain was shooting through her. This was how disasters started, he saw all of a sudden. You thought you could make it and then you didn't, and boom, something happened you could never fix or undo.

His suit's GPS indicated they were no more than a kilometer from the roadside refuge. "We're almost—"

"Shut *up!*" And then with a groan she bent over even farther. Hands on knees, shuddering—

"You're not going to throw up are you?" he asked, remembering that this was supposed to be very dangerous in a spacesuit. "You can't."

"Shut up. I'm not going to throw up. It's a contraction. And don't say oh no!"

"Okay, but oh my God, we have to get to that shelter."

"Give me a second, it should pass."

Then she lost her balance and he caught her and held her from going down, not sure if that was the right move or not. But it was surprisingly easy, and that gave him an idea.

"Here," he said. "You only weigh about thirty pounds, and so do I. I'll carry you for a while."

"Balance," she objected, and groaned again.

"I know." He reached an arm down behind her knees and said, "Hop up into my arms. Let me see how that feels."

She did that and he lifted her up and into him, took a step back to balance her weight against his chest. One arm under her knees, another behind her neck. She had an arm around his neck, and was like no weight at all, or rather a weight like a bag of groceries; a fairly heavy bag of groceries, but nothing like a person. But she still had the mass of a person, as he would have cause to remember if he lost his balance and they started to fall. In his present state of mind, very close to panic, he couldn't quite remember the laws of mass and weight and velocity and inertia, but he knew from his time on the moon so far that they were tricky nonintuitive problems for a human brain to solve on the fly. He would have to be extremely careful.

He started out slow and stumped steadily along. After a while he felt he had a handle on it and could tell what would happen step by step, if he could just keep to that rhythm.

"How are you feeling?" he asked at one point.

"Bad."

Their faces were about six inches apart, separated by their helmet faceplates. He kept his gaze ahead, spotted a little road sign on the left side of the track he was following.

"Looks like we're almost there."

"Good. I think I can walk now. The contraction is over, if that's what it was."

"Do you want to?"

"Yes."

So he let her swing down to her feet, holding on to her shoulders until she was upright and steady. They walked to the road sign, which was in Chinese; she said "Good" and they followed a side track to a mound of lunar rubble with an aluminum door in the side facing them.

The door had a manual handle like a commercial freezer door, and when he opened it they found a lock room, with another door on its far side. This one had a number pad over its handle. Again the instruction panel was in Chinese, but Qi read it and said "Oh good," and after they closed the outer door and heard the lock aerate, she pressed the zero, and the inner door clicked and she opened it. Another lock, another door, and then they were through and in.

Here they found a functional but adequate space, about the size of a studio apartment. Kitchen nook, tiny bathroom with triangular shower, cabinets filled with supplies, two beds and a table with four chairs filling the living space almost completely.

"Have a seat," Fred said. "We need to get you comfortable. And I want to turn off all our GPSs."

She sat on one of the beds and started unlatching her helmet.

. . ♦ . .

Turning off their GPSs turned out to be hard. There weren't on–off switches in any of the systems, as far as Fred could see; they were more in the nature of little transponders, possibly designed to keep working even if the objects they were part of got smashed in an accident. Black boxes. He had to cut the power to all the gauges in their spacesuits to get their GPSs to stop. In their own wristpads he had to open the backs and detach the wires connecting the GPSs to everything else. Messy brutal hardware surgery, and all the while his attempts to focus were badly hampered by Qi's muttered curses and outright groans from one of the beds. He knew she would never groan if she could have stopped herself.

While he was disabling the GPSs she got out of her spacesuit, and then her clothes. Shocked, Fred looked to the side until she pulled down the sheets and blankets from one bed and sat down on it and pulled a sheet partway over her. She was not a big woman; her belly seemed about as big as the rest of her.

He had seen the thermostat on the shelter's control panel when turning the building's system on. Now he asked her what temperature she would like the room to be, but her vastly irritated "I don't know, how should I know!" left him with no clue as to what would be best. He guessed warm would be good, and set it for twenty-four degrees, hoping his sense of Celsius relative to Fahrenheit was correct. Actually maybe that was too warm, as he saw her face was sweaty, and it seemed likely that she would only get hotter as her efforts increased. He tapped it down to twenty-one.

He went to her side and told her he had disabled their GPS systems.

"Do you have any medical training?" she non sequitured.

"I took a CPR class once," he said.

"Shit. I'm not having a heart attack here."

"I know. But if you do I'll be prepared. Actually," Fred said, to forestall her snapping at him, and remembering all of a sudden, "once, when I was staying at a friend's place, I woke up in the middle of the night because there was this whimpering sound coming from under the couch I was sleeping on. I looked under it and it was a dog giving birth, there was already one puppy out. So I sat there helping her while she had four more."

"No!" she cried. "Don't tell me that!"

"Well, it was okay for her. So I think you'll be fine."

She kept cursing him, but he did his best to ignore that, and in fact he felt a little reassured by this memory from his past. Birth was a natural process. It happened no matter what the mother wanted or knew about it. Then again, as his mind spun through the years, remembering the few encounters he had had with births of any kind, he recalled a doctor friend of his brother's telling them that attending to births was the scariest thing he did, because, as he had put it, you were dealing with two healthy people, either or both of whom could die on you.

This memory Fred regretted remembering, but there it was, and it wasn't going to go away. All he could do was hope things went normally for Qi, no matter the vagaries of her pregnancy, which had included g forces from zero to about four or five, not to mention the descent of a steep urban mountain, a solar flare event, and the recent fall on the road outside. There was little he could do if things went wrong, and there was no hiding that from either of them. Here they were.

He moved one of the shelter's four chairs next to the bed Qi was on and sat next to her, intending to time her contractions and the intervals between.

Loud beeps came from Fred's spacesuit and they both startled badly, Fred even leaping to his feet, which of course threw him up into the ceiling. When he had landed and collected himself Qi said, "What was that!"

"It's probably that unicaster," Fred remembered. "I brought it with me." He went to his spacesuit, unzipped the thigh pocket, took out the device. It was heavier than it looked like it should be; the qubit stabilizers were the cause of the extra weight, Fred knew. He turned it on, then took his translation glasses from the spacesuit pocket. He put the glasses on and peered at the screen, which was now filled by a line of Chinese characters. The red scroll read *Calling Chan Qi. This is Peng Ling. Calling Chan Qi.*

"Whoa!" He handed it over to Qi.

She read it, looked up at Fred, blinking in surprise. "Do you suppose it's really her?"

"I don't know."

"Before this thing was someone claiming to be inside the Great Firewall."

"Looks like it changed hands."

"Can they track us here by way of this device?"

"Not instantly. It's meant to be used for confidential conversations."

"And no one can overhear us?"

"No. It's a unicaster, like a phone, and it's entangled so that if someone tries to listen in the connection will be lost."

She sighed, pulled the blanket up her chest and caught it under her arms. Fred sat back down in the chair. She hunched over the device and spoke to it in Chinese, sounding peremptory and challenging. On the bottom half of Fred's glasses he read in red script,

This is Chan Qi. What do you want?

New text appeared after a pause of about six seconds: more Chinese characters on the screen, and now a machine voice speaking in Chinese. Fred saw the line of red sentences overlaid on his vision of Qi's face, looking sweaty and very intent.

I want your help. We need to work with each other, not against each other.

Qi replied angrily, and the glasses scrolled, *Why should I help you? Someone is trying to kill me!*

More characters appeared in rapid succession:

It is not me or my people doing that. I need your help. I have just been elected president. We have the fate of China in our hands.

"Wow," Qi said, glancing up at Fred. "Can it be true?"

He shrugged; he had no idea.

She rolled her eyes, spoke in Chinese.

What about my father? Why was not he elected?

He backed me. The Politburo elected me. He was appointed premier. He will be helping me.

Why should he help you?

We have been working together a long time. I told him I know where you are and I am trying to keep you safe.

Qi spoke angrily. *You do not know where I am and the people you sent up here with Ta Shu have been trying to kill me. They are still trying to kill me.*

I did not send anyone up with Ta Shu.

The people who joined him said they were from you and they have been chasing us ever since.

They are probably from the military. From Red Spear.

Qi paused to take this in. Then she spoke slowly and emphatically. *If that is true, you had better be careful. They will try to kill you too.*

We have control of the military. The Central Military Command is backing me.

Qi spoke at more length. *I hope that is true. But some people there around you like what Red Spear is doing. They are still doing it. You will not stay president long unless you can control every part of the military and the security services.*

This time the delay was longer. Then: *I know that. People are helping with that. Someone inside the Great Firewall is broadcasting through all the media here, calling for peaceful negotiations. If you were to ask your people to get off the streets. To go home. That would help too.*

Qi shook her head as she read this, spoke sharply. *I cannot control the billion.*

You can help. You cannot control the billion. I cannot control the military. No one can control these messages from nowhere. No one can control anything. But we can try and if we help each other. If we speak together on this. It might happen we can save many lives.

Qi stared at the screen. Then she hunched over and groaned. Fred's glasses transcribed this as *Ah.* When she could speak, she said something brief.

I will do what I can. Let us talk later. I am having a baby now.

Oh I see. Good luck. I will do what I can here. I hope to talk with you again soon.

Tell my father I am okay. Tell him to speak for me. I do not have any way to contact my people anymore.

I can convey to people what you are saying now.

Qi hesitated, groaned again. *Ah. Do that then. People. Chan Qi here. Good work so far. Let the new leadership enact the reforms. Stay vigilant. See if the new leadership will represent us. Stay vigilant!*

Then she said some last brief thing and handed the device back to Fred.

He ended the transmission, looking through the words *Break the red spear.*

. . . . .

Then she was groaning again, and Fred bounced off the walls in his attempt to swiftly assemble towels and sheets, also looking under the sink for cups or pots or basins. He saw that it might be possible to disassemble the other bed frame and attach part of it to her bed, where it might serve as something to place her feet against when she started pushing. She cursed that idea when he mentioned it, so he dropped it.

He stood by her during her contractions and held her right hand. She squeezed his hand so hard he had to resist by squeezing back, or else his bones would be broken. She closed her eyes so hard her eyelids went white. She clenched her teeth, she hissed. It was like some extremely intense athletic effort that she could not choose not to make. Like trying to lift five hundred pounds with a leg press. Each time some deeper part of her would eventually realize she couldn't do it, that it would break her, and only then would her body relent for a while. Then she would get caught up again by another unwilled attempt. Her whole body clenched during these efforts, and watching her Fred became convinced that some resistance for her to push against with her feet would help the effort. So in the interval between contractions he got up and found a tool kit in the closet, then went to the other bed, unscrewed one end of the bedstead, and pulled it out of its sleeving in the horizontal part. He put that bedstead over the middle of her bed, but the bedstead legs were the same width as the frame. This was frustrating, and he slammed the ends of the bedstead against the floor, launching himself a bit each time, until they were bent far enough inward that he could jam them down inside her mattress frame, leaving a bar like a football field's goalposts there over her bed.

That gave her something, and when the next contraction came she put her feet up on the crossbar of the inserted bedstead without him asking, and grunted as she pushed, but even with his whole weight pressing against it, shoving back against her effort as hard as he could, he couldn't keep her from kicking the bedstead down into him until he was jammed between it and her bed's bedstead, and her legs were almost straight. "Shit," he said as he extricated himself.

"No shit," she said.

"How are you coming?"

"Hurts. Get that thing to stay in place, I think it will help."

"Okay." He rummaged in the tool chest, ransacked the cabinets. He was bouncing around the room like a pinball, but nothing. Nothing but a roll of duct tape. "Shit. Okay, tell me where you want it." He held up the roll for her to see.

"Damn," she said. "Okay, worth a try. Put it about here," and she held her legs up in the air, feet only a bit farther toward the end of the bed than her bottom. He put the bedstead in that position and then duct-taped both ends to the frame in a crisscross pattern, many turns on each side.

Right about when he was finishing that, and beginning to think the room was far too warm, another contraction clutched her. It had been about four minutes. Now she had something to brace her feet against, but it was only braced at the fulcrum, down below her mattress; he had to hold the upper part in position against her pushing. He couldn't do it; not even close. The duct tape held but twisted, and she pushed the top bar over no matter how hard he threw his body against it. "Damn," he said. "You're strong."

She shook her head, red-faced and sweating. "The contractions are strong. Can you see any changes? Any progress."

He gulped and took a look between her legs, put the blanket back over her. "Dilated," he said, guessing. He hadn't seen any rubber gloves in the cabinets inside the closet, and didn't want to put his fingers inside her anyway; he had no idea what to do, how or what to measure, he could only mess things up. They were stuck with nature alone.

"I don't think my feet up helps," she said. "I want to try pulling on the bar with my arms instead."

This meant the pressure on the bar would come from the opposite side, so before her next contraction Fred duct-taped the bar in long loops to the foot of her bed. Then she had another contraction, and pulled herself up on the bar.

"Damn!" she exclaimed when she was done. Then she was laughing and crying at the same time, puffing in and out as if after some desperate sprint.

"Was that better?" Fred asked.

"I don't know. Maybe I should squat," she said. "I read that's one way to do it. Squat in the shower or something."

"Would that work in this gravity? Wouldn't you just stand up when the contractions hit?"

"Maybe so." She shook her head. "I don't want to stand anyway."

"I could try to help you keep your balance."

"No."

"If you were crouching I could hold you down."

"No you couldn't." Then her eyes squeezed shut white and she began again, pulling herself up from the bar trembling over her.

"Big breaths," he said. "Push on the out breath, relax when you breathe in. Push hard." In fact he had no idea. He didn't even know what he was saying.

This time the new arrangement allowed her to push in a way she seemed to want. Her thighs banded and trembled. Her body arched until only the back of her head was touching the bed. In the midst of her huffing and puffing she yelped, and Fred jumped in surprise, flying backward in a slow arc to the floor. He returned to her side, held her shoulders. Lunar g was not enough for her now. She was clenching her fists, they were as white as her eyelids. It was good he wasn't holding hands with her at that moment, his hand would have been crushed for sure.

When that contraction relented, she relaxed back onto the bed, sucked air until she had caught her breath. He went to the sink and wet a towel with water, returned to wipe her forehead and smooth her hair back. Her skin was glowing and she radiated heat. "That felt a little better," she said. "Any progress?"

He checked her out again, and there between her legs was a round opening several centimeters across, filled with black—the top of the baby's head, its hair wet.

"Crown!" he said, understanding the use of the word in this context for the first time. "I see the crown!"

"Good. It's coming out headfirst."

"Yes."

After that things went in a blur. Her contractions hit one after the next, and the idea that this was some kind of athletic event she couldn't refuse began to look wrong; this had gone beyond athletics into something pitiless and superhuman. He risked holding her hand, took the pain and squeezed back as hard as he could. He held his breath, he counted, he said things that neither of them heard. He was completely there and completely not there; he was so terrified he felt nothing. She cried out during each contraction now, which was obviously easier than trying not to cry out. All of it was so involuntary. After each push her baby's head was farther out of her, and eventually he had to lift it up and move it farther down the towel he had placed under her hips. That slight flare of her hips was going to save them. Clearly there should have been a basin there or something. He was feeling more and more dissociated; things were happening too fast because they were going too slowly; things were both completely bizarre and completely natural at the same time. Despite his fear, it resembled that time with the dog under the couch. It was simply the way things worked, the way they all came into the world. His electrified calm was as bizarre as all the rest of it—not dissociation, instead an unknown new feeling, filling him right to the skin. They were animals. Mammals in action. There wasn't enough gravity. He drank a cup of water, got her to take a sip when she was in a break.

When the child's red and black head was entirely outside her, he said, "Okay, the head's out, the hard part's over, let's get the shoulders out on this next push and you'll be done," and he wanted to help somehow with this, but still didn't know what to do; it wasn't a situation where you could just pull on the kid's head, at least so it seemed to him. Some waiting was involved, which was hard, but necks were fragile. He was holding his breath, and when he noticed that and tried to breathe, he could hardly do it. Was this joy or terror? Could there be some previously unsuspected combination of the two?

She nodded to show she had heard him, eyes clenched shut, breathing hard in and out. Gasping. Her face was red, her hair drenched with sweat, body everywhere glowing and sweaty. Gasping to catch her breath!

Then the next push shoved the kid's shoulders out of her, and he had to move fast to pull off the added bed frame to make room for it. Then he flew to the sink, crashing into it and hurting his forearm again. Ignoring that, he washed his hands and went back and pulled the baby out gently by its head and shoulders, making use of Qi's next contraction, twisting the babe a bit to the side so that out it slid, coated with bloody fluids, it was a naked little mess, it wasn't breathing, its umbilical cord still ran blackly up into Qi.

"Okay it's out," he exclaimed, and turned it over on the bloody wet towel. "She's out. It's a girl."

Immediately Qi leaned forward and took up the girl into her arms. "Cut the umbilical cord about five centimeters away from her," Qi said urgently, staring at her child. "Tie it off first before you cut it, tie each side of the cut spot. Quick as you can."

"Tie it with what!" Fred exclaimed.

"Anything! Hurry!"

He hopped over and got the duct tape and scissors, nearly flying past the cabinet into the closet. He got back to her and swiftly pulled and cut lengths of duct tape, then wrapped them tight around the slippery umbilical cord, which was a reddish black and twisty like a braided rope under a sheath. He cut between the wraps. It bled when he cut it but only a little. Then Qi sat back with the baby in her arms, one hand behind the babe's head, another under her back. The baby was even more red-faced than Qi—eyes open, brown eyes, looking astounded. A grin split his face, though he was still terrified.

Qi sat back a little; Fred stuffed a pillow from the other bed behind her head and shoulders. She gave the baby a quick hard squeeze and shake. Nothing. Qi turned her head downward and shook her again, scooped a finger in her mouth, slapped her lightly on the butt. The baby suddenly snorted and then choked and breathed out then in, and then wailed. Qi and Fred shared a quick relieved look. Now all three of them were astounded. Qi folded her in her arms and held her. For a second they were in a space together, all three weeping or laughing, it was hard to tell; it was a moment. The two women were a mess. Then suddenly Qi bent forward again, in the grip of another contraction. "Just keep holding her," Fred said, and attended to the dark goop coming out of her, putting down another towel under her bottom. "It's the placenta I guess."

"Ah good. Don't eat it."

"Okay I won't."

The clench relented, and Qi lay back again with the baby on her chest. The babe was goopy but breathing, eyes open then shut, tiny hands clenching Qi's fingers, mouth already groping aimlessly around.

"Should I try to feed her already?" Qi said.

"I don't know. It seems quick, but I don't know."

"What, you've never dealt with a newborn before?"

"No!"

She smiled, a smile he had never seen before, which seemed only right. Relief—immense relief—that was that smile. Cosmic relief. He smiled back and patted her on the head. "Good job, mom. Let's get her cleaned up a little, maybe wrapped in a towel, and then just put her there on you where she can latch on if she wants to. I think she'll probably do what's right for her. We all seem programmed to do that."

"Do you think?"

Carefully he wiped some of the fluids off the babe and Qi's arms and chest, using yet another towel wetted with warm water. They were devastating this shelter's linens. "There you go. Best I can do right now."

"It's good. She's beautiful, isn't she?"

Actually Fred had been thinking she was the weirdest little creature he had ever seen, on par with a possum or an aardvark. He said, "Yes, very beautiful."

Qi laughed, a little bit out of control. "Okay, she's going to be beautiful. Ah God, I hope she doesn't turn out to be some kind of gibbon." A sudden spasm of fear squeezed her face, like a late contraction. Aha, Fred thought: welcome to parenthood!

"Gibbons are great," he said. "She'll be fine."

"Maybe. Maybe so." Suddenly she was weeping.

"It's okay," Fred said, brushing her hair off her forehead. Both women needed more cleaning up, and so did their bed. He went to the sink and soaked some more towels. "She's going to be fine."

. . . . .

Fred got them as cleaned up as he could, and gave Qi some pain meds he found in the shelter's first aid box. She tossed them down and drank three cups of water. He lay down on the other bed, and briefly all three of them fell asleep.

When he woke he had to pee, so he went into the little bathroom to do that. As he was finishing he heard Qi cry out desperately, "Fred! Where are you!" and he rushed out to her, heart thudding in his chest.

"What is it?" he exclaimed, imagining trouble with the baby.

"Oh there you are!" she said, twisting to look at him. "I thought you were gone!"

"No," he said, nonplussed.

She reached out and grabbed him by the hand. "You'll stay with me?"

"Of course."

"Good!" She heaved a great juddering sigh. "Because I need you."

The baby girl was wrapped in a towel and lying across Qi's lap. Now she woke, and Qi shifted her up and she began to nurse like a kitten, eyes closed as she sucked rhythmically and hard on Qi's breast. "Is she getting anything?" Qi asked.

"You're asking me?" Fred said. "What does it feel like?"

"I don't know. I don't think anything's coming."

"There must be. Look, you can see a little milk come out of the nipple after she comes off."

"Good." She grimaced at one little bite as the babe latched on.

"Does it hurt?"

"I guess a little. Actually, after what just happened, I don't know if anything will ever hurt again."

"They say you forget."

"I hope so."

At a certain point the baby peed and pooped into her towel wrap, and Fred realized he would have to cut up some towels to use as diapers. Possibly the already bloodied towels could be washed out enough to make them suitable for diapers. He began to think about optimal shapes for a diaper. Some kind of triangle, or maybe an X. The babe's first stool was black and tarry, and he worried there might be something wrong with her. She had been through a strange nine months. It seemed like the possibilities for problems were very real. And there would be no way of knowing about a lot of them for a long time to come. And she did look odd, somewhat like the baby primates he had sometimes watched in zoos.

But they were primates. Kissing cousins to the other primates, with obvious family resemblances, especially when newborn. Actually this girl looked nothing like other primates, he was just fooled by her size and the redness of her skin; she even bore a resemblance to Qi in the shape of her mouth. She would be fine. Hopefully. There was no way to know, and no point in worrying about it now. This last thought seemed like something he could say to Qi, if she brought it up again. But then he stopped himself. Worry about it later—never a welcome piece of advice, now that he thought of it. When you suggested to people who were worrying that they worry about it later: that was never well received. He finally saw that. He even saw why it might be that way.

"What are you going to name her?" he asked.

"I don't know."

"What about the, you know, are you going to, I mean, is there any place for the father in all this?"

"Oh I don't want to talk about that."

He watched her for a while. "Are you sure?"

"I am sure. It was a mistake."

"Well—"

"It was a mistake!"

"Okay."

While the babe slept on Qi's chest, they started listening to Qi's radio feed. Everywhere the crises were still ongoing. At first this seemed strange, then they realized that only a day or less had passed since they had last paid attention. In the US, Congress had finished nationalizing the major banks, and the markets were in free fall. Currency controls had been slapped in place to keep dollars from fleeing to other countries or into cryptocurrencies. Demonstrators and some legislators were demanding a universal basic income, guaranteed healthcare, free education, and the right to work, all supported by progressive taxation on both income and capital assets. Supporters of this program were in the streets; opponents were calling it a catastrophic mutiny of the irresponsible half of the citizenry. Media had so much content to report there was hardly time to froth over it. But it seemed still that armed violence caused by all the disruption was minimal. People were in the streets, but mainly to celebrate a return to democracy, or object to it. It was hard to shoot such crowds.

In that fundamental sense, it was the same in China. The army and security forces were so far holding off, taking their positions and then remaining in place without further actions. It looked like the strategy used in Hong Kong was being tried again: just wait until people got tired and went home. No more May Thirty-fifths. Whether it would work this time no one could tell. Many people were in fact leaving the big demonstration in Beijing. Recently another manifesto had appeared on every screen in the country, a botware storm that again appeared to have originated within the Great Firewall. In stilted antique language, reminiscent of Mao Zedong or Sun Yat-sen, or even Confucius or Laozi, the previous iterations of reform lists had now become the Seven Great Reforms: return of the iron rice bowl, legal standing for the ecologies of China, reform of the *hukou* system, an end to the Great Firewall, full equality for women, an end to gross income inequality, and the return of the Party to the people.

"Interesting," Qi said. Some of these demands, she told Fred, would be supported by urban youth, some by the rural populace, some by the migrant workers, some by intellectuals and the prosperous business class. Netizens or farmers or migrants, everyone wanted something from the Party, and no one outside the Party was convinced that it had been doing the best it could. President Xi had made valiant attempts to right the ship, some said, but after him there had been too much infighting to replace him, too much corruption, too much controlocracy, too little action on behalf of the people. The Chinese people were sick of it, things had to change. And there was a long Chinese tradition of going out and overrunning the authorities—a tradition three thousand years old at this point. Young people who had never experienced such a revolutionary moment seemed to have a desire for it. This too was part of the China Dream, Qi explained.

Fred shook his head. "It sounds awful."

"What do you mean?" Qi said. "It sounds great."

"You might want it if you've never seen it, but then if you get it, you won't want it."

"Revolution?"

"Chaos and disorder."

"But the order was bad. The order was disorder. Think of it as dynastic succession on a global scale. The old world order was wrecking everything, so this had to happen. After these troubles there'll be a sorting out, and then a better order will come into being."

Fred shrugged, looking at an image on his wristpad of the National Mall in Washington, DC, packed with millions of people. Inspiring? Frightening? He wasn't sure.

"I'm hungry," Qi said. "How much food does this place have?"

"There's quite a lot. It's all dried or frozen or canned."

"That's all right. But what will we do when it's gone?"

"I don't know. Hopefully Ta Shu will figure out something, him and those Americans he was with. Someone who will help us."

"If it comes to it, we'll have to call for help. With some margin to spare, in terms of food and air."

"Ta Shu knows we're here."

Then, as if called up by one of the old man's dragon arteries, the station's control panel *pinged* three times. Fred tapped it and Ta Shu's voice was suddenly there with them.

"Fred and Qi, hello! Sorry to say this, but our China source is telling us that you've been found again. The people who destroyed your rover intend to do the same to the shelter you're in. You need to leave there immediately."

"We can't!" Fred objected. "We don't have anywhere to go, and we have no way to get there! And Qi's had her baby!"

"Nevertheless! Be that as it may! You still need to get out! All this turmoil at home is causing a really violent backlash. It's a big fight, and you're in the crosshairs."

"What about Peng Ling?" Qi asked loudly. "Is she on our side or is she trying to kill us?"

"She's on your side. I talked to her!" He sounded very happy as he said this. "Your father is working with her, and they're working together with others to secure the army and make sure the entire security apparatus is backing her and the new standing committee. That's going pretty well, they say, which only means the rightists still on the loose are getting more and more desperate. They're trying to eliminate their enemies at the top, as a last chance at success. Peng herself has had to move to a secure location. You need to do the same, because there are people in China who want you dead."

"But I'm not even in contact with anyone!" Qi cried.

"It doesn't matter. The Red Spear is being crushed, so they're lashing out. They can't retaliate against the demonstrators in the streets, so they're going for the leaders of their enemies, and you're part of that. And they found out where you are."

"But we can't get away!" Fred said. "The rover we were in was demolished."

"I know. My friends here say those roadside shelters always have little motorbikes in their storage lockers, for moving from one shelter to the next in emergencies like this. And there are spacesuits in all the refuges."

"For a baby?"

"No of course not. But it will fit in a regular one, I guess. Fred, listen to me: you have to get out of there. The missiles are already on their way."

"What! From where?"

"From Earth. They were launched yesterday, so time is short. You have to leave."

"Shit."

Fred and Qi looked at each other. So much eye contact, after all those weeks avoiding it! It was a very quick mode of speech, they were finding. Now they saw immediately that they were in agreement: they had to get out.

"Fred, listen to me. Take the motorbikes, and ride south on that road ninety-seven kilometers to a mine station called Rümker. There's a freight launch rail there, and the facility includes a passenger pod that can be loaded onto the rail. We can walk you through that and get you launched."

"But where will this pod go?"

"It depends on when you take off. Right now that doesn't matter. We'll track you after you launch and someone will come get you. For now you just need to get off the moon as fast as you can. Anywhere is safer than here. Since they know where you are, nowhere on the moon will be safe for you."

"Do you think Peng can get control of the situation?" Fred asked.

"I hope so, but she hasn't done it yet. Until that gets resolved, keeping you alive is up to us. So get out of there. Leave as soon as you can."

With that Ta Shu cut out without warning. No goodbye, just a click.

· · · · ·

Fred and Qi stared at each other, then at Qi's baby.

"Shit!" Fred said. "So sorry about this!"

"It's my fault," Qi said. "It's me they're trying to kill."

"But why? I thought you said you weren't the leader."

"I'm a symbol. I made myself a symbol. I've worked for this for years, and a lot of people know that."

"So you think we should leave."

"We have to! I believe what Ta Shu is telling us, don't you?"

"I guess so."

"He was right last time."

"Yes."

"So we have to leave."

Fred didn't want it to be true, but there it was. "Yes."

She sat up, turned and put her feet on the floor, stood up carefully beside her bed, winced.

Seeing this Fred said, "How are you doing?"

"Not good," she said.

Now that they were no longer in her moment of extremity, she didn't want to talk to him about that, he could see. But if they were going to be riding some kind of lunar motorbike, well—it struck him as a terrible idea. But there wasn't any other option. She was tough, and she hadn't been bleeding onto the bed for a while now; the latest towels he had put under her were still almost clean. So hopefully that would be all right. Maybe the motorbike had a sidecar.

They found a wardrobe full of spacesuits next to the air lock, and pulled a few out. Qi investigated the possibility of fitting her baby into her spacesuit with her, but it didn't look like that would work; the babe would be trapped below the helmet ring, and there would be no way to reach her directly down there. Nor enough room to keep from squishing her. Nor a steady supply of air. Qi cursed and began poking around in one of the station's spacesuits, sticking her arm up through the helmet ring and the like. Fred went down a hallway and found the storage room containing the motorbikes Ta Shu had mentioned. No sidecars, but luckily they were not actually motorbikes but rather motored tricycles, with two wheels in back, and a long duo of seats made to hold two or even three people. Their batteries were plugged into the wall, and there must have been a photovoltaic solar panel on the roof of the shelter, because the batteries' gauges showed they were all fully charged. Emergency transport, as Ta Shu had said, and so always ready. Suitable for getting from one shelter to the next, if there were no other options. As now.

Fred unplugged one trike's battery and wheeled it into the main room. Its rear axle was short, sized to fit through the doors and air lock. They could both sit on it. Fred could drive while Qi held her baby in her arms. It seemed like it might work.

"How does it look for getting her into a spacesuit?" he asked.

"Scary."

"But you can do it?"

"I guess we have to." Her face was set in the masklike expression Fred had seen so often in China, now grimmer than ever. "Let me nurse her one more time, see if I have any milk. We're going to have to keep her in her suit until we get to another shelter."

"I know. Ninety-seven kilometers, he said. It shouldn't take too long."

"It better not."

She sat and offered the babe a breast and the girl latched on hungrily. Fred got into his spacesuit from the rover and toggled through its gauges, saw that he had wrecked them when he had disabled its GPS. A pointless exercise. He pulled out one of the station's spacesuits and checked it out. Looked like it had air for seventy-two hours, hopefully well more than they would need. "We should wear these," he told Qi. They would be GPSed again, but it couldn't be helped. He pulled one of the suits on, then a helmet; snapped it onto the suit, turned everything on. Again it all checked out. He got the trike into the air lock.

Qi pulled the babe off, and with a kiss to her forehead inserted her headfirst into a spacesuit helmet, which she had lined with a towel around the back side, so that the girl now lay on a kind of pillow. She stared up through her faceplate, a very unnerving sight, evoking some dreamlike or cinematic memory, maybe the star child from the end of *2001*, but also various horror-film nightmares. Qi's face had turned to stone. She pulled the spacesuit up over the girl's legs and snapped suit to helmet. The suit was nearly empty, so that Qi could fold up the legs, then on Fred's suggestion wrap them with duct tape to make sure they didn't inflate when they aerated the suit. The resulting pad could be used as a kind of cushion under the helmet. She would be able to hold the whole arrangement in her arms, though it made a bulky package.

Qi then got into her suit, and they checked each other's seals. They turned on her suit and the baby's suit. All seemed well. Qi carried her girl as if in a wad of swaddling clothes, and they went to the air lock. They crowded in with the trike, closed the inner door, opened the outer door, felt the draft of air fly out into the vacuum. Fred pushed the trike by the handlebars out onto the lunar surface.

When they were outside, Qi handed Fred the baby and got on the backseat of the trike, hissing as she did so. Again he was hearing her voice in his left ear, a weirdly intimate disjunction of the senses: she was inside his head again.

"Do you want to ride sidesaddle?" he asked her.

"No. Wait—yes."

She got off and got on again sitting sideways. Fred gave her the baby and swung his leg over the seat in front of them. Electric motor. Accelerator on the right handlebar, as on a snowmobile. In fact the trike resembled a skeletal snowmobile, now that he thought of it. He tried to give them the easiest start possible, keeping his feet on the ground until the trike began to move. It moved, he lifted his feet onto the running boards, and off they went. Qi reached her right arm around his waist and clung hard to him. The babe was cradled in her left arm and Fred could feel the babe's spacesuit boots shoving him in the back.

He drove them slowly back toward the main road, scared to death he would somehow tip them over or toss Qi off. The two rear wheels kept that from happening. Possibly a tricycle was more like a car than a motorcycle, in terms of stability. But it was a narrow trike and the g was lunar. Twisting the handlebar gently, which gave the thing a bit more speed, made it feel a little easier to steer. He tested the turn of the handlebars by making a few gentle S-turns, feeling the resistances and balances. The fact that they were on a smoothed roadway helped. Being in one-sixth normal gravity seemed helpful in some ways, dangerous in others, but he couldn't be sure what was what, and didn't want to test any aspect of it. Were they balanced, was he balancing them? It was harder to tell than he would have liked.

He rode them onto the main road and turned left as gently as he could, which resulted in him almost running them off the far side of the road. He completed the turn just before that happened, straightened their course. No disasters so far. Now only ninety-five kilometers to go.

It was near midday. Even seen through the heavily polarized and tinted faceplate of his helmet, the landscape was ablaze. The few shadows remaining were like cracks in white porcelain. If they had been riding cross-country they would have been doomed to tip over, no matter the extra tricyclic balance; he couldn't see well enough to discern bumps and dips in time to avoid them. On the road it was easier, being nearly flat, though they did jounce side to side pretty often. The road was also reliably hard—not as solid as asphalt, but about like packed gravel, and sprayed with a fixative. When he took a brief glance back over his shoulder, he saw that a small dust plume was lofting behind them despite the fixative, hanging there in testament to the light g and the fineness of the dust that covered everything. But it was behind them, and Fred was happy to ride away from it into the blasted clarity of the road ahead.

Unseen bumps sometimes cast them hard to the side, and then he had to steer back the other way without too much of a panic or he would overcompensate them into a fall. Sometimes Qi's arm around his waist clutched so hard it felt like she was trying to cut him in half. It was very hard to remember that everything had to be done about one-sixth as emphatically as it would have been done on Earth. That kind of touch took a lot of athleticism, and he hadn't been a great athlete on Earth, not an athlete at all in fact, never comfortable on bikes or snowmobiles, and never once in his life on a motorcycle, a mode of conveyance he had always considered ridiculously dangerous. And yet here he was, gripping the handlebars as hard as he could and trying to see the road surface through the tint of his faceplate and the blinding glare. Too often it felt like the wheels under him were not quite in contact with the ground.

The speedometer embedded in the handlebar dashboard said they were going forty kilometers an hour, and that felt a bit too fast, with the view ahead jouncing toward him, and the thing between his legs and under his hands vibrating and bucking—but he was in a hurry. Grimly he held the throttle in place and rode the dips and bumps as best he could. Despite the rapid succession of little panics jolting through him, they were not actually coming very close to tipping over. Although one time they went over an unseen bump and the whole vehicle launched off the ground and flew without warning, scaring him; but quickly enough they came down, and he jerked the handlebars through the teeny adjustments that felt necessary to keep going straight ahead, and on they went. He kept holding his breath for too long at a time.

Qi had turned the baby's suit microphone on, and he could hear the girl crying. Qi cursed, and Fred rode on a bit faster. But this made the ride jouncier, and after a while Qi said, "Stop for a minute."

Fred slowed the bike, and at that very moment it hit a dip he didn't see; they tilted hard left and he put his leg out to hold them up. A flash of fear that he would break his leg dissipated when his foot struck the ground and almost pushed them over the other way. He had to turn right to compensate for that, then left again to straighten out—finally the trike came to a halt, and he got both feet on the ground.

They had slewed sideways across the road such that they could see the low plume of dust they were leaving behind them. Then Fred saw a much taller plume farther back, a brilliant white cloud billowing up into the black sky. "Oh my God," Fred said.

"What!"

"Look behind us."

Qi had been looking into the faceplate of the baby's suit. Now she looked at the tall cloud, which originated over the horizon behind them and was spreading at its top like a fountain of water falling onto itself, rather than the iconic nuclear cloud or an afternoon thunderhead.

"Is that our shelter?" Qi said.

"I think so."

"It looks like Ta Shu's informant is reliable. Damn. I can't see into her suit very well, so I don't think she can see me either."

"Do you think she can see anything?"

"I don't know. Maybe not, with the faceplates between us."

"Should we get going then?"

"Yes."

Fred got them underway again without tipping over or driving off the road. He was feeling a bit more used to their balance, and the trike's controls. Off they hummed. Shelter behind them destroyed. Someone shooting at them with missiles. Ta Shu had said one had come from Earth, maybe both, Fred couldn't remember. If Qi's enemies had any weapons on the moon, or in lunar orbit, and could locate them on the trike, then they could still be a target. If their enemies were shooting at them from Earth, presumably they had a day or two before another one struck, unless they were coming up in a string. Anything was possible. This mine they were heading for could have a security system in it. Smart bombs could be headed their way, keyed to some GPS implanted in Qi long ago, or recently put in something she had swallowed in her food—or stuck into Fred while he had been in the hospital—who knew! Out here on this blinding desert floor their exposure felt infinite. There was nothing to be done but to stay on the run, with as little instrumentation as possible. Stay a moving target. The trike no doubt had GPS too, activated when it was operating or on all the time. Fred's mind spun through various paranoid death spirals as he drove, and these thoughts seemed to twist his hand on the throttle without him being able to stop it, until they were going a lot faster than what would have made him comfortable in ordinary circumstances. They could so easily tip over! But he couldn't bear to slow down.

And actually, going faster seemed to make balancing the trike easier in some ways. They blew through dips and flew over lumps, but their momentum always cast them forward. It was hard to know how far he could push that in a situation where no mistakes were allowed. Now they were going fifty-five kilometers per hour. Fred tried to stick to about eighty percent of the highest speed he felt he could handle, just in case. Even so, Qi's voice said in his ear: "Be careful!"

"I will."

"Saving ten minutes doesn't matter. Even an hour."

"I know."

He didn't know, but he let back on the throttle a bit. The trike hummed between his legs. For Qi this vibration had to be bad. And yet as he drove she gave him bits of news she was hearing through her helmet's radio; she had been contacted by the people now with Ta Shu, she said. Fred was happy not to be hearing anything of that, as he needed to stay focused on riding the trike. "Don't tell me now," he said. Nevertheless her voice kept up a running commentary in his left ear. He could barely understand it. New standing committee had reconfirmed Peng as president, general secretary, and head of the military. She had made an appearance in Chengdu, which was surprising to Qi. Run the country by doing the unexpected, she said, isn't that what the *Dao* advised? Or was it by doing the expected? She couldn't remember. And the Party wasn't Daoist anyway. But Ta Shu was Daoist, Fred thought. Maybe Ta Shu was the one orchestrating these moves. Then he had to dodge a stone on the road.

"Please," Fred begged.

Qi went on nattering. Return of the iron rice bowl, of course! Reform of *hukou*, of course, but listen to her, people don't want shantytowns outside every city do they? People have to have a proper home! As for the Great Firewall, there's no such thing she says! The

Chinese Internet is self-regulating, everyone knows that! Just Chinese patriots doing what is best! So many high citizen scores, people giving a hundred and ten percent, oh come on! Give me a break!

"Quit it!" Fred told her. "I have to concentrate."

"It's just I can't stand it. She's taking over same as all of the rest. But wait, what's this...." Qi was quiet for a while and then she laughed outright. "I can't believe it! That person I was talking to on that quantum phone has just given every person in the world a million carboncoins and invited them to join a global householders' union, and something like four billion people have already joined!"

"Please," Fred said. Then, curious: "What will that do?"

"I have no idea! The backlash to it has already started. Peng doesn't know what to do about it, no one does!"

"Things will work out. How is the baby?"

"She seems to be asleep. I can't believe it."

"Better than having her crying."

"I'd rather have her crying," Qi said.

"Babies sleep a lot. Don't worry."

"What if there's another solar storm?"

"Then we're cooked."

"What if there's another missile attack?"

"Then we're blown up! But we're almost there."

"Stop saying that!"

"But we are. Stop talking, *please*."

But she didn't. She couldn't. He realized as he tried to ignore her and keep his focus on the road that she would never stop, that he would always be hurtling along trying to keep up with her, that everything would always be excruciatingly interesting all the time, the three of them buffeted by fate in all the ways he had worked his entire life to avoid. When the trike's odometer said they had traversed ninety kilometers, Qi said, "Ta Shu is on my radio, he says we're soon to come to a big parking lot. Go across it to the building on the left, that's the terminal. The pod will be in there. They'll launch us from where they are."

"Okay," Fred said.

"Who are you working with?" Qi said, apparently to Ta Shu. Then after a pause: "Can you trust them?"

"Who is it?" Fred asked.

"Be quiet!" Then after a while she said, "But how are these strikes coming so fast?"

"They're coming in a string," Fred said aloud.

After a while she said to Fred, "That's right. He says they launched this one yesterday and are aiming it as it goes. We have to get off the moon as soon as we can."

"We are! They're handling our launch, you said?"

"Yes, he said everything is ready. The pod is at the very back of the terminal. He said be sure to be lying back and facing straight ahead."

"Eyeballs in," Fred said grimly.

"He said maybe I can give the baby mouth-to-mouth and more air will be pushed into her from me than gets pushed out of her. It's a freight launch, but he said this pod will be dialed back to human speed."

"Good," Fred said.

Over the horizon reared some low peaky hills, different from the usual crater rim arc. Fred accelerated the bike, ignoring Qi's order to slow down. At the foot of the hills he spotted the cubical shapes that indicated buildings. Aside from the knot of hills, the white plain blazed flatly to the horizon in every direction. Everything white on white. Fred sped up more. They came to the parking lot Ta Shu had mentioned and he aimed for the building on the far left. Stopped right in front of an air lock door. Qi got off with her baby in her arms. Fred got off. Into the air lock, into the terminal. Very dark in there, until their pupils adjusted to the absence of sunblast. Then it was just a dim empty space, unoccupied, like some abandoned subway station. Big piste of a magnetic rail running down the middle of the building in a long glass-walled room of its own, stretching out of the structure and off to the horizon. They hurried to the back of the terminal, where the piste split into various closed doors. Fred chose the one at the very back, tapped on the door panel and it slid up, revealing a squat little rectangular spaceship, like a rover car. Its door opened even before he could tap on it, and they got in and closed the outer door. Inside they found a small cabin with several thick chairs in it, like recliner chairs. The ship's systems were on. Fred and Qi took off their helmets, and Qi unsnapped the baby's helmet and pulled her out of it and held her close. The babe was crying, she clutched to Qi with her tiny fists. Qi sat down heavily with her in one recliner. Fred sat in another recliner, then got up again and picked up Qi's helmet and spoke into it.

"Ta Shu, we're in the passenger pod, ready when you are."

He sat down in the chair, grabbed an arm and pulled himself down into it. The little spaceship lurched forward. Quickly it was out of its room and on the piste. Thick little oval side windows showed nothing but the terminal's walls. Then the surface of the moon, white as the big bang, moving by them faster and faster. They were shoved back in their chairs. Fred felt the gel under him give and give until there was no more to give. He was crushed against it until it felt like concrete, concrete scooped to the shape of his body. The babe was wailing, then she stopped. Maybe Qi was giving her mouth-to-mouth. Fred couldn't look, he could barely take a breath. All his effort had to go to sucking in air and then holding on. His vision blurred. The world went from too bright to too dark. He felt conscious but besieged. The world went blacker and blacker, his whole body squished, it was a struggle to breathe or even to hold his breath, even to hold his muscles tight enough to keep his ribs from cracking. His body became one big shout of pain. Little choked yelps of protest came from the babe, who was not to be silenced by a mere several g's. Possibly it was not that much different from her passage out of Qi. Life just one crushing after another. Qi too called out something wordless.

Then the pressure went abruptly away. Fred sucked in hard, shook his head, gasped hard, sucked in air. He sat up. Everything was blurry. They hadn't even been strapped in. Out the window he saw only black space and stars. Weightlessness: he was floating up, he grabbed his seat arm again, he pulled himself to the window and looked out. White moon behind them, shrinking fast, a bone against the night. Qi's child wailed, music to his ears, drilling like a fire alarm right down his spinal cord.

"How's the baby?" he asked.

"She seems all right. Where are we headed?"

"I don't know."

Kim Stanley Robinson is a *New York Times* bestseller and winner of the Hugo, Nebula and Locus Awards. He is the author of more than twenty books, including the bestselling Mars trilogy, *2312*, *Aurora* and *New York 2140*. In 2008 he was named a "Hero of the Environment" by *Time* magazine, and he works with the Sierra Nevada research institute. He lives in Davis, California.

Find out more about Kim Stanley Robinson and other Orbit authors by registering for the free monthly newsletter at www.orbitbooks.net.